INTRODUCTION

Until 1929, when the publication of *Ultima Thule* completed the trilogy *The Fortunes of Richard Mahony*, Henry Handel Richardson considered herself a failure. Her two earlier novels *Maurice Guest* (1908) and *The Getting of Wisdom* (1910), had aroused only temporary interest, and some speculation about the author. The first two volumes of the trilogy *Australia Felix* (1917) and *The Way Home* (1925) were possibly too remote from each other in time of publication, and too inconclusive to warrant serious critical attention. Richardson herself recorded that opinion on *Australia Felix* 'ranged from "a dull but honest volume" to "might have been written by a retired grocer" ', and that *The Way Home* 'was pronounced "intelligent but dull", "a thick crumby slice of life, but no story" '. Her character Richard Mahony, she reports, was thus dismissed: ' "Mr Richardson has lost all control of his hero.... The situation has become so stupidly hopeless that it ceases to interest the most sympathetic reader ... it is difficult to believe he has taken any trouble to arrange his thoughts or construct his character..." ' Even Nettie Palmer, who was later to become Richardson's most ardent and persuasive advocate in Australia, wrote of *The Way Home* that '... at worst it might be considered rather too much like a historical picture – a little flat and lacking in atmosphere'.

The original failure of these two books is easily enough explained. Neither is self-contained. *Australia Felix* abandons Richard Mahony at a point where he imagines that a chapter of his history is complete, and that he has 'got off scot-free' from his colonial experiences. But for the reader this can at best be an inconclusive pause in a narrative whose future is unpredictable, and was in fact far off. *The Way Home* ends on a downward turn of Mahony's fortunes, but even the knowledge of his financial ruin hardly prepares one for the complete dis-

v

integration of his personality which is the subject of *Ultima Thule*. Nor is there sufficient impetus in *The Way Home* to compensate for its incompleteness, and even when it is viewed in its proper perspective as the central movement of Mahony's life, it is still the least compelling of the three sections, though it was Richardson's favourite one. It is not surprising that its failure convinced Richardson that she was 'as far from making good as ever', and that, after nearly thirty years as a novelist 'there was nothing for it ... but to resign myself to failure *in perpetuum*'.

*

Ethel Florence Lindesay Richardson was born on 3 January 1870 in Melbourne. Her Irish grandmother, who was devoted to Handel, called her son Henry Handel and from him Richardson took her pen name. In 1940 Richardson explained herself thus:

I was bent on keeping my identity a secret. There had been much talk in the press of that day [i.e. at the time *Maurice Guest* was completed] about the ease with which a woman's work could be distinguished from a man's; and I wanted to try out the truth of the assertion.

Her father, Walter Lindesay Richardson, was born in Dublin, studied medicine in Edinburgh, and emigrated to Australia in the early 1850s in the hope of making his fortune on the goldfields. Her mother arrived from Leicester at about the same time. Ethel was born fifteen years after her parents' marriage, at a time of prosperity for them. When she was three, she and her younger sister were taken to England, and while they were there her father learnt of the collapse of his financial affairs, and returned abruptly to Australia, as Richard Mahony does at the end of *The Way Home*. Thereafter Ethel Richardson was a victim of his financial and psychological instability, as he took his family from place to place in a vain attempt to recoup his losses and recover his professional and personal prestige. Almost every year saw a move to a new house, as he wandered about Victoria in search of his lost hopes. He died insane in 1879, and was buried in the small country town of Koroit in the Western District of Victoria.

Ethel Richardson's Australian childhood gave her memories of the Australian countryside that lived with her for the rest of her life; a love of books that she attributed to her father's passion for reading; experience of the tensions and anxieties of family life, and an unusually mature view of the suffering and misery that are part of that experience; and a conviction, gained largely from her experience of boarding school, that she did not conform to the comfortable pattern of youthful pleasures and interests which seemed to satisfy her fellow-pupils. She presents her view of herself as an adolescent schoolgirl in *The Getting of Wisdom*. This novel and the closing sections of *The Fortunes of Richard Mahony*, where she appears as Cuffy, are her only substantial fictional recollections of her Australian youth.

In 1888 Mrs Richardson took her two daughters abroad, so that Ethel could continue her musical studies at Leipzig Conservatorium. She spent most of the next sixteen years in Germany, which became and largely remained her spiritual home. In Leipzig she met J. G. Robertson whom she married in 1895, and who became first Professor of German Literature in the University of London. In Leipzig too she experienced failure as a musician, and her own account of these years clearly suggests that she turned to writing as a refuge from the public life of the executant musician. In Germany, both before and after her marriage, she absorbed with relish the musical and intellectual life of the day, and her mind was stimulated and nourished as it had never been before. She read widely in European literature, and in the late 1890s, under the influence of her husband's suggestion that she should turn her experience of the musical life of Leipzig to good account by writing about 'a musician who failed to make good', she began *Maurice Guest* (1908). The sense of rootlessness and insecurity, and, in her musical and literary interests, of isolation from her fellows, that had marked her childhood in Australia, vanished in the active cultural life first of Leipzig, and then of Strasbourg.

The pattern of Richardson's life changed again, however, when her husband took up his appointment in London in 1904. From then until her death in 1946 Richardson lived in England. After the formative, full years in Germany, life in England more and more became a withdrawal into solitude. In the guarded seclusion of her London study she began work on *The Fortunes of Richard Mahony*, which was to occupy nearly twenty years of her life. In 1912, when *Australia Felix* was completed though not yet revised, she made a short visit to Australia to refresh her memories and to check certain details that she had written into the novel. She did not return to Australia again. After her husband's death in 1933, she moved to Sussex, where she died in 1946.

Australia had given her an understanding of the restlessness and suffering that were Mahony's destiny; Germany had widened her intellectual interests and enabled her to find her vocation; England gave her the isolation and stability she needed for writing. It is open to question whether any of the three countries between which her life was divided gave her a home. It is at least possible to speculate that the rootlessness she describes so well in Mahony, she understood with her heart as well as her mind.

*

Henry Handel Richardson began her literary career as a translator, first of J. P. Jacobsen's *Niels Lyhne* (1896) and then of Björnson's *Fiskerjenten* (1896). At the same time she produced a few critical articles on music and literature. Some time in 1906 or 1907 she began work on *Maurice Guest*. It is a compelling story of a young Englishman who comes to Leipzig to study music. His love affair with a passionate and possessive Australian girl absorbs and finally obsesses him, so that his work is destroyed, and he becomes a helpless victim of his own jealousy and fear. Richardson fills the novel with detail about the musical life of Leipzig, and the book is charged with the excitement of student days, over which the shadows of failure and despair gradually lengthen. Though it is essentially a novel about passionate love and jealousy, it also offers some comment on the distinction between genius and talent. Maurice Guest is unable to meet the demands of a musical career; and Richardson emphasizes his failure by contrasting it with the success of the brilliant but arrogant Schilsky, whose ruthless drive and selfishness win him success in music and love.

Richardson began her autobiographical novel *The Getting of Wisdom* 'partly as a relief from that book's [i.e. *Maurice Guest*] growing gloom'. By contrast it is a light novel. It relates the escapades of an adolescent girl at boarding school, but essentially, as its title suggests, it is about the difference between learning and wisdom. Laura Rambotham, Richardson's fictional version of herself, is a 'writer in the making'. As Richardson later wrote:

... in her small way the child came up against some of life's knottiest problems: crime and punishment; the workings of sex; passionate love. She was driven to ask herself Pilate's hoary question about truth; to put her faith to the test and find it wanting. Also, by dint of sad experience she discovered, unaided, the art and craft of realistic fiction.

Once again, as in *Maurice Guest*, though in a very different temper, Richardson is looking at the relationship between art and life. Laura Rambotham is bewildered by the apparent inconsistency of a world which demands one kind of truth from the artist, and another from real life, and which rewards the artist's lies with praise, and the ordinary person's lies with censure.

The years between *The Fortunes of Richard Mahony* and her last novel, *The Young Cosima* (1939), saw the publication of a number of short stories, most of which were collected in *The End of a Childhood* (1934). The title story in this book carries on the account of Cuffy's childhood from the point where she had left it at the end of *Ultima Thule*. In *The Young Cosima* Richardson turned to historical sources once more, this time to reconstruct the history of Wagner's relationship with Cosima Liszt and Hans von Bülow. And here again she turns to the problem of the artist, seeing in Wagner the man possessed by his genius, driven on against his will by the demands of his art. Wagner tells of his sacrifice:

Free will? There's no such thing: not for the artist. Of all living mortals he's the most unfree; stands powerless in the face of his own powers.

One cannot, of course, ascribe Wagner's views to Richardson. But *The Young Cosima* draws attention yet again to her preoccupation with the artist's role, and with the inner forces that bring a man to success, and whose absence spells artistic and personal failure.

By the time Richardson wrote *The Young Cosima*, she had exhausted the materials that her own life and experience could supply. In each of the earlier novels she had been steadily driving back into her past for the substance of her fiction. Her years in Leipzig and a youthful passion gave her the factual and emotional sources of *Maurice Guest*. In *The Getting of Wisdom* she reconstructed and shaped four years of her school life. In *The Fortunes of Richard Mahony* she journeyed back further still, into her family's past and the history of her country, and to her own earliest memories.

*

The Fortunes of Richard Mahony is without question Richardson's most important work. It covers some twenty-seven years of Mahony's life, from his arrival in Australia in 1852 to his death. In the first volume Richardson links Mahony's personal history closely to the history of the colony of Victoria, and of Ballarat in particular, in the years from 1852 to the later 1860s. The controlling force and centre of *Australia Felix* is, arguably, not the character of Mahony, but the life and history of the colony. Richardson's thorough and systematic account of the development of Ballarat from a ramshackle mining community into a provincial city is more than mere background to Mahony's personal history. Colonial life is the source of his prosperity and an important reason for his incurable dissatisfaction with whatever happens to be his present state. It is, in effect, the condition of his existence: and while Richardson makes quite explicit the weaknesses and conflicts, the ambitions and ideals, and the changing, indefinable aspirations which are at the centre of Mahony's character and personal relationships, these are not permitted to overshadow the social and environmental influences which are at work upon him. Thus Mahony, a severe critic of the feverish, grasping ambition of the goldfields, and the fecklessness and instability of the diggers, is himself as much a victim of the gambling instinct as are those he despises, and just as little able to control his conflicting passions as the most ignorant miner. In *Australia Felix* Mahony is a point of reference for the history of a period in which so many gave themselves thoughtlessly into the hands of fortune.

But when (in *The Way Home*) Mahony travels for the second time from England back to Australia, Richardson does not attempt to sustain the historical background of the narrative. Instead she concentrates on the social environment in which Mahony lives as a prosperous medical practitioner in Melbourne. He does not belong, nor aspire to, 'the stylish set' that revolved around Government House. His social life is that of the small intellectual group whose centre is Bishopscourt. Here Mahony discusses the lively intellectual issues of the day, particularly the debate between science and religion provoked by the publication of Darwin's theories.

By eliminating historical events, and concentrating upon Mahony's social contacts, Richardson narrows the range of the novel in such a way that she is able to close in on Mahony. This effect is reinforced by the chronology of the trilogy. In *Australia Felix* she covers some fifteen years of Mahony's life. The timespan for the rest of the novel is twelve years — approximately eight years for *The Way Home* and four for *Ultima Thule*. In this last volume she moves closer still to Mahony's inner life, so that gradually even the landscape becomes a subjective reflection of his state of mind. Thus, by narrowing her perspective from the broad historical view offered in *Australia Felix* to the more concentrated social context of *The Way Home* and finally to Mahony's psychological world, Richardson conveys through the design of the novel an essential part of its meaning. It is an accurate reflection of Mahony's increasing preoccupation with his mental states, and gradual separation from the historical events and environment which have shaped him.

In another way too, the structure of *The Fortunes of Richard Mahony* reflects the dilemma of the wayward man who is its centre. Looked at from one point of view, the novel is the fullest and most coherent expression in Australian fiction of the divided sensibility which is the persistent affliction of migrant populations and expatriates. At the beginning of the novel Mahony arrives in Australia as an adventurer. He affects an attitude of critical superiority to the raw society of the goldfields, and is patronizingly indulgent towards the miners' struggle for justice epitomized in the account of the Eureka Stockade. By the end of *Australia Felix* he has acquired enough wealth (as did so many of his real life contemporaries) to return 'home' after some fifteen years in exile to what he still calls 'the dear old mother-country'. Up to this point Mahony's migrant story is comparable to that of the squatters in Henry Kingsley's *The Recollections of Geoffry Hamlyn*, whose sole purpose for migrating is to make enough money out of the colony to be able to return to a comfortable existence in Devonshire.

But the next phase of Mahony's career, recorded in *The Way Home*, is a study in disillusionment. The one thing Mahony has not been able to predict is the effect upon him of his years at the end of the world. He has forgotten the simple fact that it is often harder to go back than to go on. His memories of the past do not match the present reality; England, whose greenness and tidiness he had pined for after the boundless, undefined, straggly, dry Australian landscape, seems small and cramped. After the open cheerfulness of his Australian friends (crude though he often found them) the English seem enervated by provincial snobbery, and paralysed by the pointless polite formalities of their existence. So he returns to Australia, longing, as he would never have believed possible, for the sun.

When, at this period in his life, Mahony finds himself a rich man, he again does what others of his time and since did in real life. He sets off on the grand tour of Europe. From this he is recalled to Australia by the collapse of his fortunes, this time compelled back to the adopted country to which, ironically enough, he would have returned voluntarily. By this time Mahony is already losing the battle against his environment. Though without stating it directly, Richardson makes it plain enough that Mahony has been captured by Australia, and that he is enslaved as much by his failures as by his successes. So it is that in the end the country of his exile becomes his last home and his obscure but permanent resting-place.

The geography of the novel, then, reflects the complex vacillations of Mahony's attitudes. Ambition drives him from England, and nostalgia drives him back. The next movement is from failure in England to triumphant success in Australia. His very success drives him back to Europe once more, and his final exile begins, not with ambition and hope, but with disaster and despair. From despair to total defeat is the record left by *Ultima Thule*. In meticulously depicting the divided loyalties of Mahony, reluctantly and painfully surrendering his homeland and yielding to the fatal enticements of an alien world, Richardson points to the complicated mixture of love and hatred, admiration and fear which is to be found even in the modern inheritors of Mahony's world.

The writing of *Australia Felix* was, for Richardson, a major research undertaking. She was once asked whether she considered herself to be a realist, to which she replied: 'Perhaps you might call me a "realist", if by that word you mean some one who endeavours to set down the truth as she sees it!' But her answer is not quite accurate. For she aimed both to tell the truth as she saw it, and to tell the truth as it was. So she prepared herself for the writing of *Australia Felix* by reading a collection of important histories and memoirs of Victoria and the gold-diggings in the 1850s. She noted even the smallest details of the dress, language and habits of the diggers, and collected in meticulously indexed note form far more information than she was able to use.

Writing about the methods of modern novelists in *The Experimental Novel*, Emile Zola describes at some length how a naturalistic novelist would go about writing a novel on theatrical life. He would first, argues Zola, set out with this general idea. Then he would make notes about everything relevant to the theatrical world. He would interview people, collect their stories, pictures and expressions. He would then consult documents. And after all this, he would visit the theatre himself, examine it minutely, and accumulate first-hand knowledge to support his research.

In that passage Zola might be describing Richardson's approach to the writing of *Australia Felix*. In her years in Germany she read widely in European fiction. In Jacobsen's *Niels Lyhne* she had found 'a romanticism imbued with the scientific spirit and essentially based on realism'. The scientific spirit expresses itself in her methodical and detailed descriptions of the goldfields, and even in her determination accurately to reproduce the contours of the landscape. The evidence of her diary shows that when she visited Australia in 1912, one of her aims was to check the details of her descriptions of Ballarat. For example she made the train journey from Ballarat to Melbourne that Mahony in *Australia Felix* made, and noted in her diary the precise point in the journey at which he would make the speech she had already written for him.

Of equal interest, however, is her way of using the historical material she accumulated. Sometimes it is possible to trace in the text of the novel the exact sources of her descriptions. Sometimes the exact wording of a phrase or sentence is derived from her source. This is true even of the descriptions she carried into the novel from her own diary. Her method is rather to accumulate and organize fact than to absorb and recreate it. When, for example, she gives a full description of the contents of Mahony's store in *Australia Felix*, her method recalls Balzac's patient accumulation of detail.

The effect of this practice is, of course, the creation of a world undeniably clear in its outlines, and solidly authentic. It raises, however, the difficult question of significant detail. Zola distinguished between Balzac and Flaubert on this point, seeing in the latter a 'discreet equilibrium' between descriptive detail and character. Zola's formula for the control of detail – that it should always complete or explain a character – would disallow some of the description in *The Fortunes of Richard Mahony*, perhaps particularly in *The Way Home*, where the lengthy account of Mahony's English experience, presented in considerable detail, does not seem justified by the relatively small gain in knowledge of his character. In this section there is the added difficulty that Richardson has committed herself to stock notions about English and colonial attitudes, and these are never explored in sufficient depth to expand one's view of Mahony's inner conflict. Much more effective are those passages, of which the Proem to *Australia Felix* is the most notable example, where Richardson controls the details by a point of view, thus giving them a meaning and shape without sacrifice of accuracy.

To observe the operation of Richardson's 'scientific spirit' in *The Fortunes of Richard Mahony* is to be reminded that only part of the novel is to be accounted for in this way. Though as has already been suggested, the relationship of historical and social context to Mahony's development varies within the novel as a whole, *The Fortunes of Richard Mahony* remains *his* story. It is *his* fortunes that are its subject. At the level of material facts, the trilogy progresses with chronological exactitude from beginning to end. But another order of facts is embodied in the structure of the novel, the mental facts of Mahony's progress towards insanity. The external events of the novel, accurate and realistic in themselves, are at the same time a means of projecting the internal events, and the chronology of these is not nearly so simple.

Mahony's mental chronology cuts across the actual time-scheme of the novel in *The Way Home*, which in terms of his mental journey should be called 'The Way Back'. The way home, it turns out, is the way to rejection and disillusionment, and to the discovery that the past is irrecoverable. It is a nightmare journey back into his own past. Only when Mahony arrives at the threshold of his childhood in Dublin does he realize that he has postponed his journey back for so long because he has 'a nervous aversion' from returning. He emerges from this underworld, feeling, as James Joyce did, that he was one of the living returning to the dead.

In Edinburgh where he had been a medical student his experience is the opposite. Here he is a 'shade permitted to revisit the haunts of men'. His lost youth, in the form of his successors, rebukes him with opportunities lost and hopes unfulfilled, and conscious of his deficiencies, he retreats from making contact with the eminent men of his profession. And even while Mahony pauses, ruminating on a vanished past, he is being propelled into a future which, like the past, will swallow up his hopes. At this point the forward pressure of the novel shows very clearly Mahony's indecisiveness, and his very limited capacity for self-analysis.

Yet he is not without aims or ambitions. When speculations in shares bring him wealth, he spends his money on books, and his leisure pondering current controversies, annotating 'The Book of Genesis', considering papers for the medical journal, and actively exploring spiritualism. Yet none of these activities is productive. He is constantly frustrated by his own inadequate grasp of reality. His pride makes him aspire to conditions beyond his capacity. He is a dreamer whose dreams refuse to take on definition; a romantic whose aspirations remain distant clouds.

Richardson establishes the central problems of Mahony's character by presenting a whole range of other characters whose lives impinge on his. The most important of these is, of course, his wife Mary. The course of their relationship clarifies Mahony's strengths and weaknesses, and plots his deterioration. As his character weakens, so Mary's gains in strength, until finally their roles are reversed and he ends in the kind of dependence on her that, from the beginning, he expected to be her relationship to him. Perhaps Richardson's dedication of *Ultima Thule* to Mary Mahony may be taken as acknowledging the reversal of their responsibilities. From this, Mahony's most intimate relationship, Richardson moves out to his friend of the early days, Purdy Smith, to his wife's family the Turnhams, to his Ballarat friends the Ococks, and further still to his employee in the store Hempel, and to patients and casual acquaintances such as the chemist Tangye. This large range of characters, all carefully delineated, is however marshalled to testify to Mahony's character. Each, from his different vantage point, as friend, relative or acquaintance, has something to contribute to the explication of Mahony's character. He is reflected in a number of different mirrors, carefully angled and placed.

Up to this point, where Richardson concentrates on the establishment of Richard Mahony's character by means of a number of reference points outside him, the realistic method serves her well. The sheer weight and accuracy of details of landscape, history, society, conversations, and events of daily life, create the conviction that substantial and reliable actuality is being described. Richardson has the capacity to direct her reader's sympathies, to place him firmly within the conflicts of the main characters, sometimes to be made irritated and impatient by Richard's moods, tantrums, complaints and pompousness, sometimes by Mary's obstinate common sense, taste for trivialities, and short-sighted pragmatism. These shifts in sympathy are managed without any direct intervention by the author. Richardson had learnt the lesson of European naturalism well. It had reinforced her attachment to literal fact, and to objectivity. There is truth in Nettie Palmer's statement that 'there seemed a dogged determination in her to pursue the method beyond the customary bounds' . . . and her explanation of this is compelling:

Or perhaps it would be truer to say that she was so absorbed by her own experience and had brooded so long and deeply upon it that she could hardly imagine going beyond it for materials for her art.

When she did go beyond it, in *The Young Cosima*, she found it 'a very heavy job', and the novel bears witness to her labour.

For a long time, however, Richardson did not disclose that her own experience was involved in *The Fortunes of Richard Mahony*. When Nettie Palmer visited her in London in 1935 she recorded her insistence that '*Maurice Guest* and *Mahony* are works of fiction'. When in 1940 Richardson wrote some notes on her books for the *Virginia Quarterly Review* she said that 'except for a vague memory, the only material I had to draw on was about a dozen old family letters'. It was not until she began writing her fragment of autobiography *Myself When Young* (1948) (which was cut short by her death), that she revealed that Richard Mahony was a portrait of her own father. Recent research has disclosed how closely Richardson kept to the actual chronology of Walter Richardson's life, and makes it clear that the novel is as much fictional biography as it is history. Its structure, therefore, is controlled both by the actual historical events which form its background, and by the events of Walter Lindesay Richardson's life with which they interlock. Richardson has used the facts to guide her steps through a past of which she had no first-hand knowledge. Her claim of objectivity extends to her insistence that she speaks in the novel for the generation about whom the book is written, and that it is *their* view, not her own, that the novel advances.

There are, however, difficulties in regarding the novel with quite the detachment Richardson herself demands. Even had she not confessed (again in *Myself When Young*) to the truth of her husband's assertion that in drawing the portrait of Richard Mahony 'I had drawn no other than my own', one could hardly fail to see it, together with her other novels, as the expression of certain consistent preoccupations. One key to these is the extent to which Richardson departs from the known facts in *The Getting of Wisdom* and *The Fortunes of Richard Mahony*. *The Getting of Wisdom* contained, as she herself said, 'a very fair account of my doings at school and of those I came in contact with'. By any ordinary standards Ettie Richardson was a success in the last five years of her school life. She was intelligent, and regularly carried off prizes. She excelled at tennis, and was a promising pianist and composer. In her last year at school she earned reviews in the main Melbourne papers for the performance of one of her own compositions. Yet in the novel her academic success is only glancingly (and somewhat slightingly) referred to, she is pronounced a failure in sport, and her musical achievements are not mentioned at all. The chief successes which, as a schoolgirl, Ethel Richardson scored, are omitted from her autobiographical fiction. The whole emphasis of the novel is placed upon her failure in human relationships, her sense of isolation from her fellows, and her conviction that she was considered 'odd and unaccountable'.

Similar omissions of fact support the main bias of *The Fortunes of Richard Mahony*. It seems clear from recent research that in the early 1870s, when Walter Lindesay Richardson was prosperous, and in his earlier days in Ballarat, he was an active man in certain areas of public life, and a man with a wide circle of friends. It is true that both in *Australia Felix* and *The Way Home* Richardson refers to his outside activities, and to the fact that he was in demand for his musical skills and speech-making. But these minor successes are given much less weight than his psychological difficulties, and the uneasiness with which he handles personal contacts. Similarly, Mahony's aspirations to intellectual activity are constantly frustrated. He never turns his ideas into actuality. Walter Richardson, on the other hand, did contribute to scientific journals; and the intellectual interest Mahony shows in spiritualism was, for Richardson, a real one. He was President of the Victorian Association of Progressive Spiritualists, and a contributor to its journal. So it seems that in dealing with her father's past, as with her own, Richardson has censored or considerably restricted those facts which bring her subjects into too easy a relationship with their fellows, or offer them the comforts of worldly success. She seals them within their conviction of their own uniqueness and difference from others; giving to Laura Rambotham the kind of failure which might be the beginning of the discovery of herself as a writer; and to Richard Mahony the failure which ends in total psychological and spiritual defeat.

Richardson was nowhere more explicit about her intentions in *The Fortunes of Richard Mahony* than when, in her article for the *Virginia Quarterly Review*, she wrote:

So far, all the novels about Australia that had come my way had been tales of adventure, and successful adventure: monster finds and fortunes made in the gold fields, the hair-raising exploits of bushrangers, and so on. But there was another and very different side to the picture, and one on which, to my knowledge, no writer had yet dwelt. What of the failures, to whose lot neither fortunes nor stirring adventures fell? The misfits, who were physically and mentally incapable of adapting themselves to this strange hard new world? I knew of many such; and my plan was to tell the life-story of one of them . . .

That is not to be taken as an exact reflection of the nature of Australian fiction at the time Richardson began the trilogy. Her knowledge of the literature of her own country was slight; as late as 1930 she wrote to Nettie Palmer: '. . . am beginning to feel that I really know something of Australian writers at last – by name at least.' While it was true that there were many success stories of life in the Colony – Magwitch in *Great Expectations* typifies one kind of legend about the prospects of making a fresh start and striking wealth – the dark side of the picture was presented by such writers as Marcus Clarke, Price Warung, Henry Lawson and Barbara Baynton. In any case it is questionable whether Richardson would so readily have turned to the theme of failure had she not already explored it in *Maurice Guest* and experienced it in her own life.

For she was a very introspective writer, for all her objectivity. She traced her understanding of the destructive love so meticulously dissected in *Maurice Guest* to an adolescent passion she herself had experienced. It also has clear affinities with the passionate attachment to a school friend which casts a sombre shadow over the last section of *The Getting of Wisdom*. Her representations of jealousy and emotional deprivation have the force of actual experience, not of acquired knowledge. As such, they have a very different tone from those passages in which she describes Mahony's intellectual speculations, or even his religious gropings. Possibly because she is in these instances attempting a historical reconstruction, her writing has a cool, calculating impartiality very different in pace and temper from the tension of the prose in parts of the earlier novels; but certainly there are occasions in which Mahony's morbid sensitivity is described with an insight that can only be the result of personal suffering. In 1912 Richardson stood outside the post-office in Koroit where her father had died, and asked herself:

Why do I feel so strongly about him? An early Victorian man, with all the prejudices and limitations of his time. But I see him as a seeker, with all the higher needs in him crushed physically, dissipated mentally, dazed and confused by the ultimate demands of life. He was never once equal to it.

In *The Getting of Wisdom* Laura Rambotham too is confused, young though she is, by the demands of her fellows. One of the lessons she learns is that while lying in real life earns the contempt of one's fellows, lying in fiction is essential for their approval. Even in this light treatment of a schoolgirl's life, Richardson sets the one against the many, the 'seeker' against the 'demands of life'. Again in *Maurice Guest*, her hero's personal qualities are unequal to the demands he and the world make upon them. He fails as a musician (as Richardson herself had done) and as a lover, and finally destroys himself, yielding to the desperate remedy from which Mahony manages to pull himself back. In each of these novels Richardson draws deeply on her own inner emotional experience as well as on her knowledge, first-hand or acquired, of the external circumstance of the world she creates. In each case it is the suffering of failure, the acute isolation of the individual who cannot find comfort in his fellows, that she most powerfully conveys.

If Richard Mahony's failure were merely a matter of worldly misfortune, the naturalistic method that Richardson chiefly employs might be adequate to her purpose. But Mahony is susceptible to forces larger than himself, and it is clear from her own comments and from the epigraphs to each book of the trilogy that Richardson sees him as representative of the common fate of humanity. She sees him, as Hardy sees his characters, battling a destiny to which, in the end, he must succumb. (It is interesting to note that she admired 'intensely' Hardy's *The Dynasts*.) Hence the novel is designed, not simply in terms of the chronological progression of historical and biographical events, nor in terms of the more complex history of Mahony's inner life, but as a pattern of interlocking ironies. One's attention is drawn to this underlying pattern by the titles of the trilogy and the separate volumes. Mahony's fortunes are misfortunes, and even his prosperity is a snare for a man of his temperament. *Australia Felix*, the name Thomas Mitchell gave to the colony of Victoria in deference to its fertility, in the end is seen by Mahony as a curse, not as a blessing, and Mitchell's vision becomes Mahony's nightmare. *The Way Home* is the way to rejection and disillusionment. 'Ultima Thule', the name Mahony gives to the grand house which acknowledges his material success and at the same time assists his material failure, becomes too a sign for his own mental journey to the utmost limits of endurance. Supporting the major ironies inherent in these titles are many incidental ones. Mahony's nightmare at the end of *Ultima Thule* picks up a scene from *Australia Felix*; the conversation with Tangye in *Australia Felix* prefigures Mahony's fate, as does his angry attack on his friend Purdy as a 'crazy lunatic'. Again and again in the organization of detail such as this Richardson insists upon the inevitability of Mahony's progress towards defeat.

This aspect of the novel is given its most significant dimension, however, by the relationship between the Proem to *Australia Felix* and the last page of *Ultima Thule*. The novel opens, as it ends, with burial. The unknown digger whose grave is a mine shaft, is, to the Mahony of *Australia Felix*, one of the common herd from whom Mahony feels himself so remote. Yet he shares his fate, and like him, a grave 'indistinguishable from the common ground'. Richardson intends an ironic comparison between the men and the comparison is a just one. Mahony claims goals for himself which are not those of a materialistic society. The diggers who flocked to the Ballarat goldfields in the 1850s were, as Richardson says, driven by ambition and greed. No doubt their values helped to create those of the society that grew up around them. It was a society more notable for its pursuit of material prosperity than for its appreciation of intellectual attainment. Mahony distinguishes himself from the dominant materialistic drives of the society in which he lives. His aspirations are intellectual and imaginative. His values are intangible, and hence both difficult to define and to achieve.

In this respect there is very little point of contact between him and the unknown digger whose grave Mahony's own grave recalls. But for all his protestations Mahony himself is as addicted to materialism as are the people he despises. The diggers gamble with their lives to acquire wealth. Mahony's gambling is of a more sophisticated kind, but it too involves his own life, and the lives of his family. He is as heavily committed to a desire for prosperity and wealth, and as reckless in squandering it as any of the diggers. Indeed, the Proem as a whole establishes a connection between the feverish insecurity of life on the goldfields and Mahony's own temperamental restlessness, the effect of which is to make him a part of the world he felt to be so hostile and alien. He, too, is 'ensorcelled', and in asserting the power of the land to lead men into captivity without chains Richardson makes Mahony, individual though he is, one of the many who have no memorial in the history of Australia.

Richardson named the Proem as one of the only two places in the trilogy in which she is not speaking 'for the generation of whom the works are written'. (The other is the descriptive paragraph at the beginning of *Ultima Thule*.) It is of some significance then that this passage is rather differently constructed from those many others in *Australia Felix* in which Richardson draws heavily on source material. It is different in kind from the catalogue of the contents of Mahony's store. If the latter passage seems to have something in common with what Zola described as Balzac's 'long appraiser's enumerations', then the Proem exhibits the 'discreet equilibrium' he praises in Flaubert. The detail is accurate, and can be traced to various of the sources listed in Richardson's notebooks. But it is controlled by a strict design, and used to exemplify a point of view. It bears to the novel something of the relationship that an overture has to an opera. It establishes a particular tone, and enunciates themes which are to sound throughout the work.

It may be said then that by adapting her naturalistic method in this way, and by the ironic repetition of incidents, Richardson lends emphatic support to a notion of the inescapable destiny of Mahony, and at the same time gives him a representative role, without robbing him of his individuality. Whether she is as successful in displaying Mahony's spiritual aspirations is open to doubt. In order to depict Mahony as a 'seeker' Richardson needs to probe his intellectual life, and to enter that difficult area where a man's intellectual aspirations and spiritual doubts and hopes feed each other, and influence his emotional stability. In his moody moments, Mahony sees Mary as 'instinctively antagonistic to the imaginative and speculative sides of life'. There is truth in his accusation, as there is in the fact that were this not so, Mahony might much earlier have lost his grip on actuality, and his ability to struggle against misfortune. Richardson does not, however, really manage to enter Mahony's imaginative and speculative mental life, and give it reality. This is in part a failure of method. In a discussion of spiritualism Mahony quotes at Mary with some asperity 'Commonplace minds usually condemn everything that is beyond the scope of their understanding'. But unfortunately for the force of Mahony's argument at this point, and still more for the sense of him as a man whose 'higher needs' are crushed by the circumstances of his life, one is not always confident that his mind is superior to those he condemns.

In analysing Mahony's intellectual aspirations the reader is faced with two related problems – the quality of Mahony's thinking and the quality of his expression. Richardson stocks Mahony's mind with some of the intellectual equipment that was, in fact, current in the middle years of the nineteenth century. Her own notes on Mahony's reading include Lyell and Darwin, Huxley, Colenso, Renan and Strauss. She feeds into the novel what are virtually summaries of contemporary controversies about science and religion, and includes some of the scientific arguments that men of Mahony's time found difficult to reconcile with the orthodoxes of religious faith. The problem is, however, that these summaries are like the list of the contents of Mahony's store, and unlike the controlled and purposeful description of the goldfields with which the novel opens. Mere mention of this kind of intellectual background, and the fact that Mahony is shown from time to time reflecting on its consequences, does not in itself establish him as a man of a speculative and imaginative turn of mind. His private ponderings do not permeate the actions and occasions of his daily life. Rather he appears as a character who has been supplied by his creator with ideas which merely offer him temporary diversions, in the way that his collection of butterflies does.

Possibly as a consequence of this, the importance of Mahony's spiritual crisis, especially in the suicide scene, is diminished in relation to his financial and emotional crises. Nor does there seem any substantial ground for the strengthening of his faith, and his recognition that the world has a meaning and unity which is guaranteed by the existence of God. Mahony's scepticism has in the first instance seemed little more than an abstract possibility confined, as it were, to his hours of contemplation in his study, and not spreading outwards into his daily life. In the same way his spiritual crisis and revelation seem to have less to do with a man deeply stirred by intellectual problems, than with the more obvious, though of course no less real pressures of professional and financial anxieties leading to extreme nervous tension and physical strain. Richardson's careful diagnosis of Mahony's condition is not in question (for this, too, she made a characteristically thorough study of text books in abnormal psychology). What is in question is whether she has shown him to have that depth of intellectual life, and its accompaniment, that awareness of the complex human conditions of his life, that were necessary to her purposes.

If, in the last analysis, Mahony is to be denied the stature of a man of unusual imaginative and speculative capacity, to what can this failure be ascribed? The difficulty is no doubt partly due to Richardson's attempt to sketch in his intellectual background in summary form. This method gives the impression that the stature of a man is to be measured by the amount of knowledge he has managed to acquire, and that one measure of Mahony's frustration is his realization that he will not manage to read all the books or visit all the places he would like to acquaint himself with before his death. These frustrations are human enough, but they are not adequate reason for despair; and Richardson does not show Mahony as a man whose frustrations are more crippling than the fairly commonplace realities most people have to face.

In those scenes where Mahony tries to articulate his longings, and define his reasons for dissatisfaction with his lot, the problem is not, however, simply with the content of his mind, but the manner of his expression. Richardson does not define her notion of the 'prejudices and limitations' of a man of Mahony's time, but one limitation the novelist cannot afford to impose on a character of this kind is verbal inadequacy. Mahony's speech is characteristically pompous, stiff, and wooden, and it may be that in making it so Richardson was fulfilling her aim of allowing her characters to speak for themselves in the idiom of their time. If this is so, then one can only see it as a failure of the naturalistic method. But the evidence of the novel as a whole suggests that the problem of Mahony's language is in fact a problem of Richardson's own style, which is very uneven. Some passages of descriptive writing are well handled. Mahony's inner anxieties are often given forceful expression, especially in *Ultima Thule*, and when, in that volume, Mahony sees the actual landscape taking on almost human shapes of hostility and menace, the impact of his distorting vision is strong and compelling. (One curious fact is the very considerable difference in tone between Mahony's letters in *Ultima Thule*, and his thinking. His letters are lucid and simple, without the gaucheries and inversions which mark his train of thoughts.) But there are many passages in every section of the novel where the style is encumbered with syntactical oddities, mixed metaphors and clichés, which one cannot simply explain away as representing the idiom of Mahony's time. Nor is this simply a matter of grammatical pedantry, of finding literal errors. One of the reasons for the length of the trilogy (and this is especially true of the expansiveness of *The Way Home*) is that Richardson's style lacks penetration. A point which can be made in one sentence is often allowed to occupy several; and what follows the original statement is a series of slight variations, or near synonyms, adding bulk but not meaning.

The ponderous slowness of Mahony's reasoning, the flatness of his language and the sparse furnishing of his mind, do not allow him to appear as a man of deep spiritual perceptions or large imaginative capacity. In the important scene where he decides against suicide, he is not a man in the grip of a shattering personal crisis, who has reached into the depths of his own misery, and rediscovered his faith at the lowest point of his suffering. It is the *intention* of the scene to accomplish this, and to convey the force of Mahony's spiritual revelation; but its tone is the same as that which marks his private intellectual debates earlier in the novel. He is still the man of limited intellectual capacity grappling with not very complex ideas. He is not a character of delicate perceptions and fine insights battling spiritual despair and coming to terms with the bleakest moments of his experience. In this particular respect Richardson's achievement falls short of her intention. She has a view of Mahony which is only partly articulated in the novel, one which could perhaps not be expressed fully without some departure from the methods she has chosen, and a more powerful style than she is able to command. In the last analysis, the sense of Mahony's common humanity, upon which Richardson, through the epigraphs and the Proem, seems to be insisting, is stronger than the sense of his uniqueness.

For all his moodiness and unpredictability, his longing for change and impetuous actions to bring it about, Mahony is not a surprising character. Richardson's exhaustive treatment of him does not permit him a mystery. His inconsistencies are explicable. His character yields to explanation and does not offer the resistance of unresolvable paradoxes. Perhaps for this reason his failure is moving, but not in the end enlightening. The forces ranged against Mahony are immense – the country, its people, his temperament, his wife, his irreconcilable desires for permanence and change, his belief that ' "panta rei" is the eternal truth, "semper idem" the lie we long to see confirmed'. Against these forces Mahony cannot hope to triumph, and Richardson has demonstrated in the novel what she believed to be true of her father in real life, that the struggle was unequal. Indeed, some of the limitations in Richardson's depiction of Mahony may be explained by her adherence to the biographical facts of her father's life. Her general intention in writing the novel was, as she said, to explore the life of a man who failed in his colonial adventure. Once that intention became centred upon the figure of her own father a second motive entered the novel. Richardson's fidelity to historical fact includes fidelity to biographical fact, and it might be argued that the latter is not always advantageous to the fiction that she is creating. In *Ultima Thule* she plots accurately the last years of her father's life. This commits her to an immensely detailed account of his mental deterioration and his senile reversion to childishness. The effect is to prolong the misery of his life but not necessarily to sharpen the reader's awareness of his personal tragedy; to make his death a release, not the only possible resolution of a human conflict.

Richardson's concentration on the full explication of Mahony's progress to failure distinguishes *The Fortunes of Richard Mahony* from any Australian novel that has been written up to that time. When Richardson began work on the trilogy Australian fiction was over seventy years old. Though it is customary to begin accounts of it with *Quintus Servinton* (1830-1), the history of the Australian novel properly begins in the 1840s with Charles Rowcroft's *Tales of the Colonies*. Richardson's observation about the nature of Australian fiction was partly correct; many early novels, including *Tales of the Colonies*, were success stories. Others were full of information about the colonies, suitable for intending migrants and curious English readers. Such is William Howitt's *Tallangetta* (1857) whose object, as the author says, is 'to depict the various phases of Australian life and character more fully than could be done in my "Two Years in Victoria" '. But even the best of these early novelists were not concerned with the creation of a fictional world, but rather with the collection of information about life in the new country, strung along a loose romantic plot.

Nor were they concerned – and this generalization holds for Richardson's most distinguished predecessor Joseph Furphy – with the exploration of character. Even in Furphy's *Such is Life* (1903), densely populated though it is, character is sketched rather than examined. Richard Mahony is the first substantial character in Australian fiction. Shortly after the publication of *Ultima Thule* Richardson wrote:

... Interesting as the experiments are that are being made today in the novel, I never cease to believe that character-drawing is its main end and object, the conflict of personalities its drama.

She never lost sight of this belief, whatever difficulties she encountered in exercising it.

Richardson's analysis of human inadequacy, the tantalizing distance between the ideal and the achievement, and the complex web of circumstance, environment, and human frailty; her steadfast pursuit of actuality, and rejection of the comforting romantic fiction, make her one of Australia's most distinguished novelists. In *The Fortunes of Richard Mahony* she brings together knowledge of a significant period in Australian history, understanding of human weakness, and a grasp of the principles and practice of the best French, German, English and Russian writers of the nineteenth century. It is a rare combination of qualifications for the novelist, and one which had not been seen in Australian writing before. By the time *The Fortunes of Richard Mahony* was completed, fictional methods had undergone a radical transformation. The experimentalists were no longer Zola's naturalists, but Proust, Joyce and their contemporaries. Yet it is questionable whether any other approach to the historical and biographical facts of the subject Richardson chose could so well have served her purpose at the time, or made it possible for her to keep the history of a country in balance with the fate of a man. The epigraph to *Ultima Thule* '. . . and some there be which have no memorial', now takes on a meaning that Richardson can hardly have intended. For in *The Fortunes of Richard Mahony*, Mahony and the many others like him who failed, have their memorial.

LEONIE KRAMER
Professor of Australian Literature
University of Sydney

PART ONE

CHAPTER ONE

When, for the third time, Richard Mahony set foot in Australia, it was to find that the fortune with which that country but some six years back had so airily invested him no longer existed. He was a ruined man; and at the age of forty-nine, with a wife and children dependent on him, must needs start life over again.

Twice in the past he had plucked up his roots from this soil, to which neither gratitude nor affection bound him. Now, fresh from foreign travel, from a wider knowledge of the beauties of the old world, he felt doubly alien; and, with his eyes still full of greenery and lushness, he could see less beauty than ever in its dun and arid landscape. – It was left to a later generation to discover this: to those who, with their mother's milk, drank in a love of sunlight and space; of inimitable blue distances and gentian-blue skies. To them, the country's very shortcomings were, in time, to grow dear: the scanty, ragged foliage; the unearthly stillness of the bush; the long, red roads, running inflexible as ruled lines towards a steadily receding horizon . . . and engendering in him who travelled them a lifelong impatience with hedge-bound twists and turns. To their eyes, too, quickened by emotion, it was left to descry the colours in the apparent colourlessness: the upturned earth that showed red, white, puce, gamboge; the blue in the grey of the new leafage; the geranium red of young scrub; the purple-blue depths of the shadows. To know, too, in exile, a rank nostalgia for the scent of the aromatic foliage; for the honey fragrance of the wattle; the perfume that rises hot and heavy as steam from vast paddocks of sweet, flowering lucerne – even for the sting and tang of countless miles of bush ablaze.

Of ties such as these, which end by drawing a man home, Richard Mahony knew nothing. He returned to the colony at heart the stranger he had always been.

Landing in Melbourne one cold spring day in the early seventies, he tossed his belongings into a hansom, and without pausing to reflect drove straight to his old club at the top of Collins Street. But his stay there was short. For no sooner did he learn the full extent of his losses, than he was ripe to detect a marked reserve, not to say coolness, in the manner of his former friends and acquaintances. More than one, he fancied, deliberately shunned him. Bitterly he regretted his over-hasty intrusion on this, the most exclusive club in the city; to which wealth alone was the passport. (He had forgotten, over his great wanderings, how small a world he had here come back to. Within the narrow clique of Melbourne society, anything that happened to one of its members was quickly known to all; and the news of his crash had plainly preceded him.) Well! if this was a foretaste of what he had to expect – snubs and slights from men who would once have been honoured by his notice – the sooner he got out of people's way the better. And bundling his clothes back into his trunk, he drove off again, choosing, characteristically enough, not a quiet hotel in a good neighbourhood, but a second-class boarding-house on the farther side of the Victoria Parade. Here, there was no earthly chance of meeting anyone he knew. Or, for that matter, of meeting anyone at all! For these outlying streets, planned originally for a traffic without compare – the seething mob of men, horses, vehicles that had once flowed, like a living river, to the goldfields – now lay as bare as they had then been thronged. By day an occasional spindly buggy might amble along their vast width, or a solitary bullock-wagon take its tortoise way; but after dark, feebly lit by ill-trimmed lamps set at enormous distances one from another, they turned into mere desolate, wind-swept spaces. On which no creature moved but himself.

It was here that he took his decisions, laid his plans. His days resembled a blurred nightmare, in which he sped from one dingy office to the next, or sat through interviews with lawyers and bankers – humiliating interviews, in the course of which his unbusiness-like conduct, his want of *nous* in money matters was mercilessly dragged to light. But in the evening he was free: and then he would pace by the hour round these deserted streets, with the collar of his greatcoat turned up to his ears, his hands clasped at his back, his head bent against the icy south winds; or, caught by a stinging hail-shower, would seek shelter under the lee of an old, half dismantled 'Horse, Cow and Pig

Market', of which the wild wind rattled and shook the loose timbers as if to carry them sky-high.

Of the large fortune he had amassed – the fortune so happily invested, so carefully husbanded – he had been able to recover a bare three thousand pounds. The unprincipled scoundrel in whose charge he had left it – on Purdy's equally unprincipled advice – had fleeced him of all else. On this pitiful sum, and a handful of second-rate shares which might bring him in the equivalent of what he had formerly spent in the year on books, or Mary on her servants and the running of the nurseries, he had now to start life anew: to provide a home, to feed, clothe, educate his children, pay his way. One thing was clear: he must set up his plate again with all dispatch; resume the profession he had once been so heartily glad to retire from. And his first bitterness and resentment over, he was only too thankful to have this to fall back on.

The moot question was, where to make the start; and in the course of the several anxious debates he had with himself on this subject, he became ever more relieved that Mary was not with him. Her absence gave him a freer hand. For, if he knew her, she would be all in favour of his settling up-country, dead against his trying to get a footing in Melbourne. Now he was as ready as any man could be, to atone to her for the straits to which he had brought her. But – he must be allowed to meet the emergency in his own way. It might not be the wisest or the best way; but it was the only one he felt equal to.

Bury himself alive up-country, he could and would not! . . . not if she talked till all was blue. He saw her points, of course: they were like herself . . . entirely practical. There were, she would argue, for every opening in Melbourne ten to be found in the bush, where doctors were scarce, and twice and three times the money to be made there. Living-expenses would be less, nor would he need to keep up any style. Which was true enough . . . as far as it went. What, womanlike, she would overlook, or treat as of slight importance, was the fact that he had also his professional pride to consider. He with his past to condemn himself to the backwoods! Frankly, he thought he would be doing not only himself, but his children after him, an injury, did he agree to anything of the kind. No! he was too good for the bush.

But the truth had still another facet. Constrained, at his age, to buckle to again, he could only, he believed, find the necessary courage under conditions that were not too direly repellent. And since, strive as he might, he could not break down Mary's imagined disapproval, he threw himself headlong into the attempt to get things settled – irrevocably settled – before she arrived; took to scouring the city and its environs, tramping the inner and outer suburbs, walking the soles off his boots and himself to a shadow, to find a likely place. Ruefully he turned his back on the sea at St Kilda and Elsternwick, the pleasant spot of earth in which he once believed he had found a resting place; gave the green gardens of Toorak a wide berth – no room there for an elderly interloper! – and, stifling his distaste, explored the outer darkness of Footscray, Essendon, Moonee Ponds. But it was always the same. If he found what he thought a suitable opening, there was certain not to be a house within cooee fit for them to live in.

What finally decided him on the pretty little suburb of Hawthorn – after he had thoroughly prowled and nosed round, to make sure he would have the field to himself – was not alone the good country air, but the fact that, at the junction of two main streets – or what would some day be main streets, the place being still in the making – he lit on a capital building lot, for sale dirt-cheap. For a doctor no finer position could be imagined – and in fancy he ran up the house that was to stand there. Of brick, two storeys high, towering above its neighbours, it would face both ways, be visible to all comers. The purchase of the land was easily effected – truth to tell, only too easily! He rather let himself be blarneyed into it. The house formed the stumbling-block. He sped from firm to firm; none would touch the job under a couple of thousand. In vain he tried to cut down his requirements. Less than two sitting-rooms they could not possibly do with, besides a surgery and a waiting-room. Four bedrooms, a dressing-room or two, a couple of bathrooms were equally necessary; while no house of this size but had verandah and balcony to keep the sun off, and to serve as an outdoor playroom for the children.

There was nothing for it, in the long run, but to put his pride in his pocket and take the advice given him on every hand: to build, as ninety-nine out of a hundred did here, through one of the numerous Building Societies that existed to aid those short of ready money. But it was a bitter pill for a man of his former wealth to swallow. Nor did it, on closer acquaintance, prove by any means the simple affair he had been led to believe. In the beginning, a thousand was the utmost he felt justified in laying down. But when he saw all that was involved he contrived, after much anxious deliberation, to stretch the thousand to twelve hundred, taking out a mortgage at ten per cent, with regular repayment of capital.

It was at this crisis that he felt most thankful Mary was not with him. *How* she would have got on his nerves! . . . with her doubts and hesitations, her aversion to taking risks, her fears lest he should land them all in Queer Street. Women paid dearly for their inexperience: when it came to a matter of business, even the most practical could not see beyond the tips of their noses. And, humiliating though the present step might be, there was absolutely no cause for alarm. These things were done – done on every hand – his eyes had been opened to that, in his recent wanderings. By men, too, less favourably placed than he. But even suppose, for supposing's sake, that he did not succeed to the top of his expectations – get, that was, the mortgage paid off within a reasonable time – where would be the hardship in treating the interest on the loan as a rental, in place of living rent-free? (And a very moderate rent, too, for a suitable house!) But Mary would never manage to forget the debt that lay behind. And it was here the temptation beset him to hold his tongue, to say nothing to her about the means he had been forced to employ. Let her believe he had built out of the resources left to him. For peace' sake, in the first place; to avoid the bother of explanation and recrimination. (What a drag, too, to know that somebody was eternally on the qui vive to see whether or no you were able to come up to the mark!) Yet again, by keeping his own counsel, he would spare her many an hour's anxiety – a sheerly needless anxiety. For any doubts he might have had himself, at the start, vanished like fog before a lifting breeze as he watched the house go up. Daily his conviction strengthened that he had done the right thing.

It became a matter of vital importance to him that the walls should be standing and the roof on, before Mary saw it: Mary needed the evidence of her senses: could grasp only what she had before her eyes. Then, pleasure at getting so fine a house might help to reconcile her to his scheme . . . God alone knew what the poor soul would be expecting. And so, in the belief that his presence stimulated the work-people, he spent many an hour in the months that followed watching brick laid to brick, and the hodmen lumber to and fro; or pottering about among clay and mortar heaps: an elderly gentleman in a long surtout, carrying gloves and a cane; with greyish hair and whiskers, and a thin, pointed face.

Again, he cooled his heels there because he had nothing better to do. Once bitten, twice shy, was his motto; and he continued rigidly to give friends and relatives the go-by: time enough to pick up the threads when he could step out once more in his true colours. Besides, the relatives were Mary's; the friends as well. The consequence was, he now fell into a solitariness beyond compare: got the habit of solitude, and neither missed nor wanted the company of his fellows.

Since, however, every man who still stands upright needs some star to go by, he kept his eyes steadfastly fixed on the coming of wife and children. This was to be his panacea for every ill. And as the six months' separation drew to an end, he could hardly contain himself for anxiety and impatience. Everything was ready for them: he had taken a comfortably furnished house in which to install them till their own was built; had engaged a servant, moved in himself. Feverishly he scanned the shipping-lists. Other boats made port which had left England at the same time . . . and even later . . . despite gales, and calms, and contrary winds. But it was not till the middle of December that the good ship *Sobraon*, ninety-odd days out, was sighted off Cape Otway; and he could take train to Queenscliff for a surprise meeting with his dear ones, and to sail with them up the Bay.

In his hand he carried a basket of strawberries – the first to come on the market.

Standing pointing out to the children familiar landmarks on the shores of their new-old home, Mary suddenly stopped in what she was saying and rubbed her eyes.

'Why! I do declare . . . if it's not – Look, children, *look*, there's your Papa! He's waving his handkerchief to you. Wave back! Nod your heads! Throw him a kiss!'

'Papa! . . . dere's Papa!' the twins told each other, and obediently set to wagging like a pair of china mandarins; the while with their pudgy hands they wafted kisses in the direction of an approaching boat-load of men.

'Where's he? *I* don't see!' opposed Cuffy, in a spirit to which the oneness of his sisters – still more, of sisters and mother – often provoked him. But this time he had a grievance as well.

Throughout the voyage there had been ever such lots of laughing and talking and guessing, about who would reckernize Papa first: and he, as the eldest, had felt quite safe. Now Mamma, who had joined in the game and guessed with them, had spoilt everything, not played fair.

But for once his mother did not heed his pouting. She was gazing with her heart in her eyes at the Health Officer's boat, in which, by the side of the doctor coming to board the ship, sat Richard in a set of borrowed oilskins, ducking his head to avoid the spray, and waving and shouting like an excited schoolboy. In a very few minutes now the long, slow torture of the voyage would be over, and she would know the worst.

Here he came, scrambling up the ladder, leaping to the deck.

'Richard! . . . my dear! Is it really you? But *oh*, how thin you've got!'

'Yes, here I am, safe and sound! But you, wife . . . how are you? – *And* the darlings? Come to Papa, who has missed you more than he can say! – Good day, good day, Eliza! I hope I see you well! – But *how* they've grown, Mary! Why, I hardly know them.'

The Dumplings, pink and drooping with shyness but docile as ever, dutifully held up their bud mouths to be kissed; then, smiling adorably, wriggled back to Mamma's side, crook'd finger to lip. But Cuffy did not smile as his father swung him aloft, and went pale instead of pink. For, at sight of the person who came jumping over, he had been seized by one of his panicky fears. The Dumplings, of course, didn't remember Papa, they couldn't, they were only four; but he did . . . and somehow he remembered him *diffrunt*. Could it be a mistake? Not that it wasn't him . . . he didn't mean that . . . he only meant . . . well, he wasn't sure what he did mean. But when this new-old Papa asked: 'And how's my big boy?' a fresh spasm of distrust shot through him. Didn't he know that everybody always said 'small for his age'?

But, dumped down on the deck again, he was forgotten, while over his head the quick, clipped voice went on: 'Perfectly well! . . . and with nothing in the world to complain of, now I've got you again. I thought you'd *never* come. Yes, I've been through an infernally anxious time, but that's over now, and things aren't as bad as they might be. You've no need to worry. But let's go below where we can talk in peace.' And with his arm round her shoulders he made to draw Mary with him . . . followed by the extreme silent wonder of three pairs of eyes, whose owners were not used any more to seeing Mamma taken away like this without asking. Or anybody's arm put round her either. When she belonged to them.

But at the head of the companion-way Mahony paused and slapped his brow.

'Ha! . . . but wait a minute. . . . Papa was forgetting. See here!' and from a side pocket of the capacious oilskins he drew forth the basket of strawberries. These had suffered in transit, were bruised and crushed.

'What, strawberries? – already?' exclaimed Mary, and eyed the berries dubiously. They were but faintly tinged.

'The very first to be had, my dear! I spied them on my way to the train. – Come, children!'

But Mary barred the way . . . stretched out a preventing hand. 'Not just now, Richard. Later on, perhaps . . . when they've had their dinners. Give them to me, dear.'

Jocularly he eluded her, holding the basket high, out of her reach. 'No, this is *my* treat! – Now who remembers the old game? "Open your mouths and shut your eyes and see what Jacko will send you!"'

The children closed in, the twins displaying rosy throats, their eyes faithfully glued to.

But Mary peremptorily interposed. 'No, no, they mustn't! I should have them ill. The things are not half ripe.'

'What? Not let them eat them? . . . after the trouble I've been to, to buy them and lug them here? Not to speak of what I paid for them.'

'I'm sorry, Richard, but – ssh, dear! surely you must see . . .' Mary spoke in a low, persuasive voice, at the same time frowning and making other wifely signals to him to lower his. (And thus engrossed did not feel a pull at her sleeve, or hear Cuffy's thin pipe: '*I'll* eat them, Mamma. I'd *like* to!' Now he knew it was Papa all right.) For several of their fellow passengers were watching and listening, and there stood Richard looking supremely foolish, holding aloft a single strawberry.

But he was too put out to care who saw or heard. 'Well and good then, if they're not fit to eat – not even *after* dinner! – there's only one thing to be done with them. Overboard they go!' And picking up the basket he tossed it and its contents into the sea. Before the children . . . Eliza . . . everybody.

With her arm through his, Mary got him below, to the privacy and seclusion of the cabin. The same old Richard! touchy and irascible . . . wounded by any trifle. But she knew how to manage him; and, by appealing to his common sense and good feelings, soon talked him round. Besides, on this particular day he was much too happy to see them all again, long to remain in dudgeon. Still, his first mood of pleasure and elation had fizzled out and was not to be recaptured. The result was, the account he finally gave her of the state of his finances, and their future prospects, was not the rose-coloured one he had intended and prepared. What she now got to hear bore more relation to sober fact.

CHAPTER TWO

A neighbour's cocks and hens wakened him before daybreak. The insensate creatures crew and cackled, cackled and crew; and, did they pause for breath, the sparrows took up the tale. He could not sleep again. Lying stiff as a log so as not to disturb Mary, he hailed each fresh streak of light that crept in at the sides of the blinds or over the tops of the valances; while any bagatelle was welcome that served to divert his thoughts and to bridge the gap till rising-time. The great mahogany wardrobe, for instance. This began as an integral part of the darkness, gradually to emerge, a shade heavier than the surrounding gloom, as a ponderous mass; only little by little, line by line, assuming its true shape. Faithfully the toilet-glass gave back each change in the room's visibility. Later on there were bars to count, formed by unevenness in the slats of the venetians, and falling golden on the whitewashed walls.

Yes, whitewash was, so far, the only covering the walls knew. The papering of them had had to be indefinitely postponed. And gaunt indeed was the effect of their cold whiteness on eyes used to rich, dark hangings. This was one reason why he preferred the penance of immobility, to getting up and prowling about downstairs. Never did the house look more cheerless than on an early morning, before the blinds were raised, the rooms in order. One realized then, only too plainly, what a bare barn it was; and how the task of rendering it cosy and homelike had baffled even Mary. He would not forget her consternation on first seeing it; her cry of: 'But Richard! . . . how shall we *ever* fill it?' Himself he stood by dumbfounded, as he watched her busy with tape and measure: truly, he had never thought of this. She had toiled, dear soul, for weeks on end, stitching at curtains and draperies to try to clothe the nakedness – in vain. If they had not had his books to fall back on, the place would have been uninhabitable. But he had emptied the whole of his library into it, with the result that books were everywhere: on the stair-landings, in the bedrooms; wherever they could with decency stop a gap. Another incongruity was the collection of curios and bric-a-brac garnered on their travels. This included some rare and costly objects, which looked odd, to say the least of it, in a room where there were hardly chairs enough to go round. For he had had everything to buy, down to the last kitchen fork and spoon. And by the time he had paid for a sideboard that did not make too sorry a show in the big dining-room; a dinner-table that had some relation to the floor-space; a piano, a desk for his surgery and so on, he was bled dry. Nor did he see the smallest prospect, in the meantime, of finishing the job. They had just to live on in this half-baked condition, which blazoned the fact that funds had given out; that he had put up a house it was beyond his means to furnish. How he writhed when strangers ran an appraising glance over it!

No: unrested, and without so much as a cup of tea in him, he could not bring himself to descend and contemplate the evidences of his folly. Instead, the daylight by now being come, he lay and totted up pound to pound until, for sheer weariness, he was ready to drop asleep again. But eight o'clock had struck, there could be no lapsing back into unconsciousness. He rose and went down to breakfast.

They had the children with them at table now. And good as the little things were by nature, yet they rose from ten hours' sound sleep lively as the sparrows: their tongues wagged without a stop. And though he came down with the best intentions, he soon found his nerves jarred. Altering the position of his newspaper for the tenth time, he was pettishly moved to complain: 'Impossible! *How* can I read in such a racket?'

'Oh, come, you can't expect children to sit and never say a word.'

But she hushed them, with frowns and headshakes, to a bout of whispering, or the loud, hissing noise children make in its stead; under fire of which it was still harder to fix his thoughts.

Retired to the surgery he was no better off; for now the thrumming of five-finger exercises began to issue from the drawing-room, where the children were having their music-lessons. This was unavoidable. With the arrival of the patients all noise had to cease; later on, Mary was too busy with domestic duties to sit by the piano; and that the youngsters must learn music went without saying. But the walls of the house had proved mere lath-and-plaster; and the tinkle of the piano, the sound of childish voices and Mary's deeper tones, raised in one-two-threes and one-two-three-fours, so distracted him that it took him all his time to turn up and makes notes on his cases for the day. By rights, this should have been his hour for reading, for refreshing his memory of things medical. But not only silence failed him; equally essential was a quiet mind; and as long as his affairs remained in their present uncertain state, that, too, was beyond his reach. Before he got to the foot of a page, he would find himself adding up columns of figures.

The truth was, his brain had reverted to its ancient and familiar employment with a kind of malicious glee. He was powerless to control it. Cark and care bestrode him; rode him to death; and yet got him nowhere; for all the calculations in the world would not change hard facts. Reckon as he might, he could not make his dividends for the past six months amount to more than a hundred and fifty pounds: a hundred and fifty! Nor was this wretched sum a certainty. It came from shares that were to the last degree unstable – in old days he had never given them a thought. And against this stood the sum of eight hundred pounds. Oh! he had grossly over-estimated his faculty for self-deception. Now that he was in the thick of things, it went beyond him to get this debt out of his mind. Suppose anything should happen to him before he had paid it off? What a legacy to leave Mary! Out and away his sorest regret was that, in the good old days now gone for ever, he had failed to insure his life. Thanks to his habitual dilatoriness he had put it off from year to year, always nursing the intention, shirking the effort. Now, the premium demanded would be sheerly unpayable.

At present everything depended on how the practice panned out. The practice . . . Truth to tell, after close on a six months' trial, he did not himself know what to make of it. Had he been less pressed for time and money, he might have described it as not unpromising. As matters stood, he could only say that what there *was* of it was good: the patients of a superior class, and so on. But from the first it had been slow to move – there seemed no sickness about – the fees slower still to come in. If, by the end of the year, things did not look up, he would have to write down his settling there as a bad job. It was an acute disappointment that he had only managed to secure two paltry lodges. Every general practitioner knew what *that* meant. He had built on lodge-work; not only for the income it assured, but also to give a fillip to the private practice. Again: not expecting what work there was to be so scattered, he had omitted to budget for horse hire, or the hire of a buggy. This made a real hole in his takings. He walked wherever he could; but calls came from places as far afield as Kew and Camberwell, which were not to be reached on foot. Besides, the last thing in the world he could afford to do was to knock himself up. Even as it was, he got back from his morning round tired out; and after lunch would find himself dozing in his chair. Of an evening, he was glad to turn in soon after ten o'clock; the one bright side to the general slackness being the absence of night-work. Of course, such early hours meant giving the go-by to all social pleasures. But truly he was in no trim for company, either at home or abroad. How he was beginning to rue the day when he had burdened himself with a house of this size, merely that he might continue to make a show among his fellow-men. When the plain truth was, he would not turn a hair if he never saw one of them again.

Yes, his present feeling of unsociableness went deeper than mere fatigue: it was a kind of deliberate turning-in on himself. Mary no doubt hit the mark, when she blamed the months of morbid solitude to which he had condemned himself on reaching Melbourne. He had, declared she, never been the same man since.

'I ought to have known better than to let you come out alone.'

She spoke heartily; but doubts beset her. It was one thing to put your finger on the root of an ill; another to cure it. Yet a failure to do so might cost them dear. Here was Richard with his way and his name to make, a practice to build up, connections to form; and, instead of taking every hand that offered, he kept up his 'Ultima Thule' habits of refusing invitations, shirking introductions; and declined into this 'let me alone and don't bother me' state, than which, for a doctor, she could imagine none more fatal.

Of course, having to start work again at his age was no light matter, and he undoubtedly felt the strain; found it hard also, after all the go-as-you-please latter years, to nail himself down to fixed hours and live by the clock. He complained, too, that his memory wasn't what it used to be. Names, now. If he didn't write down a name the moment he heard it, it was bound to escape him; and then he could waste the better part of a morning in struggling to recapture it.

'You're out of the way of it, dear, that's all,' she resolutely strove to cheer him, as she brushed his hat and hunted for his gloves. 'Now have you your case-book? And is everything in your bag?' More than once he had been obliged to tramp the whole way home again, for a forgotten article.

The reminder annoyed him. 'Yes, yes, of course. But my thermometer . . . now where the dickens have I put that?' And testily he tapped pocket after pocket.

'Here . . . you've left it lying. Oh, by the way, Richard, I wonder if you'd mind leaving an order at the butcher's as you go past?'

But at this he flared up. 'Now, Mary, *is* it fair to bother me with that kind of thing, when I've so much else to think of?'

'Well, it's only . . . the shop's so far off, and I can't spare cook. You've just to hand in a note as you pass the door.'

'Yes, yes. A thousand and one reasons!'

'Oh well, never mind. Eliza and the children must go that way for their walk – though it does take them down among the shops.'

'And why not? Are the children everlastingly to be spared at my expense?'

He went off, banging the gate behind him. The latch did not hold; Mary stepped out to secure it. And the sight of him trudging down the road brought back her chief grievance against him. This was his obstinate refusal to keep a horse and trap. It stood to reason: if he would only consent to drive on his rounds, instead of walking, he would save himself much of the fatigue he now endured; and she be spared his perpetual grumbles. Besides, it was not the thing for a man of his age and appearance to be seen tramping the streets, bag in hand. But she might as well have talked to a post. The only answer she got was that he couldn't afford it. Now this was surely imagination. She flattered herself she knew something about a practice, and could tell pretty well what the present one was likely to throw off . . . if properly nursed. To the approximate three hundred a year which Richard admitted to drawing from his dividends, it should add another three; and on six, with her careful management, they could very well pull through to begin with. It left no margin for extravagances, of course; but the husbanding of Richard's strength could hardly be put down under that head. Since, however, he continued obdurate, she went her own way to work; with the result that, out of the money he allowed her to keep house on, she contrived at the end of three months to hand him back a tidy sum.

'Now if you don't feel you want to *buy* a horse and buggy, you can at least give a three months' order at the livery-stable.'

But not a bit of it! More, he was even angry. 'Tch! *Do*, for goodness' sake, leave me to manage my own affairs! I don't want a horse and trap, I tell you. I prefer to go on as I am.' And, with that, her economies just passed into and were swallowed up in the general fund. She wouldn't do it again.

'Mamma!'

This was Cuffy, who had followed her out and climbed the gate at her side. He spoke in a coaxy voice; for as likely as not Mamma would say: 'Run away, darling, and don't bother me. I've no time.' But Cuffy badly wanted to know something. And, since Nannan left, there had never been anyone he could ask his questions of: Mamma was always busy, Papa not at home.

'Mamma! Why does Papa poke his head out so when he walks?'

'That's stooping. People do it as they grow older.' Even the child, it seemed, could see how tiresome Richard found walking.

'What's it mean growing old – really, truly?'

'Why, losing your hair and your teeth, and not being able to get about as well as you used to.'

'Does it hurt?'

'Of course not, little silly!'

'Does Papa lose his teeth? Does Eliza? And why has he always got a bag in his hand now?'

'*What* an inquisitive little boy! He carries things in it to make people well with.'

'Why does he want to make them well?'

'To get money to buy you little folks pretty clothes and good things to eat. But come . . . jump down! And run and tell Eliza to get you ready for your walk.'

'I don't *like* going walks with Eliza,' said Cuffy and, one hand in his mother's, reluctantly dragged and shuffled a foot in the gravel. 'Oh, I *do* wis' I had my little pony again.'

'So do I, my darling,' said Mary heartily, and squeezed his hand. 'I'm afraid you'll be forgetting how to ride. I must talk to Papa. Then perhaps Santa Claus . . . or on your birthday . . .'

'Ooh! Really, truly, Mamma?'

'We'll see.' – At which Cuffy hopped from side to side up the length of the path.

And Mary meant what she said. It was unthinkable that *her* children should come short in any of the advantages other children enjoyed. And not to be able to ride, and ride well, too, in a country like this, might prove a real drawback to them in after life. Now she had pinched and screwed for Richard's sake, to no purpose whatever. The next lump sum she managed to get together should go to buying a pony.

But this was not all. Besides riding, the children ought to be having dancing-lessons. She did so want her chicks to move prettily and gracefully; to know what to do with their hands and feet; to be able to enter a room without awkwardness; and they were just at their most impressionable age: what they now took in they would never forget, what they missed, never make good. But she could hope for no help from Richard; manlike, he expected graces and accomplishments to spring up of themselves, like wild flowers from the soil. Everything depended on her. And she did not spare herself. Thanks to her skill with her needle, they were still, did they go to a party, the best-dressed children in the room; and the best-mannered, too, Nannan's strict upbringing still bearing fruit. None of her three ever grabbed, or gobbled, or drank with a full mouth; nor were they either lumpishly shy or over-forward, like the general ruck of colonial children.

But they were getting big; there would soon be more serious things to think of than manners and accomplishments. If only Richard did not prove too unreasonable! So far, except for music-lessons, they had had no teaching at all, one of his odd ideas being that a child's brain should lie fallow till it was seven or eight years old. This meant that she had sometimes to suffer the mortification of seeing children younger than Cuffy and his sisters able to answer quite nicely at spelling and geography, while hers stood mutely by. In the Dumplings' case it did not greatly matter: they were still just Dumplings in every sense of the word; fat and merry play-babies. But Cuffy was sharp for his age; he could read his own books, and knew long pieces of poetry by heart. It seemed little short of absurd to hold such a child back; and after she had once or twice seen him put publicly to shame, Mary took, of a morning, when she was working up a flake-crust or footing her treadle-machine, to setting him a copy to write, or giving him simple lessons in spelling and sums. (Which little incursions into knowledge were best, it was understood, not mentioned to Papa.)

Her thoughts were all for her children. Herself she needed little; and was really managing without difficulty to cut her coat to suit her cloth. In the matter of dress, for instance, she still had the rich furs, the sumptuous silks and satins she had brought with her from home – made over, these things would last her for years – had all her ivory and mother-o'-pearl ornaments and trifles. True, she walked where she had driven, hired less expensive servants, rose betimes of a morning, but who shall say whether these changes were wholly drawbacks in Mary's eyes, or whether the return to a more active mode of life did not, in great measure, outweigh them? It certainly gave her a feeling of satisfaction to which she had long been a stranger, to know that not a particle of waste was going on in her kitchen; that she was once more absolute monarch in her own domain. Minor pleasures consisted in seeing how far she could economize the ingredients of pudding or cake and yet turn it out light and toothsome. Had Richard wished to entertain, she would have guaranteed to hold the floor with anyone, at half the cost.

But there was no question of this. They lived like a pair of hermit crabs; and, in spite of the size of the house, might just as well have been buried in the bush. For, having talked herself hoarse in pointing out the harm such a mode of life would do the practice, she had given way and made the best of things; as long, that was, as Richard's dislike of company had only to do with the forming of new acquaintances. When he began his old grumbles at the presence of her intimate friends and relatives, it was more than she could stand. In the heated argument that followed her perplexed: 'Not ask Lizzie? Put off the Devines?' she discovered, to her amazement, that it was not alone his morbid craving for solitude that actuated him: the house, if you please, formed the stumbling-block! Because this was still unpapered and rather scantily furnished, he had got it into his head that it was not fit to ask people to; that he would be looked down on, because of it. Now did *anyone* ever hear such nonsense? Why, half the houses in Melbourne were just as bare, and nobody thought the worse of them. People surely came to see you, not your furniture! But he had evidently chafed so long in silence over what he called the 'poverty-stricken aspect of the place', that there was now no talking him out of the notion. So Mary shrugged and sighed; and, silently in her turn, took the sole way left her, which was an underground way; so contriving matters that her friends came to the house only when Richard was out of it . . . a little shift it was again wiser not to mention to Papa. She also grew adept at getting rid of people to the moment. By the time the gate clicked at Richard's return, all traces of the visit had been cleared away.

CHAPTER THREE

Thus she bought peace. – But when the day came for putting up a guest in the house, for making use of the unused spare room, finesse did not avail; and a violent dispute broke out between them. To complicate matters, the guest in question was Richard's old bugbear, Tilly.

Tilly, whose dearest wish had been fulfilled some six months back by the birth of a child, but who since then had remained strangely silent, now wrote, almost beside herself with grief and anxiety, that she was bringing her infant, which would not thrive, to town, to consult the doctors there. And Mary straightway forgot all her schemes and contrivances, forgot everything but a friend in need, and wrote off by return begging Tilly, with babe and nurse, to make their house her own.

Mahony was speechless when he heard of it. He just gave her one look, then stalked out of the room and shut himself up in the surgery, where he stayed for the rest of the evening. While Mary sat bent over her needlework, with determined lips and stubborn eyes.

Later on, in the bedroom, his wrath exploded in bitter abuse of Purdy, ending with: 'No one belonging to that fellow shall ever darken *my* doors again!'

At this she, too, flared up. 'Oh . . . put all the blame for what happened on somebody else. It never occurs to you to blame yourself, and your own rashness and impatience. Who but you would ever have trusted a man like Wilding? – But Tilly being Purdy's wife is nothing but an excuse. It's not only her. You won't let a soul inside the doors.'

'Why should my wishes alone be disregarded? The very children's likes and dislikes are taken more account of. You consider everyone . . . only not me!'

'And you consider no one but yourself!'

'Well, this is my house, and I have the right to say who shall come into it.'

'It's no more yours than mine. And Tilly's my oldest friend, and I'm not going to desert her now she's in trouble. I've asked her to come here, and come she shall!'

'Very well then, if she does, I go!' – and so on, and on.

In the adjoining dressing-room, the door of which stood ajar, Cuffy sat up in his crib and listened. The loud voices had wakened him and he couldn't go to sleep again. He was frightened; his heart beat pit-a-pat, pit-a-pat. And when he heard somebody begin to cry, he just couldn't help it, he had to cry, too. Till a door went and quick steps came running; and then there were Papa's hands to hold to, and Papa's arms round him; and quite a lot of Hambelin Town and Handover City to make him go to sleep.

The knot was cut by Tilly choosing, with many, many thanks, to stay at an hotel in town. There Mary sought her out one late autumn afternoon, when the white dust was swirling house-high through the white streets, and the south wind had come up so cold that she regretted not having worn her sealskin. Alighting from the train at Prince's Bridge, she turned a deaf ear to the shouts of: 'Keb, Keb!' and leaving the region of warehouses – poor John's among them – made her way on foot up the rise to Collins Street. This was her invariable habit nowadays, if she hadn't the children with her: was one of the numerous little economies she felt justified in practising . . . and holding her tongue about. Richard, of course, would have snorted with disapproval. *His* wife to be tramping the streets! But latterly she had found her tolerance of his grandee notions about what she might and might not do, wearing a little thin. In the present state of affairs they seemed, to say the least of it, out of place. She had legs of her own, and was every bit as well able to walk as he was. If people looked down on her for it . . . well, they would just have to, and that was all about it!

These brave thoughts notwithstanding, she could not but wish – as she sat waiting in a public coffee-room, the door of which opened and shut a dozen times to the minute, everyone who entered fixing her with a hard and curious stare – wish that Tilly had picked on a quieter hotel, one more suitable to a lady travelling alone. She was glad when the waiter ushered her up the red-carpeted stairs to her friend's private sitting-room.

Tilly was so changed that she hardly knew her. Last seen in

the first flush of wifehood, high-bosomed, high-coloured, high-spirited, she seemed to have shrunk together, fallen in. Her pale face was puffy; her eyes deeply ringed.

'You poor thing! What you must have suffered!'

Mary said this more than once as she listened to Tilly's tale. It was that of a child born strong and healthy – 'As fine a boy as ever you saw, Mary!' – with whom all had gone well until, owing to an unfortunate accident, they had been forced to change the wet-nurse. Since then they had tried one nurse after another; had tried hand-feeding, goat's milk, patent mixtures; but to no purpose. The child had just wasted away. Till he was now little more than a skeleton. Nor had he ever sat up or taken notice. The whole day long he lay and wailed, till it nearly broke your heart to hear it.

'And me . . . who'd give my life's blood to help 'im!'

'Have you seen MacMullen? What does he say?'

Tilly answered with a hopeless lift of her shoulders. ' 'E calls it by a fine name, Mary – they all do. And 'as given us a new food to try. But the long and short of it is, if the wasting isn't stopped, Baby will die.' And, the ominous words spoken, Tilly's composure gave way: the tears came with a gush and streamed down her cheeks, dropping over into her lap, before she managed to fish a handkerchief from her petticoat pocket.

'There, there, you old fool!' she rebuked herself. 'Sorry, love. It comes of seeing your dear old face again. For weeping and wailing doesn't help either, does it?'

'Poor old girl, it *is* hard on you . . . and when you've so wanted children.'

'Yes, and'm never likely to 'ave another. Other people can get 'em by the dozen – as 'ealthy as can be.'

'Well, I shouldn't give up hope of pulling him through – no matter what the doctors say. You know, Tilly . . . it may seem an odd thing to come from me . . . but I really haven't *very* much faith in them. I mean – well, you know, they're all right if you break your leg or have something definite the matter with you, like mumps or scarlet fever – or if you want a tumour cut out. But otherwise, well, they never seem to allow enough . . . I mean, for *common-sense* things. Now what I think is, as the child has held out so long, there must be a kind of toughness in him. And there's always just a chance you may still find the right thing.'

But when, leaning over the cot, she saw the tiny, wizened

creature that lay among its lace and ribbons: ('Hardly bigger than a rabbit, Richard . . . with the face of an old, old man — no, more like a poor starved little monkey!') when, too, the feather-weight burden was laid on her lap, proving hardly more substantial than a child's doll: then, Mary's own heart fell.

Sitting looking down at the little wrinkled face, her mother eyes full of pity, she asked: 'What does Purdy say?'

' '*Im?*' Again Tilly raised her shoulders, but this time the gesture bespoke neither resignation nor despair. 'Oh, Purd's sorry, of course.'

'I should think so, indeed.'

'*Sorry!* Does being sorry *help?*' And now her words came flying, her aitches scattering to the winds. 'The plain truth is, Mary, there's not a man living who can go on 'earing a child cry, cry, cry, day and night and night and day, and keep 'is patience and 'is temper. And Purd's no different to the rest. When it gets too bad, 'e just claps on 'is 'at and flies out of the 'ouse — to get away from it. Men are like that. Only the rosy side of things for them! And Purd, 'e must be *free*. The smallest jerk of the reins and it's all up. As for a sick child . . . and even though it's 'is own — oh, I've learnt *something* about men since I married 'im, Mary! Purd's no good to lean on, not an 'apporth o' good. 'E's like an air-cushion — goes in where you lean and puffs out somewhere else. And 'ow can 'e 'elp it? — when there isn't anything *but* air in 'im. No, 'e's nothing in the world but fizzle and talk . . . a bag of chaff — an 'ollow drum.'

Mary heard her sadly and in silence. This, too. Oh, the gilt was off poor Tilly's gingerbread in earnest.

But, in listening, she had also cocked an attentive ear, and now she said: 'Tilly, there's something about that child's cry . . . there's a tone in it — a . . .'

' 'Ungry . . .!' said Tilly fiercely. ' 'E's starving — that's what it is.'

'Of course, hungry, too. But I must say it sounds to me more *angry*. And then look how he beats the air with his little fists. He's not trying to suck them or even get them near his mouth. What I'm wondering is . . . Richard can't, of course, touch the case, now it's in MacMullen's hands. But I'm going home to tell him all about it. He used to have great luck with children in the old days. There's no saying. He *might* be able to suggest something. In the meantime, my dear, keep a good heart. Nothing is gained by despairing.'

'Bless you, Mary! If anyone can put spunk into a mortal it's you.'

'Starving?' said Mahony on hearing the tale. 'I shouldn't wonder if starving itself was not nearer the mark.'

'But Richard, such a *young* child . . . do you really think . . . Though I must say when I heard that *exasperated* sort of cry . . .'

'Exactly. Who's to say where consciousness begins? . . . or ends. For all we know, the child in the womb may have its own dim sentience. Now I don't need to give *you* my opinion of the wet-nurse system. None the less, if the case were mine, I should urge the mother to leave no stone unturned to find the person who first had it at the breast. A woman of her class will still be nursing.'

'Mary! I'll give 'er the 'alf of what I 'ave. I'll make a spectacle of myself – go on me knees down Sturt Street if need be; but back she comes!' were Tilly's parting words as she stepped into the train.

And sure enough, not a week later a letter arrived to say that, by dint of fierce appeals to her motherhood and unlimited promises ('What it's going to cost me, Purd will *never* know!'), the woman had been induced to return. A further week brought a second communication to the breakfast-table, scrawled in a shaky hand and scrappily put together, but containing the glad news that the child had actually gained a few ounces in weight, and, better still, had ceased its heartrending wail. Tilly's joy and gratitude were of such a nature that Mary did not dare to deliver the message she sent Richard, as it stood. She just translated the gist of it into sober English.

And a good job, too, that she had watered it down. For Richard proved to be in one of his worst, early-morning moods; and was loud in scorn of even the little she passed on.

He ended by thoroughly vexing her. 'Never did I know such a man! Things have come to such a pass that people can't even feel grateful to you, without offending you. Your one desire is to hold them at arm's length. You ought to have been born a mole.'

In speaking she had hastily reinserted Tilly's letter in its envelope. A second letter was lying by her plate. This she read with wrinkled brows, an occasional surreptitious glance at Richard, and more than one smothered: 'Tch!' She also hesitated for some time before deciding to hand it, past three pairs of inquisitive young eyes, over the table.

'Here! I wonder what you'll say to this? It's not my fault this time, remember.'

Mahony incuriously laid aside his newspaper, took the sheet, frowned at the writing, and tilted it to the correct angle for his eyes, which were 'not what they used to be'.

The letter ran:

My dear Mrs Mahony,

My dear wife has been ordered a sea-voyage for the benefit of her health, and before sailing, wishes, as ladies will, to visit the Melbourne emporiums and make some additions to her wardrobe. It is impossible for me to accompany her, though I shall hope to bid her 'au revoir' before she sails, a fortnight hence. May I trespass upon your goodness, and request you to be Agnes's cicerone and escort, while in Melbourne for the above object? I need not dwell on her preference for you in this rôle, over everyone else.

Give my due regards to your husband,
and, believe me,
very truly yours,
Henry Ocock.

'In plain English, I presume, it's to be your duty to keep her off the bottle.'

'Richard! . . . ssh! How *can* you?' expostulated Mary, with a warning headshake; which was justified by Cuffy at once chiming in: 'Do ladies have bottles too, Mamma, as well as babies?' (Cuffy had been deeply interested in the sad story of Aunt Tilly's little one and its struggle for life.) 'Now, you chicks, Lallie untie Lucie's bib and all three run out and play. – *Not* before the children, Richard! That boy drinks in every word. You'll have him repeating what you say in front of Agnes. For I suppose what Mr Henry really means is that we are to invite her here?'

'The hint is as plain as the nose on your face.'

'Yes, I'm afraid it is,' and Mary sighed. 'I wonder what we should do. I'm very fond of Agnes; but I've got the children to think of. I shouldn't like *them* to get an inkling . . . On the other hand, we can't afford to offend an influential person like Mr Henry.'

'I know what *I* can't afford – and that's to have this house turned into a dumping-ground for all the halt and maimed of your acquaintance. The news of its size is rapidly spreading. And if people once get the idea they can use it as they used "Ultima Thule", God help us! There'll be nothing for it but to move . . . into a four-roomed hut.'

'Oh, Richard, if you would only tell me how we really stand, instead of making such a mystery of it. For we can't go on living without a soul ever entering our doors.'

'We may be glad if we manage to live at all.'

'There you go! One exaggeration after the other.'

'Well, well! I suppose if Ocock has set his mind on us dry-nursing his wife again, we've got to truckle to him. Only don't ask me to meet *him* over the head of it. I've no intention of being patronized by men of his type, now that I've come down in the world.'

'*Patronized?* When I think how ready people were to take us up again when we first came out! But you can't expect them to go on asking and inviting for ever, and always being snubbed by a refusal.'

Agnes. Sitting opposite her old friend in the wagonette that bore them from the station, watching the ugly tic that convulsed one side of her face, Mary thought sorrowfully of a day, many a year ago, when, standing at the door of her little house, she had seen approach a radiant vision in riding-habit, curls and feathers. What a lovely creature Agnes had been! . . . how full of kindliness and charm . . . and all to end in this: a poor little corpulent, shapeless red-faced woman, close on fifty now, but with the timid, uncertain bearing of a cowed child. Never should she have married Mr Henry. With another man for a husband, everything might have turned out differently.

The first of a series of painful incidents occurred when, the cab having drawn up at the gate, the question of paying the driver's fare arose. Formerly, the two of them would have had a playful quarrel over it, each disputing the privilege with the other. Now, Agnes only said: 'If you will be so good, love? . . . my purse so hard to get at,' in a tone that made Mary open her eyes. It soon came out that she had been shipped to Melbourne literally without a penny in her pocket. Wherever they went, Mary had to be purse-bearer, Agnes following meekly and shamelessly at her heels. An intolerable position for any man to put his wife in! It was true she had *carte blanche* at the big drapery stores; but all she bought – down to the last handkerchief – was entered on a bill for Mr Henry's scrutiny. Did she wish to make a present – and she was just as generous as of old – she had so to contrive it (and she certainly showed a lamentable want of dignity, the skill of a practised hand, in arranging matters with the shopman) that, for instance, one entry on the bill should be a handsome mantle, which she never bought. The result was a sweet little ivory-handled parasol for 'darling Mary'; a box of magnificent toys and books for the children, of whom she made much.

From her own she was completely divorced, both boy and girl having been put to boarding-school at a tender age. But Agnes was fond of children; and, of a morning, while Mary was shaking up the beds or baking pastry, she would sit on the balcony watching the three at play; occasionally running her fingers through the twins' fair curls, which were so like the goldilocks of the child she had lost.

She never referred to her own family; had evidently long ceased to have any motherly feelings for them. She just lived on dully and stupidly, without pride, without shame – so long, that was, as she was not startled or made afraid. The company of the children held no alarms for her; but early in the visit Mary found it necessary to warn Richard: 'Now whatever you do, dear, don't be short and snappy before her. It throws her into a perfect twitter.'

And Richard, who, for all his violence of expression, would not have harmed a fly, was thereafter gentleness itself in Mrs Henry's presence, attending to her wants at table, listening courteously to her few diffident opinions, till the little woman's eyes filled with tears and she ceased to spill her tea or mess her front with her egg. 'The doctor ... so nice, love ... so very, very kind!'

'She has evidently been bullied half out of her wits.'

Throughout the fortnight she stayed with them, Mary was the faithfullest of guardians, putting her own concerns entirely on one side to dog her friend's footsteps. And yet, for all her vigilance, she could sometimes have sworn that Agnes's breath was tainted; while on the only two occasions on which she let her out of her sight ... well! what then happened made her look with more lenience on Mr Henry's precautions. Once, Lucie had a touch of croup in the night and could not be left, so that Agnes must needs go alone to her dressmaker; and once came an invitation to a luncheon-party in which Mary was not included. Each time a wagonette was provided for Mrs Henry from door to door, and paid to wait and bring her home; while Richard even condescended to give the driver a gentle hint and a substantial tip. And yet, both times, when she returned and tried to get out of the cab . . . oh dear! there was nothing for it but to say in a loud voice, for the servants' benefit: 'I'm so sorry you don't feel well, dear. Lean on me!' to get the door of the spare room shut on her and whip her into bed.

'Jus' like a *real* baby!' thought Cuffy, who had not forgotten the remark about the bottle. Running into the spare room in search of his mother, he had found Aunt Agnes sitting on the side of the bed, with only her chemise on and a very red face, while Mamma, looking funny, rummaged in a trunk. Going to bed in the daytime? Why? Had she been naughty? And was Mamma cross with her, too? She was with him. She said: 'Go away at once!' and 'Naughty boy!' before he was hardly inside. But Aunt Agnes was funny altogether. Cook and Eliza thought so, too. They laughed and whispered things he didn't ought to hear. But he did once. And that night at the supper-table curiosity got the better of him, and he asked out loud: 'Where's Auntie Agnes too tight, Mamma?'

'Too tight? Now whatever do you mean by that?'

Mary's tone was jocosely belittling. But Cuffy was not deceived by it. Instinctively he recognized the fond pride that lurked beneath the depreciation – the amused interest in 'what in all the world the child would say next'. He was also spurred on by the attention of the Dumplings, who, remembering sad affairs of too much cake and tight pinny-bands, sat eager and expectant, turning their eyes from Mamma to him and back again.

'Why, Eliza said . . . she said Auntie Agnes was tight – too tight.'

Above his head the eyes of husband and wife met; and Mahony threw out his hands as if to imply: 'There you have it!'

But Mamma was *drefully* angry. 'How dare you repeat such a nasty, vulgar thing! I'm *ashamed* of you – you naughty boy!'

Besides really 'wanting to know', Cuffy had thought his question a funny one, which would call forth laughter and applause. He was dumbfounded, and went red to the roots of his hair. What had he said? Why was Mamma so cross? Why was it more wrong for Auntie Agnes to be tight than Lallie or Lucie? — And now he had made Mamma and Papa cross with each other again, too.

'It's not *repeating* kitchen talk that matters, Mary; but that the child should be in the way of hearing it at all.'

'Pray, how can I help it? I do my best; but it's quite impossible for me never to let the children out of my sight. I've told you over and over again they need a governess.'

As the time approached for Mr Henry's arrival, Agnes grew more and more ill at ease: her tic redoubled in violence; she could settle to nothing, and wandered aimlessly from room to room; while, on receipt of the letter fixing the day, she began openly to shake and tremble. 'You won't mention to Henry, Mary . . . I mean . . . oh, love, you understand?' and all Mary's tactful assurances did not quieten her. Her fear of her husband was painful to see; almost equally painful her barefaced relief when, at the eleventh hour, important business cropped up which made it impossible for Mr Henry to get away.

'Of course, if things have come to this pass between them, then it's much better they should be separated for a while. But that he can let *any* business interfere with seeing her off on so long a journey — well, all I can say is . . .' said Mary; and left the rest of her wrath to the imagination.

'Tut, tut! . . . when he's got someone here to do his dirty work for him. He probably never had any intention of coming.'

So the two women drove to Sandridge and boarded a sailing-vessel bound for the Cape. The best cabin amidships had been engaged for Agnes, and tastefully furnished. There were flowers in it, and several boxes of biscuits and oranges for the voyage. But Agnes did not so much as look round; she only cried and cried; and, when the time for parting came, threw her arms about Mary and clung to her as if she would never let go. It was, said Mary afterwards, just like seeing a doomed creature off for perdition.

'I don't believe she'll ever come back. Oh, it's a burning shame! Why *couldn't* he have put her in a Home?'

'My dear, that would publish his disgrace to the world. He has chosen the one polite and irreproachable way of getting rid of her . . . without a scandal.'

'You mean . . .? But surely she won't be able to get it on board ship?'

'If you think that, Mary, you will know next to nothing of

the tricks a tippler is up to!' – And how right he was, was shewn when the cook, in turning out the spare room, came upon a regular nest of bottles – empty medicine-bottles, the dregs of which bespoke their contents – tucked away inside the first bend of the chimney.

Mary wrote to Mr Henry informing him of Agnes's departure, also that the visit had passed off *without contretemps*: and shortly after, she received the gift of a photograph-album, bound in vellum and stamped in gold with her initials. It was a handsome and costly present. But Mahony waxed bitterly sarcastic over the head of it.

'An album! . . . a photograph-album! . . . as sole return for the expense we've been put to – why, cab-hire alone must have run into pounds – over *his* wife, whom we did not invite and had no wish to see. Not to speak of the strain the visit has been on you, my dear.'

'But Richard, you wouldn't have had him send us money? – ask for our *bill*?' Mary spoke heatedly to hide her own feelings, which were much the same as his. Richard singled out cab-fares; but these were but one item of many. In the course of a long day's shopping Agnes and she had needed lunch and refreshment – manlike he no doubt imagined them living on air! – and not infrequently Agnes had fancied some article in a shop where no account was run: none of which extras had been mentioned to him. The truth was, what with this, that and the other thing, Mary had been forced to make a sad hole in her savings.

'We certainly don't need Ocock's assistance in going downhill,' was Richard's parting shot.

It was true, a very hearty note accompanied the album; the pith of which was:

If at any time, my dear Mrs Mahony, an opportunity to return your great kindness to my dear wife should arise, I trust you will let me hear of it.

CHAPTER FOUR

Tomorrow was the Dumplings' birthday, and they were having a big party. But it was his, Cuffy's, party, too; for when he had first got six, they didn't have a house yet, and there was no room for a party. It was really *most* his, 'cos he was the oldest: his cake would be six storeys high, and have six lighted candles round it, and his chair be trimmed with most green leaves. Mamma said he might cut the cake his very own self, and make the pieces big or little just as he liked. She stopped in the kitchen all day, baking jam tarts and sausage-rolls, and men had taken the drawing-room carpet off and sprinkled the floor with white dust, so's you could slide on it. All his cousins were coming, and Cousin Emmy, and lots and lots of other children. But it was not of these grandeurs Cuffy thought, as he sat on the edge of the verandah, and, for sheer agitation, rocked himself to and fro. The truth was, in spite of the glorious preparations he felt anything but happy. Guiltily and surreptitiously he had paid at least a dozen visits to the outhouse at the bottom of the yard, to steal a peep inside. First, Mamma had said 'soon' for the pony, and then 'someday', and then his birthday: so tomorrow was his last hope. And this hope was growing littler and littler. If *only* he hadn't told! But he had, had whispered it in a secret to the Dumplings, and to that horrid tease, Cousin Josey, as well. And promised them rides, and let the twins draw lots who should be first; and they guessed and guessed what colour it would be; all in a whisper so's Mamma shouldn't hear.

'*I* fink it'll be black,' said Lallie; and Lucie nodded: 'Me, too! An' wiv a white tail.'

'But I *know* it'll be brown!'

'He knows it'll be bwown!' buzzed one Fatty to the other.

'Huh! I wouldn't *have* a pony with a white tail.'

But peep as he might, no little horse appeared in the shed; and Cuffy went about with a strange, empty, sinking feeling inside him — a sense of having been tricked. Nor did the several handsome presents he found beside his bed make up to him for this disappointment. He early kicked over a giraffe belonging to the giant Noah's Ark and broke its neck; flew into a tantrum when rebuked; was obstreperous about being dressed, and snarly to his sisters; till Mary said, if he didn't behave he'd go to bed instead. How he dreaded the display of the presents! Cousin Josey with her sneery laugh would be sure to blurt out in front of everybody: 'He said he was going to get a pony! Ho! Where's your pony now?' The Dumplings were easier to deal with. In answer to their round-eyed wonder he just said, in airy fashion: 'He says he can't come quite today. He didn't get born yet.'

'Have you seed him?'

'Course I have!' Which left the twins more dazzled than would have done the animal's arrival.

But it proved as lovely a party as they had ever had — lasted till past eleven, and the whole house, with the exception of the surgery, was turned upside down for it. Quite twenty children came, and nearly as many grown-ups. The drawing-room was stripped bare of its furniture but for a line of chairs placed round the walls. Verandah and balcony were hung with Chinese lanterns and dozens of coloured balloons. In the dining-room a long table, made up of several smaller tables put together, was laden with cakes and creams and jellies; and even the big people found the good things 'simply delicious'. And though, of course, Mary could not attempt to compete with some of the lavish entertainments here given for children — the Archie Whites had actually had a champagne supper for their five-year-old, the Boppins had hired a *chef* from a caterer's — yet she had spared no pains to make her children's party unique in its way. And never for an instant did she allow the fun to flag. Even the quite little tots, who soon tired of games and dancing, were kept amused. For their benefit a padded see-saw had been set up on the verandah, as well as a safe nursery swing. On the stair-landings stood a bran pie and a lucky bag; while Emmy superintended the fishing for presents that went on, with rod and line, over the back of the drawing-room sofa.

In a pause between the games Mary walked through the drawing-room, her black silk skirts trailing after her, the hands of two of the smallest children in hers; one of them John's baby-boy, a bandy-legged mite, still hardly able to toddle. Mary was enjoying herself almost as much as the children; her cheeks were rose-pink with satisfaction, her eyes a-sparkle. At this moment, however, her objective was Cuffy, who, his black eyes not a whit less glittery than her own, his topknot all askew – he was really getting too big for a topknot; but she found it hard to forgo the morning pleasure of winding the silky curl about her finger – Cuffy was utilizing the pause to skate up and down the slippery floor. He was in wild spirits: Cousin Josey had contented herself with making a hidjus face at him and pinching him on the sly: the titbit of the evening, the cutting of the cake, was still to come; and he had played his piece – 'Home Sweet Home' 'with runs' – which had earned him the usual crop of praise and applause. Now there was no holding him.

'Cuffy! Cuffy *dear*, don't romp like that! You *must* behave, and set a good example to your visitors. Listen! I think I heard Papa. Run, and tell him to slip on another coat, and come in and see the fun.'

But Cuffy jerked his arm away: Mamma was not so easily forgiven. 'Shan't! . . . don't want to!' and was off again like a flash.

'Tch! He's so excited. – Emmy, you go to your uncle; you can usually get round him. He really ought to put in an appearance. It will do him good, too . . . and amuse him.'

Emmy hesitated. 'Do you think so, Aunt Mary?'

'Why, of course.'

'I'll take Baby, then. Perhaps Uncle will let me lay him down on his sofa. It's time he had a nap; he screams so at night if he gets over-tired.'

'You're wonderful with that child, Emmy,' said Mary, watching the girl cuddle her little stepbrother in her arms, where he curled up and shut his eyes, one little hand dangling limp and sleepy over her shoulder. 'I'm sure Lizzie ought to be very grateful to you.'

'I don't know what I'd do without him.'

Emmy tapped at the surgery door. 'May I come in?'

The blind was down; she could just make her uncle out, sitting hunched and relaxed in his armchair. He gave a violent start at her entrance, exclaiming: 'Yes, yes? What is it? – Oh, you, Emmy! Come in, my dear, come in. I think I must have dropped off.' And passing a fumbly hand over his forehead, he crossed to the window and drew up the blind.

What! with all that noise? thought Emmy wonderingly. Aloud she said: 'May I stay here a little with Jacky? I want him to have a nap.'

'Surely.' And Mahony cleared the end of the sofa that she might find a place with her burden. 'And how is the little man today?'

'Oh, doing finely! He has hardly been afraid of anything this afternoon.'

'We must examine him again,' said Mahony kindly, laying a finger on the child's sweat-damp hair, and noting the nervous pucker of the little brows.

There was a pause, Emmy gazing at her nursling, Mahony at her. Then: 'How vividly you do remind me of your mother, my dear! The first time I ever saw her – she could have been little older than you are now – she held you on her lap . . . just as you hold Jacky.'

'Did she?' Emmy played meditatively with a tassel on the child's shoe. 'People are always saying that . . . that I'm like her. And sometimes, Uncle, I think it would be nicer just to be like oneself. Instead of a kind of copy.'

To no one else would she have confided so heretical a sentiment. But Uncle Richard always understood.

And sure enough: 'I can see your point, Emmy,' said he. 'You think: to a new soul why not a brand-new covering? All the same, child, do not begrudge a poor wraith its sole chance of cheating oblivion.'

'I only mean –'

'I can assure you, you've nothing to fear from the comparison, nothing at all!' And Mahony patted his niece's hand, looking fondly at her in her white, flounced tarlatan, a narrow blue ribbon round her narrow waist, a wreath of forget-me-nots in her ripe-corn hair. There was no danger to Emmy in letting her know what you thought of her, so free from vanity was she. Just a good, sweet, simple creature.

But here the girl bethought herself of her errand. 'Oh yes, Aunt Mary sent me to tell you . . . I mean she thought, Uncle, you might like to come and see what fun the children are having.'

On the instant Mahony lost his warmth. 'No, no. I'm not in the mood.'

'Uncle, the Murdochs and the Archie Whites are here . . .

people who'd very much like to see you,' Emmy gently transposed Mary's words.

'Entirely your aunt's imagination, child! In reality she knows as well as I do that it's not so. In the course of a fairly long life, my dear, I have always been able to count on the fingers of one hand, those people – my patients excepted, of course – who have cared a straw whether I was alive or dead. No, Emmy. The plain truth is: my fellow-men have little use for me – or I for them.'

'Oh, Uncle . . .' Emmy was confused, and showed it. Talk of this kind made her feel very shy. She could not think of anything to say in response: how to refute ideas which she was sure were not true. Positively sure. For they opened up abysses into which, young girl-like, she was afraid to peer. An awkward pause ensued before she asked timidly: 'Do you feel very tired tonight?'

'To the depths of my soul, child!' Then, fearing lest he had startled her with his violence, he added: 'I've had – and still have – great worries, my dear . . . business worries.'

'Is it the practice Uncle? Doesn't it do well?'

'That, too. But I have made a sad fool of myself, Emmy – a sad fool. And now here I sit, puzzling how to repair the mischief.'

Alone again, he let himself fall back into the limp attitude in which she had surprised him. It was well-being just to lie back, every muscle relaxed. He came home from tramping the streets dog-tired, and all of a sweat: as drained of strength as a squeezed lemon.

No one else appeared to disturb him. Emmy, bless her! had done her work well, and Mary might now reasonably be expected to leave him in peace. Let them jig and dance to the top of their bent, provided he was not asked to join in. He washed his hands of the whole affair. From the outset, the elaborate preparations for this party had put his back up. It was not that he wanted to act the wet-blanket on his children's enjoyment. But the way Mary went about things stood in absolutely no relation to his shrunken income. She was striving to keep pace with people who could reckon theirs by the thousand. It was absurd. Of course she had grown so used, in the latter years, to spending royally, that it was hard for her now to trim her sails. Just, too, when the bairns were coming to an age to appreciate the good things of life. Again, his reason nudged him with the reminder that any ultra-extravagance on her part was due, in the first place, to her ignorance of his embarrassments. He had not enlightened her ... he never would. He felt more and more incapable of standing up to her incredulous dismay. In cold blood, it seemed impossible to face her with the tidings: 'The house we live in is not our own. I have run myself – run you and the children – into debt to the tune of hundreds of pounds!' At the mere thought of it he might have been a boy once more, standing before his mother and shaking in his shoes over the confession of some youthful peccadillo. A still further incentive to silence was the queer way his gall rose at the idea of interference. And it went beyond him to imagine Mary *not* interfering. If he knew her, she would at once want to take the reins: to manage him and his affairs as she managed house and children. And to what was left of his freedom he clung as if his life depended on it.

Excuse enough for meddling she would have; he had regularly played into her hands. Had he only never built this accursed house! It, and it alone, was the root of all the trouble. Had he contented himself with a modest weatherboard, they might still have been upsides with fate. Mary would not have been led to entertain beyond their means – for the very good reason that she would not have had room for it – and he have enjoyed the fruits of a quiet mind. Instead of which, for the pleasure of sitting twirling his thumbs in a house that was far too large for him, he had condemned himself to one of the subtlest forms of torture invented by man: that of being under constraint to get together, by given dates, fixed sums of money. The past three months had been a nightmare. Twenty times a day he had asked himself: shall I be able to do it? And when, by the skin of his teeth, he had contrived to foot his bill and breathe more freely, behold! the next term was at the door, and the struggle had all to begin anew. And so it would go on, month after month; round and round in the same vicious circle. Or with, for sole variety, a steadily growing embarrassment. As it was, he could see the day coming when he would be able to pay no more than the bare interest on the loan. And the humiliation this spelt for him only he knew. For, on taking up the mortgage, he had airily intimated that he intended, *for a start*, making quarterly repayments of fifty pounds: while later on ... well, only God knew what hints he had dropped for later on: his mind had been in haste to forget them. Did he now fall into arrears, his ignominious financial situation would be known to everyone, and he become a marked man.

Who could have thought this place would turn out so poorly? – become a jogtrot little suburban affair that just held together, and no more. Such an experience was something new to him, and intolerable. In the early days it was always he who had given up his practices, not they him. He had abandoned them, one after the other, no matter how well they were doing. Here, the pages of his case-book remained but scantly filled. A preternaturally healthy neighbourhood. Or was that just a polite fiction of his own making? More than once recently it had flashed through his mind that, since putting up his plate, he had treated none but the simplest cases. Only the A B C of doctoring had been required of him. The fact was, specialists were all too easy to get at. But no! that wouldn't hold water either. Was it not rather he himself who, at first hint of a complication, was ready to refer a patient? . . . to shirk undue worry and responsibility? Yes, this was his own share in the failure; this, and the fact that his heart was not in the work. But indeed how should it be? When he recalled the relief with which, the moment he was able, he had forsaken medicine . . . where *could* the joy come in ever taking it up again, an older, tireder man, and, as it were, at the point of the sword? And with the heart went the will, the inclination. Eaten up by money-troubles, he had but faint interest to spare for the physicking of petty ailments. Under the crushing dread lest he should find himself unable to pay his way, he had grown numb to all else. Numb . . . cold . . . indifferent.

What did *not* leave him cold but, on the contrary, whipped him to a fury of impatience and aversion, was the thought of going on as he was: of continuing to sit, day after day, as it were nailed to the spot, while his brain, the only live part of him, burnt itself out in maddening anxieties and regrets. Oh, fool that he had been! . . . fool and blind. To have known himself so ill! *Never* was he the man to have got himself into this pitiable tangle . . . with its continual menace of humiliation . . . disgrace. What madness had possessed him? Even in his youth, when life still seemed worth the pother, he had avoided debt like the plague. And to ask himself now, as an old man and one grown weary of effort, to stand the imposition of so intolerable a strain, was nothing short of suicidal. Another half-year like the last, and he would not be answerable for himself.

He began to toy with the idea of flight. And over the mere imagining of a possible escape from his torments, he seemed to wake to life again, to throw off the deadly lethargy that paralysed him. Change ... movement ... action: this it was he panted after! It was the sitting inactive, harried by murderous thoughts over which he had lost the mastery, that was killing him. If once he was rid of these, all might again be well. And now insidious fancies stole upon him: fancies which, disregarding such accidents of the day as money and the lack of money, went straight to the heart of his most urgent need. To go away – go far away – from everything and everyone he had known; so that what happened should happen to him only – be nobody's business but his own! Away from the crowd of familiar faces, these cunning, spying faces, *which knew all*, and which Mary could yet not persuade herself to forbid the house. Somewhere where she would be out of reach of the temptations that here beset her, and he free to exist in the decent poverty that was now his true walk in life. Oh, for privacy! – privacy and seclusion ... and freedom from tongues. To be once more a stranger among strangers, and never see a face he knew again!

He had not yet found courage, however, for the pitched battle he foresaw, when something happened that fairly took his breath away. As it were, overnight, he found himself the possessor of close on two hundred and fifty pounds. Among the scrip he still held were some shares called 'Pitman's', which till now had been good for nothing but to make calls. Now they took a sudden upward bound, and, at a timely hint from a grateful patient who was in the swim, Mahony did a little shuffle – selling, buying and promptly re-selling – with this result. True, a second venture, unaided, robbed him of the odd fifty. None the less there he stood, with his next quarter's payments in his hand. He felt more amazed than anything else by this windfall. It certainly did not set his mind at rest; it came too late for that. Try as he would, he could not now face the idea of remaining at Hawthorn. He had dwelt too much by this time on the thought of change; taken too fixed an aversion to this room where he had spent so many black hours; to the house, the practice, the neighbourhood. Something within him, which would not be silenced, never ceased to urge: free yourself ... escape – while there is still time.

In these days Mary just sighed and went about her work.

Richard had hardly a word even for the children: on entering the house he retired at once to the surgery and shut himself in. What he did there, goodness only knew. But it was not possible nowadays for her to sit and worry over him, or to take his moods as seriously as she would once have done. And any passing suspicion of something being more than ordinarily amiss was apt, even as it crossed her mind, to be overlaid by, say, the size of the baker's bill, or the fact that Cuffy had again outgrown his boots. But she had also a further reason for turning a blind eye. Believing, as she truly did, that Richard's moroseness sprang mainly from pique at having to take up work again, she was not going to risk making matters worse by talking about them. Richard was as suggestible as a child. A word from her might stir up some fresh grievance, the existence of which he had so far not imagined. – But when the crash came, it seemed as if a part of her had all along known and feared the worst.

None the less it was a shattering blow: one of those that left you feeling ten years older than the moment before. And in the scene that followed his blunt announcement and lasted far into the night, she strove with him as she had never yet striven, labouring to break down his determination, to bring him back to sanity. For more, much more, than themselves and their own prosperity was now at stake. What happened to them happened equally to the three small creatures they had brought into the world.

'It's the children, Richard! Now they're there, you haven't the *right* to throw up a fixed position, as the fancy takes you . . . as you used to do. It didn't matter about me. But it's different now – everything's different. *Only* have patience! Oh! I can't believe you really mean it. It seems incredible . . . impossible.'

Mahony was indignant. 'And do you think no one considers the children but you? When their welfare is more to me than anything on earth?'

'But if that's true, how can you even *think* of giving up this place? . . . the house – our comfortable home! You know quite well you're not a young man any more. The openings would be so few. You'd never get a place to suit you better.'

'I tell you I *cannot* stop here!'

'But why? Give me a single convincing reason. – As to the idea of going up-country . . . that's madness pure and simple.

How often did you vow you'd never again take up a country practice, because of the distances . . . and the work? How will you be able to stand it now? . . . when you're getting on for fifty. You say there's nothing doing here; but, my opinion is, there's just as much as you're able for.'

This was so exactly Mahony's own belief that he grew violently angry. 'Good God, woman! is there no sympathy in you? . . . or only where your children are concerned? I tell you, if I stop here I shall end by going demented!'

'I never heard such talk. The practice may be slow to move — I think a town practice always would be — but it'll come right, I'm sure it will, if you'll *only* give it the chance.' Here, however, another thought struck her. 'But what I don't understand is, *why* we're not able to get on. What becomes of the money you make? There must be something very wrong somewhere. Hand over the accounts to me; let me look into your books. With no rent to pay, and three or four hundred coming in . . . besides the dividends . . . oh, would anyone else — anyone but you — want to throw up a certainty and drag us off up-country, just when the children are getting big and need decent companions . . . and schooling — what about their education? — have you thought of that? . . . or thought of anything but your own likes and dislikes?' And as he maintained a stony silence, she broke out: 'I think men are the most impossible creatures God ever made!' and pressing her face into the pillow burst into tears.

Mahony set his teeth. If she could not see for herself that it was a case, for once, of putting him and his needs first, then he could not help her. To confide in her still went beyond him. Mary had such a heavy hand. He could hope for no tenderness of approach; no instinctive understanding meeting him halfway. She would pounce on his most intimate thoughts and feelings, drag them out into daylight and anatomize them; would put into words those phantom fears, and insidious evasions, which he had so far managed to keep in the twilight where they belonged. He shuddered at the thought.

But Mary had not finished. Drying her eyes she returned to the charge. 'You say this place is a failure. I deny it, and always shall. But if it hasn't done as well as it might, there's a reason for it. It's because you haven't the way with you any longer. You've lost your manner — the good, doctor's manner you used to do so much with. You're too short with people nowadays; and they resent it; and go to someone who's pleasanter. I heard you just the other day with that lawyer's wife who called . . . how you blew her up! *She'll* never come again. – A morbid hypochondriac? I daresay. But in old days you'd never have told a patient to her face that she was either shamming or imagining.'

'I'm too old to cozen and pander.'

'Too old to care, you mean. – Oh, for God's sake, think what you're doing! Try to stop on here a little longer, and if it's only for six months. Listen! I've got an idea.' She raised herself on her elbow. 'Why shouldn't we take in boarders? . . . just to tide us over till things get easier. This house is really much too big for us. One nursery would be enough for the children; and there's the spare room, and the breakfast-room. . . . I could probably fill all three; and make enough that way to cover our living expenses.'

'*Boarders?* . . . *you?* Not while *I'm* above the sod!'

The children wilted . . . oh, it was a dreadful week! Papa never spoke, and slammed the doors and the gate whenever he went out. Mamma sat in the bedroom and cried, hastily blowing her nose and pretending she wasn't, if you happened to look in. And Cook and Eliza made funny faces, and whispered behind their hands. Cuffy, mooning about the house pale and dejected, was – as usual when Mamma and Papa quarrelled – harassed by the feeling that somehow or other he was the guilty person. He tried cosseting Mamma, hanging round her: he tried talking big to the Dumplings of what he meant to do when he was a man; he even glanced at the idea of running away. But none of these things lightened the weight that lay on his chest. It felt just as it had done the night Luce had the croup and crowed like a cock.

And then one afternoon Mahony came home transfigured. His bang of the gate, his very step, as it crunched the gravel, told its own tale. He ran up the stairs two at a time, calling for Mary; and, the door of the bedroom shut on them, broke into excited talk. It appeared that in a chance meeting that day with a fellow-medico ('Pincock, that well-known Richmond man!') he had heard of what seemed to him 'an opening in a thousand', a flourishing practice to be had for the asking, at a place called Barambogie in the Ovens District.

'A rising township, my dear, half mining, half agricultural, and where there has never been but one doctor. He's an old friend of Pincock's, and is giving up – after ten years in the place – for purely personal reasons . . . nothing to do with the practice. It arose through Pincock asking me if I knew of anyone who would like to step into a really good thing. This Rummel wants to retire, but will wait on of course till he hears of a successor. Nor is he selling. Whoever goes there has only to walk in and settle down. Such a chance won't come my way again. I should be mad to let it slip.'

This news rang the knell of any hopes Mary might still have nursed of bringing him to his senses. She eyed him sombrely as he stood before her, pale with excitement; and such a wave of bitterness ran through her that she quickly looked away again, unable to find any but bitter words to say. In this glance, however, she had for once really seen him – had not just looked, without seeing, after the habit of those who spend their lives together – and the result was the amazed reflection: 'But he's got the eyes of a child! . . . for all his wrinkles and grey hairs.'

Mahony did not notice her silence. He continued to dilate on what *he* had said and the other had replied, till, in alarm, she burst out: 'I hope to goodness you've not committed yourself in any way? . . . all in the dark as you are.'

'Come, come now, my dear!' he half cozened, half fell foul of her. 'Give me credit for at least a ha'p'orth of sense. You surely don't imagine I showed Pincock my cards? I flatter myself I was thoroughly off-hand with him . . . so much so, indeed, that before night he'll no doubt have cracked the place up to half a dozen others. – Come, Mary, come! I'm not quite the fool you imagine. Nor do I mean to be unreasonable. But I confess my inclination is, just to slip off and see the place, and make a few confidential inquiries. There can surely be nothing against that – can there?'

There could not. Two days later, he took the early morning train to the north.

CHAPTER FIVE

1

*The Sun Hotel,
Barambogie.*

My own dear Wife,

I hope you got my note announcing my safe arrival. I could not write more; the train was late and I tired out. The journey took eight hours and was most fatiguing. About noon a north wind came up, with its usual effect on me of headache and lassitude. The carriage was like a baking-oven. As for the dust, I've never seen its equal. Ballarat in summer was nothing to it. It rose in whirlwinds to the tops of the gums. We were simply smothered. But what a country this of ours is for size! You have only to get away from the sea-board and travel across it, to be staggered by its vastness. — And emptiness. Mile after mile of bush, without the trace of a settlement. And any townships we could see for dust, very small and mean. Of course everything looks its worst just now. There have been no rains here yet, and they are sadly needed. Grass burnt to a cinder, creeks bone-dry and so on. However as it was all quite new to me, I found plenty to interest me. The landscape improved as we got further north, grew hillier and more wooded: and beyond Benalla we had a fine view of the high ranges.

So much for the journey. As I mentioned, Rummel met me at the station, walked to the hotel with me and stopped for a chat. He is a most affable fellow, well under forty I should say, tall and handsome and quite the gentleman — I shall find considerable difficulty in coming after him. I was too tired that night to get much idea of the place, but now that I have had a couple of days to look about me, I can honestly say I am delighted with it. To begin with, I am most comfortably lodged; my bed is good, the table plentiful, landlady very attentive. It is a larger and more substantial township than those we passed on the way up; the houses are mostly of brick — for coolness in summer — and all have luxuriant gardens. There is a very pretty little lake, or lagoon as they call it here, skirted by trees and pleasant paths; and we are surrounded by wooded ranges. Vineyards cover the plains.

As to the information I had from Pincock, it was rather under than above the mark. Barambogie is undoubtedly a rising place. For one thing, there's a great mine in the neighbourhood, that has only been partially worked. This is now about to be reorganized: and when started will employ no fewer than a hundred and fifty men. Every one is sanguine of it paying. — I was out and about all yesterday and again this morning, introducing myself to people. I have met with the greatest courtesy and civility — the Bank Manager went so far as to say I should be a real acquisition. I think I can read between the lines that some will not be displeased to see the last of Rummel. He is by no means the universal favourite I should have imagined. Between ourselves, I fancy he takes a drop too much. He is still seeing patients, but intends leaving in a couple of days. The chemist says I should easily do eight hundred to a thousand per annum. And Rummel himself told me he has had as many as a hundred midwifery cases in a year. There are three or four nice families, so you, my dear, will not be entirely cut off from society. It is said to be a splendid winter climate. Even now, in late autumn, we have clear blue skies and bracing winds from the south. And we should certainly save. No one here keeps more than one servant, and grand entertainments are unknown. No clubs either, thank God! You know what a drawback they . . . or rather the lack of them has been to me at Hawthorn. They're all very well if you hold them yourself, but play the dickens with a practice if you don't. I should only be too glad to settle somewhere where they're non-existent.

The difficulty is going to be to find a house. There are only two vacant in all Barambogie. One of these is in poor repair, and the owner — the leading draper — declines to do anything to it. Besides he wants a rental of eighty pounds p.a., on a four years' lease — which of course puts it out of the question. The other is so small that none of our furniture would go into it. But where there's a will there's a way; and I have an idea — and I think a brilliant one. There's a fine old Oddfellows' Hall here, which is in disuse and up for auction. It's of brick — looks like a chapel — and is sixty feet long by twenty broad. Well, my plan is to buy this, and convert it into a dwelling-house. The body of the hall will give us six splendid rooms, with a passage down the middle, and we can add kitchen, scullery, outhouses, etc. I would also throw out a verandah. There's a fair piece of land which we could turn into a garden. The alterations will be easy to make and not cost much; and there we are, with out and away the best house in the town! — I fear, though, even under the most favourable circumstances we shall not be able to use all our furniture here. I haven't yet seen a room that would hold your wardrobe, or the dining-room sideboard.

If I decide to stay, I shall lose no time in consulting a builder. You for your part must at once see an agent and put the Hawthorn house in his hands. I feel sure we shall have no difficulty in letting it.

And now I must bring this long scrawl — it has been written at various odd moments — to a close. I have appointed to see Rummel again this afternoon, to have another parley with him. Not that I shall definitely fix on anything till I hear from you. From now on I intend to take your advice. But I do trust that what I have told you will prove to you that this is no wildgoose chase, but the very opening of which I am in search. It distresses me more than I can say, when you and I do not see eye to eye with each other. Now take good care of your dear self, and kiss the chicks for me. Forgive me, too, all my irritability and bad temper of the past six months. I have had a very great deal to worry me — far more than you knew, or than I wanted you to know. It is enough for one of us to bear the burden. But this will pass and everything be as of old, if I can once see the prospect of earning a decent income again. Which I am perfectly sure I shall do here.
                                            Your own

                                                  R.T.M.

2

                                 The Sun Hotel,
                                    Barambogie.

My dear Mary,

I must say you are the reverse of encouraging. Your letter threw me into such a fit of low spirits that I could not bring myself to answer it till today. It's bad enough being all alone, with never a soul to speak to, without you pouring cold water on everything I suggest. Of course, as you are so down on my scheme of rebuilding the Oddfellows' Hall I will let this unique opportunity for a bargain slip, and dismiss the idea from my mind. Perhaps, though, you will tell me what we are to do – with not another house in the place vacant – or at least nothing big enough to swing a cat in. As you are so scathing about my poor plans, you had better evolve some of your own.

I had the news about the mine on reliable authority; it was not, as you try to make out, a mere wild rumour. Nor is what I said about people being glad to get rid of Rummel a product of my own imagination. I received more than one plain hint to that effect, in the course of my visits.

However, since I wrote last, I have begun to doubt the wisdom of settling here. It's not the house-question alone. I've seen Greatorex the draper again, and he has so far come round as to agree to re-floor the verandah and whitewash the rooms, if I take the house on his terms. I repeat once more, it is the best house in Barambogie. Six large rooms, all necessary outhouses, a shed fitted with a shower-bath, and a fine garden – we might indeed consider ourselves lucky to get it. Rummel lives in a regular hovel; the parson in a four-roomed hut with not a foot of ground to it, nor any verandah to keep off the sun. Greatorex's is a palace in comparison. Of course though, as you express yourself so strongly against the four-years' lease, I shall give up all idea of coming to an agreement with him.

Besides, as I said above, I have practically decided not to remain. Your letter is chiefly responsible for this. I can see you have made up your mind beforehand not to like the place. And if you were unhappy I should be wretched, too, and reproach myself for having dragged you and the children into so outlandish an exile. I quite agree it would be hard work for you with but a single servant; but I can assure you, we should be eyed askance if we tried to keep more. In a place like this, where there is only one standard of living, it would render us most unpopular. But even should you change your mind, my advice would be, not to come for at least three months. By that time I should know better how the practice was shaping. Of course things may look brighter for me when Rummel goes, and I begin to get something to do. I've been here nearly a fortnight now, and he shows no more signs of leaving than at first. He is still attending patients; the people run after him in the streets. He has been extraordinarily popular; which is not to be wondered at, with his good looks and ingratiating manners. Only a few trifling cases have come my way. It is very dis-

heartening. To add to this, I have been feeling anything but well. The change of water has upset me. Then my bedroom is dark and airless; and the noise in the hotel enough to drive one crazy. It goes on till long past midnight and begins again before six.

Another thing that worries me is the fact that I should be alone of the profession here, if I stayed. I daresay I should get used to it in time; but just now, in my poor state, it would be an additional strain, never to have a second opinion to fall back on. — I don't need you to tell me, my dear, that a hundred confinements in the year would be stiff work. But they would also mean a princely income. However, I have no intention of dragging you here against your will: and shall now cast about for something else. I heard today of a place called Turramungi, where there is only one doctor and he a bit of a duffer. I will go over by coach one morning and see how the land lies.

But do try and write more cheerfully. I am sure you have no need to be so depressed — in our pleasant home, and with the children to bear you company. I am sorry to hear you have heard of no likely tenants. We ought to get a rent of at least two hundred, without taxes. As I said before, your wardrobe and the sideboard will have to be sold. Perhaps the incoming tenant will take them.

The flies are very troublesome today. I have constantly to flap my handkerchief while I write.

Shall hope to send you better news of myself next time.

R.T.M.

3

The Sun Hotel,
Barambogie.

My dear Wife,

A line in great haste. I have just seen an advertisement in the Argus calling for applications for medical officer to the Boorandoora Lodge, and have made up my mind to apply. I have written off posthaste for further particulars, in order to get my application in before Friday. After spending close on three weeks here, I have decided once and for all that it would be infinitely more satisfactory to make an extra couple of hundred a year at Hawthorn, with a decent house behind us, than to bury ourselves in this wild bush. A third lodge would give a tremen-

dous fillip to the practice. And the more I see of this place, the less I like it.

Of course, my application may not be considered. Lambert, who had the Boorandoora last, held it at twenty-one shillings a head, and found medicine. I mean to tender seventeen-and-six, without physic. Graves, I know, won't look at them under twenty. So I think I ought to stand a very good chance. Don't take any further steps about the house in the meanwhile.

Since I wrote last I have had a little more to do. I was called out several miles yesterday. And the people I went to told me that if I had not been here, they would have sent for the man at Turramungi. So you see Rummel is not persona grata everywhere. He is still about, and as much in my way as ever; for as long as he is on the spot, people won't consult anyone else. I wish to God I had not been in such a hurry to come. However, one thing makes me more hopeful: the date of his auction is fixed at last, for Monday next.

In haste
Your own

R.T.M.

4

The Sun Hotel,
Barambogie.

My darling Mary,

So you approve, do you, of my idea of putting in for the Boorandoora? I got the information I wanted from the Secretary of the lodge; and if I resolve to offer my services, shall do so for the sum I named. It is all very well, my dear, to talk about it being beneath my dignity to underbid others, and to ask how I myself should once have characterized such a proceeding. (Personally, I think you might keep remarks of this kind to yourself.) What I do is done for your sake. If I could get this third lodge, it might save you having to turn out and part with your furniture; and to make that possible I am ready to sacrifice my professional pride. There are so many others, younger men than I, who are only too ready to step in. And I look on it as my sole remaining chance to earn a decent livelihood within reach of civilization.

However, I must confess, I have again become somewhat undecided. The fact is, Rummel has gone at last: and he gave me his word, on leaving, that he would never come back. The *auction took place as arranged; house and ground selling for a hundred and ninety pounds. Since he went, I have been genuinely busy. The parson is ill with inflammation of the liver; and I was called out yesterday a distance of five miles. The hire of a buggy costs seven-and-six – less than half what I had to pay in Hawthorn. This afternoon I go by train to Mirrawarra, and shall walk back. It becomes daily more evident to me that there is a very fine practice to be done here. And everyone I meet implores me to stay. Some, indeed, grow quite plaintive at the idea of losing me.*

I have also had a pleasant surprise about the house. Greatorex now says he is willing to let for three years instead of four, if I pay the first year's rent in advance. This seems to me an extremely fair offer. You see it would only be like paying a small sum down for the practice. I am going over the house with him again tomorrow, and will then let you know what I decide. The point at issue is, should I not do better to accept this certain opening, with all its drawbacks, than take the uncertain chance of Hawthorn with a third lodge ... if I get it!

Your very own

R.T.M.

5

The Sun Hotel,
Barambogie.

My own dear Wife,

Well! the die is cast; I have finally made up my mind to remain in Barambogie. I did not put in for the lodge after all, but resolved to give this place a further ten days' trial. And well that I did! For the practice has looked up with a vengeance: it is now as plain as a pikestaff that I have capital prospects here, and should be a fool indeed to let them slide. If I had not popped in when I did, there would certainly have been others – and, for that matter, I am still not quite sure there may not be another settling. In the meantime I am seeing fresh patients daily, and have not had my clothes off for the past two nights. The day before yesterday I was called ten miles out to attend a case which Guthrie of Coora has neglected: and I have been bespoken for three future events. This morning I drove seven miles into the bush; for which I shall charge five guineas. In the month I have been here – ten days without Rummel – I have taken fifteen pounds and booked close on fifty. What do you think of that? I feel quite sure I shall easily touch a thousand a year. Of course it will mean hard work, but the mere prospect of such a thing keys me up. It was the doing nothing at Hawthorn that preyed so on my mind. If only I can earn a good income, and provide for you and the darlings in the style to which you are accustomed, I shall be a happy man once more.

The people here are overjoyed at the prospect of keeping me. They continue to declare I cannot fail to succeed. Everybody is most civil, and all invite me to drink with them. I have considerable difficulty in making them understand that I do not go in for that kind of thing. It sometimes needs a good deal of tact to put them off without giving offence: but so far I have managed pretty well. From all I now hear, Rummel must have been a seasoned drinker – a regular toper. I saw the Bank Manager today. He was very queer. Had evidently been taking nobblers. He has been in charge of the Bank here for over twenty years, and thinks there is no place like Barambogie. Vows I shall make my fortune.

Greatorex promises to set about the repairs without delay. My private opinion is, he's in high feather at securing such good and careful tenants. I went over the house with him again yesterday. The rooms are not quite as large as I thought – I will send you the exact measurements in a day or two – but all have French windows and are fitted with venetian blinds. The garden is well stocked with fruit, flowers and vegetables. I shall keep a man to look after it. I think you had better try and induce one of the servants from home to accompany you. Perhaps Eliza would come; as the children are used to her. Here there is little or nothing in that line to be had. Slipshod dollops demand ten shillings a week. The parson keeps none; has no room for any.

Archdeacon Coote of Taralga called yesterday, and made quite a fuss over me. I have also been introduced to the wife of one of the leading squatters. Like everyone else, she says it will be a red-letter day for the place if we come, and looks eagerly forward to making your acquaintance.

Now, if only we can let the house! The mere possibility of this, and of our being all together once more makes me wildly happy. Tell the chicks there is a splendid summerhouse in the new garden, and I will see to it that a swing is put up for them. They shall have everything they want here.

Your own old husband,
Richard Townshend Mahony.

The Sun Hotel,
Barambogie.

My dear Mary,

I am sorry you write in such low spirits. I agree with you, it is most unfortunate that we are obliged to break up our home; but it was blackest folly on my part ever to build that house, and now I am punished for it. I cannot say how deeply I regret having to ask you and the little ones to put up with bush life; and you may rest assured I should not do so, if I saw any other way out. But it is this or nothing.

It doesn't mend matters to have you carping at the class of person we shall need to associate with. For goodness' sake, don't go putting ideas of that kind into the children's heads! We are all God's creatures; and the sooner we shake off the incubus of a false and snobbish pride, the better it will be for us. There are good and worthy people to be found in every walk of life.

You are utterly wrong in your suspicions that I am letting myself be flattered and bamboozled into staying. But there! ... you never do think anyone but yourself has a particle of judgement.

No, there's nothing in the way of a school – except, of course, the State School. You had better find out what a governess would cost. About the house, I am afraid it is really not very much bigger than our first cottage in Webster St – the wooden one – before we made those additions to it. I enclose the measurements of the rooms. You will see that the drawing-room and chief bedroom are the same size – 12 by 13 – the others somewhat smaller. It will be as well to sell the pierglass and the drawing-room chiffonier. And it's no good bringing the diningroom table, or the big sofa ... or the tall glass bookcase. Or the three large wardrobes either; they wouldn't go in at the doors. But do try and not fret too much over sacrificing these things. A few years here, and you will be able to replace them; and then we will pitch our tent somewhere more to your liking.

I reckon the move will cost us about a hundred pounds.

I am still busy. Barambogie is anything but the dead-and-alive place you imagine. No less than six coaches a day draw up at this hotel. The weather continues fine. I have a good appetite: it suits me to be so much in the open air, instead of cooped up in that dull surgery. I wish I slept better though.

The noise in the hotel continues unabated. I have the utmost difficulty in getting to sleep, or in remaining asleep when I do. The least sound disturbs me – and then I am instantly wide awake. The other night, though, I had a very different experience. Something very queer happened to me. I dropped off towards three and had been asleep for about an hour – fast asleep – when some noise or other, I don't know what, wakened me with a terrific start . . . one of those fearful jerks awake which the nightbell used to give me. Except that in those days, I was all there in an instant. Here, I couldn't for the life of me come back, and went through a few most awful seconds, absolutely incapable of recollection. There I sat, bolt upright, my heart beating like a sledgehammer, powerless to remember who I was, where I was or what I was doing. My brain seemed like an empty shell . . . or a watch with all the works gone out of it. Or if you can imagine a kind of mental suffocation, a horrid struggle for breath on the part of the brain. And when, by sheer force of will, I had succeeded in fighting back to a consciousness of my personal identity, I still could not locate myself, but imagined I was at home, and fumbled for the matches on the wrong side of the bed! It was most unpleasant – a real dissociation for the time being – and I did not sleep again, dreading a return. I think it came from worry – I have been much upset. Your letter . . . and all you said in it . . . your grief and disappointment. Add to this that I had no proper rest the night before, having been up with a patient till three. I shall be more careful in future.

My love to the darlings,
Your own

R.T.M.

CHAPTER SIX

It was nearing eleven, and a chilly, cloudy night, when the little party, flanked by Eliza, alighted on the platform at Barambogie where for nearly an hour Mahony had paced to and fro. They were the only passengers to leave the train; which straightway puffed off again; and since the man hired by Mahony to transport the baggage was late in arriving, there was nothing for it but to wait till he came. The stationmaster, having lingered for a time, turned out the solitary lamp and departed; and there they stood, a forlorn little group, round a tumulus of luggage. It was pitch dark; not a single homely light shone out, to tell of a human settlement; not the faintest sound broke the silence. To Mary it seemed as if they had been dumped down in the very heart of nowhere.

But now came the man wheeling a truck; and straightway a wordy dispute broke out between him and Richard, in which she had to act as peacemaker. Boxes and portmanteaux were loaded up; carpet-bags, baskets, bundles counted and arranged: all by the light of a lantern. Richard, agog with excitement, had to be kept from waking the twins, who had dropped asleep again on top of the trunks. And all the while an overtired and captious Cuffy plucked at her sleeve. 'Is this the bush, Mamma? . . . is *this* the bush? *Where?* I don't see it!'

The little procession started, headed by the man with truck and lantern, the Dumplings riding one in Richard's arms, one in Eliza's, she and Cuffy bringing up the rear. Leaving the station behind them, they walked on till they came to a broad road, flour-soft to the feet, Cuffy kicking and shuffling up the dust to the peevish whine of: 'What *sort* of a bush, Mamma?' and passed in single file down a long narrow right-of-way, between two paling fences.

On emerging, they faced something flat and black and mysterious. Mary started. 'Whatever's that?'

'The Lagoon, my dear, the Lagoon! The house fronts it, you know. Has the best outlook of any in the town.'

(For the children to fall into! . . . *and* mosquitoes.)

Long after everyone else was asleep Mary lay and listened . . . and listened. It was years since she had lived anywhere but in a town; and this house seemed so lonely, so open to intruders. The leaves rustling in the garden, each fresh flap of the venetians startled her afresh; and in spite of the long, tiring journey, and the arduous days that had preceded it, she could not compose herself to sleep. And when at last she did fall into an uneasy doze, she was jerked back to consciousness in what seemed the minute after, by a shrill and piercing scream – a kind of prolonged shriek, that rent and tore at the air.

'Richard! . . . oh, Richard, what in the world is that?'

'Don't be alarmed, my dear. It's only the mill-whistle.'

'A mill? So close?'

'It's all right, Mary; you'll soon get used to it. Myself I hardly notice it now. And it doesn't last long. There! you see, it has stopped already.'

His attempt to make light of the appalling din had something pathetic about it. Mary bit back her dismay.

And it was the same in the morning, when he led her round house and garden: he skimmed airily over the drawbacks – the distance of the kitchen from the house; the poor water-supply; the wretched little box of a surgery; the great heat of even this late autumn day – to belaud the house's privacy, separated as it was from the rest of the township by the width of the Lagoon; the thickness of the brick walls; the shade and coolness ensured by an all-round verandah. And though daylight, and what it shewed up, only served to render Mary more and more dubious, she had not the heart on this first morning to damp him by saying what she really thought. Instead, her tour of inspection over, she buckled to her mammoth job of bringing comfort out of chaos: putting up beds and dressers; unpacking the crockery; cutting down curtains and carpets, and laying oilcloth; working dusty and dishevelled, by the light of a candle, till long past midnight for many a night. While Richard, his professional visits over, undertook to mind and amuse the children, who were sadly in her way, dashing about helter-skelter, pale with the excitement of the new.

For, oh what a lovely house this was! – Long before anyone else was astir, Cuffy had pattered out barefoot to explore; and, all his life after, he loved an empty house for its sake. It had nothing but doors, which spelt freedom: even the windows were doors. There were no stairs. A passage went right down the middle, with a door at each end which always stood open, and three room-doors on each side. You could run out of any of the windows and tear round the verandah, to play Hide-and-Seek or Hi-spy-hi. And not even Eliza was there to say 'Don't!' or 'You mustn't!' She was in the far-away kitchen, scrubbing or washing up. They had breakfast off a packing-case, which was great fun; and Papa was so nice, too. The very first morning he explained what the bush meant; and took them all out walking to find it; and then Cuffy learnt that it was not *one* bush he had come to see but lots of bushes; with trees so high that, even if you almost broke your neck bending back, you couldn't see the end of them.

Dancing ahead of Papa, who held hands with the Dumplings, and sometimes walking backwards to hear better, Cuffy fired question after question. How did the bush get there? Why did nobody live in it? What were all the holes full of water? Why were they abandoned? Why did people dig for gold? How did they do it? Why was money? – a fusillade of questions, to which on this day he got full and patient answers. Papa gave them each a threepenny bit, too, to spend as they liked. The twins carried theirs squeezed tight to show Mamma; but he put his in his pocket.

On the way home they went along a street where there were lots of little shops. Men were leaning against the verandah posts, smoking and spitting; and other men came to the doors and stared. Papa was very polite to them, and said 'Good morning!' to everybody with a little bow, and whether they did or not. And sometimes he said as well: 'Yes, these are my youngsters! Don't you think I've reason to be proud of them? . . . and as often as this happened, Cuffy felt uncomfortable. For these weren't the sort of men you stopped and talked to: you just said good morning and went home. Besides, they didn't seem as if they *wanted* to speak to you. They didn't take their pipes out; and some of them looked as if they thought Papa was funny . . . or silly. Two winked at each other when they thought he wasn't looking – made eyes like Cook and Eliza used to do.

Then at a hotel they met a fat, red-faced man – the landlord, Papa said – who seemed at first to be going to be nicer. When Papa pushed them forward and said: 'My young fry arrived at last, you see!' he smiled back and said: 'And a very jolly little set of nippers, too! Pleased to know you, missies! How do, sir, how do! Now what will yours be?'

'Cuthbert Hamilton Townshend-Mahony,' replied Cuffy, lightning-quick and politely. He was dumbfounded by the roar of laughter that went up at his words; not only the landlord laughed, but lots of larrikins, who stood round the bar. Even Papa laughed a little, in a funny, tight way.

Mamma didn't though. Cuffy heard them talking, and she sounded cross. 'Surely, Richard, you needn't drag the children in as well?'

Papa was snappy. 'I don't think, Mary, you quite realize how necessary it is for me to leave no stone unturned.'

'I can't help it. I'm not going to have *my* children mixed up in the affair.' When Mamma was cross she always said '*my* children'.

Cuffy didn't wait to hear more. He ran down the garden, where he mooned about till dinner-time. He wouldn't ever – no, he wouldn't! – go down the street where those horrid men were again. And if he saw them, he'd stamp his feet at them and call them nasty names. And he'd tell Papa not to – he wouldn't let him; he'd hold on to his coat. For they didn't like Papa either.

'Ooo . . . tum on! Us'll dance, too,' cried the twins. And taking hands they hopped and capered about the drawing-room, their little starched white petticoats flaring as they swung. For Papa was dancing with Mamma. He had seized her by the waist and polked her up the passage, and now was whirling her round, she trying to get loose and crying: 'Stop, Richard, stop! You'll make me sick.' But Papa just laughed and twirled on, the Dumplings faithfully imitating him, till, crash, bang! a vase of Parian marble on the big centre table lost its balance, toppled over and was smashed to atoms.

'There! . . . that's just what I expected. There's no room here for such goings-on,' said Mary as she stooped to pick up the fragments.

It came of her having called Richard in to view the drawing-room, where for over a week she had stitched and hammered, or sat perched on the top rung of a step-ladder. Herself she was not displeased with her work; though she mourned the absence of the inlaid secretaire, the card-table, the ottoman. These things were still in the outhouse, in their travelling-cases; and there they would have to remain. The Collard and Collard took up nearly the whole of one wall; the round rosewood table devoured the floor-space; everything was much too large. And the best bits, the Parisian gilt-legged tables and gilt-framed mirrors, made absolutely no show, huddled together as they were.

But Richard went into ecstasies. 'They'll never have seen a room like it! – the people here. We'll show them what's what, wife, eh? . . . make 'em open their eyes. Mary! I prophesy you'll have the whole township come trooping over the Lagoon to call. We shall need to charge 'em admission' – and therewith he had seized and swung her round. So undignified . . . before Eliza. Besides egging the children on to do likewise.

But there was no damping Richard just now. Though a fortnight had passed, he was still in the simmer of excitement into which their coming had thrown him. While she stitched, even while she turned the handle of the sewing-machine, he would stand at her side and talk, and talk, in a voice that was either pitched just a shade too high, or was husky and tremulous. The separation had plainly been too much for him. His joy at getting them again was not to be kept within bounds.

'You're absolutely all I've got, you know . . . you and the children.'

Which was quite literally true: so true that, at times, Mary would find herself haunted by the unpleasant vision of a funeral at which it was not possible to fill a single coach with mourners. Richard – to be followed to his grave by the doctor who had attended him, the parson who was to bury him . . . and not a soul besides. Her heart contracted at the disgrace of the thing: the shame of letting the world know how little he had cared for anyone, or been cared for in return.

Impatiently she shook her head and turned to listen to voices in the passage. They were those of Richard and a patient; but chiefly Richard's. For he had carried his talkative fit over to strangers as well . . . and Mary sometimes wondered what they thought of him: these small shopkeepers and farmers and vine-growers and licensed publicans. Well, at any rate, they wouldn't be able to bring the usual accusation against him, of stiff-necked reserve. The truth was, they just came in for their share of his all-pervading good humour. The children, too. Had he always made so much of the children, they would have felt more at home with him, and he have had less cause for jealous grumbles. He even unearthed his old flute, screwed the parts together, and to Cuffy's enchantment played them his one-time showpiece, *The Minstrel Boy*. And it was the same with everything. He vowed the Barambogie bread to be the best, the butter the sweetest he had ever tasted: going so far as to compliment the astonished tradespeople on their achievements. And Mary, watching in silence, thought how pleasant all this was ... and how unnatural ... and waited for the moment to come when he would drop headlong from the skies.

In waiting, her head with its high Spanish comb bent low over her work, she gave the rein to various private worries of her own. For instance she saw quite clearly that Eliza's stay with them would not be a long one. Forgetful of past favours, of the expense they had been at in bringing her there, Eliza was already darkly hinting her opinion of the place; of the detached kitchen; the dust, the solitude. Again, the want of a proper waiting-room for patients was proving a great trial. The dining-room seemed never their own. More serious was the risk the children thereby ran of catching some infectious illness. Then, she sometimes felt very uneasy about Richard. In spite of his exuberance, he looked anything but well. The bout of dysentery he had suffered from, on first arriving, had evidently been graver than he cared to admit. His colour was bad, his appetite poor; while as for sleep, if he managed four consecutive hours of a night he counted himself lucky. And even then it wasn't a restful sleep; for he had got the absurd idea in his head that he might not hear the nightbell – in this tiny house! – and at the least sound was awake and sitting up. Again, almost every day brought a long trudge into the bush, from which he came home too tired to eat. And Mary's old fear revived. Would he ever be able at his age to stand the wear and tear of the work?—especially as the practice grew, and he became more widely known.

But, even as she asked herself the question, another doubt flew at her. Was there any real prospect of the practice growing, and him retrieving his shattered fortunes? Or had he, in burying himself in this wild bush, committed the crowning folly of his life? And, of the two, this fear ate the deeper. For she thought he *might* have so husbanded his strength as to carry on for a few years; but, the more she saw of place and people, the slenderer grew her belief that there was money to be made there. How anybody in his five senses could have professed to see in Barambogie what Richard did – oh! *no* one but Richard could have so deceived himself. Of all the dead-and-alive holes she had ever been in, this was the deadest. Only two trains a day called there, with eight hours between. The railway station was mostly closed and deserted, the stationmaster to be found playing euchre at the 'Sun'. Quite a quarter of the shops in the main street were boarded up; the shafts round the township had all been worked out or abandoned. As for the tale of the big mine . . . well, she considered that had been just a bait with which to hook a simple fish. How she did wish she had somebody to talk to! Richard was no use at all . . . in his present mood. To the few feelers she threw out, he declared himself exaggeratedly well content. Though the number of patients was still not great, his calls into the bush were royally paid. It was five guineas here, ten there; as compared with the petty fees he had commanded at Hawthorn. 'Surely, my dear, if money flows in at this rate, we can put up with a few slight drawbacks?'

Such as the flour mill, thought Mary grimly. This dreadful mill! Would any but a man so complacently have planked them down next door to it? It entirely spoilt the garden, with its noise and dust. Then, the mill-hands who passed to and fro, or sat outside the fence, were a very rough lot; and five times a day you had to stop in what you were saying and wait for the shriek of the steam-whistle to subside. Except for the railway station, their house and the mill stood alone on this side of the Lagoon, and were quite five minutes' walk from the township. Richard hugged himself with his privacy, and it certainly was nicer to be away from shops and public-houses. But, for the practice, their seclusion was a real disadvantage. Rummel had lived in the main street; and his surgery had been as handy for people to drop into for, say, a cut finger or a black eye, as was now the chemist's shop. Then, the Lagoon itself . . . this view of which Richard had made so much! After the rains, when there was some water in it, it might be all right; but just now it was more than three parts dry, and most unsightly. You saw the bare cracked earth of its bottom, not to speak of the rubbish, the old tins and boots and broken china, that had been thrown into it when full. And the mosquitoes! She had been obliged to put netting round all their beds; and what it would be like in summer passed imagining.

From such reflections, in the weeks and months that followed, she had nothing but work to distract her. The society airily promised her by Richard failed to materialize. She received just three callers. And only one of these – the Bank Manager's wife, a young thing, newly wed – was worth considering. The stationmaster's . . . the stationmaster himself was an educated man, with whom even Richard enjoyed a chat; but he had married beneath him . . . a dressmaker, if report spoke true. Mrs Cameron, wife of the Clerk of the Court, had lived so long in Barambogie that she had gone queer from it. Nor was it feasible to ask the old couple over of an evening, for cards or music; for by then old Cameron was so fuddled that he couldn't tell a knave from a king. The parson was also an odd fish, and a widower without family; the Presbyterian minister unmarried. The poor children had no playfellows, no companions. Oh, not for herself, but for those who were more to her than herself, Mary's heart was often very hot and sore.

Nevertheless she put her shoulder to the wheel with all her old spirit; rising betimes to bath and dress the children, cutting out and making their clothes, superintending the washing and ironing, cooking the meals; and, when Eliza passed and a young untrained servant took her place, doing the lion's share towards keeping the house in the spotless state Richard loved and her own sense of nicety demanded. But the work told on her. And not alone because it was harder. In Hawthorn, she had laboured to some end; Richard had had to be re-established, connections formed, their own nice house tended. All of which had given her mind an upward lift. Here, where no future beckoned, it seemed just a matter of toiling for toil's sake. The consequence was, she tired much more readily; her legs ached, her feet throbbed, and the crow's-feet began to gather round her eyes. She was paying of course, she told herself, for those long years of luxury and idleness, in which Richard had been against her lifting a finger. And it was no easy thing to buckle to again, now that she was 'getting on', 'going downhill': Mary being come to within a twelve-month of her fortieth year.

CHAPTER SEVEN

'Cousin Emmy, tell about little Jacky.'

'Little Jacky what died.'

'No, *don't*! Tell what the gumtrees talk.'

Cuffy hated the tale of Baby Jacky's illness and death; for Cousin Emmy always cried when she told it. And to see a grown-up person cry wasn't proper.

The four of them were out for their morning walk, and sat resting on a fallen tree.

'Well, dears, poor little Jacky was so often ill that God thought he would be happier in heaven. His back teeth wouldn't come through; and he was so feverish and restless than I had to carry him about most of the night. The last time I walked him up and down he put his little arms round my neck, and said: "Ting, Memmy!" – he couldn't say "sing" or "Emmy" properly, you know' – a detail which entranced the Dumplings, who had endless difficulties with their own speech. 'And those were the very last words he said. In the middle of the night he took convulsions – '

'What *are* c'nvulshuns, Cousin Emmy?' The question came simultaneously, none of the three being minded, often as they had heard the story, to let the narrator skip this, the raciest bit of it.

'Why, poor darling, he shivered and shook, and squinted and rolled his eyes, and went blue in the face, and his body got stiff, and he turned up his eyes till you could only see the whites. And then he died, and we dressed him in his best nightgown, and he lay there looking like a big wax doll – with white flowers in his hands. And his little coffin was lined with white satin, and trimmed with the most *beautiful* lace . . .' And here sure enough, at mention of her nursling's last costly bed, Emmy began to cry. The three children, reddening, smiled funny little embarrassed smiles and averted their eyes; only occasionally taking a surreptitious peep to see what Cousin Emmy looked like when she did it.

With the heel of his boot Cuffy hammered the ground. He knew something else . . . about Cousin Emmy . . . something naughty. He'd heard Mamma and Papa talking; and it was about running away and Aunt Lizzie being most awfully furious. And then Cousin Emmy had come to stay with them. He was glad she had; he liked her. Her hair was yellow, like wattle; her mouth ever so red. And she told them stories. Mamma could only read stories. And never had time.

Today, however, there would be no more. For round a bend of the bush track, by which they sat, came a figure which the children were growing used to seeing appearing on their walks. It was the Reverend Mr Angus. He wore a long black coat that reached below his knees and a white tie. He had a red curly beard and pink cheeks. (Just like a lady, thought Cuffy.) At sight of the lovely girl in deep mourning, bathed in tears, these grew still pinker. Advancing at a jogtrot, their owner seated himself on the tree and took Emmy's hand in his.

The children were now supposed to 'run away and play'. The twins fell to building a little house, with pieces of bark and stones; but Cuffy determined to pick a *beeyutiful* nosegay, that Cousin Emmy would like ever so much, and say 'How pretty!' to, and 'How kind of you, Cuffy!' Mr Angus had a face like a cow; and when he spoke he made hissing noises through his teeth. The first time he heard them, Cuffy hadn't been able to tear his eyes away, and had stood stockstill in front of the minister till Cousin Emmy got quite cross. And Mr Angus said, in *his* opinion, little people should not only be seen and not heard, but not even seen.

All right then! Whistling his loudest Cuffy sauntered off. He would be good, and not go near any of the old, open shafts; quite specially not the one where the old dead donkey had tumbled in and floated. You weren't allowed to look down this hole, not even if somebody held your hand . . . like Mr Angus did Cousin Emmy's. (Why was he? She couldn't fall off a *log*.) It had a nasty smell, too. Cousin Emmy said only to think of it made her sick. And Mamma said they were to hold their noses as they passed. Why was the donkey so nasty because it was dead? What did a dead donkey *do*?

But first he would pick the flowers. It wouldn't take long, there were such lots of them. Papa said we must thank the rains for the flowers; and it had rained every day for nearly a month. The Lagoon was quite full, and the tank, too; which made Mamma glad. — And now Cuffy darted about, tearing up bits of running postman, and pulling snatches of the purple sarsaparilla that climbed the bushes and young trees, till he had a tight, close bunch in his hot little hand. As he picked, he sniffed the air, which smelt lovely . . . like honey. . . . Cousin Emmy said it was the wattle coming out. To feel it better he shut his eyes, screwed them up to nothing, and kept them tight. And when he opened them again, everything looked *new* . . . as if he'd never seen it before . . . all the white trees, tall like poles, that went up and up to where, right at the top, among whiskery branches, were bits of blue that were the sky.

With the elastic of his big upturned sailor-hat between his teeth — partly to keep it on; partly because he loved chewing things: elastic, or string, or the fingers of kid gloves — Cuffy ran at top speed to the donkey-hole. But a couple of yards from the shaft his courage all but failed him. What was he going to see? And ooh! . . . it *did* smell. Laying his flowers on the ground, he went down on his hands and knees and crawled forward till he could just peep over. And then, why, what a sell! It wasn't a donkey at all — just water — and in it a great lump that stuck out like a 'normous boiled pudding . . . oh, and a million, no, two million and a half blowflies walking on it, and a smell like — ooh, yes! just exactly like . . .

But before he could put a name to the odour, there was a great shouting and cooee-ing, and it was him they were calling . . . and calling. In his guilty fright Cuffy gave a jerk, and off went his hat with its pulped elastic — went down, down, down, while the blowflies came up. He just managed to wriggle a little way back, but was still on all fours (squashing the flowers) when they found him. Mr Angus panting and puffing with tears on his forehead, Cousin Emmy pressing her hand to her chest and saying, oh dear oh dear! Then Mr Angus took him by the shoulder and shook him. Little boys who ran away in the bush *always* got lost, and never saw their Mammas and Papas again. They had nothing to eat and starved to death, and not till years afterwards were their skeletons found. Cuffy, who knew quite well where he was, and hadn't meant to run away, thought him very silly . . . and rude.

It was the loss of the hat that was the tragedy. This made ever so many things go wrong, and ended with Cousin Emmy having to go back to live with Aunt Lizzie again, and them getting a real *paid* governess to teach them.

Hatless, squeezed close up to Cousin Emmy to be under her parasol, Cuffy was hurried through the township. 'Or people will think your Mamma is too poor to buy you a hat.'

The children's hearts were heavy. It infected them with fear to see Cousin Emmy so afraid, and to hear her keep saying: 'What *will* Aunt Mary say?'

Not only, it seemed, had the hat cost a lot of money – to get another like it Mamma would have to send all the way to Melbourne. But it also leaked out that not a word was to have been said about Mr Angus meeting them, and sitting on the log and talking.

'Why not? Is it naughty?'

'Of *course* not, Cuffy! How can you be so silly! But – '

But . . . well, Aunt Mary would certainly be dreadfully cross with her for not looking after him better. How *could* he be so dishonourable, the first moment she wasn't watching, to go where he had been strictly forbidden to . . . such a *dirty* place! . . . and where he might have fallen head-foremost down the shaft and never been seen again.

Yes, it was a very crestfallen, guilt-laden little party that entered the house.

Mamma came out of the dining-room, a needle in one hand, a long thread of cotton in the other. And she saw at once what had happened, and said: 'Where's your hat? – *Lost* it? Your nice new hat? How? Come in here to me.' The twins began to sniff, and then everything was up.

Yes, Mamma was very cross . . . and sorry, too; for poor Papa was working his hardest to keep them nice, and then a careless little boy just went and threw money into the street. But ever so much crosser when she heard where the hat had gone: she scolded and scolded. And then she put the question Cuffy dreaded most: 'Pray, what were you doing there . . . by yourself?' In vain he shuffled and prevaricated, and told about the nosegay. Mamma just fixed her eyes on him, and it was no good; Mr Angus had to come out. And now it was Cousin Emmy's turn. She went scarlet, but she answered Mamma back quite a lot, and was angry, too; and only when Mamma said she wouldn't have believed it of her, it was the behaviour of a common nursegirl, and she would have to speak to her uncle about her — at that Cousin Emmy burst out crying, and ran away and shut herself in her room.

Then Mamma went into the surgery to tell Papa. She shut the door, but you could hear their voices through it; and merely the sound of them, though he didn't know what they were saying, threw Cuffy into a flutter. Retreating to the furthest corner of the verandah, he sat with his elbows on his knees, the palms of his hands pressed against his ears.

And while Emmy, face downwards on her pillow, wept: 'I don't care . . . let them fall down mines if they want to . . . he's very nice . . . Aunt Mary isn't fair!' Mary was saying: 'I did think she could be trusted with the children — considering the care she took of Jacky.'

'Other people's children, my dear — other people's children! He might have been her own.'

Mary was horrified. 'Whatever you do, don't say a thing like that before Cuffy! It would mean the most awkward questions. And surely *we* are not "other people"? If Emmy can't look after her own little cousins. . . . The child might have been killed, while she sat there flirting and amusing herself.'

'It's not likely to happen again.'

'Oh, I don't know. When I tackled her with it, she got on the high horse at once, and said it wasn't a very great crime to have a little chat with somebody: life was so dull here, and so on.'

'Well, I'm sure that's true enough.'

'*What* a weak spot you have for the girl! But that's not all. It didn't take me long to discover she'd been trying to make the children deceive me. They were to have held their tongues about this Angus meeting them on their walks. . . . Cuffy went as near as he could to telling a fib over it. Now you must see I can't have that sort of thing going on . . . the children taught fibbing and deceiving!'

'No, that certainly wouldn't do.'

'Then, imagine a girl of Emmy's birth and upbringing plotting to meet, on the sly, a man we don't invite to the house! She'll be the talk of the place. And what if she got herself into some entanglement or other while she's under our care? John's eldest daughter and an insignificant little dissenter, poor as a church mouse, and years older than she is! *Think* what Lizzie would say!'

'My dear, Lizzie's sentiments would be the same, and were it Croesus and Adonis rolled into one.'

'Well, yes, I suppose they would. – But Emmy is far too extravagant for a poor man's wife. She changes her underclothing every day of the week. You should hear Maria grumble at the washing! Besides, she's everlastingly titivating, dressing her hair or something. She does none of the jobs one expects from a nursery-governess. And if I venture to find fault . . . I don't know, but she seems greatly changed. I think first her father's death, and then Jacky's have thoroughly spoiled her.'

'Well! to have the two mortals you've set your heart on snatched from you, one after the other, isn't it enough to dash the stoutest? . . . let alone an innocent young girl. Emmy has been through a great spiritual experience, and one result of it might very well be to mature her . . . turn her into a woman who feels her power. It will probably be the same wherever she goes, with a face like hers. In her father's house, she would of course have met more eligible men than we, in our poor circumstances, can offer her. Still, my advice would be, such as they are, ask 'em to the house. Let everything be open and above-board.'

'What! invite that little Angus? Nonsense! It would only be encouraging him. Besides, it's all very well for you to theorize; I have to look at it from the practical side. And it surely isn't what one has a governess for? . . . to smooth the way for her flirtations. I may as well tell you everything. When she first came, I used to send her running up to the station – if I needed stamps, or small change, or things like that – Mr Pendrell is always so obliging. But I had to stop it. She took to staying away an unconscionable time, and his wife must have got wind of it, she began to look so queerly at Emmy and to drop hints. Most uncomfortable. And then you've surely noticed how often old Thistlethwaite comes to see us now, compared with what he used to, and how he sits and stares at Emmy. He looks at her far too much, too, when he's preaching, and I've heard him pay her the most outrageous compliments. A clergyman and a widower, and old enough to be her *grand*father! But Emmy just drinks it in. Now, mind you, if there were any question of a decent match for her, I'd do what I could to help . . . for I don't believe Lizzie will ever let her say how-do-you-do to an eligible. But I *cannot* have her getting into mischief here – why, even the baker tries to snatch a word with her when he delivers the bread! — and being branded as forward, and a common flirt. No, the truth is, she's just too pretty to be of the least practical use.'

Mahony made no reply.

'Are you *listening*, Richard? . . . to what I say?'

'Yes, I hear.'

'I thought you were asleep. Well, perhaps you'll rouse yourself and tell me what I ought to do.'

'I suppose there's nothing for it: Emmy must go.'

'And then?'

'Then?'

'I mean about the children. Who's to give them their lessons and their music-lessons? . . . and take them out walking?'

'My dear, *can* you not teach them yourself for a bit?'

'No, Richard, I *cannot*! At the age they're at now, they need one person's undivided attention. They've simply *got* to have a governess.'

'Oh well! I suppose if you must you must . . . and that's all about it.'

The implication in these words exasperated Mary.

'If *I* must? I'm not asking anything for myself! You've never heard me utter a word of complaint. But I can't do more than I am doing. Anyone but you would see it. But you're as blind as a bat!'

'Not so blind as you think, my dear. One thing I see is that you never hesitate to load me up with a fresh expense.'

'No, that's out-and-away unfair,' cried Mary, thoroughly roused. 'I, who slave and toil . . . and when I'm not even convinced that it's necessary, either. For you're always saying you're satisfied with the practice, that the fees come in well and so on; and yet to get anything out of you nowadays is like drawing blood from a stone. I don't care a rap about myself; I'll put up with whatever you like; but I can't and won't sit by and see my children degenerate. I think that would break my heart. I shall fight for them to my last breath.'

'Yes, for them. But for me, never a trace of understanding!' — And now the quarrel began in earnest.

Cuffy, sitting hunched up on the verandah, squeezed his ears until they sang.

CHAPTER EIGHT

The day began at six . . . with the pestilential screech of the mill-whistle. This also started the children off. Birdlike sounds began to issue from their room across the passage: there was no muting these shrill, sweet trebles. And soon Miss Prestwick's thin voice made itself heard, capped by Mary's magisterial tones, and the dashing and splashing of bath-water, and small feet scampering, and Maria thudding up and down, clattering her brooms.

There was no more chance of sleep. He, too, rose.

The water of the shower-bath was tepid and unrefreshing. It had also to be sparingly used. Then came breakfast – with mushy butter, the pat collapsing on its way from the cellar; with sticky flies crawling over everything, a soiled cloth, the children's jabber, Miss Prestwick's mincing airs, and Mary checking, apportioning, deciding. Mahony ate hastily, and, there being here no morning paper or early post to engage him, retired to the surgery. His cases written up, his visits for the day arranged, he sat and waited, and listened. This was the time when a walking-patient or two might call for treatment; and the footsteps of anyone nearing the house could be heard a long way off, crunching the gravel of the path by the Lagoon, coming up the right-of-way. And as he sat, idly twirling his thumbs, it became a matter of interest to speculate whether approaching steps would halt at his door or move on towards the railway station. In waiting, he could hear Cuffy's voice proclaiming loudly and unnaturally: *'Jer suise urn petty garsong, de bun figoor.'*

After a couple of false alarms there was a knock at the door; and Maria introduced a working-man with a foreign body in his eye. A grain of mortar extracted and the eye bathed, Mahony washed, stitched and bandaged a child's gashed knee, and drew a tooth for a miner's wife. Mary's aid was needed here, to hold the woman's hands. It was Mary, too, who applied restoratives and helped to clean up the patient. After which she brushed yesterday's dust from his wideawake, held a silk coat for him to slip his arms into and checked the contents of his bag.

He set off on his morning round, following the path that ran alongside the Lagoon. Here and there the shadow of a fir-tree fell across it, and, though the season was but late spring, the shade was welcome. Emerging from the Lagoon enclosure, he entered the single street that formed the township of Barambogie. This was empty but for a couple of buggies which stood outside a public-house, their hoods white with the dust of innumerable bush journeys.

But the sound of his foot on the pavement, his shadow on the glass of the shop-windows, made people dart to their doors to see who passed. Huh! it was only 'the new doctor'; and out of *him* nothing was to be got . . . in the shape of a yarn, or a companionable drink.

One or two threw him a 'Mornin'!' The rest contented themselves with a nod. But all alike regarded his raised hat and courteous 'Good day to you!' 'Good morning, sir!' with the colonial's inborn contempt for form and ceremony. By the Lord Harry! slapdash was good enough for them.

On this particular day Mahony had three calls to make.

Arrived at the Anglican parsonage – a shabby brick cottage standing on a piece of ground that had never been fenced in – he took up the knocker, which, crudely repaired with a headless nail and a bit of twine, straightway came off in his hand. He rapped with his knuckles, and the Reverend Thistlethwaite, in nightshirt and trousers and with bare feet, appeared from his back premises, where he had been feeding fowls. Re-affixing the knocker with a skill born of long practice, he opened the door of the parlour, into which there was just room to squeeze. On the table, writing-materials elbowed the remains of a mutton-chop breakfast. Blowflies crawled over the fatted plates.

An unsightly carbuncle lanced and dressed, the reverend gentleman – he was a fleshy, red-faced man, of whom unkind rumour had it that there were times when his tongue tripped over his own name – laid himself out to detain his visitor. He was spoiling for a chat.

'Yes, yes, doctor, hard at work . . . hard at work!' – with an airy wave of the hand at pens, ink and paper. 'Must always have something fresh, you know, of a Sunday morning, to tickle 'em up with. Even the minor prophets are racked, I can assure you, in the search for a rousing heading.'

Mahony replaced lancet and lint in silence. It was common knowledge that old Thistlethwaite had not written a fresh sermon for years; but had used his stale ones again and again, some even said reading them backwards, for the sake of variety. The implements littering the table were set permanently out on view.

Insensitive to Mahony's attitude, he ran on: 'Talking of rummy texts now . . . did y'ever hear the story of the three curates, out to impress the Bishop with their skill at squeezing juice from a dry orange, who, each in turn, in the different places he visited on three successive Sundays, held forth on the theme: "Now Peter's wife's mother lay sick of fever"? You have? . . . capital, isn't it? But I'll warrant you don't know the yarn of old Minchin and the cow. It was at Bootajup in the Western District, and his first up-country cure; and Minch, who was a townbird born and bred, was officiating for the first time at Harvest Festival. The farmers had given liberally, the church was full, Minch in the reading-desk with his back to a side door that had been left open for coolness. All went well till in the middle of the Psalms, when he saw the eyes of his congregation getting rounder and rounder. Old Minch, who was propriety in person, thought his collar had come undone, or that he'd shed a private button . . . ha, ha! Whereas, if you please, it was a cow which had strayed to the door, and was being agreeably attracted by the farm produce. Minch looked round just as the animal walked in, lost his head, dropped his book and bolted; taking the altar rails at a leap, with cassock and surplice bunched up round him. Ha, ha! Capital . . . capital! It was Minchin, too, who was once preaching from the text: "And God shall wipe away all tears from their eyes" when he found himself forced to sneeze some dozen times running. Ha, ha, ha! His own eyes poured tears – ran with water. Out it came: a-tischoo, a-tischoo! The congregation rocked with laughter. – What? . . . you must be toddling? Well, well! we know you doctors are busy men. Hot? – call this hot? I wonder what you'll say to our summers! Well, good day, doctor, good day!'

' "Except ye become as little children" . . . "for of such is the kingdom of heaven." *My* God! . . . then give me earth.'

Striking off on a bush track Mahony trudged along, leaving a low trail of dust in his wake. His goal was a poor outlying wooden shanty, to treat a washerwoman's severely scalded leg and foot. The wound, some days old, was open, dirty, offensive; the woman, who sat propped up before her tubs, struggling to finish her week's work, loud-mouthed with pain.

'She don't half holler'n screech if oner the kids knocks up against it, volunteered a foxy-looking girl who stood by, sucking her thumb, and watching, with an unholy interest, the sponging off of the foul rags, the laying bare of the raw flesh.

Mahony's impatient 'Why on earth didn't you send for me sooner?' brought no coherent response; but his prescription of complete rest in a horizontal position effectually loosed the sufferer's tongue. 'Didn't I know you'd be after orderin' me some such foolery? Who's to kape us? I've no man. I'm a poor lone widder . . .'

'Apply to your priest for aid.'

'The praste? A fat lot o' good that 'ud be – the great lazy louse! We cud all starve afore *he'd* lift a finger.'

'Well, I've warned you, I can do no more.' And cutting further discussion short, Mahony put on his hat and walked out of the house.

As, however, the foxy child, thumb in mouth, lolloped after him, he took a sovereign from his pocket. 'Here, my girl, here's something to tide you over. Now see that your mother lies up. You're old enough to lend a hand.'

But before he had gone a hundred yards he turned on his heel, recalling the low, cunning look that had leapt into the girl's eyes at sight of the gold piece. 'Fool that I am! . . . the mother will never see it.'

Caught in the act of secreting the coin in her stocking, the girl went livid with fury. 'What d'you mean? D'you think I was goin' to pinch it? Ma! . . . d'you hear, Ma? . . . what he says? Ma! he's callin' me a thief.'

'A thief, indeed! My child a thief? – And you, you pesky young devil, you hand that chip over or I'll wring your neck!'

Thence to the shop of Ah Sing, the Chinese butcher, where a rachitic infant lay cramped with the colic. Mahony looked with pity on the little half-breed, slit of eye and yellow of skin, and was very short with the mother, a monstrously fat woman who stood, her arms akimbo, answering his questions with an air of sulky defiance. No, she didn't know, not she, what had caused the colic: *she'd* done nothing. But here espying an empty tin dish that had been thrust under the bed, Mahony picked it up and sniffed it. 'Ha! here we have it. What filthy messes has your husband been feeding the child on now? Haven't I told you her stomach will not stand them?'

'Mrs Ah Sing' bit back the abusive rejoinders that were given to escaping her at any reference to her child's mixed origin: Doctor's' were Sing's best customers. But the visit over, she flounced into the shop and, seizing a knife, let loose her spleen in hacking down some chops, while she vociferated for all to hear: 'Filthy mess, indeed . . . *I'll* mess him! Let him look to his own kids, say I! That boy brat of his is as white as a sheet and thin as a lizard. – Here, you Sing, weigh this and look sharp about it, you crawling slug, you!'

'Malia! me give lil baby powder – you no sendee more for doctorman, Malia!' said the soft-voiced, gentle Chinaman who owned her.

'Oh, hell take the kid! – and you along with it,' gave back Maria.

On the way home Mahony overtook his children and the governess, returning from their morning walk. The twins' short fat legs were weary. Entrusting his bag to Cuffy, who forthwith became 'the doctor', bowing graciously to imaginary patients, and only waggling the bag just the least little bit to hear the things inside it rattle, their father took his little girls by the hand. Poor mites! They were losing their roses already. Somehow or other he must make it possible to send them away when the real hot weather came. This was no place for children in summer; he heard it on every side. And his, reared to seabreezes, would find it doubly hard to acclimatize themselves. Stung by these reflections he unthinkingly quickened his pace, and strode ahead, a gaunt figure, dragging a small child at a trot on either hand. Miss Prestwick gave up the chase.

Dinner over, out he had to turn again. Back to the main street and the hotel, where a buggy should have been in waiting. It was not. He had to stand about in the sun while the vehicle was dragged out, the horse fetched, harnessed, and backed between the shafts. A strap broke in the buckling; the ostler, whistling between his teeth, leisurely repaired the damage with a bit of string.

Stiffly Mahony jerked himself up into the high vehicle and took the reins. He had a ten-mile drive before him, over the worst possible roads; it would be all he could do to reach home by dark. The horse, too, was unfresh. In vain he urged and cajoled; the animal's pace remained a dilatory amble. And the heat seemed to accumulate under the close black hood, which weighed on his shoulders like a giant hat. Yet, if he alighted to slip a rail, it was so much hotter outside that he was glad to clamber back beneath its covering. Still he did not complain. These bush visits were what brought the shekels in: not the tinkering with rachitic infants or impecunious Irish, whom, as this morning, he sometimes paid for the privilege of attending. (Ha, ha! . . . capital! . . . as that fool Thistlethwaite would have said.) And today promised to be more than ordinarily remunerative; for he had another long drive before him that evening, in an opposite direction. He could count on clearing a ten-pound note.

But when, towards six o'clock, he reached home, the summons he was expecting had not come. There was time for a bath, a change, a rest; and still the trap that should have fetched him had not appeared. He began to grow fidgety. The case was one of diphtheria. On the previous day he had given relief by opening the windpipe; it was essential for him to know the result of the operation. What could the people be thinking of? Or had the child died in the meantime . . . the membrane spread downwards, causing obstruction below the tube? 'Surely in common decency they would have let me know?'

He wandered from room to room, nervously snapping his fingers. Or sat down and beat a tattoo on chair-arm or table, only to spring up at an imaginary sound of wheels.

Mary dissuaded him from hiring a buggy and driving out to see what had happened. She also pooh-poohed his idea of an accident to the messenger. The father, a vinegrower, had several men and more than one horse and buggy at his disposal. The likelihood was, he would have come himself, had the child been worse. *Unless*, of course . . . well! it wasn't death *she* thought of. But the township of Mittagunga was not much farther than Barambogie from the patient's home; and there was another doctor at Mittagunga. She did not speak this thought aloud; but it haunted her; and, as the evening wore eventlessly away, the question escaped her in spite of herself: 'Can you have offended them? . . . in any way?'

'*Offended* them? I? — Well, if it's offensive to leave one's bed in the middle of the night for an eight-mile drive on these abominable roads, to perform a ticklish operation!' And very bitterly:

'What extraordinary ideas you do have, Mary! What on earth do you mean now?'

But Mary, repenting her slip, was not prepared to stir up the heated discussion that would inevitably follow.

She went into the dining-room and sat down to her sewing; while he fell to pacing the verandah. But though she, too, never ceased to keep her ears pricked for the noise of wheels, no sound was to be heard but that of Richard's feet tramping to and fro ('*How* tired he will be tomorrow!') and the peevish whine of a little nightwind round the corners of the house. Sorry as she felt for him, she did not again try to reason with him or console him. For when in one of his really black moods, he seemed to retire where words could not get at him. And these moods were growing on him. Nowadays, any small mishap sufficed to throw him into a state of excitement, the aftermath of which was bottomless depression. How would it all end? – Letting her work fall, Mary put her chin in her hand, and sat staring into the flame of the kerosene lamp. But she did not see it. She seemed to be looking through the light at something that lay beyond . . . something on the farther side, not only of the flame, but of all she had hitherto known of life; to be looking, in visionary fashion, out towards those shadowy tomorrows, for the first of which Richard was so surely incapacitating himself . . . an endless line of days, that would come marching upon her, with never a break, never a respite, each fuller of anxiety than the one that went before.

Till, with a shiver, she resolutely shook herself free. 'Tch! . . . it comes of listening to that silly, dismal wind.'

Yet when, on the clock striking eleven, she stepped out on the verandah, her first words were: 'Oh, what a lovely night!'

For the little wind whistled and piped out of a clear sky; and the moon, at full, drenched the earth with its radiance. Before the house the Lagoon lay like a sheet of beaten silver. Trees and bushes, jet-black on one side, were white as if with hoar frost on the other. The distant hills ran together with the sky in a silver haze. All was peace . . . except for the thudding of Richard's feet.

'My dear, I'm sure it's no use waiting up any longer. They won't come now. Do go to bed.'

'I'm too worried. I couldn't sleep.'

'But at least it would rest you. As it is, you're wearing yourself out.'

'Very easy for you to talk! But if anything should happen . . . the responsibility . . . my practice here – I can't afford it, Mary, and that's the truth . . . not yet.'

There was nothing to be done. With a sigh that was like a little prayer for patience, Mary turned away.

CHAPTER NINE

The postman handed in a letter with a mourning border fully an inch wide: there was barely room for name and address, which were squeezed in anyhow. It was from Mr Henry; and opening it in some trepidation Mary read the sad news of Agnes's death. Mr Henry was kind enough to give her full particulars. Agnes had, it seemed, stood the voyage out well. But on landing at the Cape she had met with an accident; had caught her foot in a rope and fallen heavily; and the shock had brought on an apoplexy from which she never rallied. Mr Henry wrote as one bereft of all he held dear; as the fond father whose pious duty it would henceforth be, to fill a mother's place to his orphaned children. In reading the letter aloud, Mary swallowed hard; then veiled her discomfort with an apologetic: 'Oh well, you know ... poor man, ... I daresay – ' by which she meant to imply that, with death's entry on the scene, the realities were apt to get overlaid. Mr Henry saw himself and his situation, not as they were, but as he would have wished them to be.

Richard, of course, sniffed at Ocock's layman-ish account of his wife's end. And he was right. For Tilly's gloss on the affair ran: *Purd heard from a man who was on board the same ship. It's true she did trip over a rope and come a cropper (and not the first time neither, as we know) and this brought on a violent attack of d.t.'s which carried her off. Henry hasn't looked the same man since. His relief is immense – simply immense.*

But Mary's faithful stubborn heart rebelled. For Agnes's own sake, her death was perhaps, pitifully enough, the best solution. But that, of all who had known her, none should mourn her passing; that even among her nearest it should stir only a sense of good riddance and relief: the tragedy of such a finish moved Mary to the depths. Tenderly she laid away the keepsake Mr Henry sent her for remembrance: a large cameo-brooch, at the back of which, under glass, was twined a golden curl, cut from the head of the little child whose untimely end had cost Agnes her bitterest tears.

A day or two later there came into her possession a still more pathetic memento: a letter from the dead, which had to be opened and read though the hand that wrote it was lying cold at the bottom of a grave. It had been found by Mr Henry amongst his wife's belongings – found sealed and addressed but never posted – a blotted and scrawled production and more than a little confused, but full of love and kindness; though written with the firm conviction that they would never meet again. Poor thing, poor thing! And having read, Mary hid it away at the back of a drawer, where no eyes but her own would ever see it. She could not have borne Richard's sarcastic comments on Agnes's poor spelling and poorer penmanship.

But there was nothing new in this secretiveness: she was falling more and more into the way of keeping Richard in the dark. A smash of china by the clumsy servant; Miss Prestwick's airs and insufficiencies; the exorbitant price of the children's new boots; disturbing gossip retailed by the girl: of vexations such as these, which were her daily portion, he heard not a word. It left her, of course, much freer to deal with things. But it also spared him the exhaustion of many a towering rage (under the influence of which he was quite capable of writing to the bootmaker and calling him a thief); saved him, too, from going off into one of his fits of depression when he imagined the whole world in league against him. The real truth was, he hadn't enough to occupy him; and not a soul to speak to . . . except his dreadful patients. Nor did he ever write or receive a letter. In coming here he seemed to have had but one desire: to forget and be forgotten.

She it was who sat up at night, spinning out the letters necessary to make people remember you. And it fell to her to write the note of welcome when Baron von Krause, the well-known botanist, proposed to break his journey from Sydney to Melbourne, solely to pay them a visit. – Though putting up a visitor nowadays meant considerable inconvenience: they had to turn out of their own room, she going in with the children, Richard making shift with the dining-room sofa. Still, in this case she thought the upset worth while: for Richard's sake. He had been as friendly with the Baron as it was in his nature to be with anybody; and the latter had once spoken to her, in warm terms, of Richard's intimate knowledge of the native flora, and lamented the fact that he should not have found time to systematize his studies.

The next morning, while Richard was out, she climbed the stepladder and unearthed the glass cases that contained his collections of plants, minerals and butterflies: for the first time on moving into a new house, he had not set them up in his room. But she wasn't going to let people think that, because he had come to live up-country, he was therefore running to seed. And having dusted and rubbed and polished, she ranged the cases along the walls of the passage and on the dining-room sideboard. To the delight of the children.

But she might have spared her pains. As far as Richard was concerned, the visit was a failure.

Baron von Krause arrived during the forenoon. Richard was on his rounds, and did not reach home till they were half through dinner. And then he tried to get out of coming to table! Going in search of him on his non-appearance, she found him sunk in his armchair, from which he vowed he was too tired to stir . . . let alone exert himself to entertain strangers.

'Strangers? There's only him! And he's just as nice as he always was. We're getting on capitally. The children, too.'

The Baron was a short, sturdy little man, bronzed brown with the sun — beside him Richard, who never tanned, looked almost transparent — dark of hair and beard, and with a pair of kindly blue eyes that beamed at you from behind large gold spectacles. Veteran colonist though he was, he still spoke a jargon all his own, coupled with a thick, foreign accent. He also expressed himself with extreme deliberation, using odd, archaic words ('Like the Bible,' thought Cuffy); and, could he not at once find the word he sought, he paused in what he was saying and scoured his mind till he had captured it. This, added to the fact that he did things at table that were strictly forbidden them, made him an object of enormous interest to the children; and three pairs of eyes hung entranced on him as he ate and spoke, to the detriment of their owners' own table-manners. In waiting, too, for him to be delivered of a word, three little faces went pink with a mixture of embarrassment and anticipation. In vain did Mary privately frown and shake her head. A knifeful of peas, 'me*lan*choly' for melancholy, and all three were agog again. It was a real drawback, at a time like this, to have such *noticing* children.

But with their father's entry a change came over their behaviour. Cuffy kept his eyes fixed on his plate and minded what he was doing, and Lallie and Lucie faithfully followed suit. The fun was at an end. For it wasn't at all the same when Papa forgot, in the middle of a sentence, what he was going to say (because Mamma interrupted him with a potato) and tried and tried his hardest to remember and couldn't, and got very cross with himself. Mamma thought it was funny though, for she laughed and said she believed he'd forget his head if it weren't screwed on; and then she told a story about Papa nearly going out without his collar, and how she had rushed after him and saved him . . . which made Papa cross with her as well.

It was too hot to go walking. And after dinner, Mahony having been called back to the surgery, the Baron strayed to the drawing-room, opened the piano, and put his hairy, knuckly hands on the keys. Mary thought this an excellent chance to slip away and 'see to things'; but Richard, the patient gone, first set his door ajar, then came along the passage and sat down in an armchair by the drawing-room window. Cuffy, at ball on the verandah, also crept in and took up his position close to the piano, leaning against it and staring fixedly at the player – listening, that is to say, after the fashion of children, as much with the eyes as with the ears (as if only by keeping the maker of the sounds in view can they grasp the sounds themselves) – the while he continued mechanically to tip his ball from hand to hand.

The Baron was playing something hard and ugly . . . like five-finger exercises but with more notes, oh! *lots* of notes in it . . . and to and fro went the ball, to and fro. This lasted a long time, and the Baron was hot when he'd finished, and had to wipe his neck and clean his glasses. Then he did some more; and this time it was prettier, with a tune to it, and it danced in little squirts up the piano; and Cuffy was obliged to smile . . . he didn't know why, his mouth just smiled by itself. He also left off fiddling with the ball. By now the Baron had become aware of his small listener. Musician-wise had noted, too, the child's instinctive response to the tripping scherzo. Pausing, he peered at Cuffy through his large round spectacles; and before putting his fingers in place for the third piece, leant over and patted the boy's cheek, murmuring as he did: 'Let us see then . . . yes, let us see!' To Cuffy he said: 'Hearken now, my little one . . . hearken well to this. Here I shall give you food for the heart as well as for the head.' – And then he began to play music that was quite, quite different to that before . . . and wasn't *like* music any more. It whispered in the bass, and while it whispered it growled; but the treble didn't growl: it cried.

And now something funny happened to Cuffy. He began to feel as if he'd like to run away; he didn't *want* to listen . . . and his heart started to beat fast. Like if he *had* run. The Baron 'd said he was playing to it . . . perhaps that was why . . . for it seemed to be getting bigger . . . till it was almost too tight for his chest. Letting his ball fall, he pressed his fists close to where he thought his heart must be. Something hurt him in there . . . he didn't *like* this music, he wanted to call out to it to stop. But the piano didn't care: it went on and on, and though it tried once to be different, it always came back and did the same thing over again . . . a dreadful thing . . . oh! something *would* burst in him if it didn't leave off . . . he felt all swollen . . . yes, he was going to burst. . . .

Then, without so much as taking his fingers off the keys, the Baron began to make a lot of little notes that sounded just like a wind, and throwing back his head and opening his mouth wide, he sang funny things . . . in ever such a funny voice.

> Über'm Garten durch die Lüfte
> Hört' ich Wandervögel zieh'n,
> Das bedeutet Frühlingsdüfte,
> Unten fängt's schon an zu blüh'n!

The relief, the ecstatic relief that surged through Cuffy at these lovely sounds, was too much for him. His eyes ran over and tears ran down his cheeks; nor could he help it, or stop them, when he found what they were doing.

Mamma – she had come back – made ever such big eyes at him.

'*Cuffy!* What on earth . . . Is this how you say thank-you for the pretty music?' (If only he was not going off before a visitor into one of his tantrums!)

'Nay, chide him not!' said the Baron, and smiled as he spoke: a very peculiar smile indeed, to Mary's way of thinking. And then he took no more notice of her, but bent over Cuffy and asked, in quite a *polite* voice: 'Will you that I play you again, my little one?'

'No . . . *no!*' As rude as the Baron was polite, Cuffy gave a great gulp and bolted from the room to the bottom of the garden; where he hid among the raspberry-bushes. He didn't know what the matter was; but he felt all sore; humiliated beyond the telling.

When he went back, aggressively sheepish and ashamed, Papa had gone. But Mamma and the Baron were talking, and he heard Mamma say: '... without the least difficulty ... ever since he was a tiny tot. – Oh, here we are, are we? – Now, Baron, he shall play to you.'

Something turned over in Cuffy at these words. '*No!* I won't!'

But Mamma threw him a look which he knew better than to disobey. Besides, she already had his music-book on the rack, the stool screwed up, and herself stood behind it to turn the pages. Ungraciously Cuffy climbed to the slippery leather top, from which his short legs dangled. Very well then if he must play, he must, he didn't care; but he wouldn't look at his notes, or listen to what he did. Instead, he'd count how many flies he could see in front of him, on the wall and the ceiling. One ... two ...

The piece – it dated from Mary's own schooldays – at an end, his mother waited in vain for the customary panegyric.

But the Baron merely said: 'H'm,' and again: 'H'm!' Adding as a kind of afterthought: 'Habile little fingers.'

When he turned to Cuffy, however, it was with quite a different voice. 'Well, and how many were then the flies on the *plafond*, my little one?'

Colouring to his hair-roots (*now* he was going to catch it!) Cuffy just managed to stammer out: 'Twelve blowflies and seventeen little flies.'

But the Baron only threw back his head and laughed, and laughed. 'Ha-ha, ha-ha! Twelve big and seventeen little! That is good ... that is very good!' To add mysteriously: 'Surely this, too, is a sign ... this capacity for to escape! – But now come hither, my son, and let us play the little game. The bad little boy who counts the flies, so long he plays the bad piece, shall stand so, with his face to the wall. I strike the notes – *so!* – and he is telling me their names – if Mr G or Mrs A – yes? List now, if you can hear what is this.'

'Huh, that's easy! That's C.'

'And this fellow, so grey he?'

'A – E – B.' Cuffy liked this: it was fun.

'And now how many I strike? D, F ... right! B, D sharp ... good! And here this – an ugly one, this fellow! He agree not with his neighbour.'

'That's two together . . . close, I mean. G and A.'

'*Ach, Himmel!*' cried the Baron. 'The ear, it, too, is perfect.' And swiftly crossing the room, he took Cuffy's face in his hands and turned it up. For a moment he stood looking down at it; and his brown, bearded face was very solemn. Then, stooping, he kissed the boy on the forehead. 'May the good God bless you, my child, and prosper His most precious gift!' – And this, just when Cuffy (after the fly episode) had begun to think him rather a nice old man!

Then he was free to run away and play; which he did with all his might. But later in the afternoon when it was cool enough to go walking, it was Cuffy the Baron invited to accompany him. 'Nay, we leave the little sisters at home with the good Mamma, and make the promenade alone, just we both!'

Cuffy remembered the flies, forgave the kiss, and off they set. They walked a long way into the bush, further than they were allowed to go with Miss Prestwick; and the Baron told him about the trees and poked among the scrub, and used a spyglass like Papa, and showed him things through it. It *was* fun.

Then they sat down on a log to rest. And while they were there, the Baron suddenly picked up his right hand and looked at it, as if it was funny, and turned it over to the back, and stretched out the fingers and felt the tips, and where the thumb joined on. And when he had done this he didn't let it go, but kept hold of it; and putting his other hand on Cuffy's shoulder said: 'And now say, my little man, say me why you did weep when I have played?'

Cuffy, all boy again, blushed furiously. He didn't like having his hand held either. So he only looked away, and kicked his heels against the tree so hard they hurt him. 'I dunno.'

Mamma would have said: 'Oh, yes, you do.' But the Baron wasn't cross. He just gave the hand a little squeeze, and then he began to talk, and he talked and talked. It lasted so long that it was like being in church, and was very dull, all about things Cuffy didn't know. So he hardly listened. He was chiefly intent on politely wriggling his hand free.

But the Baron looked so nice and kind, even when he'd done this, that he plucked up courage to ask something he wanted very much to know; once before when he had tried it everybody had laughed at him, and made fun.

'What does music *say*?'

But the Baron wasn't like that. He looked as solemn as church again, and nodded his head. 'Aha! It commences to stir itself . . . the inward apperception. The music, it says what is in the heart, my little one, to each interprets the own heart. That is, as you must comprehend, if the one who is making it is the *genie*, and has what in his *own* heart to say. That bad piece you have played me have said nothing — nothing at all . . . oh, how wise, how wise to count the little flies! But that what you have flowed tears for, my child, that were the sufferings of a so unhappy man — the fears that are coming by night to devour the peace — oh, I will not say them to one so tender! . . . but these, so great were they, so unhappy he, that at the last his brain has burst' (There! he *knew* he had been going to burst) 'and he have become mad. But then, see, at once I have given you the consolation. I have sung you of the nightingale, and moonshine, and first love . . . all, all of which the youth is full. Our dear madman he has that made, too. His name was Schumann. Mark that, my little one . . . mark it well!'

'Shooh man. — What's mad?'

'*Ach!* break not the little head over such as this. Have no care. The knowledge will soon enough come of pain and suffering.'

Cuffy's legs were getting *very* tired with sitting still. Sliding down from the log, he jumped and danced, feeling now somehow all glad inside. '*I* will say music, too, when I am big.'

'*Ja ja!* but so easy is it not to shake the music out of the sleeve. Man must study hard. It belongs a whole lifetime thereto . . . and much, much courage. But this I will tell you, my little ambitious one! Here is lying' — and the Baron waved his arm all round him — 'a great, new music hid. He who makes it, he will put into it the thousand feelings awoken in him by this emptiness and space, this desolation; with always the serene blue heaven above, and these pale, sad, so grotesque trees that weep and rave. He puts the golden wattle in it when it blooms and reeks, and this melancholy bush, oh, so old, so old, and this silence as of death that nothing stirs. No birdleins will sing in his Musik. But will you be that one, my son, you must first have given up all else for it . . . all the joys and pleasures that make the life glad. These will be for the others not for you, my dear . . . you must only go wizout . . . renounce . . . look on. — But come, let us now home, and I will speak . . . yes, I shall speak of it to the good Mamma and Papa!'

'Preposterous, I call it!' said Mary warmly and threw the letter on the table. The Baron's departure was three days old by now, and the letter she had just read was written in his hand. 'Only a man could propose such a thing. Why don't you say something, Richard? Surely you don't . . .'

'No, I can see it's out of the question.'

'I should think so! At *his* age! . . . why, he's a mere baby. How the Baron could think for a moment we should let a tot like that leave home . . . to live among strangers – with these Hermanns or Germans or whatever he calls them – why, it's almost too silly to discuss. As for his offer to defray all expenses out of his own pocket . . . no doubt he means it well . . . but it strikes me as very tactless. Does he think we can't afford to pay for our own children?'

'I'll warrant such an idea never entered his head. My dear, you don't understand.'

'It's you I don't understand. As a rule you flare up at the mere mention of money. Yet you take this quite calmly.'

'Good Lord, Mary! the man means it for a compliment. He not only took a liking to the boy, but he's a connoisseur in music, a thoroughly competent judge. Surely it ought to flatter you, my dear, to hear his high opinion of our child's gift.'

'I don't need an outsider to tell me that. If anyone knows Cuffy is clever it's me. I ought to: I've done everything for him.'

'This has nothing to do with cleverness.'

'Why not? What else is it?'

'It's music, my dear!' cried Mahony, waxing impatient. 'Music, and the musical faculty . . . ear, instinct, inborn receptivity.'

'*Well?*'

'Good God, Mary! . . . it sometimes seems as if we spoke a different language. The fact of the matter is, you haven't a note of music in you.'

Mary was deeply hurt. 'I, who have taught the child everything he knows? He wouldn't even be able to read his notes yet, if it had been left to you. Haven't I stood over him, and drummed things into him, and kept him at the piano? And all the thanks I get for it is to hear that I'm not capable of judging . . . haven't a note of music in me! The truth is, I'm good enough to work and slave to make ends meet. But when it comes to anything else, anything *cleverer* . . . then the first outsider knows better than I do. Thank God, I've still got my children. They at least look up to me. And that brings me back to where I started. I've got them, and I mean to keep them. Nothing shall part me from them. If Cuffy goes, I go too!'

On the verandah the three in question played a game of their own devising. They poked at each other round a corner of the house, with sticks for swords, advancing and retreating to the cry of "Shooh, man!" from the army of the twins, to which Cuffy made vigorous response: 'Shooh, woman!'

And this phrase, which remained in use long after its origin was forgotten, was the sole trace left on Cuffy's life by the Baron's visit.

CHAPTER TEN

The almond-trees that grew in a clump at the bottom of the garden had shed their pink blossom and begun to form fruit. At first, did you slyly bite one of the funny long green things in two, you came to a messy jelly . . . bah! it *was* nasty . . . you spat it out again as quick as you could. But a little later, though you could still get your teeth through the green shell, which was hairy on your tongue and sourer than ever, you found a delicious white slippery kernel inside.

Cuffy made this discovery one afternoon when Mamma had gone to the Bank to tea, and Miss Prestwick was busy writing letters. He ate freely of the delicacy; and his twin shadows demanded to eat, too. Their milk teeth being waggly, he bit the green casing through for them; and they fished out the kernels for themselves.

That night, there were loud cries for Mamma. Hurrying to them, candle in hand, Mary found the children pale and distressed, their little bodies cramped with grinding, colicky pains.

Green almonds? – 'Oh, you naughty, *naughty* children! Haven't I told you never to touch them? Where was Miss Prestwick? – There! I've always said it: she isn't *fit* to have charge of them. I shall pack her off in the morning.'

Followed a time of much pain and discomfort for the almond-eaters; of worry and trouble for Mary, who for several nights was up and down. All three paid dearly for their indulgence; but recovery was not in order of merit. Cuffy, who had enjoyed the lion's share, was the first to improve: remarkable, agreed Richard, the power of recuperation possessed by this thin, pale child. The twins, for all their sturdiness, were harder to bring round.

But at last they, too, were on their feet again, looking very white and pulled down, it was true; still, there they were, able to trot about; and their father celebrated the occasion by taking the trio for a walk by the Lagoon. The world was a new place to the little prisoners. They paused at every step to wonder and exclaim.

What happened no one knew. At the time it seemed to Mary that, for a first walk, Richard was keeping them out too long. However she said nothing; for they came back in good spirits, ate their supper of bread and milk with appetite, and went cheerily to bed.

Then, shortly after midnight, Lallie roused the house with shrill cries. Running to her, Mary found the child doubled up with pain and wet with perspiration. By morning she was as ill as before. There was nothing for it but to buckle down to a fresh bout of nursing.

Of the two lovely little blue-eyed, fair-haired girls, who were the joy of their parents' lives as Cuffy was the pride: of these, Mahony's early whimsy that a single soul had been parcelled out between two bodies still held good. Not an act in their six short years but had, till now, been a joint one. Hand in hand, cheek to cheek, they faced their tiny experiences, turning to each other to share a titbit, a secret, a smile. But, if in such oneness there could be talk of a leader, then it was Lallie who led. A quarter of an hour older, a fraction of an inch taller, half a pound heavier, she had always been a thought bolder than her sister, a hint quicker to take the proffered lollipop, to speak out her baby thoughts. Just as Cuffy was their common model, so Lucie patterned herself on Lallie; and, without Lallie, was only half herself; even a temporary separation proving as rude a wrench as though they had been born with a fleshly bond. – And it was a real trial, in the days that followed, to hear the bereft Lucie's plaintive wail: 'Where's Lallie? I want Lallie . . . I want Lallie.' 'Surely, Cuffy, you can manage to keep her amused? Play with her, dear. Let her do just as she likes,' said Mary – with a contorted face, in the act of wringing a flannel binder out of all but boiling water.

She spoke briskly; was cheerful, and of good heart. For, in the beginning, no suspicion of anything being seriously amiss crossed her mind. It was just a relapse, and as such needed carefullest nursing and attention. In the course of the fifth day, however, one or two little things that happened stirred a vague uneasiness in her. Or rather she saw afterwards that this had been so: at the moment she had let the uncomfortable impressions escape her with all speed. It struck her that the child's progress was very slow. Also she noticed that Richard tried another remedy. However, this change seemed to the good; towards evening Lallie fell into a refreshing sleep. But when next morning after a broken night she drew up the blind, something in the child's aspect brought back, with a rush and intensified, her hazy disquiets of the previous day. Lallie was oddly dull. She would not open her eyes properly or answer when spoken to; and she turned her face from the cooling drink that was held to her lips.

'She doesn't seem so well this morning.'

Mary's voice was steady as she uttered these words — this commonplace of the sickroom. But even as she spoke, she became aware of the cold fear that was laying itself round her heart. It seemed to sink, to grow strangely leaden, as she watched Richard make the necessary examination . . . ever so gently . . . she had never really known how tender his hands were, till she saw them used on the shrinking body of his own child. — 'Papa's darling . . . Papa's good little girl.' — But the sheet drawn up again he avoided meeting her eyes. As if that would help him! She who could read his face as if it were a book . . . how did he hope to deceive *her*? — and where one of her own babies was concerned.

'Richard, what is it? Do you . . .?'

'Now, my dear, don't get alarmed. There's bound to be a certain amount of prostration . . . till the dysentery is checked. I shall try ipecac.'

But neither ipecacuanha nor yet a compound mixture — administered in the small doses suited to so young a patient — had any effect. The inflammation persisted, racking the child with pain, steadily draining her of strength. It was a poor limp little sweat-drenched body, with loosely bobbing head, that Mary, had she to lift it, held in her arms. Throughout this day too, the sixth, she was forced to listen, sitting helplessly by, to a sound that was half a wail and half a moan of utter lassitude. And towards evening a more distressing symptom set in, in the shape of a convulsive retching. On her knees beside the bed, her right arm beneath Lallie's shoulders, Mary suffered, in her own vitals, the struggle that contorted the little body prior to the fit of sickness. Hers, too, the heartrending task of trying to still the child's terror — the frightened eyes, the arms imploringly outheld, the cries of 'Mamma, Mamma!' to the person who had never yet failed to help — as the spasms began anew.

'It's *all* right, my darling, my precious! Mamma's here — here, close beside you. There, there! It'll soon be better now.' — And so it went on for the greater part of the night.

In the intervals between the attacks when the exhausted child dozed heavily, Mary, not venturing to move from her knees, laid her face down on the bed, and wrestled with the One she held responsible. 'Oh, God, be merciful! She's such a little child, God! . . . to have to suffer so. Oh, spare her! . . . spare my baby.'

By morning light she was horrified to find that the little tongue had turned brown. The shock of this discovery was so great that it drove over her lips a thought that had come to her in the night . . . had haunted her . . . only to be thrust back into the limbo where it belonged. What if Richard . . . if perhaps some new remedy had been invented since last he was in practice, which he didn't know of? — he had been out of the way of things so long.

Now, a wild fear for her child's life drowned all lesser considerations. 'What . . . what about getting a second opinion?'

Mahony looked sadly at her and laid his hand on her shoulder. 'Mary . . . dear wife — ' he began; then broke off: too well he knew the agonies of self-reproach that might await her. 'Yes, you're right. I tell you what I'll do. I'll run up to the station and get Pendrell to telegraph to Oakworth. There's a man there . . . I happen to know his name.'

Never a moment's hesitation over the expense it would put him to: never a sign of hurt at the doubt cast on his own skill. From where she sat, Mary watched him go: he took a short-cut up the back yard, past kitchen and henhouse. Oh! but he had no hat on . . . had gone out without one . . . had *forgotten* to put his hat on — he who was so afraid of the sun! As she grasped what the omission meant, at the lightning-flash it gave her into his own state of mind, she clenched her hands till her nails cut her palms.

At earliest the doctor could not arrive before five o'clock. All through the long hours of that long, hot day, she sat and waited for his coming: pinning her faith to it — as one who is whirling down a precipitous slope snatches at any frail root or blade of grass that offers to his hand. Something — some miracle would . . . *must* . . . happen — to save her child. She was quite alone. Richard had to attend his patients, and in the afternoon to drive into the bush: other people could not be put off, or neglected, because his own child lay ill. The wife of the Bank Manager, hearing of their trouble, came and took away the other children. And there Mary sat, heedless of food or rest, conscious only of the little tortured body on the bed before her; sat and fanned off the flies, and pulled up or turned down the sheet, according as fever or the rigors shook the child, noting each creeping change for the worse, snatching at fantastic changes for the better. Her lips were thin and dogged in her haggard face; her eyes burned like coals: it was as if, within her, she was engaged in concentrating a store of strength, with which to invest her child. – But on going out to the kitchen to prepare fresh rice-water, she became aware that, for all the broiling heat of the day, her hands were numb with cold.

Richard came rushing home to meet the train. To warn, too, the stranger to caution. 'Not a word, I beg of you, before my wife. She is breaking her heart over it.'

But one glimpse of the man who entered the room at Richard's side brought Mary's last hope crashing about her ears; and in this moment she faced the fact that Lallie must die. The newcomer was just an ordinary country doctor – well she knew the type! – rough, burly, uncouth. Into the ordered stillness of the sickroom he brought the first disturbance. He tripped over the mat, his boots creaked, his hands were clumsy – or seemed so, compared with Richard's. Oh! the madness of calling in a man like this, when she had Richard at her side. Fool, fool that she was! Now, her only desire was to be rid of him again. She turned away, unable to look on while he handled Lallie, disarranged – hurt – her, in pulling back the sheet and exposing the distended, drum-like little body. ('Um . . . just so.') His manner to Richard, too, was galling; his tone one of patronage. He no doubt regarded him as some old hack who had doddered his life away up-country, and could now not treat even a case of dysentery without the aid of a younger man. And for this, which was all her doing, Richard would have to sit with him and listen to him till the down train went at ten. It was too much for Mary. The tears that had obstinately refused to flow for the greater grief rose to her eyes, and were so hot and angry that they scorched the back of her lids.

That night, in the stillness that followed his departure, the last torment was inflicted on the dying child in the shape of a monstrous hiccough. It started from far, far down, shot out with the violence of an explosion, and seemed as if it would tear the little body in two. Under this new blow Mary's courage all but failed her. In vain did Mahony, his arm round her bent shoulders, try to soothe her. 'My darling, it sounds worse than it is. We feel it more than she does . . . now.' Each time it burst forth an irrepressible shudder ran through Mary, as if it were she herself who was being racked. And on this night her passionate prayer ran: 'Take her, God! . . . take her if You must. I give her back to You. But oh! let it be soon . . . stop her suffering . . . give her peace.' And as hour after hour dragged by without respite, she rounded on Him and fiercely upbraided Him. 'It is cruel of You . . . cruel! No earthly father would torture a child as You are doing. . . . You, all-powerful and called Love!'

But little by little, so stealthily that its coming was imperceptible, the ultimate peace fell: by daybreak there was nothing more to hope or fear. Throughout the long day that followed — it seemed made of years, yet passed like an hour — Lallie lay in coma, drawing breaths that were part snores, part heavy sighs. Time and place ceased to exist for Mary, as she sat and watched her child die. Through noon and afternoon and on into the dark, she tirelessly wiped the damp brow and matted curls, fanned off the greedy flies, one little inert hand held firmly in her own: perhaps somehow, on this, her darling's last, fearsome journey, the single journey in her short life that she had taken unattended, something would tell her that her mother was with her, her mother's love keeping and holding her. On this day Richard did not leave the house. And their kind friend again fetched away the other children.

The *other* children? . . . what need now of this word! Henceforce, there would always and for ever be only two. Never again, if not by accident, would the proud words, 'My three', cross her lips. There she sat, committing to oblivion her motherstore of fond and foolish dreams, the lovely fabric of hopes and plans that she had woven about this little dear one's life; sat bidding farewell to many a tiny endearing feature of which none but she knew: in the spun-glass hair the one rebellious curl that would not twist with the rest; secret dimples kneaded in the baby body; the tiny birthmark below the right shoulder; the chubby, dimpled hands -- Richard's hands in miniature -- all now destined to be shut away and hidden from sight. Oh, of what was use to create so fair a thing, merely to destroy it!

(They say He knows all, but never, never can He have known what it means to be a mother.)

Midnight had struck before Mahony could half lead, half carry her from the room. Her long agony of suspense over, she collapsed, broke utterly down, in a way that alarmed him. He ran for restoratives; bathed her forehead; himself undressed her and got her to bed. Only then came the saving tears, setting free the desperate and conflicting emotions, till now so rigorously held in check, in a storm of grief of which he had never known the like. There was something primitive about it, savage even. For in it Mary wept the passion of her life – her children. And over the sacrifice she was now called on to make, her heart bled, as raw, as lacerated, as once her body had lain in giving them birth.

For long Mahony made no attempt to soothe or restrain. Well for her that she could weep! A nature like Mary's would not be chastened by suffering: never would she know resignation; or forgive the injury that had been done her. This physical outlet was her sole means of relief.

But the moment came when he put out his hand and sought hers. 'Wife . . . my own dearest! . . . it is not for ever. You . . . we . . . shall see our child again.'

But Mary would have none of it. Vehemently she tore her hand away. 'Oh, what does that help? . . . help *me*! I want her now . . . and here. I want to hold her in my arms . . . and feel her . . . and hear her speak. She will never speak to me again. Oh, my baby, my baby! . . . and I loved you so.'

'She knew it well. She still does.'

'How do *you* know? . . . how do you *know*? Those are only words. They may do for you. . . . But I was her mother. She was mine; my very own. And do you think she wanted to die . . . and leave me? They tore her away – and tortured her – and frightened her. They may be frightening her still . . . such a little child, alone and frightened . . . and me not able to get to her! – Oh, *why* should this just happen to us? Other people's children grow up . . . grow old. And we are so few . . . why, *why* had it to be?'

Mea culpa, mea maxima culpa! 'If only I had never brought you to this accursed place!'

There was an instant's pause, a momentary cessation of her laboured breathing, as the bed shook under the shudders that stand to a man for sobs, before she flung round and drew him to her.

'Mary, Mary! . . . I meant it for the best.'

'I know you did, I know. I *won't* have you blame yourself. It might have happened anywhere.' (Oh, my baby, my baby!)

Now they clung to each other, all the petty differences they laboured under obliterated by their common grief. Till suddenly a sound fell on their ears, driving them apart to listen: it was little Lucie, waking from sleep in an empty bed and crying with fear. Rising, her father carried her over and laid her down in his own warm place; and Mary, recalled from her profitless weeping by a need greater than her own, held out her arms and gathered the child in. 'It's all right, my darling. Mamma's here.'

This, the ultimate remedy. Half an hour later when he crept back to look, mother and child slept, tear-stained cheek to cheek.

His hand in his father's, Cuffy was led into the little room where Lallie lay. – 'I want them to have no morbid fear of death.'

On waking that morning – after a rather jolly day spent at the Bank . . . or what would have been jolly, if Lucie hadn't been such a cry-baby . . . where he had been allowed to try to lift a bar of gold and to step inside the great safe: on waking, Cuffy heard the amazing news that Lallie had gone away: God had taken her to live with Him. His eyes all but dropped out of his head, a dozen questions jumped to his tongue; but he did not ask one of them; for Mamma never stopped crying, and Papa looked as he did when you didn't talk to him, but got away and tried not to remember. So Cuffy sat on the edge of the verandah and felt most awfully surprised. What had happened was too strange, too far removed from the range of his experience, too 'int'resting', to let any other feeling come up in him. He wondered and wondered . . . why God had done it . . . and why He had just wanted Lallie. Now he himself . . . well, Luce *had* got so whiny!

But the darkened room and a sheet over the whole bed did something funny to him . . . inside. And, as his father turned the slats of the venetian so that a pale daylight filtered in, Cuffy asked – in a voice he meant to make whispery and small, but which came out hoarse like a crow: 'What's she covered up like that for?'

For answer Mahony drew back the double layer of mosquito-netting, and displayed the little sister's face. 'Don't be afraid, Cuffy. She's only asleep.' And indeed it might well have been so. Here were no rigidly trussed limbs, no stiffly folded arms: the heave of the breath alone was missing. Lallie lay with one little hand under her cheek, her curls tumbling naturally over her shoulder. The other hand held a nosegay, a bit of gaudy red geranium tied up with one of its own leaves – the single poor flower Mahony had found still a-bloom in the garden.

'Kiss her, Cuffy.'

Cuffy obeyed – and got a shock. 'Why's she so cold?'

'Because her spirit is flown. This dear little body, that we have known and loved, was only the house of the spirit; and now is empty and must fade. But though we shall not see her, our Lallie will go on living and growing . . . in a grace and beauty such as earth cannot show.' And more to himself than to the boy beside him Mahony murmured:

> Not as a child shall we again behold her,
>   For when, with raptures wild,
> In our embraces we again enfold her,
>   She will not be a child,
> But a fair maiden in her Father's mansions . . .

'Will she . . . do you mean . . . be grown up?' And Cuffy fixed wide, affrighted eyes on his father. For in listening to these words, he had a sudden vision of a Lallie who looked just like Miss Prestwick or Cousin Emmy, with a little small waist, and bulgings, and tight, high, buttoned boots. And against this picture – especially the boots – something in him rose and screamed with repugnance. He wanted Lallie's fat little legs in socks and strapped shoes, as he had always known them. He *would* not have her different!

'Oh, no, no . . . *no*!' And with this, his habitual defence against the things he was unwilling to face, Cuffy tore his hand away and escaped to his sanctuary at the bottom of the garden.

Here for the first time a sense of loss came over him. (It was the boots had done it.) What, never see Lallie any more? . . . as his little fat sister? It couldn't be true . . . it couldn't! 'I don't believe it . . . I *don't* believe it!' (Hadn't they told him that very morning that God had taken her away, when all the time she was in there lying on the bed?) And this attitude of doubt persisted; even though, when he got back the next afternoon from a long walk with Maria, God had kept His word and she was gone. But many and many a day passed before Cuffy gave up expecting her to re-appear. Did he go into an empty room, or turn a corner of the verandah, it seemed to him that he *must* find Lallie there: suddenly she would have come back, and everything be as it was before. For since, by their father's care, all the sinister ceremonials and paraphernalia of death were kept from them, he was free to go on regarding it solely in the light of an abrupt disappearance ... and if you could be spirited away in this fashion, who was to say if you mightn't just as easily pop up again? Also by Mahony's wish, neither he nor Lucie ever set foot in the outlying bush cemetery, where in due time a little cross informed the curious that the small mound before them hid the mortal remains of Alicia Mary Townshend-Mahony, aged five and a half years. Providing people, at the same time, with a puzzle to scratch their heads over. For, in place of the usual reference to lambs and tender shepherds, they found themselves confronted by the words: *Dans l'espoir*. And what the meaning of this heathenish term might be, none in Barambogie knew, but all were suspicious of.

*

'We've simply *got* to afford it,' was Mary's grim reply. — There she stood, her gaunt eyes fixed on Richard, the embodiment of a mother-creature at bay to protect her young.

Christmas had come and gone, and the fierce northern summer was upon them in earnest. Creeks and waterholes were dry now, rivers shrunk to a trickling thread; while that was brown straw which had once been grass. And Mary, worn down by heat and mental suffering, was fretting her heart out over her remaining baby, little Lucie, now but the ghost of her former self. Coming on top of Lucie's own illness, her twin-sister's death had struck her a blow from which she did not seem able to recover. And to see the child droop and fade before her very eyes rendered Mary desperate. This was why, to Richard's procrastinating and undecided: 'I must see if I can afford it,' she had flung out her challenge: 'We've *got* to!'

'I suppose you're right.'

'I know I am!'

Many and heartfelt had been the expressions of sympathy

from those friends and acquaintances who had read the brief notice on the front page of the *Argus*. Outsiders, too, people Mary had almost forgotten, showed that they still remembered her, by condoling with her in her loss. But it was left to dear old Tilly to translate sentiment into practical aid.

How I feel for you, my darling, words wouldn't tell. It's the cruellest thing ever happened. But oh, the blessing, Mary, that you've still got your other two. You must just remember how much they need you, love, while they're so small, and how much you are to them. – And now hark to me, my dear. I'd been planning before this to take a shanty at Lorne for the hot weather; and what I want is for you to come and share it with me – share expenses, if you like, me knowing what you are. But get the chicks away from that wicked heat you must. – Besides, helping to look after Baby'll be the best of medicines for that poor forlorn little mite, who it makes my heart ache even to think of.

Too great were the odds – in this case the welfare, perhaps the very life, of his remaining children – against him. Mahony bowed his head. And when Mary had gone he unlocked a private drawer of his table, and drew out a box in which lay several rolls of notes, carefully checked and numbered. Once more he counted them through. For weeks, nay, for months he had been laboriously adding pound to pound. In all there were close on forty of them. He had fully intended to make it fifty by New Year. Now there was no help: it would have to go. First, the doctor's fare from Oakworth; then the costs of the funeral . . . with a five-pound note to the parson. What was left after these things were paid must be sacrificed to Mary and the children. They would need every penny of it . . . and more besides.

PART TWO

CHAPTER ONE

To come back to the empty house, having watched the train carry them off ('Kiss papa good-bye! ... good-bye ... good-bye, my darlings! Come back with rosy cheeks. – Try to forget, Mary ... my poor old wife!'): to come back to the empty house was like facing death anew. All the doors, three on each side of the central passage, stood open, showing unnatural-looking rooms. Mary had done her best to leave things tidy, but she had not been able to avoid the last disorder inevitable on a journey. Odd sheets of newspaper lay about, and lengths of twine; the floors were unswept, the beds unmade; one of the children had dropped a glove ... Mahony stooped to it ... Cuffy's, for a wager, seeing that the middle finger was chewed to pulp. And as he stood holding it, it seemed as if from out these yawning doors, these dismal rooms, one or other of his little ones must surely dart and run to him, with a cry of 'Papa ... Papa!' But not a sound broke the silence, no shadow smudged the whitewash of the walls.

The first shock over, however, the litter cleared up, the rooms dressed, he almost relished the hush and peace to which the going of wife and children had left him. For one thing, he could rest on the knowledge that he had done for them all that was humanly possible. In return, he would, for several weeks to come, be spared the mute reproach of two wan little faces, and a mother's haggard eyes. Nor need he crack his brains for a time over the problem of an education for the children in this wilderness, or be chafed by Mary's silent but pregnant glosses on the practice. In a word he was *free* ... free to exist unobserving and unobserved.

But his satisfaction was short-lived: by the end of the second day the deathlike stillness had begun to wear him down. Maria was shut off in the detached kitchen; and on getting home of a late afternoon he knew that, but for the final mill-screech, and the distant rumble of the ten-o'clock train, no mortal sound would reach his ears the long night through. The silence gathered, descended and settled upon him, like a fog or a cloud. There was something ominous about it, and instead of reading he found himself listening . . . listening. Only very gradually did the thought break through that he had something to listen for. Dark having fallen, might not a tiny ghost, a little spirit that had not yet found rest afar from those it loved, flit from room to room in search of them? What more likely indeed? He strained him ears. But only his pulses buzzed there. On the other hand, about eleven o'clock one night, on coming out of the surgery to cross to the bedroom, he could have sworn to catching a glimpse of a little shape . . . vague, misty of outline, gone even as he saw it, and yet unmistakable . . . vanishing in the doorway of the children's room. His heart gave a great leap of joy and recognition. Swiftly following, he called a name; but on the empty air: the room had no occupant. For two nights after he kept watch, to waylay the apparition should it come; but, shy of human eyes, it did not show itself again. Not to be baulked, he tried a fresh means: taking a sheet of paper he let his hand lie lightly along the pencil. And, lo and behold! at the second trial the pencil began to move, seemed to strive to form words; while by the fourth evening words were coming through. *Her Mamma . . . her Luce . . . wants her Mamma.*

The kitchen clock had stopped: Maria, half undressed, stealing tiptoe into the house to see the time, a tin lamp with a reflector in her hand, was pulled up short, halfway down the passage, by the sound of voices. Hello! who was Doctor talking to? A patient at this hour? But nobody had knocked at the door. And what . . . oh, crikey! whatever was he saying? The girl's eyes and mouth opened, and her cheeks went pale, as the sense of what she heard broke on her. Pressing herself against the wall, she threw a terrified glance over her shoulder into the inky shadows cast by the lamp. –

'Ma! I was fair skeered out of me senses. To hear 'im sitting there a-talkin' to that pore little kid, what's been dead and buried this month and more! An' him calling her by her name, and saying her Ma would soon be back, and then she wouldn't need to feel lonely any more – why, I tell yer, even this mornin' in broad daylight I found meself lookin' behind me the whole time. – Go back? Stop another night there? Not me! I couldn't, Ma. I'm *skeered*.'

'You great ninny, you! What could 'urt yer, I'd like to know? . . . as long as you say yer prayers reg'lar and tells the troof. Ghosts, indeed! I'll ghost you!' – But Maria, more imaginatively fibred, was not to be won over.

Mahony listened to the excuses put forward by her mother on his reaching home that evening: listened with the kindly courtesy he kept for those beneath him who met him civilly and with respect. Maria's plea of loneliness was duly weighed. 'Though I must say I think she has hardly given the new conditions a fair trial. However, she has always been a good girl, and the plan you propose, Mrs Beetling, will no doubt answer very well during my wife's absence.

It not only answered: it was an improvement. Breakfast was perhaps served a little later than usual, and the cooking proved rather coarser than Maria's, who was Mary-trained. But it was all to the good that, supper over, Mrs Beetling put on her bonnet and went home, leaving the place clear. His beloved little ghost was then free to flit as it would, without fear of surprise or disturbance. He continually felt its presence – though it did not again materialize – and message after message continued to come through. Written always by a third person, in an unfamiliar hand . . . as was only to be expected, considering that the twins still struggled with pothooks and hangers . . . they yet gave abundant proof of their authorship.

Such a proof, for instance, as the night when he found that his script ran: *Her baby . . . nose . . . kitchen fire*.

For a long time he could make nothing of this, though he twisted it this way and that. Then, however, it flashed upon him that the twins had nursed large waxen dolls clad as infants; and straightway he rose to look for the one that had been Lallie's. After a lengthy search by the light of a single candle, in the course of which he ransacked various drawers and boxes, he found the object in question . . . tenderly wrapped and hidden away in Mary's wardrobe. He drew it forth in its white trappings and, upon his soul, when he held it up to the candle to examine it, he found that one side of the effigy's nose had run together in a kind of a blob . . . *melted* . . . no doubt through having been left lying in the sun, or – yes, *or* held too close to a fire! Of a certainty he had known nothing of this: never a word had been said, in *his* hearing, of the accident to so expensive a plaything. At the time of purchase he had been wroth with Mary over the needless outlay. Now . . . now . . . oh! there's a divinity that shapes our ends . . . now it served him as an irrefragable proof.

In his jubilation he added a red-hot postscript to his daily letter. *I have great — great and joyful — news for you, my darling. But I shall keep it till you come back. It will be something for you to look forward to, on your return to this dreadful place.*

To which Mary replied. *You make me very curious, Richard. Can North Long Tunnels have struck the reef at last?*

And he: *Something far, far nearer our hearts, my dear, than money and shares. I refer to news compared with which everything earthly fades into insignificance.*

Alas! he roused no answering enthusiasm. *Now, Richard, don't delude yourself . . . or let yourself be deluded. Of course you knew about that doll's nose. Lallie cried and was so upset. I'm sure what's happening is all your own imagination. I do think one can grossly deceive oneself — especially now you're quite alone. But oh don't trifle with our great sorrow. I couldn't bear it. It's still too near and too bitter.*

Of his little ghostly visitant he asked that night: *How shall we ever prove, love, to dear Mamma that you are really and truly her lost darling?*

To which came the oddly disconcerting, matter-of-fact reply: *Useless. Other things to do. Comes natural to some. Not to her.* But Mahony could not find it in his heart to let the matter rest there. So fond a mother, and to be unwilling . . . not to dare to *trust* herself . . . to believe!

And believe what, too? Why, merely that their little one, in place of becoming a kind of frozen image of the child they had known, and inhabiting remote, fantastic realms to which they might some day laboriously attain: that she was still with them, close to them, loving and clinging, and as sportive as in her brief earthly span. It was no doubt this homely, *undignified* aspect of the life-to-come that formed the stumbling-block: for people like Mary, death was inconceivable apart from awfulness and majesty: in this guise alone had it been rung and sung into them. For him, the very lack of dignity was the immense, consoling gain. Firmly convinced of the persistence of human individuality subsequent to the great change, he had now been graciously permitted to see how thin were the walls between the two worlds, how interpenetrable the states. And he rose of a morning, and lay down at night, his heart warm with gratitude to the Giver of knowledge.

But a little child-ghost, no longer encased in the lovely rounded body that had enhanced its baby prattle and, as it were, decked it out: a little ghost had, after all, not very much to say. A proof of identity given, assurances exchanged that it still loved and was loved, and the talk trickled naturally to an end. You could not put your arms round it, and hold it to you in a wordless content. Also, as time passed and Lallie grew easier in her new state, it was not to be denied that she turned a trifle freakish. She would not always come when called, and, pressed as to where she lingered, averred through her mentor that she was 'fossicking'. An attempt to get at the meaning of this involved Mahony in a long, rambling conversation with the elder ghost, that was dreary in the extreme. For it hinged mainly on herself and her own affairs. And, grateful though he was to her for her goodness to his child, he took no interest in her personally; and anything in the nature of a discussion proved disastrous. For she had been but a seamstress in her day, and a seamstress she remained; having, it would seem, gained nothing through her translation, either in knowledge or spirituality.

He flagged. To grip him, an occupation needed to be meaty – to give him something with which to tease his brains. And his present one, supplying none, began little by little to pall, leaving him to the melancholy reflection that, for all their aliveness, our lost ones were truly lost to us, because no longer entangled in the web called living. Impossible for those who had passed on to continue to grieve for a broken doll; to lay weight on the worldly triumphs and failures that meant so much to us; to concern themselves with the changing seasons, the rising up and lying down, the palaver, pother and ado that made up daily life. Though the roads to be followed started from a single point, they swiftly branched off at right angles, never to touch again while we inhabited our earthly shell . . . and in this connection, he fell to thinking of people long dead, and of how out of place, how *in the way* they would be, did they now come back to earth. We mortals were, for worse or better, ever on the move. Impossible for us to return to the stage at which *they* had known us.

And so it came about that one evening when, with many a silent groan, he had for close on half an hour transcribed the seamstress's platitudes (if it was himself who wrote, as Mary averred, then God help him! . . . he was in, beyond question, for cerebral softening) with never a word or a sign from Lallie: on this evening he abruptly threw the pencil from him, pushed back his chair and strode out on the verandah. He needed air, fresh air; was ravenous for it . . . to feel his starved lungs fill and expand. But the December night was hotter even than the day had been; and what passed for air was stale and heavy with sunbaked dust. The effort of inhaling it, the repugnance this smell roused in him brought him to. Like a man waking from a trance, he looked round him with dazed eyes, and ran a confused hand over his forehead. And in this moment the dreams and shadows of the past two weeks scattered, and he faced reality: it was near midnight, and he stood alone on the ramshackle verandah, with its three broken steps leading down to the path; with the drooping, dust-laden shrubs of the garden before him; the bed of dust that formed the road beyond. He had come to earth again – and with a bump.

A boundless depression seized him: a sheerly intolerable flatness, after the mood of joyous elation that had gone before. He felt as though he had been sucked dry: what remained of him was but an empty shell. Empty as the house which, but for a single lamp, lay dark and tenantless, and silent as the grave. Since the first night of Mary's departure, he had not visualized it thus. Now he was dismayed by it – and by his own solitude. To rehearse the bare facts: wife and children were a hundred and fifty miles away; his other little child lay under the earth; even the servant had deserted: with the result that there was now not a living creature anywhere within hail. This miserable Lagoon, this shrunken pool of stagnant water, effectually cut him off from human company. If anything should happen to him, if he should be taken ill, or break a limb, he might lie where he fell till morning, his calls for help unheard. And the thought of this utter isolation, once admitted, swelled to alarming proportions. His brain raced madly – glancing at fire . . . murder . . . sudden death. Why, not a soul here would be able even to summon Mary back to him . . . no one so much as knew her address. Till he could bear it no longer: jumping out of bed, he ran to the surgery and wrote her whereabouts in large letters on a sheet of paper, which he pinned up in a conspicuous place.

The first faint streaks of daylight, bringing relief on this score, delivered him up to a new – and anything but chimerical – anxiety. What was happening . . . what in the name of fortune was happening to the practice? Regarding for the first time the day and the day's business other than as something to be hurried through, that he might escape to his communion with the unseen, he was horrified to see how little was doing, how scanty the total of patients for the past fortnight. And here Mary was writing that she would shortly need more money.

Nobody at all put in an appearance that morning — though he sat out his consulting-hour to the bitter end. By this time he had succeeded in convincing himself that the newcomer, Mrs Beetling, was to blame for the falling-off. Untrained to the job, she had very probably omitted to note, on the slate provided for the purpose, the names of those who called while he was absent. Either she had trusted to her memory and forgotten; or had been out when she ought to have kept the house; or had failed to hear the bell. The dickens! What would people think of him, for neglecting them like this?

By brooding over it, he worked himself into a state of nervous agitation; and directly half-past ten struck pushed back his chair and stalked out, to take the culprit to task.

Mrs Beetling was scrubbing the verandah, her sleeves rolled up above her elbows, arms and hands newborn-looking from hot water and soda. At Mahony's approach, she sat back on her heels to let him by; then, seeing that he intended to speak to her, scrambled to her feet and dried her hands on her apron.

'I wish to have a word with you, Mrs Beetling.'

'Yes, sir?'

She was civil enough, he would say that for her. In looking up at him, too, she smiled with a will: a pleasant-faced woman, and ruddy of cheek . . . another anomaly in this pale country.

But he fronted her squarely for the first time: at their former interview he had been concerned only to cut her wordiness short. And this broad smile of hers advertised the fact that she had gums bare almost as a babe's; was toothless, save for a few black and rotten stumps in the lower jaw.

Now Mahony was what Mary called a 'fad of the first water' with regard to the care of the mouth. He never tired of fulminating against the colonial habit of suffering the untold agonies of toothache, letting the teeth rot in the head rather than have them medically attended. And the sight here presented to him so exasperated him that he clean forgot what he had come out to say, his irritation hurling itself red-hot against this fresh object of offence.

As though he had a meek and timid patient before him, he now said sternly: 'Open your mouth . . . wide!'

'*Sir!*' Mrs Beetling's smile faded in amazement. Instinctively pinching her lips, she blinked at Mahony, turned red, and fell to twiddling with a corner of her apron. (So far she had turned a deaf ear to the tales that were going the round about 'the ol' doctor'. Now . . . she wondered.)

'Your mouth . . . open your mouth!' repeated Mahony, with the same unnecessary harshness. Then, becoming vaguely aware of the confusion he was causing, he trimmed his sails. 'My good woman . . . I have only this moment noticed the disgraceful state of your teeth. Why, you have not a sound one left in your head! What have you been about? . . . never to consult a dentist?'

'Dentist, sir? Not me! Not if I was paid for it! No one'll ever get me to any dentist.'

'Tut, tut, you fool!' He snapped his fingers; and went on snapping them, to express what he thought of her. And Mrs Beetling, growing steadily sulkier and more aggrieved, was now forced to stand and listen to a fierce tirade on the horrors of a foul mouth and foul breath, on the harm done to the digestive system, the ills awaiting her in later life. Red as a peony she stood, her apron still twisting in her fingers, her lips glued tight; once only venturing a protest. 'I never bin ill in me life!' and still more glumly: 'I suppose me teeth's me own. I kin do what I like with 'em.' To and fro paced Mahony, his hands clasped behind his back, his face aflame; thus ridding himself, on his bewildered hearer, of his own distractedness, the overstimulation of his nerves; and ending up by vowing that, if she had a grain of sense in her, she would come to the surgery and let him draw from her mouth such ruins as remained. At which Mrs Beetling, reading this as a threat, went purplish, and backed away in real alarm. – Not till he was some distance off on his morning round, did it occur to him that he had forgotten his original reason in seeking her out. Never a word had he said of her carelessness in writing up the patients! The result was another wild bout of irritation – this time with himself – and he had to resist an impulse to turn on his heel. What the deuce would he do next? What tricks might his failing memory not play him?

On her side also, Mrs Beetling yielded to second thoughts. Her first inclination had been to empty her bucket on the garden-bed, let down her skirts, tie on her bonnet and bang the gate behind her. But she bit it back. The place was a good one: it 'ud be lunatic not to keep it warm for Maria. No sooner, though, did she see Mahony safely away, than she let her indignation fly, and at the top of her voice. 'Well, I'm blowed . . . blowed, that's what I am! Wants to pull out all me teef, does he? . . . the *butcher*! Blackguardin' me like that. Of all the lousy ol' ranters . . .'

'Eh, ma?' said a floury young mill-hand, and leant in passing over the garden gate. 'What's up with *you*? Bin seein' one of the spooks?'

'You git along with you, Tom Dorrigan. And take yer arms off that gate.'

'They do say Maria seed one widout a head and all. Holy Mother o' God protect us!' – and the lad crossed himself fearfully as he went.

While Mrs Beetling, still blown with spite and anger, gathered her skirt in both hands, and charging at a brood of Brahmapootras that had invaded the garden to scratch up a bed, scuttled them back into the yard.

CHAPTER TWO

His way led him through the main street. The morning was drawing towards noon, and the overheated air, grown visible, quivered and flimmered in wavy lines. He wore nankeen trousers, which looked a world too wide for him, and flapped to and fro on his bony shanks. His coat, of tussore, was creased and unfresh, there being no Mary at hand daily to iron it out. On his head he had a sun-hat hung with puggaree and fly-veil: he also carried a sun-umbrella, green-lined; while a pair of dark goggles dimmed for him the intolerable whiteness of sky, road, iron roofs. Thus he went: an odd figure, a very figure of fun, in the eyes of the little township. And yet for all his oddity wearing an air . . . an air of hauteur, of touch-me-not aloofness . . . which set him still further apart. The small shopkeepers and publicans who made up the bulk of the population had never known his like; and were given vigorously to slapping their legs and exclaiming: 'By the Lord Harry! . . . goes about with his head as high as if he owned the place.'

On this day though he passed unnoticed. In the broad, sun-stricken street, none moved but himself. The heat, however, was not the sole reason for its emptiness. He who ran might read that the place was thinning out. With the abandonment of the project to reorganize the great mine – the fairy-tale of which had helped to settle *him* there – all hope of a fresh spurt of life for Barambogie was at an end. The new Bank that was to have been opened to receive the gold, the crew of miners and engineers who should have worked the reefs, had already faded into the *limbus fatuorum* where, for aught he knew, they had always belonged. What trade there was, languished: he counted no less than four little shops in a row which had recently been boarded up.

Pluff went his feet in the smothery dust of the bush road – his black boots might have been made of white leather – the flies buzzed in chorus round his head. Of the two visits he had to pay, one was a couple of miles off. Two miles there and two back . . . on a morning when even the little walk along the Lagoon had fagged him. Oh! he *ought* to have a buggy. A country practice without a horse and trap behind it was like trying to exist without bread . . . or water. – And now again, as if on this particular day there was to be no rest or peace for him, a single thought, flashing into his brain, took entire possession of it and whizzed madly round. He plodded along, bent of back, loose of knee, murmuring distractedly: 'A buggy . . . yes, God knows, I ought to have a buggy.' But the prospect of ever again owning one seemed remote; at present it was as much as he could do to afford the occasional hire of a conveyance. What must the townspeople think, to see him eternally on the tramp? For nobody walked here. A buggy stood at every door . . . but his. They would soon be beginning to suspect that something was wrong with him; and from that to believing him unable to pay his way was but a step. In fancy he saw himself refused credit, required to hand over cash for what he purchased . . . he, Richard Mahony! . . . till, in foretasting the shame of it, he groaned aloud.

And the case he had come all this way to attend would not profit him. His patient was a poor woman, lying very sick and quite alone in a bark hut, her menfolk having betaken themselves to work. He did what he could for her; left her more comfortable than he found her: he also promised medicines by the first cart that went by her door. But he knew the class: there was no money in it; his bill would have to be sent in time after time. And the older he grew, the more it went against the grain to badger patients for his fees. If they were too mean, or too dishonest, to pay for his services, he was too proud to dun them. And thus bad debts accumulated.

On the road home, the great heat and his own depression overcame him. Choosing a shady spot he lowered himself to the burnt grass for a rest; or what might have been a rest, had not the sound of wheels almost immediately made him scramble to his feet again: it would never do for him to be caught sitting by the roadside. In his haste, he somehow pressed the catch of his bag, which forthwith opened and spilled its contents on the ground. He was on his knees, fumbling to replace these, when the trap hove in sight.

It was a single buggy, in which three people, a young man

and two young women, sat squeezed together on a seat built for two. None the less, the man jerked his horse to a stand, and with true colonial neighbourliness called across: 'Like a lift?' – to receive, too late to stop him, a violent dig in the ribs from his wife's elbow.

'Thank you, thank you, my good man! But you are full already.' Provoked at being caught in his undignified position, Mahony answered in a tone short to ungraciousness.

'Devil a bit! Bess 'ere can sit by the splashboard.'

'*No*, sir! I should not dream of inconveniencing the lady on my account.'

'O.K.!' said the man. 'Ta-ta, then!' and drove on.

'The *lady*! Did you hear 'im? Oh, Jimminy Gig! . . . ain't he a cure?' cried Bess, and bellowed out a laugh that echoed back to where Mahony stood.

'Bill, you great *goff*, didn't you feel me poke you? Don't you know 'oo that was? We don't want him up here along of us . . . not for Joe!'

Bill spat. 'Garn! It's a goodish step for th' ol' cove, and a regular roaster into the bargain.'

'Garn yerself, y'ol' mopoke! – I say! what was 'e doin' there's what I'd like to know. Did you see him, kneelin' with all them things spread out around him? Up to some shady trick or other I'll be bound.'

Bess nodded darkly. 'Nobody 'ull go near the house any more after dark. Maria Beetling sor a black figger in the passage one night, with horns and all, and heard 'im talkin' to it. She tore home screamin' like mad for her ma.'

'Ah, git along with yer bunkum! You wimmin's mouths is allers full o' some trash or other. I never *heard* such talk,' – and Bill ejected a fresh stream of juice over the side.

His wife made a noise of contempt. 'It's gospel truth. I heard ol' Warnock the other day talkin' to Mrs Ah Sing. An' they both said it was a crying shame to have a doctor here who went in for magic and such-like. Nor's that all. A fat lot o' good his doctoring kin be. To go and let his own kid die. If he couldn't cure *it*, what kin *we* hope for, 'oo he hates like poison?'

'They do say he *boiled* her,' said Bess mysteriously. 'Made her sit in water that was too hot for her, till her skin all peeled off and she was red and raw. She screeched like blue murder: Maria heard her. They had to rush out and send for another doctor from Oakworth. But it was too late. He couldn't save her. – An' then just look at his pore wife. So pale an' woe-begone! Shaking in her shoes, I guess, what he'll be doing to her next.'

'He ought to be had up for it. Instead of being let streel round with his highty-tighty airs.'

'No, gorblimey, you two! . . . of all the silly, clatterin' hens!' and leaning forward Bill sliced his horse a sharp cut on the belly. In the cloud of dust that rose as the buggy lurched forward, they vanished from sight.

'Ha! didn't I know it? their butt – their laughing-stock,' chafed Mahony in answer to the girl's guffaw; and his hands trembled so that he could hardly pick up his scattered belongings. In his agitation he forgot the rest he had intended to allow himself, and plodded on anew, the sweat trickling in runnels down his back, mouth and nostrils caked dry. Meanwhile venting his choler by exclaiming aloud, in the brooding silence of the bush: 'What next? . . . what next, I wonder! Why, the likelihood is, they'll boggle at my diagnosis . . . doubt my ability to dose 'em for the d.t.'s or the colic.' And this idea, being a new one, started a new train of thought, his hungry brain pouncing avidly upon it. Thereafter he tortured himself by tracking it down to its last and direct issues; and thus engrossed was callous even to his passage along the main street, for which, after what had just happened, he felt a shrinking distaste, picturing eyes in every window, sneers behind every door.

Safe again within the four walls of his room, he tossed hat and bag from him and sank into the armchair, where he lay supine, his taut muscles relaxed, his tired eyes closed to remembrance. And in a very few minutes he was fast asleep: a deep, sound sleep, such as night and darkness rarely brought him. Dinner-time came and went; but he slept on; for Mrs Beetling, still nursing her injuries, did not as usual put her head in at the door to say that dinner was ready; she just planked the dishes down on the dining-room table and left them there. And soon the pair of chops, which dish she served up to him day after day, lay hard and sodden in their own fat.

Hunched in his chair, his head on his chest, his mouth open, Mahony drew breaths that were more than half snores. His carefully brushed hair had fallen into disarray, the lines on his forehead deepened to grooves; on his slender hands, one of which hung between his knees, the other over an arm of the chair, the veins stood out blue and bold.

No sound broke the stillness but that of the clock striking the hours and half-hours. Only very gradually did the sleeper come up from those unfathomed depths, of which the waking brain keeps no memory, to where, on the fringe of his consciousness, a disturbing dream awaited him. It had to do with a buggy, a giant buggy, full of people; and, inverting the real event of the day on which it was modelled, he now longed with all his heart to be among them. For it seemed to him that, if he could succeed in getting into this buggy, he would hear something — some message or tidings — which it was important for him to know. But though he tried and tried again, he could not manage to swing himself up; either his foot missed the step, or the people, who sat laughing and grimacing at him, pushed him off. Finally he fell and lay in the dust, which, filling eyes, nose, mouth, blinded and asphyxiated him. He was still on his back, struggling for air, when he heard a voice buzzing in his ear: 'You're wanted! It's a patient come. Wake up, wake up!' — and there was Mrs Beetling leaning over him and shaking him by the arm, while a man stood in the doorway and gaped.

He was out of his chair and on his feet in a twinkling; but he could not as easily collect his wits, which were still dreambound. His hands, too, felt numb, and as if they did not belong to him. It took him the space of several breaths to grasp that his caller, a farmer, was there to fetch him to attend his wife, and had a trap waiting at the gate. He thought the man looked at him very queerly. It was the fault of his old poor head, which was unequal to the strain of so sudden a waking. Proffering an excuse, he left the room to plunge it in water. As he did this it occurred to him that he had had no dinner. But he was wholly without appetite; and one glance at the fatty mess on the table was enough. Gulping down a cup of tea, he ate a couple of biscuits, and then shouldering his dustcoat, declared himself ready. It was a covered buggy: he leant far back beneath the hood as they drove. This time, people should *not* have the malicious pleasure of eyeing him.

*

I send you what I can, my dear, but I advise you to spin it out and be careful of it, Mary, for it is impossible to say when more will be forthcoming. Things are very, very slack here. There is no sickness and no money. I could never have believed a practice would collapse like this, from over seventy pounds a month to as good as nothing. In this past week I have only had four patients . . . and they all poorish people. I feel terribly worried, and sit here cudgelling my brains what it will be best to do. The truth is this place is fast dying out — everyone begins to see now that it has had its day and will never recover. Two of the tradespeople have become insolvent since you left, and others totter on the brink.

The heat is unbelievable. The drought continues . . . no sign yet of it breaking, and the thermometer eternally up between 90 and 100. (And even so, no sickness.) I am getting very anxious, too, about the water in the tank, which is low and dirty. If rain does not soon come, we shall be in a pretty plight.

I sleep wretchedly; and time hangs very heavy. The peaches are ripening, grapes twopence a pound; but butter is hard to get, and unless it rains there will soon be none to be had.

I do not see that we can incur the expense of another governess. The children will either have to attend the State School, or you must teach them yourself.

I do not like your lined paper. I detest common notepaper. Go to Bradley's when you are in town, and order some good cream-laid. They have the die for the crest there.

'Oh dear, oh dear, he's at it again!' sighed Mary; and let the letter fall to her knee.

'Whatever is it now?' asked Tilly.

In the shadow cast by the palings that separated a little weatherboard house from the great golden-sanded beach, the two women, in large, shady hats, sat and watched their children play. Lucie, at her mother's side, was contentedly sorting a heap of 'grannies and cowries'; but Cuffy had deserted to the water's edge directly he spied the servant-girl bringing out the letter. He *hated* these letters from Papa; they always made Mamma cross . . . or sorry . . . which spoilt the day. And it *was* so lovely here! He wished the postman would never, never come.

'Oh, the usual jeremiad,' said Mary; and dropped her voice to keep the child from hearing. 'No sickness, weather awful, the water getting low, people going bankrupt — a regular rigmarole of grumbles and complaints.'

'Determined to spoil your holiday for you, my dear, . . . or so it looks to me.'

'I agree, it's a *dreadful* place; never should we have gone there. But he would have it, and now he's got to make the best of it. Why, the move cost us over a hundred. Besides, it would be just the same anywhere else.'

'Well, look here, Mary, my advice is — now Lucie, be a good child and run away and play with your brother, instead of sitting there drinking everything in. Feeling as you do about it, my dear, you must just be firm and stick to your guns. You've given in to 'im your whole life long, and a fat lot of thanks you've ever 'ad for it. It's made me *boil* to see you so meek . . . though one never dared say much, you always standing up for him, loyal as loyal could be. But time's getting on, Mary; you aren't as young as you were; and you've got others now to think of besides 'im. I just shouldn't stand any more of 'is nonsense.'

'Yes, I daresay it *was* bad for him, always having his own way. But now he's got to learn that the children come first. They have all their lives before them, and I *won't* sit by and see him beggar them. He says we can't afford another governess; that they must either go to the State School — *my* children, Tilly! — or I teach them myself. When my hands are so full already that I could do with a day twice as long. And then he's so unreasonable. Finds fault with my notepaper, and says I am to go to Bradley's and order some expensive cream-laid. Now I ask you!'

'Unreasonable?' flamed Tilly, and blew a gust from mouth and nose. 'There's *some* people, Mary, 'ud call it by another name, my dear!'

Mary sighed anew, and nodded. 'I'm convinced from past experience that this idea of the practice failing is just his own imagination. He's lonely, and hasn't anyone to talk to, and so he sits and broods. But it keeps me on the fidget; for it's almost always been something imaginary that's turned him against a place and made him want to leave it. And if he once gets an idea in his head, I might as well talk to the wind. Indeed, what I say only makes matters worse. Perhaps someone else might manage him better. Really I can't help wondering sometimes, Tilly, if I've been the right wife for him, after all. No one could have been fonder of him. But there's always something in him that I can't get at; and when things go badly, and we argue and argue . . . why, then the thought will keep cropping up that perhaps someone else . . . somebody cleverer than I am . . . Do you remember Gracey Marriner, who he was so friendly with over that table-rapping business? She was so quick at seeing what he meant . . . and why he did things . . . and they found so much to talk about, and they read the same books and played the piano together. Well, I've sometimes felt that perhaps she . . .' But here the tears that had gathered in Mary's eyes threatened to run over, and she had to grope for her handkerchief.

'*Her!* Lor, Mary! . . . he'd have tired of 'er and her la-di-da airs inside three months,' ejaculated Tilly, and fiercely blew her own nose in sympathy. 'If ever there's been a good wife, my dear, it's you. But a fig for all the soft sawder that's talked about marriage! The long and the short of it is, marriage is sent to *try* us women, and for nothin' on earth besides.'

The children reacted in distinctive fashion to the sight of their mother crying. Little Lucie, who had heard, if not grasped, all that passed, hung her head like a dog scolded for some fault it does not understand. Cuffy, casting furtive backward glances, angrily stamped his feet so that the water splashed high over his rolled-up knickerbockers. This not availing, he turned and deliberately waded out to sea.

Ah! then Mamma *had* to stop crying and to notice him. 'Cuffy! Come back!'

'*What* a naughty boy!' sermonized Aunt Tilly. 'When his poor mother is so worried, too.'

'Yes, my great fear is, Richard's heading for another move. Really, after a letter like this I feel I ought just to pack up and go home.'

'What? After you come down 'ere looking like a ghost, and as thin as thin? . . . I won't *hear* of it, Mary.'

'You see, last time he took me completely by surprise. I'm resolved *that* shan't happen again.'

'Hush! hark! . . . was that Baby?' And Tilly bent an ardent ear towards the verandah, where her infant lay sleeping in a hammock.

'I heard nothing. – There's another reason, too, why I want to stay there, wretched place though it is. It's the . . . I don't feel I *can* go off and leave the . . . the little grave, with nobody to care for it. It's all I've got left of her.'

'The blessed little angel!'

'Later on . . . it may be different. But to go away now would tear me in two. Though it may and probably will mean row after row.'

'Yes, till he wears you down. That's always been 'is way. –

Ah! but that *is* Baby sure enough.' And climbing to her feet, Tilly propelled her matronly form up the sandy path.

She returned in triumph bearing the child, which but half awake whined peevishly, ramming two puny fists into sleep-charged eyes; on her face the gloating, doting expression with which she was wont to follow its every movement. For her love, waxing fat on care and anxiety, had swelled to a consuming passion, the like of which had never before touched her easy-going life.

Mary rose and shook the sand from her skirts. 'I must see what I can find to say to him, to cheer him up and keep him quiet.'

'And our good little Lucie here, and Cuffy, too, shall mind darling Baby for Auntie, whilst she makes his pap.'

But the children hung back. Minding Baby meant one long fight to hinder him from putting things – everything: sand, shells, your hand, your spade – in his mouth, and kicking and screaming if you said no; and Aunt Tilly rushing out crying: 'What are they *doing* to my precious?' – Lucie had already a firm handful of her mother's dress in her grasp.

'Now, Mary! you can't possibly write with that child hanging round you.'

'Oh, she won't bother . . . she never does,' said Mary, who could not find it in her heart to drive her ewe-lamb from her.

'Oh, well then!' said Tilly, with a loveless glance at the retreating Cuffy. 'Muvver's jewel must just tum *wif* 'er, and see its doody-doody dinner cooked.' – And smothering the little sallow face, the overlarge head in kisses, she, too, sought the house.

('Really Tilly is *rather* absurd about that baby!')

('How Mary *does* spoil those children!')

With which private criticism, each of the other, Tilly fell to stirring a hasty-pudding, and Mary sat her down before pen and paper. And thus ended what, little as they knew it, was to be the last of their many confidential talks on the subject of Richard, his frowardness and crabbedness, his innate inability to fit himself to life. From now on, Mary's lips were in loyalty sealed.

CHAPTER THREE

Under the heat-veiled January skies Mahony saw his worst fears realized. His few remaining patients dropped off, no others appeared to take their place; and, with this, the practice in Barambogie virtually came to an end.

There he sat, with his head between his hands, cudgelling his brains. For it staggered credulity that every form of sickness, that the break-neck casualties inseparable from bush life, should one and all fade out in so preposterous a fashion. In the unhealthy season, too, compared with the winter months in which he had settled there. What were the people up to? What cabal had they formed against him? That some shady trick was being played him, he did not for a moment doubt. Suspiciously he eyed Mrs Beetling when she came to her job of a morning. *She* knew what was going on, or he was much mistaken: she looked very queerly at him, and often gave him the impression of scuttling hurriedly away. But he had never been any hand at pumping people of her class: it took Mary to do that. And so he contented himself, did he chance upon the woman, with fixing her in silence; and otherwise treating her with the contempt she deserved. He had more important things to occupy him. These first days of blank, unbroken idleness were spent in fuming about the house like a caged animal: up the passage, out on the verandah, round this and back to the passage. Again and again he believed he heard the front gate click, and ran to seat himself in the surgery. But it was always a false alarm. And after a few seconds' prickling suspense, in which every nerve in his body wore ears, he would bound up from his seat, hardly master of himself for exasperation. These infamous people! Why, oh why had he ever set foot among them? . . . ever trodden the dust of this accursed place! A man of his skill, his experience, wilfully to put himself at the mercy of a pack of bushdwellers . . . Chinese coolies . . . wretched half-castes! – And, striding ever more gauntly and intolerantly, he drove his thoughts back and salved his bleeding pride with memories of the past. He saw himself in his heyday, on Ballarat, famed alike for his diagnoses and sureness of hand; saw himself called in to perform the most delicate operations; robbed of his sleep by night, on the go the livelong day, until at last, incapable of meeting the claims made on him, there had been nothing left for him to do but to fly the place. And spurred by the exhilaration of these memories, he quickened his steps till the sweat poured off him.

But he was not to be done. He'd shew these numskulls whom they had to deal with . . . make them bite the dust. Ha! he had it: that case of empyema and subsequent operation for *paracentesis thoracis*, which he had before now contemplated writing up for the *Australian Medical Journal*. Now was the time: he would set to work straightway, dash the article off, post it before the sun went down that night. It would appear in the March issue of the journal; and these fools would then learn, to their eternal confusion, that they had among them one whose opinions were of weight in the selectest medical circles. With unsteady hands he turned out a drawer containing old notes and papers, and having found what he wanted, spread them on the table before him. But, with his pen inked and poised ready to begin, he hesitated. In searching, he had recalled another, rarer case: one of a hydatid cyst in the subcutaneous tissue of the thigh. This would be more telling; and going on his knees before a wooden chest, in which he stored old memoranda, he rummaged anew. Again, however, after a lengthy hunt, he found himself wavering. His notes were not as full as he had believed: there would be finicking details to verify, books to consult which he could no longer get at. So this scheme, too, had to be let drop. Ah! but now he had really hit it. What about that old bone of contention among the medical profession, homœopathy? Once on a time he had meant to bring out a pamphlet on the subject, and, if he remembered rightly, had made voluminous notes for it. Could he find these, he would be spared all brain-fag. And again he made his knees sore and his head dizzy over a mass of dusty, yellowing papers. After which, re-seating himself with an air of triumph, he ruled a line in red ink on a sheet of foolscap, and wrote above it, in his fine, flowing hand: Why I do not practise Homœopathy.

If, as is so often asserted, the system of homœopathy as practised by Hahnemann and his followers . . .

But having got thus far he came to a standstill, re-dipped a pen that was already loaded, bit the end of it, wrinkled his brows. What next? . . . what did he want to say? . . . how to end the sentence? And when he did manage to catch a glimpse of his thought, he could not find words in which to clothe it . . . the right words. They would not come at his beck; or phrases either. He floundered, tried one, then another; nothing suited him; and he grew more and more impatient: apparently, even with his notes before him, it was going to be beyond him to make a decent job of the thing. He had been silent too long. Nor could he, he now found, work up the heat, the orthodox heat with which he had once burnt: the points he had formerly made against this quack and his system now seemed flat or exaggerated. So indifferent had he grown with the years that his present attitude of mind was almost one of: let those who choose adopt Hahnemann's methods, those who will, be allopaths. And, as he sat there struggling to bring his thoughts to heel, to re-kindle the old fire, the tardy impulse to express himself died out. He threw his pen from him. *Cui bono?* Fool, fool! To think of blistering his brains for the benefit of these savages among whom his present lot was cast. What would they understand of it, many of whom were forced to set crosses where their names should have stood? And when he was so tired, too, so dog-tired physically, with his feverish runnings to and fro, and exhausted mentally with fretting and fuming. Much too tired (and too rusty) to embark on a piece of work that demanded utmost care and discrimination . . . let alone cope with the labour of writing it down. Suddenly, quite suddenly, the idea of exertion, of any effort whatever, was become odious to him . . . odious and unthinkable. He put his arms on the table and hid his face in them; and, lying there, knew that his chief desire was fulfilled: to sit with his eyes screened, darkness round him, and to think and feel just as little as he saw. But, a bundle of papers incommoding him, he raised his hand, and with a last flash of the old heat crumpled notes and jottings to balls and tossed them to the floor. There they lay till, next morning, Mrs Beetling swept them up and threw them on the kitchen fire.

And now silence fell anew – a silence the more marked for the stormy trampling that had preceded it. Said Mrs Beetling to her crony, the ostler's wife: 'I do declare, 'e's that mousy quiet, you never c'd tell there was a livin' creatur' in the 'ouse — not no more'n a triantelope nor a centipede!' No longer had she to spend time dodging her master: shrinking behind open doors to avoid crossing his path, waiting her opportunity to reach bedroom or dining-room unobserved. He never left the surgery; and she could work with a good grace, scrubbing floors that were not trodden on, cooking food the lion's share of which it fell to her to eat.

Meanwhile a burning February ran its course. To step off the verandah now was like stepping into a furnace. The sky was white with heat: across its vast pale expanse moved a small, copper-coloured sun. Or the hot winds streaked it with livid trails of wind-smitten cloud. The very air was white with dust. While, did a windstorm rise, the dust-clouds were so dense that everything — trees, Lagoon, township, the very garden itself — was blotted out. Dust carpeted the boards of the verandah, drove into the passage, invaded the rooms. But never a drop of rain fell. And then the fires started: in all the country round, the bush was ablaze: the sky hung dark as with an overhead fog; the rank tang of burning wood smarted the lungs.

In the little oven of a house the green blinds were lowered from early morning on. Behind them, in a bemusing twilight, behind the high paling-fence that defended house from road, Mahony sat isolate — sat shunned and forgotten. And as day added itself to day the very sound of his own voice grew strange to him, there being no need for him ever to unclose his lips. Even his old trick of muttering died out — went the way of his pacing and haranguing. For something in him had yielded, had broken, carrying with it, in its full, the black pride, the bitter resentment, the aggressive attitude of mind which had hitherto sustained him. And this wholesale collapse of what he had believed to be his ruling traits made him feel oddly humble ... and humiliated ... almost as if he had shrivelled in stature. Hence he never went out. For the single road led through the street of malicious eyes: and now nothing would have prevailed on him to expose himself to their fire. More and more the four walls of his room began to seem to him haven and refuge. And gradually he grew as fearful of the sound of footsteps approaching the door as he had formerly been eager for them. For they might mean a summons to quit his lair.

But no steps came.

Had he had but a dog to lay its moist and kindly muzzle on his knee, or a cat to arch ts back under his hand, the keenest edge might have been taken off his loneliness. But for more years than he could count, he had been obliged to deny himself the company of those dumb friends who might now have sought, in semi-human fashion, to relieve the inhuman silence that had settled round him. Nothing broke this – or only what was worse than the silence itself: the awful mill-whistle, which, five times a day, marked the passage of the empty hours with its nerve-shattering shriek. He learnt to hate this noise as if it had been a live and malignant thing; yet was constrained to wait for it, to listen to it – even to count the seconds that still divided him from its blast. His books lay unopened, withdrawn into their primary state of so much dead paper. And it was not books alone that lost their meaning and grew to seem useless, and a burden. He could forget to wind up his watch, to pare his nails; he ceased to care whether or no his socks were worn into holes. The one task to which he still whipped himself was the writing of a few lines necessary to keep Mary from fretting. (To prepare her, too. *Absolutely nothing doing . . . incredible . . . heartbreaking.*) Otherwise he would sit, for an hour at a time, staring at some object on the table before him, till it, the table, the room itself, swam in a grey mist. Or he followed, with all the fixity of inattention, the movements of a fly . . . or the dance of dust motes laddering a beam.

But this inertia, this seemingly aimless drifting, was yet not wholly irrational. It formed a kind of attempt, a threefold attempt, on the part of his inmost self, to recover from . . . to nerve himself anew for . . . to avoid rousing a whit sooner than need be . . . the black terrors that stalked those hours when he had not even the light of day to distract him.

*

To wake in the night, and to know that, on this side of your waking, lies no ray of light or hope . . . only darkness and fear. To wake in the night: be wide awake in an instant with all your faculties on edge: to wake, and be under compulsion to set in, night for night, at the same point, knowing, from grim experience, that the demons awaiting you have each to be grappled with in turn, no single one of them left unthrown, before you can win through to the peace that is utter exhaustion.

Sometimes he managed to get a couple of hours' rest beforehand. At others, he would start up from a profound sleep believing the night far advanced; only to find that a bare ten or fifteen minutes had elapsed since he closed his eyes. But, however long or short the period of oblivion, what followed was always the same; and after a very few nights he learnt wisdom, and gave up struggling to escape the unescapable. Rising on his pillow he drew a long breath, clenched his fists, and thrust off.

The order in which his thoughts swept at him was always the same. The future . . . what of the future? With the practice gone, with nothing saved on which to start afresh, with but the slenderest of sums in hand for living expenses and the everlasting drain of the mortgage, he could see no way out of his present impasse but through the bankruptcy court. And in this country even an unmerited insolvency, one brought about by genuine misfortunes, spelt disgrace, spelt ruin. And not for oneself alone. To what was he condemning Mary . . . and the children? . . . his tenderly reared children. Poverty . . . charity . . . the rough and ready scramble of colonial life. Oh, a man should indeed take thought and consider, before he gave such hostages to fortune! — And here, as he tossed restlessly from side to side, there came into his mind words he had read somewhere or heard someone say, about life and its ultimate meaning. Stripped of its claptrap, of the roses and false sentiment in which we loved to drape it, it had actually no object but this: to keep a roof over the heads and food in the mouths of the helpless beings who depend on us. — Burns, too . . . Bobbie Burns. — Oh, God! . . . there it was again. This accursed diminutive! Night for night he vowed he would not use it, and night for night his tongue slipped and it was out before he could help himself. Had he then no longer the power to decide what he would or would not say? Preposterous! . . . preposterous and infuriating! For the whole thing — both the slip and his exasperation — was but a ruse on the part of his mind, to switch him off the main issue. And to know this, and yet be constrained, night after night, to the mechanical repetition of so utter a futility . . . his cold rage was such that several minutes had invariably to pass before he was calm enough to go on.

A way out! . . . there *must* be a way out. Hoisting himself on the pillow, till he all but sat erect, and boring into the dark with eyes hot in their sockets, he fell feverishly to telling over his affairs; though by now this, too, had become a sheerly automatic proceeding: his lips singsonging figures and sets of figures, while his brain roved elsewhere. What he could *not* avoid was the recital of them: it formed another of the obstacles he was compelled nightly to clamber over, on the road to sleep. Bills and bad debts, shares and dividends and calls, payments on the mortgage, redemption of the capital: these things danced a witches' sabbath in his head. To them must now be added the rent of the house they lived in. He had reckoned on covering this with the rental from the house at Hawthorn. But they had had no luck with tenants: were already at their second; and the house was said to be falling into bad repair. In the Bank in Barambogie there stood to his credit, stood between him and beggary, the sum of not quite one hundred pounds. When this was done, God help them!

Why had he ever left Melbourne? What evil spirit had entered into him and driven him forth? What *was* that in him, over which he had no power, which proved incapable of adhesion to any soil or fixed abode? For he might arm himself, each time anew, with another motive for plucking up his roots: it remained mere ratiocination, a sop flung to his reason, and in no wise got at the heart of the matter. Wherein lay the fault, the defect, that had made of him throughout his life a hunted man? . . . harried from place to place, from country to country. Other men set up a goal, achieved it, and remained content. He had always been in flight. – But from what? Who were his pursuers? From what shadows did he run? – And in these endless nights, when he lay and searched his heart as never before, he thought he read the answer to the riddle. Himself he was the hunter and the hunted: the merciless in pursuit and the panting prey. Within him, it would seem, lodged fears . . . strange fears. And at a given moment one of these, hitherto dormant and unsuspected, would suddenly begin to brew, and go on growing till he was all one senseless panic, blind flight the only catholicon. No matter what form it took – whether a morbid anxiety about his health, or alarm at the swiftness with which his little day was passing – its aim was always the same: to beat him up and on. And never yet had he succeeded in defying it. With the result that, well on in years and loaded with responsibilities, he stood face to face with ruin. Having dragged with him those who were dearer to him than his own life. – But stay! Was that true? . . . and not just one of those sleek phrases that dripped so smoothly off the tongue. *Were* they dearer? In this moment of greater clarity he could no longer affirm it. He believed that the instinct of self-preservation had, in his case, always been the primary one. And digging deeper still, he got, he thought, a further insight into his motives. If this were so, then what he fled must needs be the reverse of the security he ran to seek: in other words, annihilation. The plain truth was: the life-instinct had been too strong for him. Rather than face death and the death-fear, in an attempt to flee the unfleeable he had thrown every other consideration to the winds, and ridden tantivy into the unknown.

But now all chance of flight was over. He sat here as fast a prisoner as though chained to a stake — an old and weary man, with his fiftieth birthday behind him. — *Old*, did he say? By God! not as a man's years were reckoned elsewhere. In this accursed country alone. Only here were those who touched middle age regarded as decrepit, and cumberers of the soil. Wisdom and experience availed a man nothing, where only brawn had value. As for the three-score years and ten — But no! . . . no use, no use! . . . words would not help him. Not thus could it be shirked. He had to fight through, to the last spasm, the paroxysm of terror which at this point shook him like a palsy, at the knowledge that he would never again get free; that he was caught, trapped, pinned down . . . to be torn asunder, devoured alive. His pulses raced, his breath came hard, the sweat that streamed off him ran cold. Night after night he had the same thing to undergo; and from bitter experience he knew that the fit would gradually exhaust itself, leaving him spent, inert. — But this was all. With this, his compliance ceased, and there came a block. For, below the surface here, under a lid which he never lifted, which nothing would have induced him to raise by a hair's-breadth, lurked a darker fear than any, one he could not face and live; even though, with a part of his mind, a watchful part, a part that it was impossible to deceive, he *knew* what it was.

Swerving violently, he laid the onus of his terror on a side issue: the confession that stood before him, the confession to Mary of his ruinous debt. As he pictured this, and as the borrowed emotion swelled it out, it turned to something horrible . . . monstrous . . . the performance of which surpassed his strength. How could he ever break the news to her, all unsuspecting, who shrank from debt as other women from fire or flood? What would she say? . . . hurl what bitter words at him, in her first wrath and distress? She being what she was, he believed the knowledge would well-nigh break her heart . . . as it almost broke his, to think of the anguish he must inflict on her. – And once again the years fell away, and he was a little velvet-suited lad, paling and quivering under the lash of a caustic Irish tongue. But there also came times when some such vividly recalled emotion proved the way out. Then, one or other episode from the forty-year-old past would rise before him, with so amazing a reality that he re-lived it to its flimsiest details, hearing the ominous tick of the clock on the chimney-piece, smelling the scent of lavender that went out from his mother's garments. At others, the past failing in its grip, there was nothing for it but to fight to a finish. And so he would lie, and writhe, and moan, and beat the pillow with his hands, while tears that felt thick as blood scalded his cheeks.

But gradually, very gradually this last convulsion spent itself: and, as at the approach of soft music from a distance, he was aware of the coming end . . . of the peace advancing, at which all the labour of the night had been directed. Peace at last! . . . for his raw nerves, his lacerated brain. And along with it a delicious drowsiness, which stole over him from his finger-tips, and up from his feet, relaxing knotted muscles, loosening his hands, which now lay limp and free. He sank into it, letting himself go . . . as into a pond full of feathers . . . which enveloped him, closed downily about him . . . he sinking deeper . . . ever deeper . . .

Until, angry and menacing, shattering the heavenly inertia, a scream. – Who screamed? A child? What was it? Who was hurt? – Oh God! the shock of it, the ice-cold shock! He fell back on the pillow, his heart thudding like a tom-tom. Would he *never* grow used to it? . . . this awful waking! . . . and though he endured it day after day. For . . . as always . . . the sun was up, the hour six of a red-hot morning, and the mill-whistle flayed the silence. In all he had slept for not quite three-quarters of an hour.

Thereafter he lay and stared into the dusty light as he had stared into the darkness. Needle-like pulses beat behind his lids; the muscles round eyes and mouth were a-twitch with fatigue. From the sight of food he turned with a sick man's disrelish. Swallowing a cup of milkless tea, he crossed to the surgery and shut himself in. But on this particular day his habit of drowsing through the empty hours was rudely broken through. Towards midday he was disturbed by the door opening. It was Mrs Beetling who, without so much as a knock, put her head in to say that the stationmaster had hurt his foot and wanted doctor to come and bandage it.

The stationmaster? – He had been far away, on high cliffs that sloped to the sea, gathering 'horsetails' . . . and for still an instant his brain loitered over the Latin equivalent. Then he was on his feet, instinctively fingering the place where his collar should have been. But neither coat nor collar . . . and: 'My boots, my good woman, my boots!' The dickens! Was that he who was shouting? Tut, tut! He must pull himself together, not let these spying eyes note his fluster. But there was another reason for the deliberateness with which he sought the bedroom. His knees felt weak, and he could hardly see for the tears that would keep gathering. Over three weeks now – close on a month – since anyone had sent for him. *All* were not dead against him then! Oh, a good fellow, this Pendrell! . . . a good fellow! . . . a man after his own heart, and a gentleman. – And throwing open drawers and cupboards, he made many an unnecessary movement, and movements that went wide of their mark.

In putting arnica and lint in his bag he became aware that his hands were violently a-shake. This wouldn't do. Impossible to appear before a patient in such a state. He clenched his fists and stiffened his arms; but the tremor was stronger than his will, and persisted. As a last resource, he turned to the sideboard, poured some sherry into a tumbler, and gulped it down.

Quitting the house by the back door, he went past the kitchen, the woodstack, the rubbish-heap, a pile of emptied kerosene-tins, the pigsties (with never a pig in them), the fowls sitting moping in the shrinking shade. His eyes ran water anew at the brassy glare; and phew! . . . the heat. In his haste he had forgotten to put a handful of vine-leaves in the crown of his wideawake. The sun bore down on him with an almost physical weight: he might have had a loaded sack lying across neck and shoulders. And as soon as he let the hasp of the gate fall, he was in the dust of the road; and then his feet were weighted as well.

But his thoughts galloped. Oh, that this summons might be the start of a new era for him! . . . the awful stagnation of the past month prove to have been but a temporary lull, a black patch, such as any practice was liable to; the plot he had believed hatched against him prove to have existed only in his own imagination; and everything be as before . . . he still able to make a living, pay his way. – 'Mercy! . . . dear God, a little mercy!' – But if that were so, then he, too, would need to do his share. Yes, he would make a point from now on of meeting the people here on their own level. He would ask after their doings . . . their wives and children . . . gossip with them of the weather and the vines . . . hobnob – no, drink with them he could and would not! But he knew another way of getting at them. And that was through their pockets. Fees! Quite likely he had set his too high. He would now come down a peg . . . halve his charges. They'd see then that it was to their advantage to call him in, rather than send elsewhere for a stranger. It might also be policy on his part – in the meantime at any rate – to treat trivial injuries and ailments free of charge. (Once the practice was set going again, he'd make them pay through the nose for all the worry and trouble they'd caused him.) If *only* he could get the name of being freehanded . . . easygoing – could ingratiate himself . . . become popular.

So rapt was he that though, at the level crossing, his feet paused of themselves, he could not immediately think why he had stopped, and gazed absently round. Ha! the trains, of course. But there *were* no trains at this hour of day: the station was shut up, deserted. A pretty fool he would look was he seen standing there talking to himself. He must hurry in, too, out of the sun. The heat was beginning to induce giddiness; the crown of his head felt curiously contracted. But he had still some distance to go. He spurred himself on, more quickly than before, his feet keeping time with his wingy thoughts.

Mary was hard put to it not to alarm the children. Every few minutes her anxiety got the better of her, and dropping her work she would post herself at a corner of the verandah, where she could see down the road. She had been on the watch ever since the postman handed in Richard's letter that morning, for the telegram that was to follow. Her first impulse had been to start for home without delay; and despite Tilly's reasonings and persuasions, she had begun to sort out the children's clothes. Then she wavered. It would be madness to go back before the heat broke. And, if the practice was as dead as Richard averred, there was no saying when the poor mites would get another change of air.

Still . . . Richard needed her. His letter ran: *I am afraid what I have to tell you will be a great shock to you. I was up at the stationmaster's just now and found myself unable to articulate. I could not say what I wanted. I lay down, and they brought me water. I said I thought it was a faint — that I had been out too long in the sun. I fear it is something worse. I am very, very uneasy about myself. I have been so distressed about the practice. I think that must have upset me. Intense mental depression . . . and this awful heat — what with solitude and misfortunes I have been terribly put about. All the same I should not worry you, if it were not for my dread of being taken ill alone. I am most unwilling to bring you and the children back in the meantime. The heat baffles description. I should never spend another February here — it would be as much as my life is worth. Perhaps the best thing to do will be to wait and see how I am. I will telegraph you on Monday morning early. Take no steps till you hear.*

But to this a postscript had been added, in a hand it was hard to recognize as Richard's: *Oh, Mary wife, come home, come home! — before I go quite mad.*

Down by the water's edge Cuffy played angrily. He didn't know what he loved best: the seaweed, or the shells, or the little cave, or the big pool on the reef, or the little pool, or bathing and lying on the sand, or the smell of the ti-trees. And now — oh, *why* had Papa got to go and get ill, and spoil everything? *He'd* seen Mamma beginning to pack their things, and it had made him feel all hot inside. Why must just *his* clothes be packed? He might get ill, too. Perhaps he would, if he drank some sea. Aunt Tilly said it made you mad. (Like Shooh man.) All right then, he would get mad . . . and they could see how they liked it! And so saying he scooped up a palmful of water and put it to his mouth. It ran away so fast that there was hardly any left; but it was enough: ugh! wasn't it nasty? He spat it out again, making a 'normous noise so that everybody should hear. But they didn't take a bit of notice. Then a better idea struck him. He'd give Mamma the very nicest things he had: the two great big shells he had found all by himself, which he kept hidden in a cave so that Luce shouldn't even touch them unless he said so. He'd give them to Mamma, and she'd like them so much that she'd never want to go home — oh well! not for a long, long time. Off he raced, shuffling his bare feet through the hot, dry, shifty sand.

But it was no good: she didn't care. Though he made her shut her eyes tight and promise not to look, while he opened

her hand and squeezed the shells into it and shut it again, like
you did with big surprises. She just said: 'What's this? Your
pretty shells? My dear, what should I do with them? No, no!
. . . you keep them for yourself,' – and all the while she wasn't
really thinking what she said. And he couldn't even tell her
why, for now Aunt Tilly shouted that the telegram-boy was
coming at last; and Mamma just pushed the shells back and
ran out into the road, and tore open the telegram like anything,
and smiled and waved it at Aunt Tilly, and they both laughed
and talked and wiped their eyes. But then everything was all
right again; for it was from Papa, and he had telegrammed: *Am
better, do not hurry home.*

CHAPTER FOUR

In spite, however, of this reassurance Mary could not rest. And one fine morning not long after, the trunks were brought out again, and she and Tilly fell to packing in earnest.

Cuffy's resentment at being torn from the sea a whole fortnight too soon did not stand before the excitements of a journey: first in a coach and then in a train. Besides, Mamma had given him a little box to himself, to pack his shells in. Importantly he carried this, while she and Aunt Tilly ran about counting the other luggage. There was so much – portmanteaux and bundles, and baskets and bonnet-boxes, and beds and mattresses, and buckets and spades and the perambulator – that they were afraid there wouldn't be room for it in the coach. But there was: they had it all to themselves. And di*reck*ly the door was shut the lunch-basket was opened; for one of the most 'squisite things about a journey was that you could eat as much as you liked and whenever you liked. Mamma was so nice, too, and didn't scold when you and Luce rushed to look first out of one window and then the other. But Aunt Tilly said you trod on her feet and knocked against Baby, and you were a perfect nuisance; in all her born days she'd never known such fidgets. But Mamma said it was only high spirits, and you couldn't be always carping at children, wait till Baby got big and she'd see! And Aunt Tilly said she'd take care he wasn't brought up to be a nuisance to his elders. Cuffy was afraid they were going to get cross, so he sat down again, and only waggled his legs. He didn't like Aunt Tilly much. He didn't like fat people. Besides, when Baby squawked she thought it was lovely, and gave him everything he wanted to put in his mouth. They were in the train now, and *wouldn't* it be fun to pinch his leg! But he couldn't, 'cos he wasn't sitting next him. But he stuck his boot out and pressed it as hard as ver he could against Baby's foot, and Aunt Tilly didn't see but Baby did, and opened his eyes and looked at him . . . just horrid!

Then came Melbourne and a fat old lady in a carrriage and two horses, who called Mamma my dearie. She lived in a *very* big house with a nice old gentleman with a white beard, who took his hand and walked him round 'to see the grounds' (just as if he was grown up). He was a very funny man, and said he owed (only he said it 'h'owed') everything to Papa, which made Cuffy wonder why, if so, he didn't pay him back. For Papa was always saying he hadn't enough money. But Mamma had told them they must be specially good here, and not pass remarks about *anything*. So he didn't. One night they went to a Pantomime called *Goody Two-Shoes* – not Mamma, she was still too sorry about Lallie being dead – and once to hear music and singing in a theatre. The old Sir and Lady took them both times, and at the music Luce was a donkey and went to sleep, and had to be laid down on a coat on the floor. He didn't! He sat on a chair in the front of a little room like a balcony, and listened and listened to a gipsy singing in a voice that went up and up, and made you feel first hot and then cold all over. Afterwards people made a great noise clapping their hands, and he did it, too, and made more noise than anybody. And the gipsy came by herself and bowed her head to everyone, and then she looked at him, and smiled and blew him a kiss. He didn't much care for that, because it made people laugh; and he didn't know her. They all laughed again when they got home, till he went red and felt more like crying. He didn't, though; he was too big to cry now; everybody said so. The funny thing was, lots of big people did cry here; there seemed always to be someone crying. Aunt Zara came to see them all dressed in black, with black cloths hanging from her bonnet and a prickly dress that scratched – like Papa's chin when he hadn't shaved. This was because she was a widder. She had a black streak on her handkerchief, too, to cry on, and felt most awfully sorry about writing to Mamma on paper that hadn't a 'morning border', but what with one thing and another . . . Cuffy hoped Mamma wouldn't mind, and asked what a morning border was, but was only told to run away and play. He didn't. He stopped at the window and pretended to catch flies, he wanted so much to hear. Aunt Zara said she lit'rally didn't know where to turn, and Mamma looked sorry but said if you made beds you must lie on them. (That *was* rummy!) And Aunt Zara said she thought she had been punished enough. Mamma said as long as she had a roof over her head she wouldn't see anyone belonging to her come to want, and there *were* the children, of course, and she was at her wits' end what to do about them, but of course she'd have to consult Richard first, and Aunt Zara knew what he was, and Aunt Zara said, only too well, but there was nothing she wouldn't do, she'd even scrub floors and wash dishes.

'Maria always scrubs our floors!'

It just jumped out of him; he did so want her to know she wouldn't have to. But then she said the thing about little pitchers and Mamma got cross as well, and told him to go out of the room at *once*, so he didn't hear any more.

Then Cousin Emmy came, and she cried too – like anything. He felt much sorrier for her than Aunt Zara. He had to sniffle himself. She was so nice and pretty, but when she cried her face got red and fat, and Mamma said if she went on like this she'd soon lose her good looks. But she said who'd she got to be good-looking for, only a pack of kids, which made him feel rather uncomfortable and he thought she needn't have said that. But it was very int'resting. She told about somebody who spent all her time dressing in 'averdipoy', and was possessed by a devil (like the pigs in the Bible). He longed to ask what she meant, but this time was careful and didn't let anything hop out of him, for he was going to hear just *everything*. Mamma seemed cross with Cousin Emmy, and said she was only a very young girl and must put up with things, and one day Mister Right would come along and it would be time enough, when that happened, to see what could be done. And Cousin Emmy got very fierce and said there'd never be any Mister Right for her, for a man was never allowed to show so much as his nose in the house. (Huh! *that* was funny. Why not his nose?) Mamma said she'd try and make *her* see reason, and Cousin Emmy said it'd be like talking to a stone statue, and it would always be herself first and the rest nowhere, and the plain truth was, she was simply crazy to get married again and there'd never be any peace till she had found a husband. And Mamma said, then she'd have to look out for someone with lots of money, your Papa's will being what it was. And Cousin Emmy said she was so sick and tired of everything that sometimes she thought she'd go away and drown herself. And then she cried again, and Mamma said she was a very wicked girl, even to *think* of such a thing. He had to wink his own eyes hard when she said that, and went on getting sorrier. And when she was putting on her hat to say good-bye he ran and got his shells, and when he was allowed to go to the gate with her he showed her them, and asked if she'd like to have them 'for keeps'. And Cousin Emmy thanked him most awfly but couldn't think of robbing him of his beautiful shells . . . oh well then, if he wanted it *so* much, she would, but only one, and he should keep the other and it would be like a philippine, and they wouldn't tell anybody; it would just be their secret. Which it was.

Next day they went to see Aunt Lizzie, where Cousin Emmy lived with 'John's cousins' . . . no, he meant 'John's children'. They couldn't see John, for he was dead. In the wagonette Mamma told him all about the 'squisite songs Aunt Lizzie used to sing him when he was quite a young child, and he hoped she would again; but when he asked her, when she had finished kissing, she clapped her hands and said law child, her singing days were over. It was Aunt Lizzie who was averdipoy – he knew now it meant fat, and not putting on something, for he had asked Mamma at dinner and Mamma had told him; but she had been cross, too, and said it was a nasty habit and he *must* get out of it, to listen to what his elders said, especially if you repeated it afterwards. He didn't like Aunt Lizzie much. She had a great big mouth to sing with, and she opened it so wide when she talked you could have put a whole mandarin in at once; and she had rings on her fingers that cut you when she squeezed.

And then Mamma and her wanted to talk secrets, and they were told to go and play with their cousins. Cousin Emmy took them. Two of them were nearly grown-up, with their hairs in plaits, and they didn't take much notice of them but just said, what a funny little pair of kids to be sure, and whatever was their Mamma thinking of not to put them in 'morning' for their sister. They all had great big staring black eyes and it made him sorry he had. Cousin Josey was as horrid as ever. She said she guessed he was going to be a dwarf and would have to be shown at an Easter Fair, and Luce looked a reg'lar cry-baby. Cousin Emmy told her not to be so nasty, and she said her tongue was her own. Cousin Josey was only ten, but *ever* so big, with long thin legs in white stockings and black garters which she kept pulling up; and when she took off her round comb and put it between her teeth, her hair came over her face till she looked like a gorilla. When she said that about the cry-baby he took hold of Luce's hand to pertect her, and squeezed it hard so's she shouldn't cry. But then Cousin Josey came and pinched Luce's nose off between her fingers and showed it to her, and she pinched so hard that Luce got all red and screwed up her eyes like she really was going to cry. Cousin Emmy said she was not to take any notice what such a rude girl did, and then Cousin Josey stuck out her tongue, and Cousin Emmy said she'd box her ears for her if she didn't take care. And then Cousin Josey put her fingers to her nose and waggled them – which was most awfly wicked – and Cousin Emmy said no it was too much and tried to catch her, and she ran away and Cousin Emmy ran too, and they chased and chased like mad round the table, and the big girls said, go it Jo, don't let her touch you, and first a chair fell over and then the tablecloth with the books on it and the inkstand, and it upset on the carpet and there was an awful noise and Aunt Lizzie and Mamma came running to see what was the matter. And Aunt Lizzie was furious and screamed and stamped her foot, and Cousin Josey had to come here, and then she boxed her ears on both sides fit to kill her. And Mamma said oh Lizzie don't and something about drums, and Aunt Lizzie said she was all of a shake, so she hardly knew what she was doing, but this was just a specimen, Mary, of what she had to put up with, they fought like turkey-cocks, and Cousin Emmy wasn't a bit of good at managing them but just as bad as any of them, and there was never a moment's peace, and she wished she'd seen their father at Jericho before she'd had anything to do with him or his spoilt brats. And the other two winked at each other, but Cousin Emmy got wild and said she couldn't wish it more than she did, and she wouldn't stand there and hear her father ubbused, and Aunt Lizzie said for two pins and if she'd any more of her sauce she'd box *her* ears as well though she *did* think herself so grand. And Cousin Emmy said she dared her to touch her, and it was *dreadful*. He was ever so glad when Mamma said it was time to go home, and he put on his gloves in a hurry. And when they got home Mamma told the Lady about it and said it was a 'tragedy' for everybody concerned. He didn't like Cousin Emmy quite so well after this. And that night in bed he told Luce all about the shells and the philippine, and Luce said if he'd given it to her she'd have given it him back and then he'd still have had two. And he was sorry he hadn't.

Uncle Jerry was a nice man . . . though he didn't have any whiskers. Mamma said he looked a perfect sketch, and he'd only cut them off to please Aunt Fanny who must always be ahlamode. Mamma said he had to work like a nigger to make money, she spent such a lot, but he gave him and Luce each a shilling. At first it was only a penny, and first in one hand, then in the other, but at the end it was a shilling, to spend *exactly* as they liked.

And then they had to go home, and got up ever so early to catch the train. This time it wasn't so jolly. It was too hot: you could only lie on the seat and watch the sky run past. Mamma took off their shoes and said, well, chicks, we shall soon be seeing dear Papa again now, won't that be lovely? And he said, oh yes, won't it. But inside him he didn't feel it a bit. Mamma had been so nice all the time at the seaside and now she'd soon be cross and sorry again . . . about Lallie and Papa. She looked out of the window, and wasn't thinking about them any more . . . thinking about Papa. – Well, he *was* glad he hadn't spent his shilling. He nearly had. Mamma said what fun it would be if he bought something for Papa with it. But he hadn't. For Papa wrote a letter and said for God's sake don't buy *me* anything, but Mamma did . . . a most beautiful silver fruit knife. Luce had bought her doll new shoes . . . perhaps some day he'd buy a kite that 'ud fly up and up to the sky till you couldn't see a speck of it . . . much higher than a swing . . . high like a . . .

Good gracious! he must have gone to sleep, for Mamma was shaking his arm saying come children, wake up. And they put on their shoes again and their hats and gloves and stood at the window to watch for Papa, but it was a long, long time till they came to Barambogie. Papa was on the platform, and when he saw them he waved like anything and ran along with the train. And then he suddenly felt most awfly glad, and got out by himself di*reck*ly the door was open, and Mamma got out too, but as soon as she did she said oh Richard, what *have* you been doing to yourself? And Papa didn't say anything, but only kissed and kissed them, and said how well they looked, and he was too tired to jump them high, and while he was saying this he suddenly began to cry. And the luggage-man stared like anything and so did the stationmaster, and Mamma said, oh dear whatever is it, and not before everybody Richard, and please just send the luggage after us, and then she took Papa's arm

and walked him away. And Luce and him had to go on in front
... so's not to see. But he did, and went all hot inside, and felt
most awfly ashamed.

And Papa cried and cried ... he could hear him through the
surgery door.

CHAPTER FIVE

When Mary came out of the surgery and shut the door behind her, she leaned heavily up against it for a moment, pressing her hand to her throat; then, with short steps and the blank eyes of a sleep-walker, crossed the passage to the bedroom and sat stiffly down. She was still in bonnet and mantle, just as she had got out of the train: it had not occurred to her to remove them. And she was glad of the extra covering, for in spite of the heat of the day she felt very cold. Cold . . . and old. The scene she had just been through with Richard seemed, at a stroke, to have added years to her age. It had been a dreadful experience. With his arms on the table, his head on his arms, he had cried like a child, laying himself bare to her, too, with a child's pitiful abandon. He told of his distraction at the abrupt stoppage of the practice; of his impression of being deliberately shunned; of his misery and loneliness, his haunting dread of illness – and, on top of this, blurted out pell-mell, as if he could keep nothing back, as if, indeed, he got a wild satisfaction out of making it, came the confession of his mad folly, the debt, the criminal debt in which he had entangled them, and under the shadow of which, all unknown to her, they had lived for the past year. Oh! well for him that he could not see her face as he spoke; or guess at the hideous pictures his words set circling in her brain; the waves of wrath and despair that ran through her. After her first spasmodic gasp of: '*Richard! Eight hundred pounds!*' the only outward sign of her inner commotion had been a sudden stiffening of her limbs, an involuntary withdrawal of the arm that had lain round his shoulders. Not for a moment could she afford to let her real feelings escape her: her single exclamation had led to a further bout of self-reproaches. Before everything, he had to be calmed, brought back to his senses, and an end put to this distressing scene. What would the children think, to hear their father behave like this? . . . his hysterical weeping . . . his loud, agitated tones. And so, without reflection, she snatched at any word of comfort that offered; repeated the old, threadbare phrases about things not being as black as he painted them; of everything seeming worse if you were alone; of how they would meet this new misfortune side by side and shoulder to shoulder – they still had each other, which was surely half the battle? With never a hint of censure; till she had him composed.

But as she sat in the bedroom, with arms and legs like stone, resentment and bitterness overwhelmed her . . . oh, a sheerly intolerable bitterness! Never! not to her dying day, would she forgive him the trick he had played on her . . . the deceit he had practised. On her . . . his own wife. So *this* was why he had left Hawthorn! – why he had not been able to wait to let the practice grow – *this* the cause of his feverish alarm here, did a single patient drop off. Now she understood – and many another thing besides. Oh, what had he done . . . so recklessly done! . . . to her, to his children? For there had been no real need for this fresh load of misery: they could just as easily – more easily – have rented a house. His pride alone had barred the way. It wouldn't have been good enough for him; nothing ever *was* good enough; he was always trying to outshine others. No matter how she might suffer over it, who feared debt more than anything in the world. But with him it had always been self first. Look at the home-coming he had prepared for her! He had hardly let her step inside before he had sprung his mine. Of course he had lost his head with excitement at their arrival . . . had hardly known what he was saying. Yes! but no doubt he had also thought to himself: at the pass to which things were come, the sooner his confession was made, the better for him. *What* a home-coming!

Further than this, however, she did not get. For the children, still in their travelling clothes and hot, tired and hungry, were at the door, clamouring for attention. With fumbly hands she took off her bonnet, smoothed her hair, pinned on her cap, tied a little black satin apron round her waist; and went out to them with the pinched lips and haggard eyes it so nipped Cuffy's heart to see.

Her pearl necklace would have to go: that was the first clear thought she struck from chaos. It was night now: the children had been fed and bathed and put to bed, the trunks unpacked, drawers and wardrobes straightened, the house – it was dirty and neglected – looked through, and Richard, pale as a ghost but still pitifully garrulous, coaxed to bed in his turn. She sat alone in the little dining-room, her own eyes feeling as if they would never again need sleep. Her necklace... even as the thought came to her she started up and, stealing on tiptoe into the bedroom, carried her dressing-case back with her... just to make sure: for an instant she had feared he might have been beforehand with her. But there the pearls lay, safe and sound. Well! as jewellery she would not regret them: she hadn't worn them for years, and had never greatly cared for being bedizened and behung. Bought in those palmy days when money slid like sand through Richard's fingers, they had cost him close on a hundred pounds. Surely she ought still to get enough for them – and for their companion brooches, rings, chains, ear-rings and bracelets – to make up the sums of money due for the coming months, which he admitted not having been able to get together. For consent to let the mortgage lapse she never would: not if she was forced to sell the clothes off her back, or to part, piece by piece, with the Paris ornaments, the table silver... Richard's books. It would be sheer madness; after having paid out hundreds and hundreds of pounds. Besides, the knowledge that you had this house behind you made all the difference. If the worst came to the worst they could retire to Hawthorn, and she take in boarders. She didn't care a rap what she did, so long as they contrived to pay their way.

How to dispose of the necklace was the puzzle. To whom could she turn? She ran over various people but dismissed them all. Even Tilly. When it came to making Richard's straits public, she was hedged on every side. Ah! but now she had it: *Zara!* If, as seemed probable, Zara came to take up her abode with them to teach the children, she would soon see for herself how matters stood. (And at least she was one's own sister.) Zara... trailing her weeds – why yes, even these might be turned to account. Widows did not wear jewellery; and were often left poorly off. People would pity her, perhaps give more, because of it.

And so, having fetched pen, ink and paper, Mary drew the kerosene lamp closer and set to writing her letter.

It wasn't easy; she made more than one start. Not even to Zara could she tell the unvarnished truth. She shrank, for instance, from admitting that only now had she herself learnt of Richard's difficulties. Zara might think strange things . . . about him and her. So she put the step she was forced to take, down to the expenses of their seaside holiday. Adding, however, that jewellery was useless in a place like this where you had no chance of wearing it; and even something of a risk, owing to the house standing by itself and having so many doors.

The letter written she made a second stealthy journey, this time to the surgery, where she ferreted out Richard's case-books. She had a lurking hope that, yet once more, he might have been guilty of his usual exaggeration. But half a glance at the blank pages taught her better. Things were even worse than he had admitted. What *could* have happened during her absence? What had he done, to make people turn against him? Practices didn't die out like this in a single day — somehow or other he must have been to blame. Well! it would be her job, henceforth, to put things straight again: somehow or other to re-capture the patients. And if Richard really laid himself out to conciliate people — he *could* be so taking, if he chose — and not badger them . . . Let him only scrape together enough for them to live on, and she would do the rest: her thoughts leapt straightway to a score of petty economies. The expenses of food and clothing might be cut down all round; and they would certainly go on no more long and costly holidays: had she only known the true state of affairs before setting out this summer! But she had been so anxious about the children . . . oh, she was forgetting the children. And here, everything coming back to her with a rush, Mary felt her courage waver. Merciless to herself; with only a half-hearted pity for Richard, grown man that he was and the author of all the trouble; she was at once a craven and wrung with compassion where her children were concerned.

At the breakfast-table next morning she sat preoccupied; and directly the meal was over put the first of her schemes into action by sending for the defaulting Maria and soundly rating her. But she could get no sensible reason from the girl for running away — or none but the muttered remark that it had been 'too queer' in the house with them all gone. After which, tying on her bonnet Mary set out for the township, a child on either hand. Lucie trotted docilely; but Cuffy was restive at being buttoned into his Sunday suit on a week-day, and dragged back and shuffled his feet in the dust till they were nearly smothered. Instead of trying to help Mamma by being an extra good boy!

'But I don't *feel* good.'

Once out of sight of the house, Mary took two crêpe bands from her pocket and slipped them over the children's white sleeves. Richard's ideas about mourning were bound to give ... had perhaps already given offence. People of the class they were now dependent on thought so much of funerals and mourning. But he never stopped to consider the feelings of others. She remembered how he had horrified Miss Prestwick, with his heathenish ideas about the children's prayers. All of a sudden one day he had declared they were getting too big to kneel down and pray 'into the void', or to 'a glorified man'; and had had them taught a verse which said that loving all things big and little was the best kind of prayer and so on; making a regular to-do about it when he discovered that Miss Prestwick was still letting them say their 'Gentle Jesus' on the sly.

Here she righted two hats and took Cuffy's elastic out of his mouth; for they were entering the township; and for once the main street was not in its usual state of desertedness, when it seemed as if the inhabitants must all lie dead of the plague ... or be gone *en masse* to a fairing. The butcher's cart drove briskly to and fro; a spring-cart had come in from the bush; buggies stood before the Bank. The police-sergeant touched his white helmet; horses were being backed between the shafts of the coach in front of the 'Sun'. Everybody of course eyed her and the children very curiously, and even emerged from their shops to stare after them. It was the first time she had ever walked her own children out, and on top of that she had been absent for over two months. (Perhaps people imagined she had gone for good! Oh, could *that* possibly be a reason?) However she made the best of it: smiled, and nodded, and said good day; and in spite of their inquisitive looks everyone she met was very friendly. She went into the butcher's to choose a joint, and took the opportunity of thanking the butcher for having served the doctor so well during her absence. The man beamed: and showed the children a whole dead pig he had hanging in the shop. She gave an order to the grocer, who leaned over the counter with two bunches of raisins, remarking 'A fine little pair of nippers you have there, Mrs Mahony!' To the baker she praised his bread, comparing it favourably with what she had eaten in Melbourne; and the man's wife pressed sweets on the children. At the draper's, which she entered to buy some stuff for pinafores, the same fuss was made over them . . . till she bade them run outside and wait for her there. For the drapery woman began putting all sorts of questions about Lallie's illness, and what they had done for her, and how they had treated it . . . odd and prying questions, and asked, with a strange air. Still, there was kindness behind the curiosity. 'We did all feel that sorry for *you*, Mrs Mahony . . . losing such a fine sturdy little girl!' And blinking her eyes to keep the tears back, Mary began to think that Richard must have gone *deliberately* out of his way to make enemies of these simple, well-meaning souls. Bravely she re-told the tale of her loss, being iron in her resolve to win people round; but she was thankful when the questionnaire ended and she was free to quit the shop. To see what the children were doing, too. She could hear Cuffy chattering away to somebody.

This proved to be the Reverend Mr Thistlethwaite, who had engaged the pair in talk with the super-heartiness he reserved for what he called the 'young or kitchen fry' of his parish. In his usual state of undress – collarless, with unbuttoned vest, his bare feet thrust in carpet slippers he was so waggish that Mary could not help suspecting where his morning stroll had led him.

'Good morning, madam, good morning to you! Back again, back again? *And* the little Turks! Capital . . . quite capital!'

He slouched along beside them, his paunch, under its grease spots, a-shake with laughter at his own jokes. The children of course were all ears; and she would soon have slipped into another shop and so have got rid of him – you never knew what he was going to say next – if a sudden bright idea had not flashed into her mind.

It came of Mr Thistlethwaite mentioning that the Bishop was shortly expected to visit the district; and humorously bemoaning his own lot. For, should his Lordship decide to break his journey at Barambogie on his way home, he, Thistlethwaite would be obliged to ask him to share his bachelor quarters. 'Which are all very well for hens and self, Mrs Mahony . . . hens and self! But for his Lordship? Oh dear, no!'

Privately Mary recognized the ruse. The piggery in which Thistlethwaite housed had stood him in good stead before now: never yet had the parsonage been in fit state to receive a brother cleric. But at the present crisis she jumped at the handle it offered her.

'But he must come to us!' cried she. 'The doctor and I would be only too delighted. And for as long as he likes. Another thing: why not, while he *is* here, persuade him to give us a short lecture or address? We might even get up a little concert to follow, and devote the money to the fencing fund.' — For the church still stood on open ground. In the course of the past year but a meagre couple of pounds had been raised towards enclosing it; and what had become of these, nobody knew.

And now Mary's ideas came thick and fast; rising even to the supreme labour of a 'Tea-meeting'. And while Thistlethwaite hummed aloud in ever greater good humour, mentally cracking his fingers to the tune of: 'That's the ticket . . . women for ever! The work for them, and the glory for us,' Mary was telling herself that to secure the Bishop as their guest would go far towards restoring Richard's lost prestige. He would be reinstated as the leading person in the township; and the fact of his Lordship staying with them would bring people about the house again, who *might* turn to patients. At any rate Richard and he would be seen in the street together, and at concert or lecture it would naturally fall to Richard to take the chair.

Striking while the iron was hot, she offered her services to mend the altarcloth; to darn and 'get up' a surplice; to over-sew the frayed edges of a cassock. She would also see, she promised, what could be done to hide a hole in the carpet before the lectern, in which the Bishop might catch his foot. For this purpose they entered the church. It was pleasantly cool there, after the blazing heat out of doors; and having made her inspection Mary was glad to rest for a moment. The children felt very proud at being allowed inside the church when it wasn't Sunday; and Thistlethwaite actually let Cuffy mount the pulpit-steps and repeat: 'We are but little children weak,' so that he could see what it felt like to preach a sermon. Cuffy spoke up well, and remembered his words, and Mr Thistlethwaite said they'd see him in the cloth yet; but all the time he, Cuffy, wasn't *really* thinking what he was saying. For he spied a funny little cupboard under the ledge of the pulpit, and while he was doing his hymn he managed to finger it open, and inside he saw a glass and a water-jug and a medicine-bottle. And next Sunday he watched the water Mr Thistlethwaite drank before he preached, and saw he put medicine in it first. But when he asked Mamma if he was ill, and if not, why he took it, she got cross and said he was a very silly little boy, and he was to be sure and not say things like that before people.

There was still Richard to talk over on getting home. And he was in a bad temper at their prolonged absence. 'All this time in the township? What for? Buying your own eatables? What on *earth* will people think of you? – Not to speak of dragging the children after you like any nursemaid.'

'Oh, let me go my own way to work.'

To reconcile him to the Bishop's visit was a tough job. Gloomily he admitted that it might serve a utilitarian end. But the upset . . . to think of the upset! 'It means the sofa for me again. While old M., who's as strong as a horse, snores on my pillow. The sofa's like a board; I never sleep a wink on it; it sets every bone in my body aching.'

'But only for one night . . . or at most two. Surely you can endure a few aches for the good that may come of it? Oh, Richard, *don't* go about thinking what obstacles you can put in my way! I'm quite sure I can help you, if you'll give me a free hand.'

And she was right . . . as usual. The mere rumour that so important a visitor was expected – and she took care it circulated freely – brought a trickle of people back to the house. By the end of the week, Richard had treated four patients.

CHAPTER SIX

They were at breakfast when the summons came — breakfast, the hardest meal of any to get through without friction. Richard invariably ate at top speed and with his eyes glued to his plate; in order, he said, not to be obliged to see Zara's dusty crêpe and bombazine, the mere sight of which on these hot mornings took away his appetite. But he also hoped by example to incite Zara to haste: now she was there, the meals dragged out to twice their usual length. For Zara had a patent habit of masticating each mouthful so-and-so many times before swallowing; and the children forgot to eat, in counting their aunt's bites. With their ears cocked for the click at the finish. Mamma said it was her teeth that did it, and it was rude to listen. Aunt Zara called her teeth her *mashwar*. Why did she, and why did they click? But it was no good asking *her*. She never told you anything . . . except lessons.

Yes, Mary had got her way, and for a couple of weeks now, Zara had been installed as governess. As a teacher she had not her equal. She also made a very good impression in the township, looking so much the lady, speaking with such precision and all that. But — well, it was a good job nothing had been said to Richard of her exaggerated offer to wash dishes and scrub floors. How he would have crowed! Apart from this, she had landed them in a real quandary by arriving with every stick of furniture she possessed: her bed, her mahogany chest of drawers, a night-commode. In the tiny bedroom which was all they had to offer her, there was hardly room to stand; while still unpacked portmanteaux and gladstone-bags lined the passage, Zara having turned nasty at a hint of the outhouse. And directly lessons were over, she shut herself up among her things with a bottle of French polish.

Of course, poor soul, they were all that was left her of her own home: you couldn't wonder at her liking to keep them nice. And the main thing was, the children were making headway. Reward enough for her, Mary, to hear them gabbling their French of a morning, or learning their steps to Zara's: 'One, two, *chassez*, one!' Such considerations didn't weigh with Richard though. Just as of old, everything Zara said or did exasperated him. He was furious with her, too, for grumbling at the size of her room. — But there! It wasn't only Zara who grated on his nerves. It was everybody and everything.

On this particular day all her tact would be needed. For the message Maria had looked in during breakfast to deliver was a summons to Brown's Plains; and if there was one thing he disliked more than another, it was the bush journeys he was being called on to face anew. 'What! . . . *again*? Good God!' he looked up from his gobbling to ejaculate. Which expression made Zara pinch her lips and raise her eyebrows; besides being so bad for the children to hear. She, Mary, found his foot under the table and pressed it; but that irritated him, too, and he was nasty enough to say: 'What are you kicking me for?' Breakfast over, she sent Maria to the 'Sun' to bespeak a buggy; looked out his driving things, put likely requisites in his bag — as usual the people hadn't said what the matter was — and, her own work in the house done, changed her dress and tied on a shady hat. Now that Zara was there to mind the children, she frequently made a point of accompanying Richard on these drives.

The buggy came round: it was another of her innovations to have it brought right to the door; he had nothing to do but to step in. But at the gate they found Cuffy, who began teasing to be allowed to go, too. He had no one to play with; Lucie was asleep and Maria was busy, and Aunt Zara shut up in her room; and he was *so* tired of reading. Thus he pouted, putting on his special unhappy baby face; and as often as he did this it got at something in his mother, which made her weak towards her first-born. So she said, oh, very well then, if he wanted to so much, he might; and sent him in to wash his hands and fetch his hat. Richard, of course, let loose a fresh string of grumbles: it would be hot enough with just the pair of them, without having the child thrown in. But Mary, too, was cross and tired, and said she wasn't going to give way over every trifle; and so Cuffy, who had shrunk back at the sharp words, was hoisted up and off they set. — And soon the three of them, a tight fit in the high, two-wheeled, hooded vehicle, had left the township behind them, and were out on bush tracks where the buggy rocked and pitched like a ship on the broken waters of a rough sea.

Cuffy had never before been so far afield, and his spirits were irrepressible. He twisted this way and that, jerked his legs and bored with his elbows, flinging round to ask question after question. It fell to Mary to supply the answers; and she had scant patience with the curiosity of children, who hardly listened to what you told them in their eagerness to ask anew. But her 'I wonder!' 'How do *I* know?' and 'Don't bother me!' failed to damp Cuffy, who kept up his flow till he startled her by exclaiming with a vigorous sigh: 'Ugh! I *do* feel so hot and funny.' His small face was flushed and distressed.

'That's what comes of so much talking,' said Mary, and without more ado whisked off his sailor-hat, with its cribbing chin-elastic, undid his shoes, slid his feet out of his socks.

Thus much Cuffy permitted. But when it came to taking off his tunic, leaving him to sit exposed in his little vest, he fought her unbuttoning hands.

'*Don't*, Mamma – I won't!'

'But there's nobody to see! And it wouldn't matter if they did – you're only a little boy. No, you *would* come. Now you must do as I tell you.'

And when she knew quite well how he felt! Why, not even Lucie was allowed to see him undressed. Since they had slept in the same room she had always to go to bed first, and turn her face to the wall, and shut her eyes tight, while he flew out of his clothes and into his nightshirt. To have to sit in broad daynight with naked arms, and his neck, too, and his braces showing! All his pleasure in the drive was spoiled. At each turn in the road he was on thorns lest somebody should be there who'd see him. Oh, *why* must Mamma be like this? Why didn't she take her own clothes off? His belonged to him. (He *hated* Mamma.)

Nursing this small agony, he could think of nothing else. And now there was silence in the buggy, which lurched and jolted, Richard taking as good as no pains to avoid the foot-deep, cast-iron ruts, the lumpy rocks and stones. Over they went sideways, then up in the air and down again with a bump. 'Oh, gently, dear! *Do* be careful.' He wasn't the driver for this kind of thing. She never felt really safe with him. – And here there came to her mind a memory of the very first time they had driven together: on their wedding journey from Geelong to Ballarat.

How nervous she had been that day . . . how home-sick and lonely, too! . . . beside someone who was little more than a stranger to her, behind a strange horse on an unknown road, bound for a place of which she knew nothing. Ah well, it was perhaps a wise arrangement on the part of Providence that you *didn't* know what lay ahead . . . or you might never set out at all. Could *she* have foreseen all that marriage was to mean: how Richard would change and the dance he would lead her; all the nagging worry and the bitter suffering; then, yes then, poor young inexperienced thing that she was, full of romantic ideas, and expecting only happiness as her lot, she might have been excused for shrinking back in dismay. – Her chief objection nowadays to driving was the waste of time. To make up for having to sit there with her hands before her, she let her mind run free, and was deep in her usual reckonings – reducing grocer's and butcher's bills, making over her old dresses for the children – when a violent heave of the buggy all but threw her from her seat: she had just time to fling a protective arm round Cuffy, to save the child from pitching clean over the dashboard. Without warning, Richard had leant forward and dealt the horse a vicious cut on the neck. The beast, which had been ambling drearily, started, stumbled, and would have gone down, had he not tugged and sawed it by the mouth. For a few seconds they flew ahead, rocking and swaying, she holding to the child with one hand, to the rail with the other. – 'Do you want to break our necks?'

Mahony made no reply.

Gradually the rough canter ceased, and the horse fell back on its former jog-trot. It was a very poor specimen, old and lean; and the likelihood was, had been in harness most of the morning.

Again they crawled forward. The midday heat blazed; the red dust enveloped them, dimming their eyes, furring their tongues; there was not an inch of shade anywhere. Except under the close black hood, where they sat as if glued together.

Then came another savage lash from Richard, another leap on the part of the horse, more snatching at any hold she could find, the buggy toppling this way and that. Cuffy was frightened and clung to her dress, while she, outraged and alarmed, made indignant protest.

'Are you crazy?' If you do that again, I shall get out.'

For all answer Richard said savagely: 'Oh, hold your tongue, woman!' Before the child, too!

But her hurt and anger alike passed unheeded. Mahony saw nothing — nothing but the tremulous heat-lines, which caused the whole landscape to quiver and swim before him. His head ached to bursting: it might have had a band of iron round it, the screws in which were tightened, with an agonizing twist, at each lurch of the vehicle, at Cuffy's shrill pipe, Mary's loud, exasperated tones. Inside this circlet of pain his head felt swollen and top-heavy, an unnatural weight on his shoulders: the exact reverse of an unpleasant experience he had had the night before. Then, as he went to lay it on the pillow it had seemed to lose its solidity, and, grown light as a puff-ball, had gone clean through pillow, bolster, mattress, drawing his shoulders after it, down and down, head-foremost, till he felt as if he were dropping like a stone through space. With the bed-curtain fast in one hand, a bed-post in the other, he had managed to hold on while the vertigo lasted, his teeth clenched to hinder himself from crying out and alarming Mary. But the fear of a recurrence had kept him awake half the night, and today he felt very poorly, and disinclined for any exertion. He would certainly have jibbed at driving out all this distance, had it not been for Mary and her hectoring ways. He was unable to face the fuss and bother in which a refusal would involve him.

If only they could reach their destination! They seemed to have been on the road for hours. But — with the horse that had been fobbed off on him . . . old, spiritless, and stubborn as a mule. . . . And there he had to sit, hunched up, crushed in, with no room to stir . . . with hardly room to breathe. One of Mary's utterly mistaken ideas of kindness, to dog his steps as she did. To tack the child on, too. . . . Because *she* liked company. . . . But his needs had never been hers. Solitude . . . solitude was all he asked . . . to be left alone the greatest favour anyone could now do him. Seclusion had become as essential as air or water to the act of living. His brain refused its work were others present. Which reminded him, there was something he had been going to think over on this very drive: something vital, important. But though he ransacked his mind from end to end, it remained blank. Or mere disconnected thoughts and scraps of thought flitted across it, none of which led anywhere. Enraged at his powerlessness he let the horse taste the whip; but the relief the quickened speed afforded him was over almost as soon as begun, and once more they ambled at a funeral pace. Damnation take the brute! Was he, because of it, to sit for ever on this hard, narrow seat, chasing incoherencies round an empty brain? ... to drive for all eternity along these intolerable roads? ... through this accursed bush, where the very trees grimaced at you in distorted attitudes, like stage ranters declaiming an exaggerated passion – or pointed at you with the obscene gestures of the insane ... obscene, because so wholly without significance. – And again he snatched up the whip.

But the prolonged inaction was doing its work: a sense of unreality began to invade him, his surroundings to take on the blurred edges of a dream: one of those nightmare-dreams in which the dreamer knows that he is bound to reach a certain place in a given time, yet whose legs are weighed down by invisible weights ... or which feel as if they are being dragged through water, tons of impeding water ... or yet again the legs of elephantiasis ... swollen, monstrous, heavy as lead: all this, while time, the precious time that remains *before* the event, is flying. Yes, somewhere ... far away, out in the world ... life and time were rushing by: he could hear the rhythm of their passing in the beat of his blood. He alone lay stranded – incapable of movement. And, as always at the thought of his lost freedom madness seized him: dead to everything but his own need, he rose in his seat and began to rain down blows on the horse: to beat it mercilessly, hitting out wherever the lash found place – on head, neck, ears, the forelegs, the quivering undersides. In vain the wretched creature struggled to break free, to evade the cut of the thong: it backed, tried to rear, dragged itself from side to side, ducked its defenceless head, the white foam flying. But for it, too, strapped down, buckled in, there was no chance of escape. And the blows fell ... and fell.

'*Richard!* Oh, *don't!* – don't beat the poor thing like that! How can you? What are you doing?' For, cruellest of all, he was holding the animal in to belabour it, refusing to let it carry out its pitiful attempts to obey the lash. 'You who pretend to be so fond of animals.' There was no anger now in Mary's voice: only entreaty, and a deep compassion. – And in the mad race that followed, when they tore along, in and out of ruts, on the track and off, skimming trees and bushes, always on the edge of capsizing, blind with dust: now, frightened though she

was, she just set her teeth and held fast and said never a word
... though she saw it was all Richard could do to keep control:
his lean wrists spanned like iron.

Brought up at length alongside a rail-and-post fence, the
horse stood shaking and sweating, its red nostrils working like
bellows, the marks of the lash on its lathered hide. And Richard
was trembling too. His hand shook so that he could hardly
replace the whip in its socket.

With an unspoken 'Thank God!' Mary slid to the ground,
dragging Cuffy after her. Her legs felt as if they were made of
pulp.

'I think this must be the place . . . I think I see a house. . . .
No, no, you stop here. I'll go on and find out.' (Impossible for
him to face strangers in the state he was in.) 'Hush, Cuffy! It's
all right now.' Saying this she made to draw the child under a
bush; he was lying sobbing just as she had dropped him.

But Cuffy pushed her away. 'Leave me alone!' He only
wanted to stop where he was. And cry. He felt so *dread*fully
miserable. For the poor horse . . . it couldn't cry for itself . . . only
run and run – and it hadn't *done* anything . . . 'cept be very old
and tired . . . prayeth best who loveth best . . . oh! everything
was turned all black inside him. But for Papa, too, because . . .
he didn't know why . . . only . . . when Mamma had gone and
Papa thought nobody would see him, he went up to the horse's
neck and stroked it. And that made him cry more still.

But when he came and sat down by him and said 'Cuffy,'
and put out his arms, then he went straight into them, and Papa
held him tight, so that he could feel the hard sticking-out bone
that was his shoulder. And they just sat and never spoke a
word, till they heard Mamma coming back; and then Papa let
him go, and he jumped up and pretended to be looking at something on the ground.

Mary carried a dipper of water.

'Yes, this is it right enough. There's been an accident – the
son – they're afraid he's broken his leg. Oh, *why* can't people
send clearer messages! Can you rig up some splints? A man's
bringing a bucket for the horse. Come, let me dust you down.
No, I'll wait here . . . I'd rather.'

Richard went off bag in hand: she watched him displacing
and replacing slip-rails, walking stiffly over the rough ground.
Just before he vanished he turned and waved, and she waved
back. But this last duty performed, she sat heavily down, and

dropped her head in her hands. And there she sat, forgetful of where she was, of Cuffy, the heat, the return journey that had to be faced: just sat, limp and spent, thinking things from which she would once have shrunk in horror.

All the way home Cuffy carried in his pocket half one of the nicest sugar-biscuits the people had sent him out by Papa. It was a present for the horse. But when the moment came to give it, his courage failed. Everybody else had forgotten: the horse, too: it was in a great hurry to get back to its stable. He didn't like to be the only one to remember, to make it look as if he was still sorry. So, having feebly fingered the biscuit – the sugary top had melted and stuck to his pocket – he ate it up himself.

CHAPTER SEVEN

For some time after this, Cuffy fought shy of his father; and tried never, if he could help it, to be alone with him. It wasn't only embarrassment at having been nursed and petted like a baby. The events of the drive had left a kind of fear behind them: a fear not of his father, but for him: he was afraid of having to see what Papa was feeling. If he was with him, he didn't seem able not to. And he didn't *like* it. For he wanted so awf'ly much to be happy – in this house that he loved, with the verandah, and the garden, and the fowls, and the Lagoon – and when he saw Papa miserable, he couldn't be. So he gave the end of the verandah on which the surgery opened a wide berth; avoiding the dining-room, too . . . when it wasn't just meals. For there was no sofa in the surgery, and if Papa had a headache he sometimes went and lay down in the dining-room.

But he couldn't *always* manage it.

There was that day Mamma sent him in to fetch her scissors, and Papa was on the sofa with the blind down and his eyes shut, and his feet sticking over the end. Cuffy walked on the tips of his toes. But just when he thought he was safe, Papa was watching him. And put his hand out and said: 'Come here to me, Cuffy. There's something I wish to say to you.'

The words struck chill. With resistance in every limb, Cuffy obeyed.

'Pull up the hassock; sit down.' And there he was, alone in the dark with Papa, his heart going pit-a-pat.

Papa took his hand. And held on to it. 'You're getting a big boy now; you'll soon be seven years old . . . when I was not much older than that, my dear, I was being thrashed because I could not turn French phrases into Latin.'

'What's Latin?' (Oh, perhaps after all it was just going to be about when Papa was little.)

'Latin is one of the dead languages.'

'How can it ... be dead? It isn't a ... a man.'

'Things perish, too, child. A language dies when it is no longer in common use; when it ceases to be a means of communication between living people.'

This was too much for Cuffy. He struggled with the idea for a moment, then gave it up, and asked: 'Why did you have to? And why did your Mamma let you be thrashed?' (Lots and lots of questions. Papa always told.)

'Convention demanded it ... convention and tradition ... the slavish tradition of a country that has always rated the dead lion higher than the live dog. And thralls to this notion were those in whose hands at that time lay the training of the young. The torturing rather! A lifetime lies between, but I can still feel something of the misery, the hopelessness, the inability to understand what was required of you, the dread of what awaited you was your task ill done or left undone. A forlorn and frightened child ... with no one to turn to, for help or advice. That most sensitive, most delicate of instruments – the mind of a little child! Small wonder that I vowed to myself, if ever I had children of my own ... to let the young brain lie fallow ... not so much as the alphabet ... the A B C ...' Thus, forgetful of his little hearer, Mahony rambled on. And Cuffy, listening to a lot more of such talk (nasty talk!), kept still as a broody hen, not shuffling his feet, or sniffling, or doing anything to interrupt, for fear of what might come next.

Then Papa stopped and was so quiet he thought he'd gone to sleep again. He hoped so. He'd stay there till he was *quite* sure. But through his trying too hard not to make a noise, a button squeaked, and Papa opened his eyes.

'But ... this wasn't what I brought you here to say.' He looked fondly at the child and stroked his rough, little-boy hand. 'Listen, Cuffy. Papa hasn't felt at all well lately, and is sometimes very troubled ... about many things. And he wants you, my dear, to promise him that if anything should ... I mean if I should' – he paused, seeking a euphemism – 'if I should have to leave you, leave you all, then I want you to promise me that you will look after Mamma for me, take care of her in my place, and be a help to her in every way you can. Will you?'

Cuffy nodded: his throat felt much too tight to speak. Dropping his head he watched his toe draw something on the carpet.

To hear Papa say things like this made him feel like he did when he had to take his clothes off.

'Your little sister too, of course, but Mamma most of all. She has had so much to bear ... so much care and trouble. And I fear there's more to come. Be good to her, Cuffy! – And one other thing. Whatever happens, my little son ... and who knows what life may have in store for you ... I want you never to forget that you are a gentleman – a gentleman first and foremost – no matter what you do or where you go, or who your companions may be. *Noblesse oblige.* With that for your motto you cannot go far wrong.'

'What a lot of little hairs you've got on your hand, Papa!'

Cuffy blurted this out, hardly knowing what he said. Nobody ... not even Papa ... had the right to speak such things to him. They *hurt*.

Free at last he ran to the garden, where he fell to playing his wildest, merriest games. And Mahony, lying listening to the childish rout, thought sadly to himself: 'No use ... too young.'

That Papa might be going away stayed Cuffy's secret: he didn't even tell Lucie. Or at least not till she got a secret, too. He saw at once there was something up; and it didn't take him half a jiffy to worm it out of her. They sat on the other side of the fowl-house; but she whispered, all the same. 'I fink Mamma's going away.'

Cuffy, leaning over her with his arm round her neck, jerked upright, eyes and mouth wide open. *What?* ... Mamma, too? Oh, but that couldn't be true ... it couldn't! He laughed out loud, and was very stout and bold in denial because of the fright it gave him. 'Besides, if she did, she'd take us with her.'

But his little sister shook her head. 'I heard her tell Papa yesterday, one of vese days she'd just pack her boxes an' walk outer the house an' leave bof him an' the child'en. An' then he could see how he liked it.' And the chubby face wrinkled piteously.

'Hush, Luce! they will hear you – don't cry, there's a good girl. I'll look after *you* ... always! An' when I'm a big man I'll ... I'll marry you. So there! Won't that be nice?'

But Cuffy's world tottered. Papa's going would be bad enough ... though ... yes ... *he'd* take care of Mamma so well that she'd never be worried again. But that *she* should think of leaving them was not to be borne. Life without Mamma! The nearest he could get to it was when he had once had to stop alone at a big railway station to mind the luggage, while Mamma and Luce went to buy the tickets. It had taken so long, and there were so many people, and he was so sure the train would go without them . . . or else they might forget him, forget to come back . . . or get into a wrong train and he be left there . . . standing there for always. His heart had thumped and thumped . . . and he watched for them till his eyes got so big they almost fell out . . . and the porters were running and shouting . . . and the doors banging . . . oh dear, oh dear!

He knew what the row had been about – a picture Cousin Emmy had painted quite by herself, and sent as a present to Mamma. Mamma thought it was a lovely picture, and so did he: all sea and rocks, with little men in red caps sitting on them. But Papa said it was a horrible dorb, and he wouldn't have it in *his* house. And Mamma said that was only because it was made by a relation of hers, and if it had been one of his, he would have liked it; and it was an oil painting, and oil paintings were ever so hard to do; and when she thought of the time it must have taken Emmy, and the work she had put into it . . . besides, she'd always believed he was fond of the girl. And Papa said, Good God, so he was, but what had that to do with 'heart'? And Mamma said, well he might talk himself hoarse, but she meant to hang the picture in the drawing-room, and Papa said he forbade it . . . and then he'd run away so as not to hear any more, but Luce didn't, and it was then she heard.

He hated Aunt Zara. Aunt Zara said, with them quarrelling as they did, the house wasn't fit to live in. He went hot all over when she said this. And that night he got a big pin and stuck it in her bed with the point up, so it would run into her when she lay down. And it must have; because she showed it to Mamma next day and was *simply furious*. And he had to say yes he'd done it, and on purpose. But he wouldn't say he was sorry, because he wasn't; and he stopped naughty, and never did say it at all.

For then the Bishop came to stay, and everyone was nice and smiley again.

The Bishop was the same genial, courtly gentleman as of old. Tactfulness itself, too: in the three days he was with them never, by word or by look, did he show himself aware of their changed circumstances. He admired house and garden, complimented Mary on her cooking, and made much of the children. Especially Lucie. 'I shall steal this little maid before I'm finished, Mrs Mahony. Pop her in my pocket and take her home as a present to my wife!' And the chicks were on their best behaviour – they had had it well dinned into them beforehand not to comment on the Bishop's attire. But even if it had been left to his own discretion, Cuffy would in this case have held his tongue. For, truth to tell, he thought the Bishop's costume just a *little rude*. To wear your legs as if you were still a little boy, and then . . . to have something hanging down in front. Mamma said it was an apron and all Bishops did – even a 'sufferin'' Bishop like this one. But surely . . . surely . . . if you were a grown-up gentleman . . .

Zara, too, did her share. At table, what with looking after Maria and the dishes, keeping one eye on the children, the other on the Bishop's plate, Mary's own attention was fully occupied. Richard sat for the most part in the silence that was now his normal state; he was, besides, so out of things that he had little left to talk about. Hence it fell to Zara, who was a fluent conversationalist and very well read, to keep the ball rolling. The Bishop and she got on splendidly (Zara had by now, of course, returned to the true fold). Afterwards, he was loud in her praises. 'A very charming woman, your sister, Mrs Mahony . . . very charming, indeed!' And falling, manlike, under the spell of the widow's cap, he added: 'How bravely she bears up, too. So sad, so *very* sad for her losing her dear husband as she did. Still! . . . God's ways are not our ways. His Will, not ours, be done!'

At which Mary winced. For he had used the self-same words about their own great grief, had worn the same sympathetic face, dispensed a like warm pressure of the hand. And this rankled. It was true she did not parade her loss in yards of crêpe. But that anyone who troubled to think could compare the two cases! A little child, cut prematurely off, and Hempel, poor old Hempel, Zara's *pis aller*, who had had one foot in the grave when she married him, whom she had badgered and bullied to the end. But these pious phrases evidently formed the Bishop's stock-in-trade, which he dealt out indiscriminately to whoever suffered loss or calamity. And now her mind jumped back to the afternoon of his arrival, when after tea Richard and he had withdrawn to the surgery. 'A most delightful chat,' he subsequently described the hour spent in there; though she, listening at the door, knew that Richard had hardly opened his mouth. At the time, she had thought it most kind of the Bishop so to make the best of it. Now, however . . .

And when, later on, he returned from a visit to church and parsonage, and still professed himself well content, she began to see him with other eyes. It was not so much tact and civility on his part, as a set determination not to scratch below the surface. He didn't want to spoil his own comfort by being forced to see things as they really were.

Of course this turn of mind made him the pleasantest of guests. (Fancy, though, having to live perpetually in such a simmer of satisfaction!) And even here his wilful blindness had its drawbacks. Had he been different, the kind of man to say: 'Your husband is not looking very well,' or: 'Does Dr Mahony find the climate here try him?' or otherwise have given her an opening, she might have plucked up courage to confide in him, to unburden herself of some of her worries – oh! the relief it would have been to speak freely to a person of their own class. As it was, he no doubt firmly refused to let himself become aware of the slightest change for the worse in Richard.

Well, at least her main object was achieved: if wanted, the Bishop had to be sought and found at 'Doctor's'. She also so contrived it that Richard and he were daily seen hobnobbing in public. Each morning she started them off together for the township: the short, thickset, animated figure, the tall, lean, bent one.

And now the crown was to be set on her labours by a public entertainment. First, a concert of local talent; after which his Lordship had promised to give them a short address.

But at the very last minute, if Richard didn't threaten to undo all her work! For, if he did not take the chair at this meeting, she would have laboured in vain. Just to think of seeing that fool Thistlethwaite in his place! Or old Cameron, who as likely as not would be half-seas over.

But Richard was as obstinate as a mule. 'I *can't*, Mary,' . . . very peevishly . . . 'and what's more, I won't! To be stuck up there for all those yokels to gape at. For God's sake, let me alone!'

She could cheerfully have boxed his ears. But she kept her temper. 'All you've got to do, dear, is to sit there . . . at most to say half-a-dozen words to introduce his Lordship. You, who're such a dab hand at that sort of thing!' – Until, by alternate wheedling and bullying, she had him worn down.

But when the evening came she almost doubted her own wisdom. By then he had worked himself up into a sheerly ridiculous state of agitation: you might have thought he had to appear before the Queen. His coat was too shabby, his collar was frayed; he couldn't tie his cravat or get his studs in – she had everything to do for him. She heard him, too, when he thought no one was listening, feverishly rehearsing the reading which the Bishop, at a hint from her, had duly persuaded him into giving. No, she was much feared Richard's day for this kind of thing was over.

The hall at the 'Sun' was packed. From a long way round, from Brown's Plains and the Springs, farmers and vinegrowers had driven in with their families: the street in front of the hotel was blocked with buggies, with wagonettes, spring-carts, shandrydans and drays. And the first part of the evening went off capitally. There was quite a fund of musical talent in the place: the native-born sons and daughters of tradesmen and publicans had many of them clear, sweet voices, and sang with ease. It was not till the turn came of the draperess, Miss Mundy, that the trouble began – they hadn't ventured to leave her out, for she was one of the main props of the church and head teacher in the Sunday School. But she had no more voice than a peahen; and what there was of it was not in tune. Then, though elderly and very scraggy, she had dressed herself up to the nines. She sang *Comin' Thro' the Rye* with what she meant to be a Scotch accent . . . said jin for gin, boody for buddy . . . and smirked and sidled like a nancified young girl. To the huge delight of the audience, who had her out again and again, shouting 'Brave-o!' and 'Enkor!'

And the poor silly old thing drank it all in, bowed with her hand on her heart, kissed the tips of her gloves – especially in the direction of the Bishop – then fluttered the pages with her lavender kids and prepared to repeat the song. This was too much for Richard, who was as sensitive to seeing another person made a butt of, as to being himself held up to ridicule. From his seat in the front row he hissed, so loudly that everybody sitting round could hear: 'Go back, you fool, go back! Can't you see they're laughing at you?'

It was done out of sheer tenderheartedness, but . . . For one thing the Bishop had entered into the fun and applauded with the rest; so it was a sort of snub for him, too. As for Miss Mundy, though she shut her music-book and retired into the wings, she glared at Richard as if she could have eaten him; while the audience, defrauded of its amusement, turned nasty, and started to boo and groan. There was an awkward pause before the next item on the programme could be got going. And when Richard's own turn came – he was reading selections from *Out of the Hurly-Burly* – people weren't very well disposed towards him. Which he needed. For he was shockingly nervous; you could see the book shaking in his hands. Then, too, the light was poor, and though he rubbed and polished at his spectacles and held the pages up this way and that, he couldn't see properly, and kept reading the wrong words and having to correct himself, or go h'm . . . h'm while he tried to decipher what came next. And through his stumbling so, the jokes didn't carry. Nobody laughed; even though he had picked out those excruciatingly funny bits about the patent combination step-ladder and table, that performed high jinks of itself in the attic at night; and the young man who stuck to the verandah steps when he went a-courting: things that usually made people hold their sides.

If only he would just say he couldn't see, and apologize and leave off . . . or at least cut it short. But he was too proud for that; besides, he wouldn't think it fair, to fail in his share of the entertainment. And so he laboured on, stuttering and stumbling, and succeeding only in making a donkey of himself. Suppressed giggles were audible behind Mary; yes, people were laughing now, but not at the funny stories. Of course at the finish, the audience didn't dare not to clap; for the Bishop led the way; but the next minute everybody broke out into a hullabaloo of laughing and talking; in face of which the Bishop's 'Most humorous! Quite a treat!' sounded very thin.

The exertion had worn Richard out: you could see the perspiration trickling down his face. The result was, having immediately to get on his feet again to introduce the Bishop, he clean forgot what he had been going to say. Nothing came. There was another most embarrassing pause, in which her own throat went hot and dry, while he stood clearing his and looking helplessly round. But, once found, his words came with a rush – too much of a rush: they tumbled over one another and got all mixed up: he contradicted himself, couldn't find an end to his sentences, said tomorrow when he meant today, and *vice versa*; which made sad nonsense. The Bishop sat and picked his nose, or rather pinched the outside edge of one nostril between thumb and middle finger, looking, as far as a man of his nature could, decidedly uncomfortable. Behind her, a rude voice muttered something about somebody having had 'one too many'.

And things went from bad to worse; for Richard continued to ramble on, long after the Bishop should have been speaking. There was no one at hand to nudge him, or frown a hint. His subject had of course something to do with it. For the Bishop had elected to speak on 'Our glorious country: Australia', and that was too much for Richard. How could he sing a *Te Deum* to a land he so hated? The very effort to be fair made him unnecessarily wordy, for his real feelings kept cropping up and showing through. And then, unluckily, just when one thought he had finished, the words 'glorious country' seized on his imagination; and now the fat was in the fire with a vengeance. For he went on to say that any country here, wonderful though it might be, was but the land of our temporary adoption; the true 'glorious country' was the one for which we were bound hereafter: 'That land of which our honoured guest is one of the keepers of the keys.' Until recently this Paradise had been regarded as immeasurably distant . . . beyond earthly contact. Now the barriers were breaking down. – 'If you will bear with me a little, friends, I will tell you something of my own experiences, and of the proofs – the irrefragable proofs – which I myself have received, that those dear ones who have passed from mortal sight still live, and love us, and take an interest in our doings.' – And here if he didn't give them . . . didn't come out in front of all these scoffing people, with that foolish, ludicrous story of the doll . . . Lallie's doll! Mary wished the floor would open and swallow her.

The giggling and tittering grew in volume. ('Sit down, Richard, oh, sit down!' she willed him. '*Can't* you see they're laughing at you?') People could really hardly be blamed for thinking he had had a glass too much; he standing there staring, with visionary eyes, at the back of the hall. But by now he had worked himself into such a state of exultation that he saw nothing . . . not even the Bishop's face, which was a study, his Lordship belonging to those who held spiritualism to be of the devil.

'Where's dolly?' 'Want me mammy!' 'Show us a nose!' began

to be heard on all sides. The audience was getting out of hand. The Bishop could bear it no longer: rising from his seat he tapped Richard sharply on the arm. Richard gave a kind of gasp, put his hand to his forehead, and breaking off in the middle of a sentence sat heavily down.

Straightway the Bishop plunged into his prepared discourse; and in less than no time had his audience breathlessly engrossed, in the splendid tale of Australia's progress.

CHAPTER EIGHT

Wept Mary, his Lordship's visit having ended in strain and coolness: 'How could you! . . . how *could* you? Knowing what he thinks – and him a guest in the house! And then to hold our poor little darling up to derision – for them to laugh and mock at – oh! it was cruel of you . . . cruel. I shall never forget it.'

'Pray would you have me refuse, when the opportunity offers, to bear witness to the faith that is in me? Who am I to shrink from gibes and sneers? Where would Christianity itself be today, had its early followers not braved scorn and contumely?'

'But *we're* not early Christians! We're just ordinary people. And I think it's perfectly dreadful to hear you make such comparisons. Talk about blasphemy . . .'

'It's always the same. Try to tell a man that he has a chance of immortality . . . that he is not to be snuffed out at death like a candle . . . and all that is brutal and ribald in him comes to the surface.'

'Leave it to the churches! . . . it's the churches' business. You only succeed in making an utter fool of yourself.'

Immortality . . . and a doll's nose! Oh, to see a man of Richard's intelligence sunk so low! For fear of what she might say next, Mary flung out of the room, leaving him still haranguing, and put the length of the passage between them. At the verandah door she stood staring with smouldering eyes into the garden. Telling herself that, one day, it would not be the room only she quitted, but the house as well. She saw a picture of herself, marching with defiant head down the path and out of the gate, a child on either hand. (Oh! the children went, too: she'd take good care of that.) Richard should be left to the tender mercies of Zara: Zara who, at first sound of a raised voice, vanished behind a locked door. That might bring him to his senses. For things could not go on as they were. Never a plan did she lay for his benefit but he somehow crossed and frustrated it. And as a result of her last effort, they were actually in a worse position than before. Not only was the practice as dead as a doornail again, but a new load of contempt rested on Richard's shoulders.

The first hint that something more than his spiritistic rantings might be at work, in frightening people off, came from Maria. It was a couple of weeks later. Mary was in the kitchen making pastry, dabbing blobs of lard over a rolled-out sheet of paste, and tossing and twisting with a practised hand, when Maria, who stood slicing apples, having cast more than one furtive glance at her mistress, volunteered the remark: 'Mrs Mahony, you know that feller with the broke leg? Well, they do say his Pa's bin and fetched another doctor, orl the way from Oakworth.'

'What boy? Young Nankivell? Nonsense! He's out of splints by now.'

'Mike Murphy told the grocer so.'

'Now, Maria, you know I won't listen to gossip. Make haste with the fruit for this pie.'

But it was not so easy to get the girl's words out of her head. Could there possibly be any truth in them? And if so, did Richard know? He wouldn't say a word to her, of course, unless his hand was forced.

At dinner she eyed him closely; but could detect no sign of a fresh discomfiture.

That afternoon, though, as she sat stitching at warm clothing – with the end of March the rains had set in, bringing cooler weather – as she sat, there came a knock at the front door, and Maria admitted what really seemed to be a patient again at last, a man asking imperiously for the doctor. He was shown into the surgery, and even above the whirring of her sewing-machine Mary could hear his voice – and Richard's, too – raised as if in dispute, and growing more and more heated. She went into the passage and listened, holding her breath. Then – oh! what was that? . . . who? . . . *what?* . . . *a horse-whipping?* Without hesitation she turned the knob of the surgery door and walked in.

'What is it? What's the matter?' With fearful eyes she looked from one to the other. In very fact the stranger, a great red-faced, burly fellow, held a riding-whip stretched between his hands.

And Richard was cowering in his chair, his grey head sunk

between his shoulders. Richard . . . *cowering?* In an instant she was beside him, her arm about his neck. 'Don't mind him! . . . don't take any notice of what he says.'

Roughly Mahony shook himself free. 'Go away . . . go out of the room, Mary. This is none of your business.'

'And have him speak to you like that? I'll do nothing of the sort. Why don't you turn him out?' And as Richard did not answer, and her blood was up, she rounded on the man with: 'How dare you come here and insult the doctor in his own house? You great bully, you!'

'*Mary!* – for God's sake! . . . don't make more trouble for me than I've got already.'

'Now, now, madam, I'll trouble you to have a care what you're saying!' – and the network of veins on the speaker's cheeks ran together in a purplish patch. 'None of your lip for me, if you please! As for insults, me good lady, you'll have something more to hear about the rights o' that. You've got a boy of your own, haven't you? What would you say, I'd like to know, if a bloody fraud calling himself a doctor had been and made a cripple of him for life?'

(*That* hit. Cuffy? . . . a cripple? Oh, Richard, Richard, what *have* you done?)

'As fine a young chap as ever you see, tall and upstanding. And now 'tis said he'll never walk straight again, but'll have to hobble on crutches, with one leg four inches shorter than the other, for the rest of his days. – But I'll settle you! I'll cork your chances for you! I'll put a stop to your going round maiming other people's children. I'll have the lor on you, that's what I'll do. I'll take it into court, by Jesus I will!'

'You'll ruin me.'

'I'll never stop till I have . . . so help me, God! . . . as you've ruined me boy. You won't get the chance to butcher no one else – you damned, drunken old swine, you!'

Richard sat motionless, head in hand, and the two fingers that supported his temple, and the skin on which they lay, looked as though drained of every drop of blood. But he said not a word – let even the last infamous accusation pass unchallenged. Not so Mary. With eyes so fierce that the man involuntarily recoiled before them, she advanced upon him. 'How dare you? . . . how *dare* you say a thing like that to my husband? You! . . . with a face which shows everybody what your habits are . . . to slander someone who's never in his life been the worse for drink? Go away . . . we've had enough of you . . . go away, I say!' – and throwing open the door she drove him before her. – But on the garden path he turned and shook his fist at the house.

Richard had not stirred; nor did he look up at her entry. And to her flood of passionate and bewildered questions, he responded only by a toneless: 'It's no use, Mary; what he says may be true. A case of malunion. Such things do happen. And surgery has never been one of my strong points.' Try as she would, there was nothing more to be got out of him.

In despair she left him, and went to the bedroom. Her brain was spinning like a Catherine wheel. Yet something must be done. They could not – oh, they *could* not! – sit meekly there, waiting for this new and awful blow to fall. She must go out, track the man, follow him up; and snatching her bonnet from the drawer she tied it on – it had a red rose on a stalk, which nodded at her from the mirror. She would go on her knees to him not to take proceedings. He had a wife. *She* might understand . . . being a woman, be merciful. But . . . Cuffy . . . a cripple . . . would *she* have had mercy? What would *her* feelings have been, had she had to see her own child go halt and lame? No, Richard was right, it was no good: there was nothing to be done. And tearing off her wraps she threw herself face downwards on the bed, and wept bitterly.

She did not hear the door open, or see the small face that peered in. And a single glimpse of the dark mass that was his mother, lying shaking and sobbing, was enough for Cuffy: he turned and fled. Frightened by the angry voices, the children had sought their usual refuge up by the henhouse. But it got night, and nobody came to call them or look for them, and nobody lit the lamps; and when they did come home the table wasn't spread for supper. Cuffy set to hunting for Mamma. But after his discovery his one desire was not to see anything else. In the dark drawing-room, he hid behind an armchair. Oh, *what* was the matter now? What *had* they done to her? It could only be Papa that hurt her so. *Why* did he have to do it? Why couldn't he be nice to her? Oh, if only Papa – yes, if . . . if only Papa *would* go away, as he said, and leave them and Mamma together! Oh, pray God, let Papa go away! . . . and never, never come back.

But that night – after a sheerly destructive evening, in which Mary had never ceased to plead with, to throw herself on the mercy of, an invisible opponent: I give you my word for it, he wasn't himself that day . . . what with the awful heat . . . and the length of the drive . . . and the horse wouldn't go . . . he was so upset over it. And then the loss of our little girl . . . that was a blow he has never properly got over. For he's not a young man any more. He's not what he was . . . *anyone* will tell you that! But they'll tell you, too, that he has never, never neglected a patient because of it. He's the most conscientious of men . . . has always worked to the last ounce of his strength, put himself and the state of his own health last of all . . . I have known him tramp off of a morning when anybody with half an eye could see that he ought to be in bed. And so kindhearted! If a patient is poor, or has fallen on evil days, he will always treat him free of charge. Oh, surely people would need to have hearts of stone, to stand out against pleas such as these? – Or she lived through, to the last detail, the horrors of a lawsuit: other doctors giving evidence against Richard, hundreds of pounds having to be paid as damages, the final crash to ruin of his career. And when it came to the heritage of shame and disgrace that he would thus hand on to his children, her heart turned cold as ice against him. But that night every warring feeling merged and melted in a burning compassion for the old, unhappy man who lay at her side; lay alarmingly still, staring with glassy eyes at the moonlit window. Feeling for his hand she pressed it to her cheek. 'Don't break your heart over it, my darling. Trust me, I'll win him round . . . *somehow!* And then we'll go away – far away from here – and start all over again. No one need ever know.'

But she could not get at him, could not rouse him from the torpor in which this last, unmerited misfortune had sunk him. And there they lay, side by side, hand in hand, but far as the poles apart.

The court, airless and fetid, was crowded to the last place. With difficulty he squeezed into a seat on a hard, backless bench . . . though he was too old and stiff nowadays to sit for long without a support. The judge – why, what was this? He knew that face . . . had surely met him somewhere? . . . had dined with him perhaps, or tilted a table in his company – the judge held a large gold toothpick in his hand, and in the course of the proceedings must have picked in turn every tooth he had in his head. Foul teeth . . . a foul breath . . . out of such a mouth should judgement come? He felt in his pocket to see if, in a species of prevision, he had brought his forceps with him; and sharply withdrew his hand from a mess of melting jujubes. (The children of course . . . oh, devil take those children! They were always in his way.) Believing himself unseen, he stealthily deposited the sticky conglomerate on the floor. But his neighbour, a brawny digger, with sleeves rolled high above the elbow and arms behaired like an ape's, espied him, and made as if to call the attention of the usher to his misdeed. To escape detection he rose and moved hurriedly to the other side of the court; where, oddly enough, there seemed after all to be plenty of room.

Here he was seated to much better advantage; and pulling himself together, prepared to follow the case. But . . . again he was baffled. Plaintiff's counsel was on his feet; and once more the striking likeness of the fellow to somebody he had known distracted him. Hang it all! It began to look as if everyone present was more or less familiar to him. Secretly he ran his eye over the assembly, and found that it was so . . . though he could not have put a name to a single manjack of them. However, since nobody seemed to recognize him, he cowered down and trusted to pass unobserved. But, from now on, he was aware of a sense of mystery and foreboding; the court and its occupants took on a sinister aspect. And even as he felt this, he heard two rascally-looking men behind him muttering together. 'Are you all right?' said one. To which the other made half-audible reply: 'We are, if that bloody fool, our client – ' Ha! there was shady work in hand; trouble brewing for somebody. But what was *he* doing here? What had brought him to such a place?

Wild to solve the riddle, he made another desperate attempt to fix his thoughts. But these haunting resemblances had unnerved him; he could do nothing but worry the question where he had met plaintiff's counsel. The name hung on the very tip of his tongue; yet would not out. A common, shoddy little man, prematurely bald, with a protruding paunch and a specious eye – he wouldn't have trusted a fellow with an eye like that farther than he could see him. Most improperly dressed, too; wearing neither wig nor gown, but a suit of a loud, horsey check, the squares of which could have been counted from across a road.

This get-up it was, which first made it plain to him that the case under trial had some secret connection with himself. Somehow or other he was involved. But each time, just as he thought he was nearing a clue, down would come a kind of fog and blot everything out.

Through it, he heard what sounded like a scuffle going on. It seemed that the plaintiff was drunk, not in a fit state to give evidence . . . though surely that was his voice protesting vehemently that he had never been the worse for drink in his life? The two cut-throats in the back seat muttered anew; others joined in; and soon the noise from these innumerable throats had risen to an ominous roar. He found himself shouting with the rest; though only later did he grasp what it was all about: they were calling for the defendant to enter the witness-box. Well, so much the better! Now at last, he would discover the hidden meaning.

The defendant proved to be an oldish man, with straggly grey hair and whiskers, and a round back: he clambered up the steps to the witness-box, which stood high, like a pulpit, with a palpable effort. This bent back was all that could be seen of him at first, and a very humble back it looked, threadbare and shiny, though brushed meticulously free of dust and dandruff. Surely to goodness, though, he needn't have worn his oldest suit, the one with the frayed cuffs? . . . his second-best would have been more the thing . . . even though the coat did sag at the shoulders. Edging forward in his seat he craned his neck; then half rose, in his determination to see the fellow's face – and, having caught a single glimpse of it, all but lost his balance and fell, with difficulty restraining a shriek that would have pealed like the whistle of a railway-engine through the court, and have given him away . . . beyond repair. For it was himsef he saw, himself who stood there perched aloft before every eye, holding fast, with veined and wrinkled hands, to the ledge of the dock: himself who now suddenly turned and looked full at him, singling him out from all the rest. His flesh crawled, his hairs separated, while something cold and rapid as a ball of quicksilver ran from top to bottom of his spine. – Two of him? God in heaven! But this was madness. *Two* of him? The thing was an infamy . . . devilish . . . not to be borne. *Which was he?*

And yet, coeval with the horror of it, ran an obscene curiosity. So *this* was what he looked like! *This* was how he presented himself to his fellow-men. Smothering his first wild fear, he took in, coldly and cruelly, every detail of the perched-up figure, whose poverty-stricken yet sorrily dandified appearance had been the signal for a burst of ribald mirth. He could hear himself laughing at the top of his lungs; especially when, after a painful effort to read a written slip that had been handed to him, his double produced a pair of horn-rimmed spectacles, and shakily balanced them on the tip of his long thin nose. Ha, ha! This was good . . . was very good. Ha, ha! A regular owl! . . . exactly like an old owl. A zany. A figure of fun.

Then, abruptly, his laughter died in his throat. For hark! . . . what was this? . . . what the . . .! God above! he was pleading now – *pleading?* nay, grovelling! – begging abjectly for mercy. He whined: 'Me Lud, if the case goes against me I'm a ruined man. And he has got his knife in me, me Lud! . . . he's made up his mind to ruin me. A hard man . . . a cruel man! . . . if ever there was one. Oh, spare me, me Lud! . . . have pity on my poor wife and my two little children!' The blood surged to his head, and roared in neck and temples till he thought they would burst. *Never!* . . . no, never in all his days had he sought either pity or mercy. And never, no matter what his plight, would he sink so low. The despicable sniveller! The unmanly craven! . . . he disowned him – loathed him – spat at him in spirit: his whole being swam in hatred. But even as, pale with fury, he joined in the hyena-like howl against clemency that was raised, a small voice whispered in his ear that his time was running short. He must get out of this place . . . must escape . . . save himself . . . from the wrath to come. Be up and away, head high, leaving his ghost to wring its hands . . . and wail . . . and implore. Long since he had lifted his hat to his face, where he held it as if murmuring a prayer. But it was no longer the broad-brimmed wideawake he had brought with him into court; it had turned into a tall beaver belltopper, of a mode at least twenty years old, and too narrow to conceal his face. He tossed it from him as, frantic with the one desire, he pushed and struggled to get out, treading on people's feet, crushing past their knees – oh! was there no end of their number, or to the rows of seats through which he had to fight his way? . . . his legs growing heavier and heavier, more incapable of motion. And then . . . just when he thought he was safe . . . he heard his own name spoken: heard it said aloud, not once but many times, and, damnation take it; by none other than old Muir the laryngologist, that pitiful old fossil, that infernal old busybody, dead long since, who it seemed had been in court throughout the proceedings and now recognized him, and stood pointing at him. Again a shout rose in unison, but this time it was his name they called, and therewith they were up and on his heels, and the hue and cry had begun in earnest. He fled down Little Bourke Street, and round and up Little Collins Street, running like a hare, but with steadily failing strength, drawing sobbing breaths that hurt like blows; but holding his left hand fast to his breast-pocket, where he had the knife concealed. His ears rang with that most terrifying of mortal sounds: the wolf-like howl of a mob that chases human game and sees its prey escaping it. For he *was* escaping; he would have got clean away if, of a sudden, Mary and the children had not stood before him. In a row . . . a third child, too. He out with his knife . . . *now* he knew what it was for! But a shrill scream stayed his hand . . . who screamed? who screamed? . . . and with such stridency. Mary . . . it could *only* be Mary who would so deliberately foul his chances. For this one second's delay was his undoing. Someone dashed up behind and got him by the shoulder, and was bearing him down, and shaking, shaking, shaking . . . while a fierce voice shrieked in his ear: 'Richard . . . oh, *Richard*, do wake up! You'll terrify the children. Oh, what dreadful dream have you been having?'

And it was broad daylight, the mill-whistle in full blast, and he sitting up in bed shouting, and drenched in sweat. The night was over, a new day begun, in which had to be faced, not the lurid phantasmagoria of a dream-world that faded at a touch, but the stern, bare horrors of reality, from which there was no awakening.

CHAPTER NINE

The facts of the case, brought to light by vigorous action on Mary's part, were these. The boy had been removed to the Oakworth hospital, where he was to be examined. Only when this was done could the surgeon in charge say whether there was any possibility of correcting the malunion, by re-breaking and re-setting the limb; or whether the patient would have to remain in his present degree of shortness. He hoped to let them know in about three days' time. It might, of course, be less.

'There's nothing for it; we must have patience,' said Mary grimly and with determination, as she re-folded the telegram and laid it back on the table.

Patience? Yes, yes; that went without saying; and Mahony continued to feign busyness with pencil and paper till the door had shut behind her.

Alone, he fell limply back in his chair. So this was it . . . this was what it had come to! His fate had passed out of his own keeping. Another – a man his junior by several years – would sit in judgement on him, decide whether or no he was competent to continue practising the profession to which he had given up the best years of his life. In the course of the next three days. – Three days. What *were* three days? . . . in a lifetime of fifty years. A flea-bite; a single tick of time's clock. An infinitesimal fragment chipped off time's plenty, and for the most part squandered unthinkingly. In the ecstasy of happiness – or to the prisoner condemned to mount the scaffold – a breath, a flash of light, gone even as it came. – *Three days!* To one on the rack to learn whether or no he was to be found guilty of professional negligence, with its concomitants of a court of law, publicity, disgrace; to such a one, three days were as unthinkable as infinity: a chain of hours of torture, each a lifetime in itself.

For long he sat motionless, wooden as the furniture around him; sat and stared at the whitewashed walls till he felt that, if he did not get out from between them, they might end by closing in on him and crushing him. Pushing back his chair he rose and left the house, heading in the direction of the railway station: never again would he cross the Lagoon path to show his face in the township. From the station he struck off on a bush track. This was heavy with mud; for it had rained in torrents towards morning: the hammering of the downpour on the iron roof no doubt accounted for some of the sinister noises of which his dream had been full. Now, the day was fine: a cool breeze swung the drooping leaves; the cloudless sky had deepened to its rich winter blue. But to him the very freshness and beauty of the morning seemed a mockery, the blue sky cruel as a pall. For there was a blackness under his lids, which gave the lie to all he saw.

He trudged on, with the sole idea of somehow getting through the day . . . of killing time. And as he went he mused ironically, on the shifts mortals were put to, the ruses they employed, to rid themselves of this precious commodity, which alone stood between them and an open grave.

Then, abruptly, he stopped, and uttering an exclamation swung round and made for home. *It might, of course, be less.* Who knew, who knew? By this time it was just possible that another telegram had arrived, and that he was tormenting himself needlessly. Was he not omitting to allow for the fellow-feeling of a brother medico, who, suspecting something of what he was enduring, might hasten to put him out of suspense? (How his own heart would have bled for such a one!) And so he pushed forward, covering the way back in half the time, and only dropping his speed as he neared the gate. For the children sat at lessons in the dining-room, and three pairs of eyes looked up on his approach. At the front door he paused to dry his forehead, before stepping into the passage where the life-giving message might await him. But the tray on the hall-table was empty; empty, too, the table in the surgery. His heart, which had been palpitating wildly, sank to normal; and simultaneously an immense lassitude overcame him. But without a moment's hesitation he turned on his heel and went out again . . . with stealthy, cat-like tread. The last thing he wanted to do was to attract Mary's attention.

He retraced his steps. But now so tired was he that every hundred yards or so he found himself obliged to sit down, in order to get strength to proceed. But not for long: there was a demon in him that would not let him rest; which drove him up and on till, in the end, he was seized and spun by a fit of the old vertigo, and had to throw his arms round a tree-trunk to keep from falling. 'Drunk again! . . . drunk again.'

He was done for . . . played out. Home he dragged once more, sitting by the wayside when the giddy fits took him, or holding fast to the palings of a fence. It was one o'clock and dinner-time when he reached the house. Well! in any case, he would not have dared to absent himself from the table. (Oh, God, on such a day to have been free and unobserved!)

But he had over-rated his powers of endurance. The children's prating, Mary's worried glances in his direction, the clatter of the dishes, Zara's megrims: all this, the ordinary humdrum of a meal, proved more than his sick nerves could bear. His usual weary boredom with the ritual of eating turned to loathing: of every word that was said, every movement of fork to mouth, of the very crockery on the table. Halfway through, he tossed his napkin from him, pushed his chair back, and broke from the room.

To go out again was beyond him. Entering the surgery, he took his courage in both hands; and, not with his nerves alone, but with every muscle at a strain, braced himself to meet the slow torture that awaited him, the refined torture of physical inaction; the trail of which may be as surely blood-streaked as that from an open wound. With his brain on fire, his body bound to the rack, he sat and watched the hands of the clock crawl from one to two, from two to three and three to four; and the ticking of the pendulum, and the beat of his own pulses, combined to form a rhythm – a conflicting rhythm – which wellnigh drove him crazy. As the afternoon advanced, however, there came moments when, with his head bedded on his arms, he lapsed into a kind of coma; never so deeply though, but what his mind leapt into awareness at the smallest sound without. And all through, whether he waked or slept, something in him, inarticulate as a banshee, never ceased to weep and lament . . . to wail without words, weep without tears.

Later on, a new torture threatened; and this was the coming blast of the mill-whistle. For a full hour beforehand he sat anticipating it: sat with fingers stiffly interlocked, temples a-hammer, waiting for the moment when it should set in. Nor was this all. As the minute-hand ticked the last hour away, stark terror seized him lest, when the screech began, he, too, should not be able to help shrieking; but should be forced to let out, along with it, in one harsh and piercing cry, the repressed, abominable agony of the afternoon. At two minutes to the hour he was on his feet, going round the table like a maddened animal, wringing his hands and moaning under his breath: it is too much . . . I am not strong enough . . . my God, I implore Thee, let this cup pass! And now, so sick and dazed with fear was he, that he could no longer distinguish between the murderous din that was about to break loose, and the catastrophe that had befallen his life. When, finally, the hour struck, the whistle discharged and the air was all one brazen clamour, he broke down and wept, the tears dripping off his face. But no sound escaped him.

Supper time. – He wanted none; was not hungry; asked only to be left in peace. And since Mary, desperate, too, after her own fashion, could not make up her mind to this, but came again and yet again, bringing the lamp, bringing food to tempt him, he savagely turned the key in the lock.

Thereafter, all was still: the quiet of night descended on the house. Here, in this blissful silence, he took his decision. Numbed to the heart though he was – over the shrilling of the siren something in him had cracked, had broken – he knew what he had to do. Another day like this, and he would not be answerable for himself. There was an end to everything . . . and his end had come.

Mary, stealing back to remind him that it was close on midnight, found him stooped over a tableful of books and papers. 'Don't wait for me. I'm busy . . . shall be some time yet.'

Relieved beyond the telling to find his door no longer shut against her, and him thus normally employed, she put her arm round his shoulders and laid her head against his. 'But not too late, Richard. You must be so tired.' Herself she felt sick and dizzy with anxiety, with fatigue. It was not only what had happened, but the way Richard was taking it . . . his secrecy . . . his morbid self-communing. God help him! . . . help them all.

Desperately Mahony fought down the impulse to throw off her hampering arm, to cry out, to her face, the truth: go away . . . go away! I have done with you! And no sooner had the bedroom door shut behind her than he brushed aside his brazen pretence at work – it would have deceived no one but Mary – and fell to making the few necessary preparations. Chief of these was the detaching of a couple of keys from his bunch of keys, and laying them in a conspicuous place. After which he sat and waited, for what he thought a reasonable time, cold as a stone with fear lest she, somehow sensing his intention, should come back to hinder him. But nothing happened; and cautiously unlatching the door, he listened out into the passage. Not a mouse stirred. Now was the time! Opening the French window he stepped on to the verandah. But it had begun to rain again; a soft, steady rain; and some obscure instinct drove him back to get his greatcoat. This hung in the passage; and had to be fetched in jerks – a series of jerks and pauses. But at last he had it, and could creep up the yard and out of the back gate.

His idea was, to get as far from the house as possible . . . perhaps even to follow the bush track he had been on that morning. (That morning only? It seemed more like a century ago.) But the night was pitch dark: more than once he caught his foot, tripped and stumbled. So, groping his way along outside the palings of the fence, and the fence of the mill yard, he skirted these, and doubled back on the Lagoon. To the right of the pond stood a clump of fir-trees, shading the ruins of what had once been an arbour. It was for these trees he made: an instinctive urge for shelter again carrying the day.

Arrived there, he flung himself at full length on the wet and slimy ground. (No need now, to take thought for tic or rheumatism, or the other bodily ills that had plagued him.) And for a time he did no more than lie and exult in the relief this knowledge brought him – this sense of freedom from all things human. *Fear no more the heat of the sun*, nor the stranglecoils in which money and money-making had wound him, nor Mary's inroads on his life, nor the deadening responsibilities of fatherhood. Now, at long last, he was answerable to himself alone.

But gradually this feeling died away, and an extraordinary lucidity took its place. And in his new clearness of vision he saw that his bloodiest struggle that day had been, not with the thing itself, but with what hid it from him. Which was Time. He had set up Time as his bugbear, made of it an implacable foe, solely to hinder his mind from reaching out to what lay beyond. That, he could not face and live. He saw it now, and was dying of it: dying of a mortal wound to the most vital part of him – his pride . . . his black Irish pride. That he, who had held himself so fastidiously aloof from men, should be forced down into the market-place, there to suffer an intolerable notoriety; to know his name on people's lips ... see it dragged through the mud of the daily press ... himself branded as a bungler, a botcher! God! no: the mere imagining of it nauseated him. Dead, infinitely better dead, and out of it all! Life and its savagery put off, like a garment that had served its turn. Then, let tongues wag as they might, he would not be there to hear. In comparison, his death by his own hand would make small stir. A day's excitement, and he would pass for ever into limbo; take his place among those pale ghosts of whose earth-life every trace is lost. None would miss him, or mourn his passing — thanks to his own *noli me tangere* attitude towards the rest of mankind. For there had been no real love in him: never a feeler thrown out to his fellow-men. Such sympathy as he felt, he had been too backward to show: had given of it only in thought, and from afar. Pride, again! — oh! rightly was a pride like his reckoned among the seven capital sins. For what *was* it, but an iron determination to live untouched and untrammelled ... to preserve one's liberty, of body and of mind, at the expense of all human sentiment. To be sufficient unto oneself, asking neither help nor regard, and spending none. A fierce, Lucifer-like inhibition. Yes, this ... but more besides. Pride also meant the shuddering withdrawal of oneself, because of a rawness ... a skinlessness ... on which the touch of any rough hand could cause agony; even the chance contacts of everyday prove a source of exquisite discomfort.

Thus he dug into himself. To those, on the contrary, whose welfare had till now been his main solicitude, he gave not a thought. For this was *his* hour; the hour between himself and his God: the end of the old life, the dawn, so he surely believed, of the new. And now that release was in sight — port and haven made, after the desolate, wind-swept seas — he marvelled at himself for having held out so long. At the best of times small joy had been his: while for many a year never a blink of hope or gladness had come his way. Weary and unslept, he had risen, day after day, to take up the struggle; the sole object of which was the grinding for bread. The goal of a savage: to one of his turn of mind; degradation unspeakable. A battle, too, with never a respite — interminable as time itself. (Why, the most famous Agony known to history had lasted but for three hours, and a sure Paradise awaited the great Martyr.) Even the common soldier knew that the hotter the skirmish, the sooner it would be over, with, did he escape with his life, stripes and glory for a finish. Ah! but with this difference, that the soldier was under duress to fight to the end: for those who flung down their muskets and ran, crying, hold! enough! the world had coined an evil name. And at this thought, and without warning, such a red-hot doubt transfixed him, such a blazing host of doubts, that he fell to writhing, like one in the grip of insufferable physical anguish. These doubts brought confusion on every argument that he had used to bolster up his deed. What was he doing? ... what was he about to do? He, a coward? ... a deserter? ... abandoning his post when the fire was hottest? – leaving others to bear the onus of his flight, his disgrace? ... and those others the creatures he had loved best? Oh, where was here his pride!

Besides: no Lethe awaits me, but the judgement seat. How shall I face my Maker? – The phrasing was that of his day; the question at issue one with which men have tortured themselves since the world began. Have I the right to do this thing? Is my life my own to take? – And in the fierce conflict of which he now tossed the helpless prey, he dug his left hand into the earth until what it grasped was a compact mass of mud and gravel. (His right, containing the precious phial, was under him, held to his breast.) Only little by little, with pangs unspeakable, did the death-throes of his crucified pride cease, and he emerge from the struggle, spent and beaten, but seeing himself at last in his true colours. Too good ... too proud to live? Then, let him also be too proud to die: in this ignominious fashion ... this poltroon attempt to sneak out of life by a back door. Should it be said of him, who had watched by so many a deathbed, seen the humblest mortals rise superior to physical suffering, that, when his own turn came, he was too weak to endure? – solely because the torments he was called on to face were not of the body but the mind? Pain ... anguish ... of body or of mind ... individual pain ... the pangs of all humanity. Pain, a state of being so interwoven with existence that, without it, life was unthinkable. For, take suffering from life, and what remained? Surely, surely, what was so integral a part of creation could not spring from blind chance? ... be wholly evil? ... without value in the scheme of things? A test! – God's acid test ... failing to pass which, a man might not attain to his full stature. And if this were so, what was *he* doing to brush the cup from his lips, to turn his back on the chance here offered him? But oh! abhorrent to him was the pious Christian's self-abasement: the folded hands, the downcast eyes, the meek 'God wills it!' that all too often cloaked a bitter and resentful spirit. Not thus, not thus! God would not be God, did He demand of men grovelling and humiliation. Not the denial of self was called for, but the affirmation: a proud joy (here, surely, was the bone for his own pride to gnaw at?) at being permitted to aid and abet in the great Work, at coupling, in full awareness, our will with His. So, then, let it be! And with a movement so precipitate that it seemed after all more than half involuntary, he lifted his hand and threw far from him the little bottle of chloroform, which he had clutched till his palm was cut and sore. It was gone: was lost, hopelessly lost, in rain and darkness. He might have groped till morning without finding it.

But such a thought did not cross his mind. For now a strange thing happened. In the moment of casting the poison from him, he became aware – but with a sense other than that of sight, for he was lying face downwards, with fast closed eyes, his forehead bedded on the sleeve of his greatcoat – became suddenly aware of the breaking over him of a great light: he was lying, he found, in a pool of light; a radiance thick as milk, unearthly as moonlight. And this suffused him, penetrated him, lapped him round. He breathed it in, drew deep breaths of it; and, as he did so, the last vestiges of his old self seemed to fall away. All sense of injury, of mortification, of futile sacrifice was wiped out. In its place there ran through him the beatific certainty that his pain, his sufferings – and how infinitesimal these were, he now saw for the first time – had their niche in God's Scheme (pain the bond that linked humanity: not in joy, in sorrow alone were we yoke-fellows) – that all creation, down to the frailest protoplasmic thread, was one with God; and he himself, and everything he had been and would ever be, as surely contained in God, as a drop of water in a wave, a note of music in a mighty cadence. More: he now yearned as avidly for this submergedness, this union of all things living, as he had hitherto shrunk from it. The mere thought of separation became intolerable to him: his soul, ascending, sang towards oneness as a lark sings its way upwards to the outer air. For, while the light lasted, he *understood*: not through any feat of conscious perception, but as a state – a state of being – a white ecstasy, that left mere knowledge far behind. The import of existence, the mysteries hid from mortal eyes, the key to the Ultimate Plan: all now were his. And, rapt out of himself, serene beyond imagining, he touched the hem of peace at last . . . eternal peace . . . which passeth understanding.

Then, as suddenly as the light had broken over him, it was gone, and again night wrapped him heavily round; him, by reason of the miracle he had experienced, doubly dark, doubly destitute. (But I have *known* . . . *nothing* can take it from me!) And he had need of this solace to cling to, for his awakening found his brain of an icy clearness, in which no jot or tittle of what awaited him was veiled from him. As if to test him to the utmost, even the hideous spectre of his blackest nights took visible form, and persisted, till, for the first time, he dared to look it in the face. – And death seemed a trifle in comparison.

But he struggled no more. Caked in mud, soaked to the skin, he climbed to his feet and staggered home.

*

What a funny noise! . . . lots of noises . . . people all talking at once; and ever so loud. Cuffy sat up, rubbing his eyes, for there were lights in them. Stars . . . no, *lanterns!* Huh! *Chinese* lanterns? But it wasn't Christmas! He jumped out of bed and ran to the door, opened it and looked out; and it was two strange men with lanterns walking up and down the passage and round the verandah. And Mamma was there as well, in her red dressing-gown with the black spots on it, and her hair done for going to bed, and she was crying, and Aunt Zara (oh, she *did* look funny when she went to bed) was blowing her nose and talking to the men. And when she saw him, she was most awfully angry and said: 'Go back to bed at once, you naughty boy!' And Mamma said: 'Be good, Cuffy . . . for I can bear no more.' And so he only just peeped out, to see what it was. And it was Papa that was lost. *Papa* . . . *lost?* (How *could* grown-up people be lost?) in the middle of the night . . . it was dark as dark . . . and he might never come back. Oh no! It couldn't be true. Only to think of it made him make such a funny noise in his throat that Luce woke up, and wanted to know, and cried and said: 'Oh dear Papa, come back!' and was ever so frightened. And they both stopped out of bed and sat on the floor and listened. And the men with the lanterns – it was the sergeant and the constable – went away with them, and you could only hear Mamma and Aunt Zara talking and crying. And he waited till it seemed nearly all night, and his toes were so cold he didn't feel them. Luce went to sleep again, but he couldn't. And all the time his heart thumped like a drum.

Then he thought he saw a monkey in a wood, and was trying to catch it, when somebody shouted like anything; and first it was Maria on the verandah, and then Aunt Zara in the passage, and she called out: 'It's all right, Mary! They've got him . . . he's coming!' And then Mamma came running out and cried again, and kept on saying: 'I must be brave . . . I must be brave.' And then one's heart almost jumped itself dead, for there was Papa, and he couldn't walk, and the police were holding him up, and he had no hat on, and was wet, the water all running out of him, and so muddy, the mud sticking all over his greatcoat and in his face and hair – just like the picture of Tomfool in the 'King of Lear'. And Mamma began to say dreadfully: 'Oh, *Richard!* How *could* – ' And then she stopped. For as soon as Papa saw her he pulled himself away and ran to her, and put his arms round her neck and said: 'Oh, Mary, my Mary! . . . I couldn't do it. . . . I couldn't do it.' And then he nearly fell down, and they all ran to hold him up, and put him in the bedroom and shut the door. And he didn't see him again, but he saw Maria and Aunt Zara carrying in the bath, and hot water and flannels. And Papa was found. He tried to tell Luce but she was too sleepy, and just said: 'I fought he would.' But he was so cold he couldn't go to sleep again. And then something in him got too big and he had to cry, because Papa was found. But – What did it mean he said he *couldn't* be lost? Why not?

CHAPTER TEN

On one of the numerous packing-cases that strewed the rooms – now just so much soiled whitewash and bare boards – Mary sat and waited for the dray that was to transport boxes and baggage to the railway station. Her heart was heavy: no matter how unhappy you had been in it, the dismantling of a home was a sorry business, and one to which she never grew accustomed. Besides, this time when they left, one of them had to stay behind. As long as they lived here, her child had not seemed wholly gone; so full was the house of memories of her. To the next, to any other house they occupied, little Lallie would be a stranger.

Except for this, she was as thankful as Richard to turn her back on Barambogie – and he had fled like a hunted man, before he was really fit to travel. For the first time in their lives, the decision to leave a place had come from her; she had made up her mind to it while he was still too ill to care what happened. By the next morning the tale of his doings was all over the town: he would never have been able to hold up his head there again. For it wasn't as if he had made a *genuine* attempt . . . at . . . well, yes, at suicide. To the people here, his going out to take his life and coming back without even having *tried* to, would have something comic about it . . . something contemptible. They would laugh in their sleeves; put it down to want of pluck. When what it really proved – fiercely she reassured herself – was his fondness for her, for his children. When the moment came he couldn't find it in his heart to deal them such a blow.

But for several days she did no more than vehemently assert to herself: we go! . . . and if I have to beg the money to make it possible. Richard paid dearly for those hours of exposure: he lay in a high fever, moaning with pain and muttering lightheadedly. As soon, however, as his temperature fell and his cough grew easier, she made arrangements for a sale by auction, and had a board with 'To let' on it erected in the front garden.

Then, his keys lying temptingly at her disposal, she seized this unique opportunity and, shutting herself up in the surgery, went for and by herself into his money-affairs; about which it was becoming more and more a point of honour with him to keep her in the dark. There, toilfully, she grappled with the jargon of the law: premiums, transfers, conveyances, mortgagor and mortgagee (oh, *which* was which?), the foreclosing of a mortgage, rights of redemption. Grappled, too, with the secrets of his pass-book. And it was these twin columns which gave her the knock-out blow. As far as ready money went, they were living quite literally from hand to mouth – from the receipt of one pound to the next. In comparison, the deciphering of his case- and visiting-books was child's play. And here, taking the bull by the horns, she again acted on her own initiative. Risking his anger, she sent out yet once more the several unpaid bills she came across, accompanying them by a more drastic demand for settlement than he would ever have stooped to.

For the first time, she faced the possibility that they might have to let the mortgage lapse. Already she had suspected Richard of leaning towards this, the easier solution. But so far she had pitted her will against his. And, even yet, something stubborn rose in her and rebelled at the idea. As long as the few shares he held continued to throw off dividends, at least the interest on the loan could be met. While the rent coming in from the house at Hawthorn (instead of being a source of income!) would have to cover the rent of the house they could no longer live in, but had still to pay for. Oh, it sounded like a bad dream – or a jingle of the House-that-Jack-built order.

None the less, she did not waver in her resolution: somehow to cut Richard free from a place that had so nearly been his undoing. And, hedge and shrink as she might, fiercely as her native independence, her womanish principles – simple, but still the principles of a lifetime – kicked against it, she had gradually to become reconciled to the prospect of loading them up with a fresh burden of debt. The matter boiled down to this: was any sacrifice too great to make for Richard? Wasn't she really, at heart, one of those women she sometimes read of in the newspapers, who, rather than see their children starve, *stole* the bread with which to feed them?

Yet still she hesitated. Until one night, turning his poor old face to her Richard said: 'It's the sea I need, Mary. If I could just get to the sea, I should grow strong and well again. — But there! . . . what's the use of talking? As the tree falls, so it must lie!' On this night casting her scruples to the winds, Mary sat down to pen the hated appeal.

For Richard's sake, Tilly, and only because I'm desperate about him, I'm reduced to asking you if you could possibly see your way to lend me a hundred and fifty pounds. I say 'lend' and I mean it, though goodness knows when I shall be able to repay you. But Richard has been so ill, the practice has entirely failed, and if I can't get him away from here I don't know what will happen.

Tilly's answer, received by return, ran: *Oh, Mary love, I feel that sorry for you I can't say. But thanks be I can 'do' my dear, and I needn't tell you the money is yours for the asking. As for 'lending' — why, if it makes your poor mind easier put it that way: but it won't worry me if I never see the colour of the oof again, remember that. All I hope is, you'll make tracks like one o'clock from that awful place, and that the doctor'll soon be on his legs again. — But Mary! aren't I glad I kept that nest-egg as you know of! You were a bit doubtful at the time, love, if you remember. But if I hadn't, where should I be today? Something must have warned me, I think: sit up, you lovesick old fool you, and take thought for the time when it'll be all calls and no dividends. Which, Mary, is now. The plain truth being, his lordship keeps me that tight that if I didn't have what I do, I might be sitting in Pentridge. And he, the great loon, imagines I come out on what he gives me! — Oh, men are fools, my dear, I'll say it and sing it to my dying day — and if it's not a fool, then you can take it from me it's a knave. There ought to be a board up warning us silly women off. — Except that I've got my blessed Babe. Which makes up for a lot. But oh! if one could just get children for the wishing, or pick 'em like fruit from the trees, without a third person having to be mixed up in it. (I do think the Lord might have managed things better.) And I won't deny, Mary, the thought has come to me now and then just to take Baby and my bit of splosh, and vamoose to somewhere where a pair of trousers'll never darken my sight again.*

And now, for several mornings running, the postman handed in a couple of newspapers, the inner sheets of which contained the separate halves of a twenty-pound note: this being Tilly's idea of the safest and quickest means of forwarding money.

'Just something I'd managed to lay past for a rainy day,' Mary lied boldly, on handing Richard his fare to town and ten pounds over for expenses. And pride, scruples, humiliation, all faded into thin air before the relief, the burning gratitude, her gift let loose in him. 'Wife! you don't . . . you *can't* know what this means to me!' And then he broke down and cried, clinging like a child to her hand.

Restored to composure, he burst into a diatribe against the place, the people. What it had done to him, what they had made of him . . . him, whose only crime was that of being a gentleman. 'Because I wouldn't drink with them, descend to their level. Oh, these wretched publicans! . . . these mill-hands, and Chinese half-castes . . . these filthy Irish labourers! Mary, I would have done better to go to my grave, than ever to have come among them. And then the climate . . . and this waterhole they call a Lagoon . . . and the mill-whistle – that accursed whistle! It alone would have ended by driving me mad. But let me once shake the dust of the place off my feet, and Richard will be himself again. A kingdom for a horse? Mine – no kingdom, but a cesspool – for the sea! The sea! . . . elixir of life . . . to me and my kind. Positively, I begin to believe I'm one of those who should never live out of earshot of its waves.'

This new elation held up to the very end (when the thought of being recognized or addressed by any of those he was fleeing from threw him into a veritable fever). In such a mood he was unassailable: insensitive alike to pain or pleasure. Hence, the report that finally reached them from the Oakworth hospital didn't touch him as it ought to have done . . . considering that the affair had all but killed him. He really took it very queerly. The surgeon wrote that the operation had been successful; there was now every hope that, the overlapping corrected, perfect union would be obtained; which, as the lad's father also professed himself satisfied, would no doubt lift a weight from Dr Mahony's mind. But Richard only waxed bitterly sarcastic. 'Coming to their senses at last, are they? . . . now it's too late. Beginning to see how a gentleman ought to be treated?' Which somehow wasn't like him . . . to harp on the 'gentleman'.

He even came back on it, in a letter describing an acquaintance he had made (Richard and chance acquaintances!) in sailing down the Bay to Shortlands Bluff. This was a fellow medico: *Like myself a gentleman who has had misfortunes, and is now obliged to resume practice.* Still more disconcerting was it to read: *'I told him about Barambogie and mentioned the house being to let and the sale of the furniture, and said there was a practice ready to hand. Rather quiet just now, but certain to improve. If he took it, all I should ask would be a cheque for fifty pounds at the end of the year. I put our leaving down entirely to the climate. Should he write to you, be sure and do not put him off.* At which Mary winced. – And yet . . . Another man might get on quite well here; someone who understood better how to deal with the people. So she answered guardedly; being loath to vex him and spoil his holiday, which really seemed to be doing him good. He boasted of sound nights and improved appetite: *As usual the sea makes me ravenous.* And so it went on, until the time came when it was no longer possible to shirk the question: what next? Then, at once, they were at loggerheads again.

In passing through Melbourne, Mahony had seen an advertisement calling for tenders for a practice at a place named Narrong; and with her approval had written for particulars. To Mary this opening seemed just the thing. More than three times the size of Barambogie, Narrong stood in a rich, squatting district, not very far north of Ballarat. The practice included several clubs; the climate was temperate: if Richard could but get a footing there – the clubs alone represented a tidy income – the future might really begin to look more hopeful.

And at first he was all in favour of it. Then, overnight as it were, he changed his mind, and, without deigning to give her a single reason, wrote that he had abandoned the idea of applying. It was the sea that had done it; she could have sworn it was: this sea she so feared and hated! Besides, the usual thing was happening: no sooner did Richard get away from her than he allowed himself to be influenced by every fresh person he met. And taking advantage of his credulity, people were now, for some obscure purpose of their own, making him believe he could earn three or four hundred a year at Shortlands Bluff . . . though it was common knowledge that such seaside places lay dead and deserted for nine months out of the twelve. Besides, there was a doctor at Shortlands already; though now close on seventy, and unwilling to turn out at night.

The one valuable piece of information he gave her was that the billet of Acting Health Officer, with a yearly retaining-fee and an additional couple of guineas for each boarding, was vacant. All else, she felt sure, was mere windy talk. Thus, people were advising him, if he settled there, not only to keep a horse and ride round the outlying districts, but also to cross twice or thrice weekly to the opposite side of the Bay, and open consulting-rooms at some of the smaller places. *With my love of sailing this would be no toil to me . . . sheerly a pleasure.* It was true, old Barker intended to hang on to the two clubs in the meanwhile; but by Christmas he might hope to have these in his own hands. He had found the very house for them – a great piece of good luck this, for private houses were few. She would do well, though, to part with some of the heavier furniture; for the rooms were smaller than those they were leaving. Also to try to find a purchaser for the 'Collard and Collard' – since coming here he had learned that an 'Aucher Frères' was better suited to withstand the sea air. The climate, of course, was superb – though very cold in winter – the bathing excellent: *In summer I shall go into the sea every day.* Best of all they were within easy reach of Melbourne . . . and that meant civilization once more. *I feel very happy and hopeful, my dearest. Quite sure my luck is about to turn.*

Angry and embittered, Mary made short work of his fallacies. And now high words passed between them: she believing their very existence to be at stake; he fighting, but with considerable shuffling and hedging (or so it seemed to her), to defend his present scheme. And neither would give way.

Till one morning she held the following letter in her hand.

I see it's no use my beating about the bush any longer – you force me, by writing as you do, to tell you what I did not mean to worry you with. The truth is, I have not been at all well again. My old enemy, for one thing – requiring the most careful dieting – the old headaches and fits of vertigo. I have also fallen back on very poor nights; no sleep till four or five . . . for which however I must say your letters are partly responsible. Feeling very low the other day, I went to Geelong and saw Bowes-Smith who visits there; and it was his opinion that I should be totally unfit to cope with the work at Narrong. Which but confirms my own. Of course, as you are so set on it, I might try it for three months – alone. But I cannot do impossibilities, and I feel more and more that I am an old and broken man. (Another thing, I should again have no one to consult with – and . . . as you ought to know by now . . . I am not well up in surgery.) My poor head has never recovered the shock it got last summer . . . when you were away. No doubt I had a kind of fit. And though

I have said nothing about it, I have been sensible of some unpleasant symptoms of a return of this, on more than one occasion since. My affection, which was aphasia, may come on again at any time. It may also end in . . . well, in my becoming a helpless burden . . . to you and everyone. Nothing can be done; there is no treatment for it but a total absence of worry and excitement. So if you regret Narrong, you must forgive me; it was done for your sake.

One other thing. Everyone here takes boarders during the season: there is no disgrace attached to it. You could probably fill the house . . . and in that way I should not feel that I was leaving you entirely unprovided for. There is no dust or dirt here either: whereas at Narrong I should need to keep two horses and a man and buggy.

Send me some warmer underclothing, the continual blow of the equinoctial gales.

There is sure to be plenty of sickness when the visitors come. Shortlands will lead to strength, Narrong to the Benevolent Asylum.

Your loving husband,
R.T.M.

P.S. I am so worried I hardly know what I am writing for God's sake cheer up.

At which Mary threw the letter on the table and laughed aloud. Hear how ill I am, but be sure not to take it to heart! Oh, it wasn't fair of him . . . it wasn't fair. He had her down and beaten, and he knew it: to such a letter there could be but one reply. Picking it up she re-read it, and for a moment alarm riddled her. Then with a jerk she pulled herself together. How often Richard had . . . yes! over and over again. Besides, you could just as easily deceive yourself with bad dreams as with rosy ones. *How much of what he wrote was true?* His health had certainly suffered; but that was all due to this place. He'd said so himself. Let him once get away from here. . . . Places. And if she now insisted on his going to Narrong, even on his definitely applying for the practice, there would be more swords held over her head, more insidious hints and threats. He complained of not being able to find his words: well, would anyone think that surprising, did they know the life he had led here? . . . how he never went out, never spoke to a soul, but sat, for days on end, gloomily sunk in himself.

His airy suggestion that she should open the house to boarders stung and aggrieved her . . . coming from him. The idea was her own: she had mooted it long ago. *Then*, it had outraged his feelings. 'Not as long as *I* live!' Which attitude, bereft of common sense though it was, had yet something very soothing in it. Now, without a word of excuse, he climbed down from his perch and thrust the scheme upon her . . . as his own! Blown into thin air was his pride, his thoughts for her standing, his care for the children's future. Her heart felt dark and heavy. Of course if the worst *should* come to the worst . . . but then she would be doing it for *them*, not for him . . . or rather, not just in order that he might somehow get his own way. Oh, he had cried wolf too often. And a desperate bitterness; the sensation of being 'had', of him baulking at no means to achieve his end, was upon her again, clouding her judgement. She simply did not know what to think.

And this attitude of doubt accompanied her through all the dreary weeks of uprootal; down to the day when the bellman went up and down the main street crying the sale; when the auction-flag flew from the roof; and rough, curious, unfriendly people swarmed the house, to walk off with her cherished belongings. And as she worked, watched, brooded, a phrase from Tilly's letter kept ringing and buzzing through her head. *Sometimes the thought has come to me, just to take Baby and my bit of splosh and go off somewhere where* . . .

For nothing in the world would she have her children defrauded of their piano. Every toy they possessed, too, went with them; she saw to that. (*He* never thought of parting with his books!) While the Paris ornaments were her share of the spoils. (But anyhow it would have been casting pearls before swine, to offer them for sale here.) – As, one by one, she took apart the gilt-legged tables, the gilt candelabra, to lay the pieces between soft layers of clothing, memories of the time when they were bought came crowding in on her. She saw the Paris shops again, the salesman bowing and smirking, the monkey-like little courier who had acted as interpreter. But most vividly of all she saw Richard himself. The very clothes he had worn were plain to her: there he stood, erect and handsome, a fine and dignified figure. And then, in pitiful contrast, a vision of him as, a few weeks back, he had slunk up to the railway station: a shamed and humiliated old man. Dear God! . . . these passionate angers he roused in her, the unspeakable irritations she was capable of feeling with him, were things of the surface only. Dig deeper, and nothing mattered . . . *but* him. Aye, dig only deep enough, and her heart was raw with pity for him. Let what might, happen to her; let the children go short, run wild; let him drag them at his heels the whole world over: she would submit to everything, endure everything, if she could only see him – Richard, her own dear husband – hold up his head once more, carry himself with the old confidence, fear to meet no one's eye, knowing that he had never yet wilfully done any man hurt or wrong.

PART THREE

CHAPTER ONE

'Papa, papa – the flag! The flag's just *this* minnit gone up.'

'The flag! Papa's this minnit gone up.'

The children came rushing in with the news, Lucie in her zeal to echo Cuffy bringing out her words the wrong way round. But *how* funny! Papa was fast asleep in his chair, and at first when he waked up couldn't tell where he was. He called out quite loud: 'Where am I? Where the dickens am I?' and looked as if he didn't know them. But as soon as he did, he ran to the window. 'Quite right! Splendid! So it is. – Now who saw it first?'

'Lucie,' said Cuffy stoutly; for he had seen first *all* the times; Luce never would, not if she was old as old. And so Lucie received the hotly coveted penny, her little face, with the fatly hanging cheeks that made almost a square of it, pink with pleasure. But also with embarrassment. Would God be *very* angry with Cuffy for tellin' what wasn't true? (She thought God must look just like Papa when he was cross.)

Papa scuttled about. Shouting.

'Mary! Where are you? The flag's gone up. Quick! My greatcoat. My scarf.'

'Yes, yes, I'm coming. – But . . . why . . . you haven't even got your boots on! Whatever have you been doing since breakfast?'

'Surely to goodness, I can call a little time my own? . . . for reading and study?'

'Oh, all right. But fancy you having to go out again today. With such a sea running! And when you got so wet yesterday.'

'It's those second-hand oilskins. I told you I ought to have new ones. – Now where are my papers? – Oh, these confounded laces! They *would* choose just this moment to break. It's no good; I can't stoop; it sends the blood to my head.'

'Here . . . put up your foot!' And going on her knees, Mary laced his boots. *Till* she got him off! The fuss – the commotion!

Standing in the doorway Cuffy drank it all in. This *was* an exciting place to live. To have to rush like mad as soon as ever a flag went up. If only someday Papa would take him with him. To go down to the beach with Papa, and row off from the jetty – Papa's own jetty! – and sit in the boat beside him, and be rowed out by Papa's own sailors, to the big ship that was waiting for him. Waiting just for Papa. When he was a big man he'd be a doctor, too, and have a jetty and a boat of his own, and be rowed out to steamers and ships, and climb on board, and say if they were allowed to go to Melbourne. – But how *funny* Papa was, since being here. When his voice got loud it sounded like as if he was going to scream. And then . . . he'd said he was busy . . . when he was really asleep. He believed Papa was afraid . . . of Mamma. Knew she'd be cross with him for going to sleep again directly after breakfast. It made him want to say: Oh, *don't* be afraid, Papa, big men never do be . . . only little children like Lucie. (Specially not one's Papa.)

Slamming the driving-gate behind him – with such force that it missed the latch, and swinging out went to and fro like a pendulum – Mahony stepped on to the wide, sandy road, over which the golden-flowered cape weed had spread till only a narrow track in the centre remained free. It was half a mile to the beach, and he covered the ground at a jog-trot; for his fear of being late was on a par with his fear that he might fail to see the signal: either through a temporary absence of mind, or from having dozed off (the sea air was having an unholy effect upon him) at the wrong moment. Hence his bribe to the children to be on the look-out. – Now on, past neat, one-storeyed weatherboards, past Bank and church and hotels he hurried, breathing heavily, and with a watchful eye to his feet. For his left leg was decidedly stiffish; and, to spare it, his pace had to be a long, springing step with the right, followed by a shorter one with the left: a gait that had already earned him the nickname in Shortlands of 'Old Dot-and-go-one'.

Taking the Bluff, with its paths, seats and vivid grass-carpet, in his stride, he scrambled down the loose sand of the cliff, through the young scrub and the ragged, storm-bent ti-trees, which were just bursting into pearly blossom. And the result of this hurry-scurry was that he got to the beach too soon: his men had only just begun to open up the boat-shed. Fool that he was! But it was always the same . . . and would be tomorrow, and the day after that: when his fears seized him, he was powerless against them. Having irritably snapped his fingers and urged on the crew with an impatient: 'Come, come, my good men, a little more haste, if you please!' he retired to the jetty, where he paced to and fro.

But at last the boat was launched, the sailors had grasped their oars: he, too, might descend the steps and take his seat. — And now he knew that all the press and fluster of the past half-hour had been directed towards this one, exquisite moment: in which they drew out to ride the waves. Of the few pleasures left him, it was by far the keenest: he re-lived it in fancy many a night when his head lay safe on the pillow. Today was a day, too, after his own heart. A high sea ran, and the light boat dived, and soared, and fell again, dancing like a cockleshell. The surface of the water was whipt by a wind that blew the foam from the wave-crests in cloudlets of steam or smoke. The salt spray was everywhere: in your eyes, your mouth, your hair. Overhead, between great bales of snowy cloud, the sky was gentian-blue; blue were the hills behind the nestling white huts of the quarantine-station on the other side of the Bay; indigo-blue the waters below. Intoxicated by all this light and colour, at being one again with his beloved element, he could have thrown back his head and shouted for joy; have sent out cries to match the lovely commotion of wind and sea. But there was no question of thus letting himself go: he had perforce to remain as dumb as the men who rowed him. Above all, to remember to keep his eyes lowered. For the one drawback to his pleasure was that he was not alone. He had a crew of six before him, six pairs of strange eyes to meet; and every time he half-closed his own and expanded his nostrils, the better to drink in the savour of the briny, or, at an unusually deep dip, let fly a gleeful exclamation, they fixed him stonily, one and all. There was no escaping them, pinned to his seat as he was: nor any room for his own eyes . . . nowhere to rest them . . . except on the bottom of the boat. Only so could he maintain his privacy. — Eyes . . . human eyes. Eyes . . . *spies*, ferreting out one's thoughts . . . watchdogs on the qui vive for one's smallest movement . . . spiders, sitting over their fly-victims, ready to pounce. Eyes. Slits into the soul; through which you peered, as in a twopenny peepshow, at clandestine and unedifying happenings. A mortal's outside the *ne plus ultra* of dignity and suavity . . . and then the eyes, disproving all. Oh! it ought not to be possible, so to see into another's depths; it was indecent, obscene: had he not more than once, in a woman's comely countenance, met eyes that were hot, angry, malignant? . . . unconscious betrayers of an unregenerate soul. None should outrage him in like fashion: he knew the trick and guarded against it, by keeping his own bent rigidly on the boards at his feet . . . on the boot-soles of the men in front of him. But smiles and chuckles were not so easily subdued: they would out . . . and out they came.

As the boat drew nearer the vessel that lay to, awaiting them, a new anxiety got the upper hand. Wrinkling his brows, he strained to see what was in store for him. Ha! he might have known it: another of those infernal rope ladders to be scaled. He trembled in advance. For you needed the agility of an ape to swing yourself from the tossing boat to the bottom rung of the ladder; the strength of a navvy to maintain your hold, once you were there, before starting on the precarious job of hoisting yourself, rung by rung, up the ship's steep side. And today, with this wild sea running, it was worse than ever – was all the men could do to bring the boat close enough, yet not too close, alongside, for him to get a grip on the rope. The seat he stood on was slippery, his oilskins encumbered him: he made one attempt after another. Each time, before he had succeeded in jerking himself across, the gulf opened anew. Finally, in most undignified fashion, he was laid hold of, and pushed and shoved from behind; and thereafter came a perilous moment when he hung over the trough of sea, not knowing whether his muscles would answer to the strain, or whether he would drop back into the water. Desperately he clung to the swaying rope; what seemed an eternity passed before he could even straighten himself let alone climb out of reach of the waves. – Deuce take it! you needed to be at least twenty years younger for acrobatics of this kind.

Hanging over the side, the ship's crew followed his doings with the engrossed and childish interest of men fresh from the high seas. As he came within reach, however, willing hands were thrust forth to help him. But he was shattered by his exertions, the deck was wet, and no sooner did he set foot on it than his legs shot from under him, and he fell heavily and awkwardly on his back. And this was too much for the onlookers, just suited their elephantine sense of humour, already tickled by his un-seamanlike performance on the ladder: one and all burst into a loud guffaw. Bruised and dazed he scrambled to his feet, and, hat and bag having been restored him, was piloted by a grinning seaman to the captain's cabin.

There had been no single case of sickness on the outward voyage: the visit was a mere formality; and the whole affair could have been settled inside five minutes – had he not been forced to ask the captain's leave to rest a little, in order to recover before undertaking the descent: his hips ached and stung, his hand shook so that he had difficulty in affixing his signature. He thought the captain, a shrewd-eyed, eagle-nosed Highlander, whose conversation consisted of a series of dry: 'Aye, aye's!' looked very oddly at him on his curt refusal of the proffered bottle. 'Thank you, I never touch stimulants.'

As he hobbled home wet and chilled, his head aching from its contact with the deck, arm and shoulder rapidly stiffening: as he went, he had room in his mind for one thought only: I've taken on more than I can manage. I'm not fit for the job – or shan't be . . . much longer. And then? . . . my God! . . . *and then?* – But hush! Not a word to Mary.

Entering the dining-room he pettishly snatched off the dish-cover. '*What?* . . . hash again? I declare of late we seem to live on nothing else!'

Mary sighed. 'If I serve the meat cold, you grumble; if I make it up, you grumble, too. I can't throw half a joint away. What am I to do?'

He suppressed the venomous: 'Eat it yourself!' that rose to his lips. 'I've surely a right to expect something fresh and appetizing when I get back after a hard morning's work? You know I loathe twice-cooked meat!'

'I thought you'd bring such an appetite home with you that you'd be equal to anything. Other times you do. But you don't know your own mind from one day to the next.'

'If *that's* all you have to say, I won't eat anything!' – And despite her expostulations and entreaties: 'Richard! come back, dear, don't be so silly,' he banged out of the room.

Instantly Cuffy pushed his plate away. 'I don't like it either, Mamma.'

Glad of a scapegoat, Mary rounded on the child with a: 'Will *you* kindly hold your tongue, sir?' letting out not only her irritation with Richard, but also the exhaustion of a morning's governessing: a task for which she was wholly unfitted by nature. 'You'll not leave the table till you've eaten every scrap on your plate.'

And Cuffy, being really very hungry – he had only said like Papa to try and make Mamma think Papa wasn't *quite* so bad – obeyed without a further word.

Afterwards, he had to go to the butcher's with a basket to buy a chop – a big one and not too fat, Papa didn't eat fat – and then, when the whole house smelt good with frying, to go in and say to Papa that dinner was ready.

But Papa was asleep and snoring; and he didn't like to wake him. He fidgeted about and made a noise for a bit, and then went out and said so.

But Mamma sent him back: the chop was cooked and had to be eaten. So he put his hand on Papa's arm and shook it. But Papa knocked it off, and jumped up calling out: 'What is it? ... what is it now?' And very angry: '*Can't* you let me be? – Oh, it's you, my dear? – What? Not I! Tell your mother I want nothing.'

And then Mamma came marching in herself, and was furious. 'And when I've sent out specially to get it! I never heard such nonsense. Going the whole day without food just to spite me!'

She was quite close up to Papa when she talked this; and they were both dreadfully angry; and then ... then Cuffy dis*tink*ly saw Papa's foot fly out and hit her ... on her knee. And she said: '*Ooh!*' and stooped down and put her hand to it, and looked at him, oh! so fierce ... but she didn't say any more, not a word (and he knew it was because he was there), but turned on her back and walked out of the room. And he felt frightened, and went away, too; but not before he'd seen Papa put his face in his hands, just as if he was going to cry.

They kept a goat now: it was chained up in the back yard to eat the grass and things, which would have smothered them if it hadn't. Well, he went out to the goat – it was tied up and couldn't run away – and kicked it. It maa-ed and tore round like mad: but he just didn't care; he kicked it again. Till Luce came out and saw him and made awful eyes, and said: 'Oh, *Cuffy*! Oh, poor little Nanny! Oh, you bad, wicked boy! I'll go wight in and tell Mamma what you're doin'.'

But Mamma could not be got at. She was in the bedroom with the door locked; and she wouldn't come out, though you called and called, and rattled the handle. (But she wasn't dead, 'cos you could hear them talkin'.)

With his arms round her, his face on her shoulder, Richard

besought her: 'Mary, Mary, what is it? What's the matter with me? Why am I like this? – oh, why?'

'God knows! You seem not to have an atom of self-control left. When it comes to kicking me . . . and in front of the children . . .' Her heart full to bursting, Mary just stood and bore his weight, but neither raised her arms nor comforted him.

'I know, I know. But it isn't only temper – God knows it isn't. It's like a whirlpool . . . a whirlwind . . . that rises in me. Forgive me, forgive me! I didn't mean it. I had a nasty fall on the deck this morning. I think that knocked the wits out of me.'

'A fall? How? Were you hurt?' Mary asked quickly. At any hint of bodily injury, and was it but a bruise, she was all sympathy and protection.

Meekly now, but with only the ghost of an appetite, Mahony sat down to the congealed chop, which he sliced and swallowed half-chewed, while Mary moved about the room, her lids red-rimmed and swollen. And the children, having snatched one look at her, crept away with sinking hearts. Oh, Mamma, dear, dear, don't . . . *don't* be unhappy!

In telling of his fall and making it answerable for his subsequent behaviour, Mahony failed to mention one thing: the uneasiness his leg was causing him. Some perverse spirit compelled him to store this trouble up for his own tormenting – that night when he lay stiff as a corpse, so as not to deprive Mary of her well-earned rest. This numbness . . . this fatal numbness. . . . He tried to view himself in the light of a patient: groped, experimented, investigated. What! cutaneous anaesthesia as well? For he now found he could maltreat the limb as he would; there was little or no answering sensation. Positively he believed he could have run a pin into it. Sick with apprehension he put his hand down to try yet once more, by running his finger-nails into and along the flesh – and was aghast to hear a shrill scream from Mary. '*Richard!* What *are* you doing? Oh, how you have hurt me!'

He had drawn blood on her leg instead of on his own.

CHAPTER TWO

Mary waited, as for the millennium, for the opening of the summer season. In the meantime Shortlands lay dead to the rest of the world: the little steamer neither brought nor took off passengers; the big ships all went by. But on every hand she heard it said: let the season once begin and there would be work for everyone; the life of a year was crowded into three brief months. If only they could manage to hold out till then! For December was still two months off, and of private practice there was as good as none. The place was so healthy for one thing (oh, there must surely be something very wrong about a world in which you had to feel *sorry* if people weren't ill!) and the poorer classes all belonged to the clubs, which Richard hadn't got. His dreams of keeping a horse and riding round the district, of opening consulting-rooms on the other side, had, as she had known they would, ended in smoke: the twice he had crossed the Bay he had not even covered his fare. She wondered, sometimes, if such sickness as there was did not still find its way to Dr Barker, retired though the old man professed to be. It was certainly owing to him that nightwork had become extinct here. Through him refusing to leave his bed, the inhabitants had simply got out of the way of being taken ill at night.

And Richard did nothing to mend matters. On the contrary. At present, for instance, he was going about in such a simmer of indignation at what he called the trick that had been played on him – the misleading reports of the income to be made here – that he was apt to let it boil over on those who did approach him. Then, too, the dreadful habit he had fallen into, of talking to himself as he walked, put people off. (From something the servant-girl let drop, she could see that he was looked on as *very* odd.) But when she taxed him with it he flared up, and vowed he had never in his life been guilty of such a thing; which just shewed he didn't know he was doing it. If he had, he would have been more careful; for he liked the place (hardly a day passed on which he did not sigh: 'If I can *only* make a living here!) in spite of its deadness . . . and also of the cold, which found out his weak spots. And for once in their lives they were in agreement: she liked it, too. They were among people of their own class again by whom she had been received with open arms. Though, as she could see, this very friendliness might have its drawbacks. For Richard had been quite wrong (as usual): the members of this little clique did not let lodgings, most emphatically not; they drew, indeed, a sharp line between those who did and those who didn't. Well! she would just have to see . . . when the time came. If the practice did *not* look up. – But oh! how she hoped and prayed it would: she could hardly trust herself to think what might happen if it did not.

One afternoon as they sat at tea – it was six o'clock on a blustery spring day – they heard the click of the gate, and looking out saw someone coming up the path: a short, stoutish man in a long-skirted greatcoat, who walked with a limp.

Mary rubbed her eyes. 'Why . . . why, Richard!'

'What is it? . . . who is it?' cried Mahony, and made as if to fly: he was in one of those moods when the thought of facing a stranger filled him with alarm.

'Why . . . I . . .'

'He's walking right in,' announced Cuffy.

'An' wavin' his hand, Mamma.'

Sure enough, the newcomer came up the verandah steps and unceremoniously tapped on the window-pane. 'Hullo, good people all! . . . how are you?' And *then*, of course, he with his hat off, shewing a head innocent of hair, there was no mistaking him.

With one eye on Richard, who was still capable of trying to do a bolt, one on the contents of her larder-shelves, Mary exclaimed in surprise. 'Well, of all the . . . Purdy! Where have you sprung from? Is Tilly with you?'

'*Tilly?* Mrs P. Smith? God bless my soul, no! My dear, this wind 'ud give 'is Majesty the bellyache for a month; we'd hear tell of nothing else. Lord bless you, no! We never go out if it blows the least little tiddly-wink, or if there's a cloud in the sky, or if old Sol's rays are too strong for us. We're a hothouse plant, *we* are. What do you say to that, you brawny young nippers, you?'

It was the same old Purdy: words just bubbled out of him.

And having taken off his coat and chucked the children under the chin — after first pretending not to know them because of their enormous size, and then to shake in his shoes at such a pair of giants — he drew in his chair and fell to, with appetite, on the toothsome remains of a rabbit-pie and the home-baked jam tarts that Mary somehow conjured up to set before him. 'These sea-voyages are the very devil for makin' one peckish. I've a thirst on me, too ... your largest cup, Polly, if you please, will just about suit my measure.' — As she listened to his endless flow, Mary suspected him of already having tried to quench this thirst on the way there.

In eating, he told of the business that had brought him to Shortlands; and at greater length than was either necessary or desirable; for there was a lot in it about 'doing' a person, in revenge for having been 'done' by him, and the children of course drank it all in. Mary did her best to edge the conversation round, knowing how strongly Richard disapproved of their being initiated, before their time, into the coarse and sordid things of life. But what followed was even worse. For now Purdy started indulging in personalities. 'I say, you two, isn't this just like old times ... eh?' he said as he munched. 'Just like old times ... except of course that we're all a good bit thicker in the tummy and thinner on the thatch than we were, ha, ha! ... your humb. serv. in partic.! *Also*' — and he winked his right eye at the room at large — 'excepting for the presence of the young couple I observe sitting opper*site*, who were *not* on the tappis, or included in the programme, in those far-off days — eh, Poll? Young people who insisted on putting in an appearance at a later date, unwanted young noosances that they were!' (At which Cuffy, flaming scarlet, looked anxiously at his mother for a denial: she had told him over and over again how enjoyed she and Papa had been to see him.) 'Well, well! such little accidents will happen. But far from us was it to think of such ... all those many ... now *how* many years was it ago? Thirty — for a cert! Ah, no hidin' your age from me, Mrs Poll ... after the manner of ladies when they come to the sere and yellow leaf. I've got you nailed, me dear!'

Colouring slightly (she thought talk of this kind in sorry taste before the children), Mary was just about to say she didn't mind who knew how old she was, when Richard, who till now had sat like a death's-head, brought his fist down on the table with a bang. 'And I say, not a day over twenty-five!' He did make them jump.

Purdy, so jovial was he, persisted in taking this to refer, not to the date, but to her age, and bantered harder than ever, accusing Richard of trying to put his wife's clock back. And what with Richard arguing at the top of his voice to set him right, and Purdy waggishly refusing to see what was meant, it looked for a moment as if it might come to an open quarrel between them.

'Richard! . . . hush, dear!' frowned Mary, and surreptitiously shook her head. 'What can it matter? Oh, don't be so silly!' For he was agitatedly declaring that he would fetch out his old casebooks and prove the year, black on white. She turned to Purdy: 'You've told me nothing at all yet about Tilly and the boy.'

But Purdy had plainly no wish to talk of wife or child, and refused to let himself be diverted from the course of reminiscence on which he had embarked. To oblige her, he dropped his mischievous baiting with a: 'Well, well, then, so be it! I suppose I'm getting soft in the uppers,' but continued to draw on his memories of the old days, spinning yarns of things that had happened to him, and things she was quite sure hadn't, egged on by the saucer eyes of the children. 'Remember this, Poll? . . . remember that?' she vainly endeavouring to choke him off with a dry: 'I'm afraid I don't.' She sat on pins and needles. If only he wouldn't work Richard up again. But it almost seemed as if this was his object; for he concluded his tale of the Stockade and his flight from Ballarat, with the words: 'And so afeared for his own skin was our friend old Sawbones there, that he only ventured out of an evening, after dark; and so the wound got mucky and wouldn't heal. And that's the true story, you kids, of how I came to be the limping-Jesus I am and ever shall be, world without end, amen!'

Of all the wicked falsehoods! (Or had he *really* gone about nursing this belief?) Such expressions, too! . . . before the children. Thank goodness, Richard hadn't seemed to hear: otherwise she would have expected him to fly out of his chair. A stolen glance shewed him sitting, head on chest, making patterns on the tablecloth with the point of his knife. And having failed thus to draw him, if Purdy didn't now dish up, with several unsavoury additions, the old, old story of the foolish bet taken between the two of them as young men, that Richard wouldn't have the pluck to steal of kiss from her at first meeting; and how, in the darkness of the summer-house, he had mistaken one girl for the other and embraced Jinny instead. 'Putting his arms round her middle – plump as a partridge she was too, by gum! – and giving 'er a smack that could have been heard a mile off. Killing two birds with one stone I call it! . . . gettin' the feel of a second gal under his hands, free, gratis and for nothing.'

At such indelicacy Mary held her breath. But what was this? Instead of the furious outburst for which she waited, she heard a . . . chuckle. Yes, Richard was laughing – his head still sunk, his eyes fixed on the tablecloth – laughing and nodding to himself at the memory Purdy had called up. And then – oh, no! it was incredible: to her horror, Richard himself added a detail, the grossness of which sent the blood to her cheeks.

What was more, he was going on. 'Run away and play, children. At once! Do you hear?' For Cuffy was listening openmouthed, and laughing, too, in an odd, excited way. She had them off their chairs and out of the room in a twinkling. Herself she stood for a moment in the passage, one hand pressed to her face. Oh! by fair means or foul – 'You're wanted, Richard! Yes, immediately!' And after that it was not hard to get Purdy up from the table and sent about his business.

But as soon as the children were in bed, she went into the surgery, and there, shutting fast the door, let out her smothered wrath, making a scene none the less heated because it had to be carried on under her breath. To her stupefaction Richard flatly denied the charge. What was she talking about? No such words had ever crossed *his* lips! 'Before my children? Whose every hair is precious to me?' He was as perturbed as she, at the bare idea. Oh, what was to be done with a person whose memory was capable of playing him such tricks? In face of his indignation, his patent honesty, you couldn't just rap out the word 'liar!' and turn on your heel.

Yes, a disastrous visit from start to finish. The children alone got pleasure from it. Purdy took a great liking to them – he who hadn't a word to say for his own child – and on the verandah next morning the trio were very merry together. Cuffy's laugh rang out again and again.

For Cuffy thought Mr Purdy a *very* nice man . . . even if his head *was* shiny like an egg, and he was nearly as fat as that ol' Sankoh in the big book with the pictures. (Papa, he was like Donk Quick Shot, who tried to kill the windmills.) He had two be*aut*iful big diamond rings on his fingers, and a watch that struck like a clock, and a whole bunch of things, little guns and swords and seals, hanging on his chain. He gave them each half-a-crown and said not to tell Mamma, and rode Luce to market on his foot, and sang them a lovely song that went:

> A man whose name was Johnny Sands
> Had married Betty Hague,
> And though she brought him gold and lands,
> She proved a terrible plague;
> For O she was a scolding wife,
> Full of caprice and whim,
> He said that he was tired of life,
> And she was tired of him.

Ever so much of it, all about these people, till she fell into the river and asked him to pull her out, and Johnny Sands would have, but:

> I can't my dear, tho' much I wish,
> For you have tied my hands

He and Luce jumped about and sang it, too. Oh, wasn't it nice when somebody was happy and jolly and funny? – instead of always being sorry, or cross. He thought he could *nearly* have asked Mr Purdy what it meant when you said: the female nobleman obliges. It belonged to him, Papa had said it did; but he hadn't ever dared ask anybody about it; people like Aunt Zara laughed so, when you didn't understand. But he was going to . . . some day. –

The climax came next morning when, the front door having closed behind the guest, the children came running out of the dining-room crying gleefully: 'Look, Mamma! Look what he's left on the table!' For an instant Richard stood and stared incredulously at the five-pound note Cuffy was holding aloft; the next, with a savage exclamation he had snatched it from the child's hand, and was through the porch and down the path, shouting at the top of his voice: 'Here you, sir, come back! How dare you! Come back, I say! Do you take my house for an hotel?'

But Purdy, already on the other side of the gate and limping off as hard as he could go, only made a half-turn, waved one arm in a gesture that might have meant anything, and was out of sight. Short of running down the street in pursuit, or of mixing one of the children up in it . . . Beside himself with rage, Richard threw the note to the ground and stamped on it, then plucking it up, tore it to bits.

Taking him by the arm, Mary got him indoors. But for long she could not calm him. (Oh, was there *ever* such a tactless fool as Purdy? Or was this just another of those spikey thrusts at Richard which he seemed unable to resist?)

'Does he think because he's gone up in the world and I've come down that it gives him the right to insult me in this way? — him, the common little ragamuffin I once picked out of the gutter? (Oh, no, Richard!) To come here and offer me alms! . . . for that's what it amounts to . . . pay his few shillingsworth of food with a present of pounds? Why, I would rather rot in my grave than be beholden to him!' (Oh, how Richard did at heart despise him!) '*Charity!* — from *him* to *me!*'

'He shall never come again, dear.' (Though how were you to help it, if he just walked in?)

Behind the locked door (she seemed always to be locking doors now) she sat, wide-lapped in her full skirts; and, when Richard had railed himself tired, he knelt down before her and laid his face on her dress. Her hands went to and fro over the grey head, on which the hair was wearing so thin. What could she do for him? . . . what was to become of him? . . . when every small mischance so maddened, so exasperated him. That a stupid, boorish act like Purdy's could so shatter his self-control! Her heart wept over him; this heart which, since the evening before, had lain under the shadow of a new fear; a fear so ominous that she still did not dare to put it into words; but against which, for her children's sake, she might need to take up arms . . . to lock, so to speak, yet another door.

The upshot of the matter was that she had to replace the destroyed note by one from her jealously guarded store. This Richard haughtily sealed up and posted back, without a single covering word.

There was, however, one bright side to the affair. And again it was the children who benefited.

In running them out after breakfast to buy some lollipops, Purdy had got permission from the postmaster, an old friend of his, to take them up the lighthouse; and so the three of them went up and up and up a staircase that twisted like a corkscrew, hundreds of steps, till they came to where the great lamp was that shone at night; and then, tightly holding hands, they walked round the little narrow platform outside and looked down at the sea, all bubbly and frothy, and the white roofs of the houses. They found their own, and it didn't look any bigger than a doll's-house. Afterwards they were asked inside the post office – right inside! – and they peeped through the little window where the stamps were sold, and saw the holes where the letters were kept; and the two tel'graph machines that went click, click; and how tape ran away on wheels with little dots and dashes on it, that the postmaster said were words. And then he took them into his house behind to see his Mamma and his four grown-up sisters, who were ever so nice, and asked their names, and said Cuffy *was* a big boy for his age, and Luce was a cuddly darling; and they cut a cake specially for them, and showed them a ship *their* Papa had made all by himself, even the little wooden men that stood on the decks. They laughed and joked with Mr Purdy, and they had the most lovely teeth, and sang songs for them till Cuffy was wild with delight.

Thus, through Purdy's agency, a house was opened to the children the like of which they had never known: a home over which no shadow brooded; in which the key was set to laughter and high spirits, and the nonsensical gaiety that children love. Cuffy and Lucie, petted and made much of, completely lost their hearts to their new friends, and talked so much of them, teasing to be allowed to visit them, that Mary felt it incumbent on her to tie on her bonnet and pay a call in person. She came back entirely reassured. The daughters, one and all Australian-born, were charming and accomplished girls; while in old Mrs Spence, the widow of an English university man who in the early days had turned from unprofitable gold-digging to Government service, she found one who, in kindliness and tolerance, in humour and common sense, reminded her vividly of her own mother, long since dead.

To the children this old lady early became 'Granny'; and even Cuffy, who had begun to fight shy of his mother's knee, was not above sitting on hers. A Granny was diffrunt . . . didn't make you feel such a baby. And it was of her kind old face that he eventually succeeded in asking his famous question.

'Bless the child! . . . now what can he mean?' Then, noting the sensitive flush that mounted, Granny cried: 'Pauline, come you here! – Pauline will know, my dear. She's ever so much cleverer than a silly old woman like me.'

And pretty Pauline – they were all four so pretty and so nice that Cuffy couldn't tell which he liked best – knelt down before him, he sitting on Granny's lap, and, with her dress bunching out round her and her hands on his knees, explained, *without laughing a bit*. *Noblesse oblige* didn't mean the obliging female nobleman at all: he had got it mixed up with poet and poetess. 'What it says, Cuffy dear, is that people who are born to a high rank . . . like Kings and Queens . . . must always remember who they are and act accordingly. Little gentlemen must always behave *like* gentlemen, and never do anything low or mean. Do you see?'

And Cuffy nodded . . . and nodded again. Yes, now he knew. And he never would! – But he knew something else, too. He loved Pauline more'n anybody in the world.

CHAPTER THREE

'There you go . . . tripping again. You keep one in a perfect fidget,' sighed Mary.

'It's these confounded shoes. They're at least two sizes too big.'

'I told you so! But you were so set on having them easy.'

Entering the surgery Mahony kicked the inoffensive slippers from his feet, and drew on his boots. After which, having opened the door by a crack, to peer and listen, he stole into the passage to fetch hat and stick.

But Mary, in process of clearing the breakfast-table, caught him in the act. 'What? . . . going out already? I declare your consulting-hours become more of a farce every day. Well, at least take the children with you.'

'No, that I can't. They're such a drag.'

And therewith he whipped out of the house and down the path, not slackening his pace till he had turned a corner: Mary was quite capable of coming after him and hauling him back. And escape he must – from the prison cell that was his room; from the laming surveillance to which she subjected him. Only out of doors, with the wind sweeping through him, the wild expanse of sea tossing in the sunlight, could he for a little forget what threatened; forget her dogging and hounding; enjoy a fictitious peace . . . dream of safety . . . forget – forget.

He made for the Bluff where, for an hour or more, he wandered to and fro: from the old grey lighthouse and flagstaff at one end, to pier and township at the other. He carried his hat in his hand, and the sea wind played with his fine, longish hair till it stood up like a halo of feathers round his head. That no chance passer-by should use them as spy-holes, he kept his eyes glued to the ground; but at the same time he talked to himself without pause; no longer mumbling and muttering as of old, but in a clear voice for any to hear, and stressing his words with forcible gestures: throwing out an open palm; thumping a closed fist in the air; silencing an imaginary listener with a contemptuous outward fling of the hand.

He was obliged to be energetic, for it was Mary he argued with, Mary he laboured to convince; and this could only be done by means of a tub-thumper's over-emphasis. Where he was in question. She believed others readily enough. But he never had her wholly with him; invariably she kept back some thought or feeling; was very woman in her want of straightness and simplicity. Even here, while shouting her down with: 'I tell you once for all that it *is* so!' he felt that he was not moving her. — But stay! What was it he sought to convince her of? Confound the thing! it had slipped the leash and was gone again: grope as he might, standing stockstill the while in the middle of the path and glaring seawards, he could not recapture it. Not that this was anything new. Nowadays his mind seemed a mere receptacle for disjointed thoughts, which sprang into it from nowhere, skimmed across it and vanished . . . like birds of the air. Birds. Of Paradise. Parrakeets . . . their sumptuous green and blue and rosy plumage. You caught one, clasped it round, and, even as you held it, felt its soft shape elude you, the slender tail-feathers glide past till but the empty hole of your curled hand remained. A wonderful flight of parrakeets he had once seen at . . . at . . . now *what* was the name of that place? – a Y and a K, and a Y. Damnation take it! this, too, had flown; and though he scoured and searched, working letter by letter through the alphabet: first the initial consonants, then the companion vowels . . . fitting them together – mnemonics – artificial memory . . . failing powers . . . proper names went first – gone, gone! . . . everything was gone now, lost in a blistering haze.

Such a frenzied racking of his poor old brain invariably ended thus . . . with a mind empty as a drum. And though he crouched, balled like a spider, ready to pounce on the meagrest image that shewed, nothing came: the very tension he was at held thought at bay. His senses on the other hand were strung to a morbid pitch; and little by little a clammy fear stole over him lest he should never again know connected thought; be condemned eternally to exist in this state of vacuity. Or the terror would shift, and resolve itself into an anticipation of what would, what *must* happen, to end the strain. For there was nothing final about it: the blood roared in his ears, his pulses thudded like a ship's engines, the while he waited: for a roar fit to burst his eardrums; for the sky to topple and fall upon his head, with a crash like that of splitting beams. Thunder – thunder breaking amid high mountains . . . echoing and re-echoing . . . rolling to and fro. Or oneself, with closed eyes and a cavernous mouth, emitting a scream: a mad and horrid scream that had nothing human left in it, and the uttering of which would change the face of things for ever. This might escape him at any moment; here and now: wind and sea were powerless against it – he could feel it swelling . . . mounting in his throat. He fought it down: gritted his teeth, balled his fists, his breath escaping him in hoarse, short jerks. Help, help! . . . for God's sake, help!

And help approached . . . in the shape of a middle-aged woman who came trapesing along, dragging a small child by the hand.

Swaying round his stick, which he dug into the gravel for a support, Mahony blocked her way, blurting out incoherencies; in a panic lest she should pass on, abandon him. 'Good morn'g, my good woman . . . good morn'g. A pleasant morn'g. Cool breeze. A nice lil girl you have there. A fine child. Know what I'm saying, speak from exp'rience . . . a father myself. Yes, yes, two little girls . . . golden curls, healthy, happy. Like criteks . . . chirking. A boy, too. Porridge for rickets . . . you've let yours walk too soon. Nothing like porridge for forming bone. The Highlanders . . . main sustenance . . . magnif'cent men. – Eh? What? Well, good day . . . good day!'

For, having edged round and past him, the woman grabbed her child and made off. Not till she had put a safe distance between them did she stop to look round. 'Well, I'm blowed! Of all the rum ol' cusses!' There he went, without a hat, his hair standing up anyhow, and talking away nineteen to the dozen. The whole time he'd spoke to her, too, he'd never so much as took his eyes off the ground.

In his wake Mahony left a trail of such open mouths. Espying a man digging a garden, he crossed the road to him and leaned over the fence. A painter was at work on the beach, re-painting a boat: he headed for him, wading ankle-deep through the loose, heavy sand.

Of these, the former spoke up sturdily. 'Can't say as I understand what you're drivin' at, mister, with them sissyfass stones you tork of. But this I do know: anyone who likes can have *my* job! An' today rather'n tomorrow.'

The painter knew the 'ol' doctor' by sight and stopped his work to listen, not impolitely, to certain amazing confidences that were made him. After which, watching the departing figure, he thrust his fingers under his cap and vigorously scratched his head. 'Crikey! So *that's* him, is it? Well, they do say . . . and dang me! I b'lieve they're not far wrong.'

Dog-tired, footsore, Mahony limped home, his devils exorcised for the time being. At the gate a little figure was on the watch for him – his youngest, his lovely one, towards whom his heart never failed to warm: her little-girl eyes had nothing of the boy's harassing stare. Holding her to him he walked up the path. Then: 'Good God! but I said I had two. What . . . *what* came over me? The creature will think I was lying . . . boasting!' Where should he find her, to put things right? . . . by explaining that one of the two no longer wore bodily form; but had been snatched from them amid pain and distress, the memories of which, thus rudely awakened, he now – in the twenty odd yards that divided gate from door – re-lived to their last detail, and so acutely that he groaned aloud.

Hot with the old pity, he laid a tender hand on Mary's shoulder; and following her into the dining-room ate, meekly and submissively, what she set before him: without querulous carping, or fastidious demands for the best bits on the dish. And this chastened mood holding, he even offered in the course of the afternoon to walk the children out for her.

Bidden to dress himself, Cuffy obeyed with the worst possible grace. It was dull enough walking with Mamma, who couldn't tell stories because she was always thinking things; but when it came to going out with Papa . . . well, Mamma never did it herself, and so she didn't know what it was like. But he couldn't ask to be let stop at home, because of Luce. He *had* to be there to pertect Luce, who was so little and so fat. Mamma was always saying take care of her.

Papa held their hands and they started quite nice; but soon he forgot about them, and walked so quick that they nearly had to run to keep up, and could look at each other across behind him. And they went round by the bay at the back, where the mussels were, and heaps of mud, and no waves at all. Luce got tired direckly. Her face hung down, very red. *Somehow* he'd got to make Papa go slower.

'Tell us a story.' – He said it twice before Papa heard.

'A story? Child, I've no stories left in me.'

('You ask him, Luce.')

'Tell 'bout when you was a little boy, Papa,' piped Lucie, and trotted a few steps to draw level.

'No, tell 'bout when you first saw Mamma.' Luce, she loved to hear how Papa's big sisters had smacked him and put him to bed without his supper; but he liked best the story of how Papa had seen nothing, only Mamma's leg in a white stocking and a funny black boot, when he saw her first; and it was jumping out of a window. He'd jumped out, too, and chased her; but then he let her go and went away; but as soon as he got home he slapped his leg and called himself a donkey, and hired a horse and galloped ever and ever so many miles back again, to ask her if she'd like to marry him. And first she said she was too young, and then she did. He'd heard it a million times; but it was still exciting to listen to . . . how in a hurry Papa had been.

But today everything went wrong. Papa began all right; but so loud that everybody who was passing could hear. But then he got mixed, and left out the best part, and said the same thing over again. And then he couldn't remember Aunt Tilly's name, and didn't listen when they told him, and got furious – with himself. He said he'd be forgetting his own name next, and that *would* be the end of everything. And then he jumped on to the funny bit in the arbour that Mr Purdy had teased him about, where he'd kissed somebody called Miss Jinny instead of Mamma . . . and this really truly *was* funny, because Mamma was so little and spindly and Miss Jinny was fat. But when he came to this he forgot to go on, and that he was telling them a story, and that they were there, and everything. He said: 'My God! how could I have done such an idiotic thing? . . . have made such an unspeakable fool of myself. Took her in my arms and kissed her – the wrong girl . . . the wrong girl. I can hear them still – their ribald laughter, their jeers and guffaws . . . their rough horseplay. And how she shrank before them . . . my shy little Polly! . . . my little grey dove. I to make her the butt of their vulgar mirth!' And then he made a noise as if something hurt him, and talked about pain-spots one shouldn't ever uncover, but shut up and hide from everybody. And then some more, in a dreadful hoarse voice, about a scream, and somebody who'd soon have to scream out loud if he didn't keep a hold on himself.

Cuffy couldn't bear it any longer; he pulled his hand away (Papa didn't notice) and let Papa and Luce go on alone. He stayed behind and kicked the yellow road-flowers till all their heads fell off. But then Luce looked back, and he could see she was crying. So he had to gallop up and take her hand. And then he called out – he simply shouted: 'Papa! Lucie's tired. She wants to go home to Mamma.'

'Tired? . . . my poor little lamb! Such short leggykins! See . . . Papa will carry her.' And he tried to lift her up, and first he couldn't, she was so heavy, and when he did, he only staggered a few steps and then put her down again. Luce had to walk home with their hands, and all the way back he made haste and asked questions hard, about the yellow flowers and why they grew on the road, and why the wind always sang in the treble and never in the bass, and always the same tune; till they got to the gate. But you didn't tell how Papa had been . . . not a word! You were too ashamed.

Shame and fear.

If you were coming home from Granny's, walking nicely, holding Luce's hand and taking care of her, and if you met a lot of big, rough, rude boys and girls coming from the State School, what did you do? Once, you would have walked past them on the other side of the road, sticking your chin up, and not taking any notice. Now you still kept on the other side (if you didn't run like mad as soon as you saw them), but you looked down instead of up, and your face got so red it hurt you.

For always now what these children shouted after you was: 'Who'd have a cranky doctor for a father? . . . who'd have a cranky doctor for a father!' and they sang it like a song, over and over, till you had gone too far to hear. And you couldn't run away; you *wouldn't* have! You squeezed Luce's hand till you nearly squeezed it off, and whispered: '*Don't* cry, Luce . . . don't let them see you cry.' And Luce sniffed and sniffed, trying not to.

You didn't tell this either; nor even speak to Luce about it. You just tried to pretend to yourself you didn't know. Like once when Miss Prestwick was new and had taken them too long a walk at Barambogie, and Luce hadn't liked to ask, and had had an accident: he'd been ever so partic'lar then not to look at her; he'd kept his head turned right round the other way. That was 'being a gentleman'. But this about Papa . . . though you tried your hardest to be one here, too, you couldn't help it; it was always there. Like as if you'd cut your finger and a little clock ticked inside. And being good didn't help either; for it wasn't your *fault*, you hadn't *done* anything. And yet were ever so ashamed . . . about somebody . . . who wasn't you . . . yet belonged to you. Somebody people thought silly and had to laugh at . . . for his funny walk . . . and the way he talked. – Oh, *why* had one's Papa got to be like this? Other children's Papas weren't. They walked about . . . properly . . . and if they met you they said: 'Hullo!' or 'How do you do?'

Something else wormed in him. Once in Barambogie he had seen a dreadful-looking boy, with his mouth open and his tongue hanging out, and bulgy eyes like a fish. And when he'd asked Marie she said, oh, he was just cranky and an idjut. But Papa wasn't like *that*! The thought that anyone could think he was, was too awful to bear.

'What's it really mean, Bridget, cranky?' he asked, out of this pain, of the small servant-girl.

And Bridget, who was little more than a child herself, first looked round to make sure that her mistress was not within hearing, then mysteriously put her mouth to his ear and whispered: 'It means . . . *what your Pa is.*'

Granny, on whose knee he sat, held him from her for an instant, then snatched him close. 'Why bother your little head with such things?'

'I just want to know.'

As usual Granny turned to Pauline for aid; and Pauline came over to them and asked: 'Who's been saying things to you, my dear? Take no notice, Cuffy. Oh, well, it just means . . . different – yes, that's what it means: different from other people.' But he saw her look at Granny and Granny at her; and his piece of cake was extra big that day, and had more currants in it than Luce's.

But a 'diffrunt doctor' didn't mean anything at all.

But now you and Luce never stopped running all the way home, and you went a long way round, so as not to have to go down the street where the State School was. And when Papa took you for a walk, you *chose* the hidjus way at the back.

When all the time you might have gone on the real beach, by the real sea.

For what a lovely place this would have been, if it hadn't been for Papa. There wasn't any wattle here to shut your eyes and smell and smell at, and you couldn't smell the sun either, like in Barambogie. But the beach and the sea made up for everything. You could have played on the beach till you died. The sand was hot and yellow and so soft that it felt like a silk dress running through your fingers; and there were big shells with the noise of the sea in them, and little ones with edges like teeth; and brown and green and red and pink seaweed; and pools to paddle in; and caves to explore when the tide went out. And soon lots of little boys and girls – *nice* ones – who you could have played with if you had been allowed, came to the seaside, too. But Mamma always said: keep to yourselves. Which meant there was only him and Luce. And then you learned to swim. The bathing-woman said you were a born fish, and you wished you were: then you could have stopped in the water for ever – and never have needed to go home again – or for walks with Papa.

Fear. All sorts of fears.

One was, when he lay in bed at night and listened to the wind, which never stopped crying. Mamma said it was because the room was at a corner of the house, and the corner caught the wind; but Bridget said it was dead people: the noise people made when they were dead. 'But my little sister Lallie's dead!' 'Well, then, it's her you hear.' (But Lallie had never cried like that.) But Bridget said it was the voice of her soul in torment, hot in hell; and though he *knew* this wasn't true, because Lallie was in heaven, he couldn't help thinking about it at night, when he was awake in the dark. Then it did sound like a voice – lots of voices – and as if they were crying and sobbing because they were being hurt. Other times it seemed as if the wind was screeching just at him, very angry, and getting angrier and angrier, till he had to sit up in bed and call out (not too loud because of Luce): 'Oh, *what's* the matter?' But it didn't stop: it just went on. And even if you stuffed your fingers in both your ears, you couldn't shut it out; it was too treble. Till you couldn't stand it any longer, and jumped out of your own bed and went to Luce's, and lifted the blankets and got in beside her – she was always fast asleep – and held on to her little fat back. And then you went to sleep, too.

But Mamma was cross in the morning when she came in and found you: she said it wasn't nice to sleep two in one bed.

'But you and Papa do!'

'That's quite different. A big double bed.'

'Couldn't Luce and me have a double bed, too?'

'Certainly not,' said Mamma; and was ashamed of him for being afraid of the dark. Which he wasn't.

Worse still were those nights when he had to lie and think about what was going to happen to them when all their money was done. Mamma didn't know; she often said: 'What *is* to become of us?' And it was Papa's fault. They never ought to have come to live here; they ought to have gone to a place called Narrong, where there was plenty of money; but Papa wouldn't; so now they hadn't enough, and quite soon mightn't have any at all. Perhaps not anything to eat either. His mind threw up a picture of Luce crying for bread, which so moved him that he had to hurry on. Maria's mother had taken in washing. But you couldn't think of Mamma doing that: standing at the tubs and mangling and ironing, and getting scolded if the buttons came off. No, he wouldn't ever let her! He'd hold her hands, so that she couldn't use the soap. Or else he'd pour the water out of the tubs.

But *quite* the most frightening thing was, when no more money was left, Mamma and Papa might have to go to prison. Once, when he was little, he'd heard them talking about somebody who couldn't pay his debts, and so had cheated people and been put in gaol. And this dim memory returning now to torture him, he rolled and writhed, in one of childhood's hellish agonies. *What* would he and Luce do? How could they get up in the morning and have breakfast, and know what to put on, or what they were to practise, without Mamma and – no! *just* without Mamma. And though he might talk big and say he wouldn't let her be a washerwoman, yet inside him he knew quite well he was only a little boy, and not a bit of use, *really*. If the sergeant came and said she had to go to prison, nothing he could do would stop her. Oh, Mamma . . . Mamma! She alone, her dear, substantial presence, stood guard between him and his shadowy throng of fears. And now, when he and Lucie raced home hand in hand of an afternoon, their first joint impulse was to make sure of Mamma: to see that she was still there . . . hadn't gone out, or . . . been taken away. Only close up to where she stood, radiating love and safety, a very pillar of strength, was it possible for their fragile minds to sustain, uninjured, the grim tragedy that overhung their home, darkening the air, blotting out the sun, shattering to ruin all accustomed things; in a fashion at once monstrous and incredible.

CHAPTER FOUR

As if struck by a beneficent blindness, Mary, alone unseeing, alone unsuspecting, held to her way. And, in excuse of her wilful ignoring of many a half-thought and passing impression, her care to keep these from coming to consciousness, there was this to be said: she knew Richard so well. Who but she had endured, for the better part of a lifetime, his whimsies, his crotchets? When had she ever thought of him, or spoken of him, but as queer, freakish, eccentric? Hence, was it now to be wondered at that, as age crept on and added its quota, his peculiarities should wax rather than wane? The older, the odder seemed but natural to her, who had never looked for anything else.

Meanwhile October passed into November, November into December; and one day – overnight, as it seemed – the season was upon them. The houses on either side were full of new faces; there was hardly a spare seat in church on Sunday; you had to wait your turn for a cabin at the baths. And the deck of the little steamer, which came daily, was crowded with lively, white-clad people. Now was the time ... if ever ... for Richard's fortunes to turn.

But the days dragged by in the old monotony; not a single new patient knocked at the door. Instead, by the end of the week Mary had definite information that old Barker was being called out again. Yes, people were actually preferring this antediluvian old man to Richard. And could one altogether blame them? Who would want to consult a doctor who went about talking to himself, and without a hat? ... who omitted to brush his hair or brush the fluff off his coat-collar, and thought nothing of appearing in public with a two-days' growth on his chin? She could imagine landladies and hotel-keepers advising their guests: 'Oh, I shouldn't have *him*, if I were you. Extremely queer! Goes nowhere.'

Boarders. It was boarders or nothing now . . . and not a moment to lose either, with a season that lasted for a bare three months. Like the majority of people in Shortlands, she would have to seize the chance and make money while she could, by throwing open her house to strangers. Grimly she tied on her bonnet and went down into the township, to hang out her name and her terms as a boarding-house-keeper; to face the curious looks, the whispers and raised eyebrows: what? . . . the grand Mrs Mahony? . . . reduced to taking in lodgers? Not till she got home again did she know how high she had carried her head, how rigidly set her jaw, over the taking of this step which would once have seemed like the end of the world to her. But, true to herself, she refused to allow her strength to be sapped by vain regrets. Instead, she turned with stubborn energy to the re-arrangement of her house. If Richard and she moved into the children's bedroom, and the children slept in a small inner room lit by a skylight, she would have two good-sized bedrooms to let, in which she could put up as many as four to five people. At two guineas a head this would bring in ten a week. Ten guineas a week for three months! . . . of which not a penny should pass out of her own hands.

On the day this happened — and in the swiftness and secrecy of her final decision there was something that resembled a dash of revenge — on this day, Richard was out as usual all the morning, strolling about on cliffs or beach. And though he came home to dinner, he was in one of his most vacant moods, when he just sat and ate — ravenously — noticing nothing of what went on around him. — But anyhow she would not at this eleventh hour have started to thresh the matter out with him. Better, first to get everything irrevocably fixed and settled.

Perhaps, though, she had a dim foreboding of what awaited her. For the next time he came back he was wider awake, and took in the situation at a glance. And then there was a scene the like of which she had never known. He behaved like a madman, stamping and shouting about the house, abusing her, and frightening the poor children out of their wits. In vain she followed him, reasoning, arguing, throwing his own words in his teeth: had the idea not been his, originally? Besides, what else was left for her to do, with no patients, no money coming in, and old Barker resuming practice? He would not listen. Frenzy seized him at the thought of his threatened privacy: strangers to occupy his bedroom, hang their hats in the passage, go in and out of his front door. Not as long as *he* lived! 'My mother . . . my sisters . . . the old home in Dublin – *they* would sooner have starved!' And as he spoke he sent hat and stick flying across the hall table, and the brass card-tray clattering to the floor. He kicked it to one side, and with an equally rough push past Mary, who had stooped to recover it, banged into the surgery and locked the door. And there he remained. She could neither get at him nor get a word out of him.

Late that night the children, their parents' neighbours now, sat miserably huddled up together. Lucie had been fast asleep; but Cuffy had so far only managed to doze uneasily, in this funny room where the window was in the roof instead of the wall: he was quite sure something would look in at him through it, or else fall down on his head. Now they sat and clung to each other, listening . . . listening . . . their little hearts pounding in their chests. 'Oh, *don't*, Papa! Oh, what's he doing to her?' To which Cuffy gave back sturdily: '*I* don't hear anything, Luce, truly I don't!' 'Oh, yes, you do! And now I know she'll go away . . . Mamma will . . . and leave us.' 'No, she won't. She told me so yesterday – promised she wouldn't ever!' Though his teeth were chattering with fear.

For Mary had at last reached what seemed the limits of human endurance. After pleading and imploring; after reasoning, as with a little child: after stabbing him with bitter words, and achieving nothing but to tear and wound her own heart, she gave it up, and, turning bodily from him, as she had already turned in mind and deed, she crushed her face into the pillow and gave way, weeping till she could weep no more; as she had not wept since the death of her child. But on this night no loving arms reached out to her, to soothe and console. Richard might have been made of stone: he lay stockstill, unmoved, staring with glassy eyes into the moonlight.

From sheer exhaustion she thought she must have sunk into a momentary unconsciousness; for, coming to with a start, she found the place beside her empty. Throwing back the sheet she jumped to the floor, her temples a-throb, and ran into the hall. There, among the lines and squares of greenish moonshine that filtered through the open doors of the rooms, stood Richard, a tall white figure, just as he had got out of bed. He was at the front door, fingering the lock, plainly on the point of leaving the house. Abominably frightened, but mindful of the sleeping children, she called to him under her breath: '*Richard!* What are you doing?'

He did not answer: she had to go up to him and shake his arm. 'What's the matter? Where are you going?'

'To find peace.'

So gaunt and old . . . the ribbed neck and stooping shoulders . . . the poor thin shanks: and once, he, too, had been young, and handsome, and upstanding. As always, did she compare present with past, an immense compassion swept through Mary, driving every smaller, meaner feeling before it. She put out her arms, put them round him, to hold, to protect. 'Oh, but not like this . . . and at this hour. Wait till morning. Come back and try to sleep. Come, my dear, come!'

But he resisted her. Only by dint of half pushing, half pulling, did she manage to get him back to bed. He seemed dazed; as if he were moving in a dream. And though, during the hours that followed, she sometimes believed he slept, she herself did not dare to close her eyes, so great was the fright he had given her.

But Mahony slept as little as she did. With his back to her, withdrawn from any chance contact, he merely put into practice an art learned in scores of wakeful nights: that of lying taut as the dead, while the long hours ticked away. Let her think what she chose . . . think him asleep – *or* dead . . . as long as she held her cruel tongue. His hatred of her passed imagining: his mind was a seething cauldron of hate and fury. Fury with himself. For he had been within an ace of deliverance, of getting through that door; beyond which lay everything his heart desired: space . . . freedom . . . peace. One and all drenched in the moon's serene light. This light it was that drew him; affecting him as do certain scenes or people which, on seeing them for the first time, you feel you have known long since . . . in dreams, in a dream life. The sea, too, lay without. Seas . . . silvered masses . . . leaping and tumbling under a great round moon. And then, at the last moment, he had been baulked of his freedom by the knowledge that he was grown too tall for the doorway. To pass through it he would have needed to risk knocking his head against the doorpost, or to stoop; and tonight either alternative was beyond him. His poor head felt so queer . . . so queer. Top-heavy, yet weightless as a toy balloon. Already on first laying it down, he had had the old sensation of sinking through the pillow; of falling head-foremost into nothingness. Hence he dared not risk a blow; or the dizzy fit stooping would entail. And so he had been caught and dragged back; made a prisoner of . . . yet once more. But this time should be the last. Revenge! . . . revenge is sweet. Vengeance is mine, saith the Lord: I will repay. Fill the house with strangers, would she? – *his* house? Cut the ground from under his feet? – deprive him of his only haven? . . . why! even a rabbit had its burrow. To be without covert; to know no place to creep to for hiding, when the fit, the burning need of escape seized him? – And then his eyes. What in God's name should he do with his eyes? Strangers at his table? On your p's and q's with strangers; aye, and on the watch, too, lest they should find you out. And for all this he had only Mary to thank – Mary, who might have been expected to show mercy. She? As well ask blood of a stone. – And now such a paroxysm of hatred shook him: the outcome, solidified, intensified, of thousands of conflicts; of the ceaseless clash and war of their opposing temperaments: that it was all he could do to master the itch his fingers felt to close round her throat. But he would be even with her yet! . . . somehow . . . somehow . . . though he did not yet know how. But . . . *it would have to do with money!* For it was money she was after: with her it had always been money, from first to last. What new tricks was she hatching this time? Was it going to *cost* money to take these lodgers in? Or was she doing it to *make* money? He was so confused tonight; his poor brain seemed smothered in cobwebs. But it didn't matter, either way would do. As long as he remembered that *it had to do with money*. And surely, surely, the long night would now soon end, and day break, and he be free to get up and set about what had to be done. (His home, his poor home, his sole refuge . . . eyes . . . greenish eyes in the moonlight, coming towards him, and, most horribly, without any accompanying face.) First, though, he would have to pull himself together to endure in silence, without an answering shriek, the blast of the mill-whistle – that thrice-accursed, infernal din! Not much more than an hour now, till it was due to sound.

At breakfast he sat silent, seemed lost in thought. And Mary, to whom the dark hours had brought no clearness – every way she turned seemed barred to her – watched him, the passion of pity that had been wakened by the sight of his poor old scraggy form at the door in the moonlight, trying to escape from her – from *her*! – still hot in her.

But the meal over, he roused to a kind of life. Taking his little favourite on his knee, he caressed her. And then, of a sudden, he grew solicitous about the children: their morning walk, their daily dip in the sea. 'Or' – to Lucie this, as he rocked her to and fro – 'we shall not have them growing up tall and sturdy!' (If only he could hold on to the fact that *it had to do with money*.)

'Trust me to look after them,' said Mary shortly, at a third repetition. Her own thoughts ran: If I can't talk to someone I shall go crazy. Something will have to be done. I know. There's old Mrs Spence. She is so wise.

Would he never be rid of them? It seemed this morning as if Mary deliberately invented jobs to detain them. He fell to pacing the dining-room, his arms a-swing . . . and each time he came to the window he lifted his eyes in alarm, lest the flag should have run up the flagstaff. A ship at this moment would ruin everything.

But . . . softly! Mary was growing suspicious. 'Are you stopping at home then?'

'Yes, yes, I'm staying in. I'll look after the house.' (Ha, ha!)

And at last gowns and towels, spades and buckets were collected, the children's hats and her bonnet tied on, and off they went. It was a radiant summer morning, with a light breeze playing, but Mary saw nothing of it: her brain continued its feverish work, in the hope of finding some way out. Suppose I induced him to leave home for a time? – to go away for a holiday? . . . and so get the house to myself. Or even persuaded him to put up at an hotel. But before she had gone any distance, she became aware of such a strange inner excitement that it was only with difficulty she mastered an impulse to turn and go back to the house. Why had he been so anxious to get rid of them? Why this sudden odd concern for the children? – and here there leapt in her mind a story she had once read, or heard, of somebody who had sent his wife and his children out for a walk, and then deliberately hanged himself on a nail behind the scullery-door. But, this half-born apprehension spoken out, she fell righteously foul of herself: her reason, her common sense, that part of her which had waged a life-long war with the fantastic, the incorporeal, rose in arms. Such *nonsense*! Really . . . if one once began to let oneself go. . . . (Besides, wasn't Bridget constantly in and out of the scullery?) Imaginings like these came solely from want of sleep. How angry Richard would be, too, if she reappeared!

So she went on, as usual making Cuffy the scapegoat for her nervous perplexity. 'Don't eat your bathing-dress, you naughty boy! How often am I to tell you . . .'

'I'm *not* eating it! Only smelling.' – He did though, sometimes. (And his sponge, too.)

'Well, that's not nice either.'

'It *is*! It's scrumptious,' cried Cuffy warmly. How did Mamma know? . . . she never bathed. The salty smell – and the taste – of damp blue serge when it was hot with the sun – ooh! too lovely for words. If he put it to his nose he could hardly keep his legs from running: it made him shiver all over, simply not able to *wait*, to be in the water. And directly they came to the Bluff he bolted: shot along the narrow wooden bridge that ran out from the beach, past the counter where gowns and towels were for hire, and into the Baths, where nothing but gowns and towels were hanging on the rails to dry, all one big salty smell. And you poked your nose into every empty cabin, to find a dry one; and then, hi! off with your clothes before Luce and Mamma got there, and into your gown, hot with the sun, and all prickly and tickly; and then you galloped round the platforms and out on the springboard, which bounced you ever so high in the air, into water they said was fifteen feet deep, but you didn't know, only if you jumped straight, and made yourself quite stiff, you went down and down, and took ever such a time to come up. Then you swam back to the steps – they were all slimy, and with seaweed washing round them, for they weren't ever out of the water – and up and off the board again, again and again, till it was time to fetch Luce, who was afraid to jump springboard.

'If I'm not back in an hour make them come out,' Mary instructed the fat bathing-woman, who knew what young water-rats the chicks were, and could be trusted to use force is necessary. – And with this she turned to go.

But she had done no more than set foot on the wooden causeway, when she saw someone dash on to it from the other end, push rudely past a group of people, a servant it was . . . and it was *Bridget*, with her hair half down, in her dirty morning apron . . . and she came rushing up to her and seized her hand, and pulled her by it, and sobbed and cried, for everyone to hear: 'Oh, Mrs Mahony, come home! . . . come home quick!

The doctor's bin and lighted a fire on the surgery table. He's burning the house down!'

'Bridget!'

Her heart, which had begun to hammer at first sight of the girl, gave a gigantic bound, then seemed to stop beating: she had to lean against the wooden railing and press both hands to it, to get it to re-start. But, even so, she heard her own voice saying: 'Be quiet! Don't make such a noise. There are people . . . I'm coming, I'm coming.'

Home! Uphill, through loose, clogging sand; a short cut over the grass of the gardens; along one reddish street and into another, and round into a third; hampered at every step by her long, heavy woman's clothing; not daring to run, for fear of exciting comment, struggling even yet, for Richard's sake, to keep up appearances; the perspiration glistening below her bonnet, her breath coming stormily; but with only one thought: that of being in time to save him. At her side Bridget, gasping out her story. If it hadn't bin that he hadn't had no matches, she'd never have known. But he'd had to come to the kitchen for some, and she'd seen at once there was something in the wind. He'd looked at her, oh, ever so queer! And first he'd tried to take 'em without her seeing him . . . and when she had, he'd laughed, and had went up the passage laughing away to himself. She'd gone after him on tiptoe to see what he was up to, and she'd peeped through the crack of the door, and he'd got that black tin box of his open, and was taking papers and tied-up things out of it, piling 'em on the table, and striking matches and setting fire to 'em. Holy Mother o' God, *how* she'd run!

There was smoke in the passage. The surgery was full of it; full of bits of flying ash and burnt papers. Through this she saw Richard. He stood at the table, the deal top of which was scorched and blackened, his dispatch-box open and empty before him, his hands in a heap of ashes which he was strewing about the room. He laughed and shouted. She heard her own name.

'*Richard!* My God! What have you done?'

Mary? . . . Mary's voice? Recoiling, he threw up his arms as if to ward off a blow, looking round at her with a face that was wry and contorted. At the sight of her standing in the doorway, he tried to shake his fist at her; but his arm crumpled up, refused to obey; tried to hurl a scurrilous word . . . to spit at her: in vain. What did happen was the thing against which, waking and sleeping, he had battled with every atom of his failing self-control: there escaped him, at long last, the scream, the insane scream, which signified the crossing of the rubicon. And, as it broke loose, ringing in his ears like the bestial cry of a wounded, maddened animal, everything turned black before his eyes. He lost his balance, staggered, caught at a chair and went down, with the chair on top of him, like an ox felled by a single blow of the pole-axe. And there he lay, in a confused and crumpled heap on the floor.

And Mary, whom no audible sound had reached, who had read into the outward fling of his arm towards her only an appeal for help, for support, was on her knees beside him, her bonnet awry, her dress in disarray, crushing the poor old head to her breast and crying: 'Richard! My *darling*! What is it, oh, what is it?'

But to these words, with which she had so often sought enlightenment, sought understanding, there was now no reply.

CHAPTER FIVE

His stertorous breathing could be heard through the house. Except for this, he might have been dead . . . behind the snow-white dimity and muslin hangings which she had put up in honour of those strangers who would now never cross the threshold. For Bowes-Smith, the well-known Melbourne physician whom she had called in on the advice of Dr Barker – yes! with Richard lying senseless at her feet she had forgotten everything but his need, and had sent Bridget flying for the old man whom she had borne so bitter a grudge; and he had come at once, and been kindness itself. So active, too: it was hard to believe that he was between twenty and thirty years Richard's senior – oh, how *did* some people manage to live so long and be so healthy! But in spite of his consoling words, she could see that he took a very grave view of Richard's case. And Bowes-Smith and he had had a sheerly endless consultation – from which, of course, they shut her out – after which the former had broken it to her that, even if he recovered from the present fit, Richard would remain more or less of a sick man for the rest of his life.

The utmost care was essential; an entire absence of excitement. 'For I cannot conceal from you that such apoplectiform attacks, which – as in this case – differ little or not at all from true apoplexy, will be liable to recur.'

He stood on the dining-room hearthrug, tall, lugubrious, sandy-whiskered, holding his gold-rimmed pince-nez in his hand, and tapping the air with it while he cast about for words, which came laboriously. They had known him well in the old days, and she remembered this habit; it had always made him seem something of a bore. Now it maddened her. For she was keyed up to hear the truth, learn the worst; and to be obliged to sit there, listening to him stumbling and fumbling! He was so bland, too, so non-committal; how differently he would have talked to Richard had she lain ill. But she was only a woman; and, doctors being what they were . . . oh, she knew something about them from the inside. Usen't Richard to say that it was etiquette in the profession to treat a patient's relatives, and particularly his womenfolk, as so many cretins?

Ignoring her blunt question: 'But if it isn't true apoplexy, then what is it?' Bowes-Smith proceeded deliberately to catechize her.

'I don't know, Mrs Mahony, whether you are . . . h'm . . . whether it is . . . er . . . news to you that I saw your husband some two or three months back? He . . . er . . . consulted me, at the time, with regard to . . . h'm . . . to an attack . . . nay, to recurring attacks of vertigo. I found him then under no . . . h'm . . . no delusion as to his own state. He said nothing to you? Did not take you into his confidence?'

'No, nothing,' said Mary dully: and inconsequently remembered the letter she had had from Richard when she was trying to induce him to settle in Narrong. She hadn't known then what to believe; more than half suspected him of writing as he did to further his own ends.

'And you have not noticed anything . . . h'm . . . out of the way? There has been no marked change in his habits? No . . . er . . . oddness, or eccentricity?' The questions lumbered along, she sitting the while fiercely knotting her fingers.

'Nothing,' she said again. Adding, though, in spite of herself: 'But then he has always been so peculiar. If he did seem a little odder of late, I merely put it down to his growing old.'

'Quite so . . . er . . . most natural.' (She was keeping things back, of course; wives always did. He remembered her well: a handsome creature she had been when last he saw her. The eyes were still very striking.) 'And now . . . er . . . with regard to the present attack. Are you aware of anything having happened to . . . er . . . cause him undue excitement . . . or agitation?'

'No,' said Mary staunchly. How could it matter now, what had brought the fit on? Wild horses would not have dragged from her any allusion to their bitter quarrel of the night before. That would have meant turning out, to this stranger, the dark side of their married life. However, she again glossed over the bluntness of her denial with: 'But he was always one to work himself up over trifles.'

'Well, well! My colleague here . . . and if, at any time, you would care to see me again, I am entirely at your disposal.' (No need to trouble the poor creature with more, at present. Yes, truly, a magnificent pair of optics!) 'Do not be . . . h'm . . . alarmed at any slight . . . er . . . stiffness or rigidity of the limbs that may ensue. That will pass.'

And I a doctor's wife! thought Mary hotly. Aloud she said: 'Oh, I'm not afraid – of paralysis or anything – as long as he is spared.' And while the two men confabbed anew, she went to the bedroom and stood looking down at Richard. Her own husband . . . and she could not even be told frankly what was the matter with him. For twenty-five years and more she had had him at her side, to give the truth if she asked for it. She had never known till now how much this meant to her.

Meanwhile she spilt no jot of her strength in brooding or repining: every act, every thought was concentrated on him alone. And not till the first signs of betterment appeared: when the dreadful snoring ceased and his temperature fell to normal; when his eyes began to follow her about the room; when he was able to move one hand to point to what he wanted, not till then did she sit down, cold and grim, to face the future.

'By God! what's to become of us?'

A pitiful forty-odd pounds standing to his credit in a Melbourne Bank, and her own poor remnant of Tilly's loan, was literally all they had in the world. In that last mad holocaust everything else had gone: deeds and mortgages, letters and securities, down to the last atom of scrip. He had piled and burnt till the dispatch-box was empty. (Who would now be able to prove what shares he had held? Or how much had been paid off on the mortgage?) The house at Barambogie was still on their hands; and almost the whole of their lease at Shortlands had still to run. How were these rents to be met? . . . and what would happen if they weren't? She would need expert advice, probably have to employ a lawyer – a thought that made her shiver. For she had the natural woman's fear of the law and its followers: thought of these only in terms of bills of costs . . . and sharp, dishonest practices.

But that must all come later. The burning question was, where to turn for ready money. The little she had would go nowhere: Richard's illness . . . presents to the doctors, the servant's wages – nor could they live on air. Boarders were out of the question now: for Richard's sake. *What* could she do? What did other women do who were left in her plight, with little children dependent on them? Driving her mind back, she saw that as a rule these 'widows and things' were content to live at somebody else's expense, to become the limpets known as 'poor relations', leaving the education of their children to a male relative. But she had not been Richard's wife for nothing. At the mere thought of such a thing, her back stiffened. Never! Not as long as she had a leg to stand on . . . mere woman though she was.

It's not money I want this time, Tilly, she wrote: and Tilly was but one of many who, the news of Richard's breakdown having spread abroad as on an invisible telegraph, came forward with offers of help. *It's work. I don't care what; if only I can earn enough to keep us together.* But here even Tilly's ingenuity failed her: women of Mary's standing (let alone her advanced age, her inexperience) did not turn out of their sheltered homes and come to grips with the world. Impossible, utterly impossible, was to be read between the lines of her reply.

And, as day after day went by without enlightenment, it began to look as if Tilly was right. Beat her brains as she would, Mary would find no way out.

To old Mrs Spence, who in this crisis had proved a friend indeed, she finally made a clean breast of her despair.

'There seems literally nothing a woman *can* do. Except teach – and I'm too old for that. Nor have I the brains. I was married so young. And had so little schooling myself. No, the plain truth is, I'm fit for nothing. Really there come moments when I can see us all ending in the Benevolent Asylum.'

It was here that Mrs Spence, nodding her sage, white-capped head in sympathy, made the tentative suggestion: 'I wonder, my dear . . . has it never occurred to you to try to enter Government service?'

Mary winced . . . she hoped not too perceptibly. 'Oh, I'm afraid that again would need more brains than I've got.' It was well meant, of course, but . . . *so* to cut oneself adrift!

Undaunted the old lady went on. 'Plenty of women before you have done it. As a postmistress, you would have a house rent-free, with free lighting and firing, all sorts of perquisites, and a fixed salary. And I think, my dear, with the many friends you have at court, it would be easy for you to skip preliminaries. My son, I know, would be only too happy to help you in any way he could.'

'You're very kind. But I feel sure I'm too old . . . and too stupid.'

But that night, as she tossed wakeful on the hard little bed she had set up beside Richard's, her friend's words came back to her, and rang in her ears till they had effectually chased away all chance of sleep: so spurred and pricked her, in fact, that she sat up in bed and, hunching her knees, propped her elbows on them and dug her clenched fists into her chin. A house rent-free . . . nothing to pay for light and firing . . . a fixed salary – she didn't know how much, of course, but it would need to be enough to support a family on, so many postmasters being married men. It would also mean that she could keep Richard and the children with her; and the fear of having to part from them was the worst she knew. And then those rents, those dreadful rents, which hung round her neck like millstones . . . might she not perhaps . . . But, oh! the come-down . . . the indignity . . . the *publicity* of the thing – in this colony where she had been so well known. A postmistress . . . she, a postmistress! . . . forced to step out into the open, become a kind of public woman. To see her name – *Richard's* name – in printed lists, in official communications. (She might even have to tell her age.) Men – strange men – would be over her, she their subordinate, answerable to them for what she did. Worse still, she herself would have men under her, young men of a class with which she had never come in contact. What would her friends and acquaintances say, to see her sink like this in the social scale? (At which her native plain-dealing jogged her elbow with the reflection that it would soon shew who were her true friends, and who not.) Oh, it was easy to *say* you didn't mind what you turned your hand to. But when it came to doing it! – And then, too, suppose she wasn't equal to the work? As she had said, and truly, she had no faith in her own abilities. Directly it came to book- or head-learning, she thought of herself as dull and slow. Though here, oddly enough, the thought perked up and declined to be quenched that, if Richard had only let her have a say, however small, in the management of his affairs, these might never have got into the muddle they had. Figures didn't come hard to her.

Thus was she tossed and torn, between a womanly repugnance, her innate self-distrust, and her sound common sense. And she got up in the morning still having failed to reconcile the combatants. It was the sight of Richard that determined her. When she saw him sitting propped up among his pillows, his lower jaw on the shake; when she heard his pitiful attempts to say what he wanted — like a little child he was having to be taught the names of things all over again — when she looked at this wreck, every other consideration fell away. What did she matter? ... what did anything or anybody matter? — if only she could restore to health and contrive to keep, in something of the comfort he had been used to, this poor old comrade of the years.

Henry Ocock held office in the present ministry; and it was to Mr Henry she turned; for they had a common bond in the memory of poor Agnes. She wrote, without hedging, of Richard's utter physical collapse; of the loss — through fire — of his papers and securities; the urgent necessity she was under of finding employment. It had been suggested to her that she might try to enter Government service. Would he, for the sake of their old friendship, do her the great kindness to use his influence, on her behalf, with the present Postmaster General? Mr Spence, in charge of the local office, had offered her the preliminary training. Had this not been so ... *for I tell you plainly I could never go in for an examination — try to pass the Civil Service or anything of that sort. It would be quite beyond me.*

Almost by return she held a page-long telegram in her hand, in which, making no attempt (as she had half feared he would) to press a loan on her, Mr Henry said that he was only too happy to be able to help her. Her request came in the nick of time. An up-country vacancy was on the point of occurring. Did she think she could be ready, with Spence's aid, to take over charge there, say, in six weeks' time? If so, the P.M.G. would put in a relieving officer for that period. The rush and hurry of the thing cut the ground from under her feet. Hardly knowing whether she stood on her head or her heels, she straightway telegraphed acceptance. — And so the die was cast.

Henceforward she was a member of the working classes. To begin with, she spent every afternoon from two till six at the Shortlands post office, learning her job.

The calvary this was to her, none but she knew. She would never have believed she was so sensitive, so touchy. A host of prejudices (many of them no doubt imbibed from Richard) which she hadn't even been aware of possessing, woke to life in her. The very fact of being tied down to leave home at a set hour, like any clerk or shopman, seemed to humiliate her, who had never come and gone but at her own sweet will. Then, everyone in the township knew, of course, where she was bound for. People eyed her and whispered about her, and pointed her out to one another as she passed: in her full skirts flounced to the waist, her dolman of silk velvet, her feathered bonnet; yes, there she went, Mrs Dr Mahony off to learn to be a postmistress! The half-mile seemed unending; before she reached her destination her pale cheeks were dyed rose-pink.

In the office she stood, a middle-aged lady (close on two-and-forty years old) bonnetless and capless, amid a posse of young clerks: the telegraph operator, the messenger, the indoor clerk, the postman: to whom she was an object of unending curiosity. All of whom, too, could do in a twinkling the things that came so hard to her. And then their manners! They jostled her, failed to apologize, kept their hats on in her presence, lolled and lounged, bandied private jokes, laughed and talked openly in disregard of her, did Mr Spence quit the office. Her courage might sometimes have failed her, had it not been that the money side of the business gave her so little trouble: she learnt in no time how to issue a money-order, to enter up a savings-book deposit, to handle postage stamps and registered letters; even to draw up the financial 'statement' that was forwarded daily and monthly to Head Office. The telegraph it was that baffled her. Oh, this awful morse code! It was like going to school again to learn one's alphabet. Her memory was weak and undeveloped: she floundered and was hopelessly at sea amid the array of dots and dashes that stood for letters. The little paper handbook containing the code grew as shabby and dog's-eared as a child's lesson-book. For she carried it with her everywhere she went, and slept with it under her pillow; of a night often starting up and striking a match to see if it was B that had three dots after its dash, or K more than one between its two. *Never* would she be able to 'take by ear'! How she marvelled at these young clerks, who could jot down a whole telegram without so much as a glance at the tape. Whereas she had painfully to puzzle the message out, letter by letter. And the 'sending' was harder still: with her lips pinched thin, her head thrown back, her black eyes fixed, in desperate concentration, on the empty air, laboriously she hammered out dash and dot, dot and dash.

All this, too, with one anxious ear turned towards home, where things grew worse instead of better. She had hoped that, once the physical effects of the stroke had worn off, and Richard was able to walk and talk again, his mind, too, would clear. Now, she began to doubt whether he would ever again be *quite* himself. Days came when he sat and brooded from morning till night: sat with his head on one thin hand, staring before him with eyes so sorrowful that it hurt you to look at them . . . though what he was thinking or remembering, she could never get him to say. At other times he was unable to be still, or to stay in the same room for a minute on end; and then it took all her influence and persuasion to keep him indoors. The children, poor mites, in whose charge she was forced to leave him while she worked, could do nothing with him, and her first question of the forlorn little pair who ran to meet her, of an evening, was invariably: 'Where's Papa?' To which more often than not the answer came: 'Gone out. He *would* go, Mamma . . . we couldn't stop him. He went to look for you.'

And then it was always: 'Run, Cuffy, run quick! . . . and find him.'

Once Cuffy had said: 'Oh, *can't* Bridget go instead of me?' but Mamma had looked so funny at him that he'd never done it again. He went; his hands cold like frogs. For he was so ashamed. Papa would be standing on the green in front of the blacksmith's, and the blacksmith had stopped work, and a whole lot of larrikins were there as well, and they were all listening to Papa . . . who was sort of play-acting to himself with his hands . . . and laughing at him and making fun. And Papa didn't see them; but *he* did. And then he wished Papa was dead, and that he didn't ever need to come and fetch him again. But he took his hand and said, quite small: 'Papa, come home! Mamma wants you.' And then he left off acting direckly, and was most awfly glad and said: 'Where is she? Where *is* Mamma?' and came away, holding on to his hand like a little girl, and nearly running to get there.

That was one thing he hated. The other was, every afternoon Mamma went out and left him and Luce quite alone . . . with Papa. (And you didn't *like* to be with Papa, since he couldn't speak right: when you heard him say a spoon and he meant a chair, it made you feel sick inside, like when you saw a snake.) You were supposed to practise while Mamma was out, and you did; but your thoughts went on thinking and thinking; and it was always the same: suppose she *never* came back? Luce cried all the time. And then Papa came and was almost crying, too, and said: 'Oh, *where* is Mamma? Will she never come home?' and he must go out and look for her. And it got tea-time, and nearly bedtime, and still she didn't come; and every time you looked at the clock only five minutes had gone, and it seemed like an hour. And at last it got so bad you went and stood down at the gate, or a little way in the road, and waited for the first bit of her to come round the corner. And then, oh, how they ran! At least Luce did. He just whistled. For each time, once he saw Mamma safe again, he didn't seem to care a bit any more.

The day she told them they'd got to go away and live where there wasn't any sea, he'd been naughty. He'd cried and stamped and pushed people when they tried to comfort him. But it wasn't a *real* 'naught': it was just something inside him and he couldn't stop it happening. No more springboard, no more lovely blue water to jump down into, no more hot salty smells. In his prayers at night, and in secret prayers offered up in corners of the garden, he begged and prayed God to let them stop there, or at least to let there be another sea where they were going. But God just didn't seem to hear.

They weren't to take their toys with them, either, their great big best toys. They had to be sold. Mamma was sorry; but they simply hadn't got enough money for what it would cost to take the rocking-horse . . . or the doll's house . . . or Cuffy's big grocer's-shop . . . or Luce's huge doll's-p'rambulator. Each of them would have needed a packing-case to itself.

Both he and Luce prayed about this, kneeling down in the long thick grass that grew behind the closet, with their eyes tight shut and their hands put properly together; and he told Luce what to say. But it was no good. God wasn't there.

Or if He was, He liked Luce best. For by-and-by she was allowed to take her doll with her, the big, baby one. Mamma said it was because she could carry it; but he b'lieved it was because Luce had cried so much. Of course you couldn't carry Dobbin or the shop; but, my! it *did* hurt to think of anybody else sitting on the saddle, or using the scales. He took a pencil and wrote 'My horse' in big letters under Dobbin's stomach, and cut a bunch of hairs out of his tail for a keepsake. And then, as God still didn't do anything, he *stole* something; took away a little bag of sugar and a tiny wee tin of biscuits out of the shop, and hid them; and when he told Luce, she did, too, and took a little sofa from the doll's-house drawing-room. But afterwards a man came with a pencil and book, and Mamma said he was going to write down the name of every single thing that was for sale, and then Luce got afraid, and told, and asked

Mamma if she might keep it, and Mamma said no, it wouldn't be honest; and so she put it back. But he didn't; he stayed a thief; and said if Luce told on him, he'd put out both her doll's eyes.

Mamma, she didn't leave things behind . . . what *she* wanted. When Bridget fetched down from the top of the wardrobe those dirty old cork-boards with butterflies pinned to them — most of them had got their wings knocked off them now — and old glass boxes with bits of stone in them, and dead flowers, and asked Mamma what to do with all this rubbish, Mamma said, give them here, and how she wouldn't part with them not for anything in the world. And he said, then he didn't see why he couldn't take his horse; and Mamma was cross, and said little boys didn't know everything, but when he was as old as she was he'd understand. But he did now: it was because they were Papa's. And when he said so, she sat back on her legs and went very red, and looked angry at him, and said: 'What in the name of fortune is all this fuss for about that wretched animal? You know you hardly ever ride it now! It's too small.'

'I don't care . . . it's mine!'

'Well, *I* think that's a very selfish way of looking at it. — Besides where we're going, if we arrive with big, expensive toys, people will think we've come there under false pretences.'

'And then?'

'Then we might be turned out.'

Cuffy paled. 'Is that because it's going to be a post office?'

'Yes. And now I hope you'll leave off pestering.'

The day the oxshun was, millions of people walked about the house just as if it was theirs. He and Luce went to Granny's; and Pauline took them for a bathe and let them stop in till his teeth trembled. But a few days after they had to get up again in the middle of the night, and a buggy came to the door and Mamma and Papa got in, and all their trunks and portmanteaux, and drove to the pier. A funny little steamer was there to take them to Melbourne, and it was pitch dark; they had to go on board with a lantern. And they sat in a teeny-weeny saloon that was the shape of a heart, with one lamp hanging in the middle; and it was so dark you could hardly see your faces. And there was nobody else. Luce went to sleep; and Mamma was sick; but in between, when she felt better, she tried to pull the rug up round Papa — it would slip off . . . she was always very kind to Papa now. But Papa was angry. He said: 'I don't *like* this,

Mary; it's not what I've been accustomed to. There's something hole-and-corner about it.' And she patted his hand: 'But so nice and private, dear. We've got it all to ourselves.' But Papa went on talking about who he was, and the kind of ships he'd travelled in, till Mamma told him how cheap it was, and what a lot of money it was going to save her. And then he began to cry, and cried and cried – and the captain (Mamma said) came in and looked at him – till he went to sleep. But *he* couldn't sleep. He'd always thought, even if they had to go away, there would be the beautiful steamer to sail on, with a big deck, and lots of people, and the band playing. Now he knew, because of Papa they weren't good enough for big steamers any more. And it seemed just hours he lay and watched the lamp swing, and listened to Mamma being sick, and the waves making a noise on the sides; and always more strange men – sailors and things – came in and pretended to be busy. But he believed just so they could take a good look at Papa, who was asleep now, with his head hanging down and his mouth wide open, making funny noises . . . not like a grown-up gentleman any more.

CHAPTER SIX

Their final destination was a place called Gymgurra in the Western District, some two hundred miles from Melbourne; to be reached either by a night's sea voyage – round Cape Otway and along the wild coast – or by a combined train and coach journey. With the ordeal of 'taking over charge' before her, Mary dared not risk the physical upset of a voyage. So at Colac she got out of the train and into the mail coach, to lumber, the night through, over the ruts and jolts of bush roads, Lucie a dead weight on her lap, Cuffy lying heavily up against her.

There were only the three of them; Richard had had to be left behind. It had torn her heart to part from him, to hand him over to strangers; but not only Bowes-Smith, everyone she consulted had advised against the fatigues of the journey for him in his present state. So she had yielded – and not for his sake alone. In the beginning she would need to give her whole mind to her new work. Richard would be better looked after where he was. Thanks to Bowes-Smith, she had managed to get him into a kind of private hospital, where he would live in comfort under a doctor's eye.

At Toorak, the place was, standing in its own beautiful grounds: there were shrubberies and summer-houses, a croquet-lawn, a bowling-green, fruit- and flower-gardens; the mere sight of which had a good effect on Richard. He brightened up, carried himself more erectly – even gave himself proprietary airs as they walked together through the gardens. None the less, when the time for parting came he wept bitterly, clinging like a child to her skirts. She had to romance about how soon she was coming back to fetch him: all the doctor thought it wise for him to be told, in the meanwhile, was that she was travelling on ahead to set the new house in order; he surely remembered how he hated the bother and confusion of moving? And by now he was too deeply sunk in himself to put awkward questions. Not once, since his attack, had he troubled his head about ways and means, or where tomorrow's dinner was to come from. It was pitiable to see; and yet . . . she couldn't find it in her heart to grudge him the peace and content this indifference brought him. The doctors called it euphoria.

The one thing he did ask, again like a timid child, was: 'Mary, it's not that place . . . that other place, Mary . . . the one with the whistle . . . and the . . . the . . . the canal, we're going back to, is it?'

'No, no, dear, indeed it's not! It's somewhere quite new; where there'll be all sorts of fresh things for you to see and do. And till then, Richard, think how comfortable you're going to be here. Your own room, your own books; and this armchair by the window, so that you can sit and look out at the flowers, and watch the croquet, and see all that happens.'

But something else still wormed in him. 'Who will – Mary, will you . . . will they let me . . . clean . . . clean collars, Mary . . . and those other things . . . hankchiefs?'

Here one had a glimpse of the old Richard, with his fastidious bodily habits. Mary got a frog in her throat over it. But she answered sturdily enough: 'Of course, they will. As many as you like. And be sure, my darling, if there's anything you don't feel quite happy about, let me know, and I'll have it put right at once.'

As indeed there should be no difficulty in doing, considering what she was paying. Though this, again thanks to Bowes-Smith – and the fact of Richard being a medical man – was only the half of what was charged an ordinary patient: five guineas a week instead of ten. Even so, it was a desperately heavy drain. She had put by as much as she dared towards it – seventy pounds – from the sale of the furniture, so in the meantime he was safe. When this was gone, she could but hope and pray he would be well enough to come home.

Out of what remained of the auction money, together with Richard's deposit and her own small savings, she had at once paid off a quarter's rent on each of the houses. Neither was yet due . . . and when Sir Jake heard what she had done, he rather called her over the coals for so unbusiness-like a proceeding. But he didn't know – how could he? – the load it took from her mind to know these things settled. With her, in the coach, she carried three little packets of notes, two of which, screwed up in old pieces of newspaper and tied securely and privately to her body, were towards the next quarter again. The third lay in her sealskin handbag, and was for the expenses of the journey and the purchasing of a few sticks of furniture. It had been a sad blow to learn that the salary attached to the Gymgurra post office was only eighty pounds a year. Eighty pounds! Could she and the children possibly live on that? And what, when Richard came too? Of course there was always a chance the house at Shortlands might find a tenant — houses were so scarce there — even though the summer was by now half over. In which case she would be some pounds to the good. Jerry, too, in whose hands she had left the affair of the perished documents, did not despair of retrieving *something* from the general ruin. But herself add a single penny to her income she could not; as a Government servant her hands were tied.

Over these reckonings the night wore away. (It would be money, always money now, she supposed, to the bitter end.) Still, she did not fail to send a warm thought back to the dear friends who had stood by her in her trouble. The Devines had not only housed them all, but had called in their own medical man to Richard, had helped her to make arrangements at the hospital, to interview doctor and matron. Lady Devine, too — notwithstanding her corpulence — had promised to visit Richard weekly and report on his progress. Old Sir Jake, with her hand in both of his, had gone as near as he dared towards offering her a substantial loan. Mr Henry had driven out to tell her that Mr Vibert, the Deputy P.M.G., was in receipt of special instructions with regard to her case; while the postmaster at the nearest town of any size to Gymgurra had orders to give her what help she needed. More, said he, the house of Gymgurra had been enlarged by three rooms. Then dear old Tilly had travelled down from Ballarat to see her; Jerry come all the way from Wangaratta. Not to speak of many a kindness shewn her by less intimate acquaintances. — And yet, in spite of this, Mary felt that she was seeing more than one of them for the last time. Still was she Mrs Townshend-Mahony, the one-time member of Melbourne society. From now on, as plain Mrs Mahony, postmistress, she would sink below their ken: she read it in their eyes when she announced what she was going to do; announced it bluntly, even truculently; for she was determined not to sail under false colours.

It was the same with her relatives. Lizzie, for instance: Lizzie who still traded on past glories — and also, alas! went on hoarding up poor John's children – was loud in praise of her courage and independence. But a blind man could have seen her relief when she learnt that these virtues were to be practised at a distance. Jerry, of course, like the sensible fellow he was, ranged himself on her side – if he did seem a trifle unsure of Fanny – but Zara made no bones of her horrification.

'Have you really thought *seriously*, Mary, of what you are about to do? Of the publicity, the notoriety it will entail? For, no matter what has happened, you are still our poor, dear Richard's wife. And my one fear is, the odium may redound on him.'

'Zara, I've thought till I could think no more. But it's either this or the workhouse. People who are too good to know me any longer must please themselves. To tell the truth, I don't very much care. But as for what I'm doing reflecting on *Richard* ... no, that's too absurd!'

It wasn't really Richard, it was herself Zara was concerned for; and in how far having a postmistress for a sister would damage her prospects. Besides, never again, poor thing, would she be able to give Richard's name as a reference. Ah, had Zara only been different! Then the two of them, sisters, and bound by one of nature's closest ties, might have combined forces; Zara have managed the house, taught the children, even perhaps have augmented their slender joint incomes by opening a little school.

Thinking these things Mary found she must have dozed off; for when, feeling extremely cold, she opened her eyes again, it was broad daylight. Daylight: and all around her what seemed to her the flattest, barest, ugliest country she had ever had the misfortune to see. Not a tree, not a bit of scrub, hardly so much as a bush broke the monotony of these plains, these immeasurable, grassy plains: here, flat as pancake, there, rolling a little up and down, or rising to a few knobbly hillocks, but always bare as a shorn head – except for lumps of blackish rock that stuck up through the soil. You could see for miles on every side, to where the earth met the sky. Another ugly feature was the extreme darkness of the soil: the long, straight road they drove was as black as all the other roads she had known had been white or red. A cloudy sky, black roads, bare earth: to Mary, lover of towns, of her kind, of convivial intercourse, the scene struck home as the last word in loneliness and desolation.

Even the children felt it. 'Why are there no trees?' demanded

Cuffy aggressively, the crosspatch he always was after a broken night. 'I don't *like* it without.'

And Lucie's echoing pipe: 'Why are there no trees, Mamma?'

And then the place itself.

'Is *this* it? Is this *all*?' more resentfully still. 'Then I think it's simply hidjus!'

'Oh, come! Don't judge so hastily.'

But her own courage was at zero when, having clambered down from the coach with legs so stiff that they would hardly carry her, she stood, a child on either hand, and looked about her. — Gymgurra! Two wide, ludicrously wide cross-roads, at the corners of which clustered three or four shops, a Bank, an hotel, the post office, the lock-up; one and all built of an iron-grey stone that was almost as dark as the earth itself. There were no footpaths, no gardens, no trees: indeed, as she soon learnt, in Gymgurra the saying ran that you must walk three miles to see a tree; which however was not quite literally true; for, on the skyline, adjoining a farm, there rose a solitary specimen . . . a unicum.

Their new home, the 'Post and Telegraph Office', with on its front the large round clock by which the township told the time, stood at one of the corners of the cross-roads. Facing it was a piece of waste ground used for the dumping of rubbish: thousands of tins lay scattered about, together with old boots, old pots, broken crockery: its next-door neighbour was the corrugated-iron lock-up. Until now, it had consisted only of an office and two small living-rooms. For her benefit a three-roomed weather-board cottage had been tacked on behind. This poor little dingy exterior was bad enough; inside, it was even worse. The former postmaster had been a bachelor; and before she and the children could live in the rooms he had left, these would have to be cleaned from top to bottom, and the walls given a fresh coat of whitewash, to rid them of greasy smears and finger-marks, of the stains of flies and squashed spiders. In the wooden portion – two small bedrooms and a kitchen – all the workmen's sawdust and shavings still lay about. From the back door three crude wooden steps led to a yard which, except for the water tank, held only rubbish: bottles galore, whole and broken; old boxes; boots and crockery again; with, she thought, every kerosene-tin that had been emptied since the house was first built. Never a spadeful of earth had been turned.

Thank God, she had not brought Richard with her. The mere

sight of such a place might have done him harm. By the time he came, poverty-stricken though it was, she would engage to have it looking very different. And this thought gave her the necessary fillip. Mastering her dismay, throwing off her discouragement with bonnet and mantle, she pinned back her skirts and fell to work. With the help of an old, half-blind woman – women seemed very scarce here – she swept and scrubbed and polished, in an effort to make the little house clean and sweet; to free it of a dirty man's traces. Then, perched on top of a step-ladder, with her own hands she whitewashed walls and ceilings. After this, taking coach to the neighbouring coast town, she bought the few simple articles of furniture they needed. – And, for all her preoccupation over trying to make one pound go as far as two, she could not help smiling at Cuffy's dismay as he watched her purchase of a kitchen-table for use in the dining-room. 'But we can't eat our dinner off *that*, Mamma!' he nudged her, politely and under his breath lest the shopman should hear, but with his small face one wrinkle of perplexity.

And her whispered assurance that a cloth would hide the deal top didn't help. Cuffy continued sore and ashamed. It wasn't only this table. There was the dressing-table, too; and the washstand: they were both *really* only empty packing-cases, stood on their sides and covered with pink s'lesha and book-muslin, to look nice. And for long he lived in dread of some inquisitive person lifting up cloth or curtain to peep underneath. It would be like seeing Mamma found out in a story. (If he were there, he would tell that one of the legs had come off the real things and they were away being mended. It didn't matter about *him*. But to think of Mamma turning cheat gave him a funny stiff ache in his chest.)

He wasn't, he knew, being very good just now; he didn't seem able to help it. It was so dull here; there was nothing to do – not even a piano to play your pieces on. Out of chips and blocks of wood left by the builders he cut little boats, which he and Lucie sailed in the wash-tubs by the back door . . . with matches for masts, and bits of paper for sails. But you couldn't go on doing that always. And Lucie soon got tired, and went to see that Mamma hadn't run away. You weren't allowed in the office, where there would have been the machine to look at, and letters in the pigeon-boxes (had somebody once kept pigeons in them?) and to see how stamps were sold. And the yard had palings round it so high that you couldn't see over them, only peep through the cracks. You weren't supposed to go out in the street. You did. But there wasn't anything there either. The streets were all just bare.

This was the first time they hadn't had a garden; and fiercely Cuffy hated the gaunt, untidy yard; the unfinished back to the house. There hadn't been much at Shortlands either, only pear-trees and grass; but he liked grass; specially if it nearly covered you when you sat down in it. At Barambogie there had been flowers, and the verandah, and lots of paths . . . and heaps and heaps of trees and wattle to go out and walk in. He could remember it quite well. And in a kind of vague way he remembered other things, too. Somewhere there had been straight black trees like steeples, that swept their tops about when the wind blew; lawns with water spraying on them; hairy white strawberries that somebody made you open your mouth to have popped into. And vague and faint as these memories were, as little to be caught and held as old dreams, they had left him a kind of heritage, in the shape of an insurmountable aversion to the crude makeshifts and rough slovenliness of colonial life. His little sister, on the other hand, carried with her, as the sole legacy of her few years, only a wild fear lest, one sure prop having given way, the other should now also fail her. Except at her mother's side, little Lucie knew no rest. She had, as it were, eternally to stand guard over the parent who was left. And to her baby mind the one good thing about this poor, ugly place was that Mamma never went out. Not even to church: a state of things that threw Cuffy who, ever since he could toddle, had been walked to church on his mother's hand, into fresh confusion. What would God think? It wouldn't do for Him not to *like* Mamma any more, now she was so poor. And He'd said as plain as plain, Remember the Sabbath Day to keep it holy. Oh dear! he was only a little boy and nobody took any notice of him; but what with boxes dressed up as tables, and a table that pretended to be mahogany, and now none of them going to church, he felt as if his world was turning upside down. And that it was one's *Mamma* who did it . . . who ought to know better; be perfect, without sin. . . .

Mary was unaware of these vicarious sufferings on her behalf: had neither time nor thought to spare for a child's imaginary torments. She was never off her feet – from seven in the morning till long past midnight. For when the office closed, she had still the main part of her work to do: food to prepare for the next day; to wash and iron and sew: whatever happened, her children must be spotlessly turned out.

Very soon after arriving she had given the relieving officer his congé. The man's manners were intolerable. It also came to her ears that he was going about the township saying: 'By the Lord Harry, there's a pair of eyes for you!' Which explained why he and the boy who was her sole assistant sat stolidly by, not budging to help, while she answered knocks at the little window: to dole out a single penny stamp, sell a postcard, repeat till she was tired: 'Nothing today,' to inquiries for letters. She thought every man in the place must have come rapping at the wooden shutter . . . to take a look at her. Once alone with the lad, however, she had small difficulty in keeping him in his place. He was a heavy, lumpish youth; clerk, operator, telegraph messenger rolled in one. The trouble was, he was so often absent. For though no letters were carried out, yet, had a telegram to be delivered, what with the long distances to be covered on foot and the lad's incurable propensity for gossip, she would find herself deserted for hours at a time on the run between 'key' and window, getting her 'statement' made up at any odd moment. Luckily enough, the money side of the business continued to come easy to her. Figures seemed just to fall into line and to add up of themselves.

Had there been the day's work only to contend with, she would not have complained. It was the nights that wore her down. The nights were cruel. On every one of them without exception, between half-past one and a quarter to two, there came a knocking like thunder at the front door. This was the coach arriving with the night mail: she had to open up the office, drag a heavy mail-bag in, haul another out. Not until this was over could there be any question of sleep for her.

Almost at once it became a nervous obsession (she who had had such small patience with Richard's night fancies!) that, did she even doze off, she might fail to hear the knocking – calculated though this was to wake the dead! – fail in her duty, lose her post, bring them all to ruin. Hence she made a point of sitting up till she could sit no longer, then of lying down fully dressed, watching the shadows thrown by the candle on walls and ceiling, listening to the children's steady breathing, the wind that soughed round the corners of the house.

Then when the coach had rumbled off, the sound of wheels and hoofs died away, and she might have slept, she could not.

The effort of rising, of pulling the bags about and exchanging words with the driver, had too effectually roused her. Also, the glimpse caught through the open door of the black darkness and loneliness without alarmed her each time afresh. For the country was anything but safe. The notorious Kellys had recently been at work in the district, and not so very far from Gymgurra either; the township still rang with tales of their exploits. And after the Bank, the post office was the likeliest place to be stuck up, if not *the* likeliest; for the Bank Manager had a strong-room, and no doubt a revolver, too . . . besides being a man. While she was only a defenceless woman, with no companions but two small children. If the bushrangers should appear one night, and order her to 'bail up' while they rifled the office, she would be utterly at their mercy.

The result of letting her mind dwell on such things was that she grew steadily more awake; and till dawn would lie listening to every sound. Never did the cheering fall of a human foot pass the house. Unlit, unpatrolled, the township slept the sleep of the dead. Only the dingoes snarled and howled; at first a long way off, and then, more shrilly, near at hand. Or the old volcano that stood in its lake some three miles away – it was said to be extinct, but really one didn't know – would suddenly give vent to loud, unearthly rumblings; which sometimes became so violent that the jugs on the washstand danced and rattled. And then the children, who had learned to sleep through the bustle of the coach, would wake up, too, and be frightened; and she would have to light the candle again and talk to them, and give them drinks, and re-arrange their pillows.

'It's all right, chicks. There's nothing to be afraid of. Mamma's here.'

This satisfied them: Mamma was there, hence all was well . . . as though she were a kind of demigod, who controlled even the eruptions of volcanoes! With Lucie cuddled tight in her arms, all the fragrance of the child's warm body mounting to her, she lay and thought of her children with a pity that left mere love far behind. They trusted her so blindly; and she, what could she do for them? Except for this imagined security, she had nothing to give. And, should anything happen to her, while they were still too young to fend for themselves – no! that simply did not bear thinking of. She had seen too much of the fates of motherless children in this country. Bandied from one home to another, tossed from pillar to post . . . like so much unclaimed baggage. Rather than know hers exposed to such a destiny . . . yes, there came moments when she could understand and condone the madness of the mother who, about to be torn away, refused to leave her little ones behind. For, to these small creatures, bone of her bone and flesh of her flesh, links bound Mary that must, she felt, outlast life itself. Through them and her love for them, she caught her one real glimpse of immortality.

CHAPTER SEVEN

But these were night thoughts. By day, when the children were their very human selves – high-spirited, quarrelsome, up to endless mischief – the question of Richard and Richard's welfare again took first place in her mind.

The improvement she had so hoped for him, in his pleasant, carefree surroundings, did not come to pass. She saw this, not so much from what the doctors wrote – they were painfully guarded – as from his own letters to her. Week by week these grew more incoherent; not words only, whole sentences were now being left out. They were written, too, in a large, unformed, childish hand, which bore no likeness to his fine, small writing; were smudged and ill-spelt. She felt them as shameful, and directly she had deciphered them hid them away: no eye but hers should see to what depths he had sunk.

And the doctors kept up their non-committal attitude to the end: the end, that was, of the three months for which she had their fees laid by. Then, they were forced to come out of their shell; and, to her letter saying that she could no longer afford to leave her husband in their charge and asking for a frank opinion on his case, they wrote her what she had feared and foreseen: there was no hope of recovery for Richard. His mental deterioration, since coming under their notice, had been marked; signs of arterial degeneration were now to be observed as well. Did she seriously contemplate removing him, they could only advise his further restraint in one of the public institutions. They trusted, however, that she would reconsider her decision to remove him. On all points it would be to the patient's advantage.

In her distress, Mary crushed the letter to a ball in her hand. To re-read it, she had to stroke and smooth it flat again. For the step they were urging upon her meant the end of everything: meant certification; an asylum for the insane. (The children's father a certified lunatic!) Yet, just because of the children ...

This was an objection the doctors had raised, in telling her that Richard might last for years – in his present state – when she first proposed keeping him with her. They would be doubly against it now. And for days she went irresolute, torn between pity for Richard and fear for her children. In the end it was once more Bowes-Smith who got the better of her. He pointed out how little, for all her devotion, she could do to ameliorate her husband's lot, compared with the skilled nursing he would receive from properly trained attendants. Besides, Richard was, he assured her, by now too far gone in inattention, really to miss her or to need her. There seemed nothing for it but gratefully to accept his offer, himself to take the affair in hand. Thanks to his influence, Richard had a chance of being lodged in one of the separate cottages at the asylum, apart from the crowd: he would be under a special warder, have a bedroom more or less to himself. And so, with a heavy heart Mary gave her consent; the various legal and medical formalities were set in motion; and, soon after, the news came that the change had been made and Richard installed in his new quarters. His books and clothing were being returned to her. (Prisoners – no, she meant patients – were not allowed any superfluous belongings. Nor, bitter thought! need she now rack her brains where the new suit was to come from, for which his late nurse had pressed, because of his growing habit of spilling his food. From now on, he would wear the garb of his kind.) But after this she heard no more: with the shutting of the gates behind him silence fell – a horrible, deathlike silence. Never again did one of his pitiful little letters reach her; and the authorities blankly ignored her requests for information. Finally, in response to a more vigorous demand than usual, she received a printed form stating that reports were issued quarterly, and hers would reach her in due course. Grimly she set her teeth and waited; meanwhile laying shilling to shilling for the journey to Melbourne which she could see lay before her. – But, when the time came, she had to part with a little brooch to which she had clung, because it had been one of Richard's first gifts to her after marriage. Mr Rucker, the clergyman, bought it of her for his wife.

Her story was, of course, common property in Gymgurra by now; and it was just an example of people's kindness, when the very next day Mrs Rucker brought the brooch back and, with her own hands, pinned it on again, saying things that made it impossible to take offence. Yes, Mary never ceased to marvel at the way in which friends sprang up round her in her need, and put themselves out to help her. These Ruckers, for instance – they had no family of their own – were constantly taking the children off her hands. Hence, when the week's leave of absence for which she had applied was granted, she could part from Cuffy and Lucie with an easy mind.

And one cold spring night towards two o'clock, she put on her warmest travelling clothes and climbed into the coach for Colac. She had bespoken a seat . . . and a good job, too! For an election had taken place in the district, and the coach was crammed with men, some coming from the polling, others on their way to a cattle market. She sat, the night through, jammed in among them, her arms pinned to her sides, half suffocated with smoke, and deafened by their talk. Not till daybreak was she joined by one of her own sex. Then, on stopping at a wayside public-house, they found a thinly clad, elderly woman waiting for the coach, a little bundle in her hand. But there was not room for a mouse in among them, let alone an old woman: one rude voice after another bawled the information. At which the poor thing began to cry, and so heartbrokenly that Mary was touched. Elbowing her way to the window, she leaned out and questioned the woman. At what she heard, and at the continued crude joking of her fellow-travellers, she lost her temper, and rounding on them cried: 'Do you mean to say there isn't one of you who's man enough to give up his seat?' And as, though the laughter ceased, none offered, she said hotly: 'Very well then, if you won't, I will! I'm on my way, too, to see a sick person, but I'll take my chance of getting a lift later in the day. – I'm glad I'm not a man . . . that's all!'

'Now then, missis, keep your hair on.' And a lanky young fellow, with hands like ploughshares and a face confusion-red at his own good deed, gawkily detached himself and stepped out. 'Here y'are, ma, in you get! I'll toddle along on Shanks' p's.'

The two women made the rest of the journey in company, Mary even treading underfoot the prejudice of a lifetime and going second-class in the train. (There was no Richard now, to cast up his eyes in horror.) The poor soul at her side told a sad story: one's own troubles shrank as one heard it. She was bound for the Melbourne Hospital, where her son, her only child, lay dying: he had got 'the water' on his chest, and the doctors had telegraphed she must come at once if she wanted to see him alive. Her husband had been killed at tree-felling only a few months back; and, her son gone, she would be alone in the world. Mary, feeling rich in comparison, shared with her her travelling-rug, her packet of sandwiches, her bottle of cold tea; and at Spencer Street station, having saved considerably on her fare, was able to put the poor mother in a wagonette and pay for her to be driven straight to the hospital. For she could see the bush-dweller's alarm at the noise and bustle of the city.

On parting, the woman kissed her hand. 'God bless you, ma'am . . . God bless and keep you, the kindest lady ever I met! – and may He restore your poor gentleman to his right mind! I shan't never forget what you've done for me this day. And if ever there come a time when I c'ld do su'thing for you . . . but there! not likely – only Bowman's my name – Mrs Bowman, at Sayer's Thack, near Mortlake.'

For Mary the Devines' carriage and pair was in waiting. The old coachman smiled and touched his hat and said: 'Very glad to see you again, ma'am!' tucked the black opossum-rug round her, and off they rolled, she lying back on the springy cushions. And all the time she was in Melbourne this conveyance stood freely at her disposal, Lady Devine being by now grown too comfortable even for 'carriage exercise'. 'By the time I've buttoned me boots, dearie, and put on me plumes, I'm dead beat. An' there are the 'orses eatin' their 'eads off in the stable. You can't do Jake and me a greater kindness 'n to use 'em.'

Without this mechanical aid: to expedite her hither and thither, to wait for her while she kept appointments, to carry her on anew, Mary could impossibly have got through what she did in the days that followed: looked back on, they resembled the whirligig horrors of a nightmare. She had come to Melbourne tired, sad, and anxious enough, in all conscience. But in the hard-faced, unscrupulous woman with which, at the end of the time, her glass presented her, she hardly recognized herself. Never in her life had she fought for anything as now for Richard's freedom.

The morning after her arrival, she drove out to the asylum. The way led through lovely Toorak, with its green lawns and white houses, up Richmond Hill, and down into the unattractive purlieus of Collingwood. The carriage came to a standstill on a stretch of waste land, a kind of vast, unfenced paddock, where hobbled horses grazed. It could go no farther, for, between them and the complex of houses, cottages, huts which formed the asylum, flowed the unbridged river. Rain had fallen during the night, and the reddish, muddy stream, which here turned and twisted like a serpent, ran so high that the weeping willows (Richard's favourite *Salix babylonica*) which lined the bank, dragged their branches deep in the flood. The houses, overhung by the ragged, melancholy gums, looked shabby and neglected; one and all in need of a coat of paint. Mary's heart fell.

Seating herself in the ferry, she was conveyed across the water.

She had not announced her visit. Her intention was to see for herself how Richard was lodged and cared for, at those times when the place was closed to the public. Had the authorities known beforehand that she was coming, they might have dressed and dolled him up for her. (Yes! she was fast turning into a thoroughly suspicious and distrustful woman.) For passport, she had armed herself with a letter to the head doctor from Sir Jake Devine.

And well that she had. Great its virtue was not, but, without it, she would hardly have got over the threshold. And once inside the front door she had to fight her way forward, step by step: it needed all her native obstinacy, her newly acquired aggressiveness, not to allow herself to be bowed out by the several assistants and attendants who blocked her path. But having vowed to herself that she would see someone in authority, see him she did; though in the end they fobbed her off with a youngish fellow, to whom – he had cod's eyes and a domineering manner – she took an instant and violent dislike.

By this time, too, her blood was up; and the incivility of her reception seemed the last straw. A good log-fire burnt in the fireplace – the rest of the building struck her as very damp and chill – a comfortable armchair was suitably placed, but he did not invite her to approach the fire or to take a seat. He stood while he spoke . . . and kept her standing. She had, he presumed, already been informed that this was not a visiting-day – and certainly not an hour for visitors. But as he understood that she had made a special journey from up-country, they had stretched a point. What did she want?

'To know how my husband is.'

His fish eyes bulged still more. Was that all? When the report would have been so shortly in her hands?

'I preferred to come myself. I wish to speak to my husband.'

'For that, ma'am, you will need to present yourself at the

proper time.' (Then it was as she thought. They were *not* going to let her see Richard unprepared.)

As, however, she made no movement to withdraw, but stood her ground with, for all her shabby dress and black gloves showing white at the finger-tips, the air of a duchess, and an answer for everything (danged if he knew how to treat such a bold, bouncing woman!), he crossed the room, took a ledger from a rack, and asked in tones of exasperation: 'Well, what in thunder is it then? . . . your husband's name?'

'Quite so . . . exactly!' he cut her reply short. 'If you think, madam, with the dozens of patients we have on our hands . . . it is possible to remember . . . the details and antecedents of each individual case . . .' As he spoke he was running a fat finger down column after column. 'Ha! here we have it.' Transporting the book to the central table, he laid it flat and faced her over it. 'Here it is; and I regret to inform you that the report we should presently have sent you would have been of a highly unsatisfactory nature.'

'Why? Is he so much worse?' With difficulty her dry lips framed the words.

'I refer not to his state of health – the disease is running a normal course – but to his conduct. Ever since being admitted to the asylum, your husband has proved to the last degree obstreperous and unruly.'

'Well, that I cannot understand!' gave back Mary hotly. 'Where he was – before he came here – they had only good to say of him.'

'No doubt, no doubt! A patient worth his eight or ten guineas a week –'

'*Five*, if you please! He received special terms . . . as a medical man.'

'All of which is beside the point. The fact remains that, to us, he is a constant source of trouble. We have been obliged more than once to place him in solitary confinement. His behaviour is such as to corrupt the other patients.'

'*Corrupt?*'

'Corrupt.'

'Well, all I can say is . . . there must be something very wrong in the way he's treated. He would never willingly give trouble. By nature he's one of the gentlest and politest of men.'

'Perhaps you would like to hear his warder on the subject?'

And going to the fireplace the young man rang a bell and instructed a servant: 'Send 97B's keeper here to me.'

(97B? . . . why B? . . . why not A? Mary's mind seized on the trivial detail and held fast to it, so as not to have to face the . . . the degradation the numbering implied.)

The warder entered touching his forelock: a coarse, strongly built fellow, with a low forehead and the under-jaw of a prize-fighter. Her heart seemed to shrivel at thought of Richard . . . Richard! . . . in the power of such a man.

She hung her head, holding tight as if for support to the clasp of her sealskin bag, while the warder told the tale of Richard's misdeeds. 97B was, he declared, not only disobedient and disorderly; he was extremely abusive, dirty in his habits (here the catch of the handbag snapped and broke), would neither sleep himself at night nor let other people sleep; also he refused to wash himself, or to eat his food. 'It's always the same ol' story. No sooner I bring him his grub than he up and pitches the dishes at me head.'

She thought she had the fellow there. 'Do you mean to tell me he . . . that you give him fresh crockery to break every day?'

'Crockery? Ho, no fear! The plates and cups is all of tin.'

At this Mary laughed, but very bitterly. 'Ah! now I see. That explains it. For I know my husband. Never would you get him . . . nothing would induce him, . . . to eat off tin.'

'Needs Sèvres no doubt!'

'No! All he needs is to be treated like a gentleman . . . by gentlemen.'

But she had to keep a grip on her mind to hinder it from following the picture up: Richard, forced by this burly brute to grope on the floor for his spilt food, to scrape it together, and either eat it or have it thrust down his throat. So she shut her ears, made herself deaf to their further talk, stood as it were looking through the speakers and out beyond – at her ripening purpose.

But when at the end of the interview she made a last, passionate appeal to be allowed to see her husband, she was not too absorbed to catch the glance, alive with significance, that passed between the men. Sorry, said the keeper, but the patient was in bed resting after a very bad night: he couldn't on any account have him woke up again. At which excuse, things (old things), that she had heard from Richard about the means used to quell and break the spirits of refractory lunatics, jumped into her mind. There was not only feeding by force, the strait-jacket, the padded cell. There were drugs and injections, given to keep a patient quiet and ensure his warders their freedom: doses of castor oil so powerful that the unhappy wretch into whom they were poured was rendered bedridden, griped, thoroughly ill.

But she saw plainly, here was nothing to be done. Her fight to get him back would have to be carried on outside the walls of the asylum. Buttoning her gloves with shaky, fumbling fingers, she confronted her opponents in a last bout of defiance. 'I find it hard to believe a word of what you've said. But I know this: my husband shall not stay here. I'll take him home and look after him myself. He shall never leave my side again.'

They all but laughed in her face. The idea was a very woman's! No alienist would ever be got to revoke this particular patient's certificate . . . or advise his release. In his fits of mania 97B was dangerous, and not merely to those about him; he needed protection against himself, which could only be given him by men trained to the job. Impossible! . . . utterly impossible.

She left them at it, turned her back and marched out of the room and down the corridor, through innumerable doors, not one of which she could afterwards remember having opened or shut (they were as insubstantial as the people she met on her passage), made her way to the ferry and up the other side, where she was helped into the carriage. And even while she bowled forward again, she continued to sit rigid and insensible, her sole movement being to pull off her gloves – they incommoded her – that she might lock her fingers . . . in an iron grip. The skin of her face felt stretched: like a mask that was too tight for it. But she shed not a tear, either here or when, having reached home, she paced the floor of the room and told her story. Something stronger than herself had control of her: she was all one purpose, one flame. Her old friend it was who wept. 'Oh, just to *think* of 'im being come to this! . . . 'im, the 'andsomest man I ever saw, and the best as well.'

But she, too, said: 'Impossible! Oh no, my dear, it *couldn't* be done,' when she heard of Mary's determination. 'Your children – you 'ave your children to consider.'

'Oh, I can take care of them. But should I ever again know a moment's peace, if I left him in that awful place? Richard? . . . my poor old husband? As it is he'll believe I've deserted him . . . forgotten him . . . left off caring. No: I mean to get him out or die in the attempt.'

And when the old lady saw the blazing eyes, the dilated nostrils, the set jaw with which this was said, she bowed before the iron will made manifest, and went over heart and soul to Mary's side. 'Well, then, my love and my dearie, if nothing else will do – and, oh my dear, I feel in the bottom of my 'eart you're right – then what I say is, we – Jake and me – 'ull do everything that lies in our power to 'elp you. *I'll* manage Jake; you go on to the rest. Get 'old of 'em somehow, and give 'em no quarter . . . and though they talk till all's blue about their laws and certificates. What's laws for, I'd like to know, if not to be got round?'

But this was the sole word of encouragement Mary heard. The rest of the world combined to iterate and reiterate the doctor's verdict of impossible, utterly impossible.

She battered at every likely door. All sense of pride having left her, any influential or well-known person who in former years had broken bread at her table, or whom she had casually met at another's, she now waylaid or ran to earth. For along with her pride went also the retiring modesty, the shrinking from prominence, that had hallmarked her years of wifehood. She was no longer the 'lady', watchful of her steps. She was a tiger fighting for her young – did not Richard, in his present state, stand for the youngest and most helpless of her children? – and she now found to her astonishment that she was quite capable of standing up to men, of arguing with them, of talking them down, and, if necessary, of telling them what she thought of them.

The medical profession, of course, furnished her with her most implacable opponents. The doctors to whom she turned acted as if *she* were the crazed one; or else they smiled good-humouredly at her, as at a child . . . or a woman. But if she stood firm, refusing to be browbeaten or cajoled, they gave her short shrift. To remove an insane person with notedly violent periods – a perfectly proper subject for detention – from medical safe-keeping, in order to place him in inexperienced lay-hands: such an act would be a criminal proceeding on the part of any medical man found to sanction it. Her ignorance of matters medical alone acquitted her. Nor could she get them to credit the ill-treatment to which Richard was being subjected. Again it was sheer ignorance on her part that made her take this view. The asylum authorities were doubtless fully justified in what they did: you could not *reason* with the deranged. And so on . . . and on. How she came to hate and dread the words Certification,

Lunacy Laws, Lunacy Authorities! Their very sound seemed to shut away for ever, from the rest of humanity, from every human feeling, those unfortunates who had fallen beneath the ban.

Giving the doctors up as a bad job, she turned her attention to other influential people she had known: members of parliament, bankers, the clergy. And here she was received with the utmost consideration, no one of these old friends and acquaintances reminding her, by so much as a look, that she was now but a poor up-country postmistress. All alike deplored Richard's fate, and offered her their heartfelt sympathy; but from none of them could she wring a promise of help or interference. Their concern was entirely for her, her personal safety, and that of her children. While the Bishop and his brethren spoke in muted voices of God's Will, this mysterious Will to which it was one's duty to submit — till she could have flung her bag at their heads. A stone for bread, indeed, when her only cry was: 'Give me back my husband!'

Sir Jake, who had been won over — though rather half-heartedly, and solely as a result of endless, nagging curtain-lectures — did what he could; but he no longer held office and his influence was slight. And the person on whom Mary had built most, the one member of the present ministry she knew intimately, Henry Ocock, was not to be got at. Though she called every day, and sometimes twice a day, at his chambers, it was always to learn that business still detained him in Ballarat.

She applied for a second week's leave of absence — and got it. And when but forty-eight hours of this remained and she had still achieved as good as nothing, she sent Mr Henry a page-long telegram, imploring him, in the name of their old friendship, to grant her an interview.

He travelled to Melbourne by the next train. She met him one cold, dusty autumn afternoon, in a private sitting-room at Scott's Hotel.

He came towards her with outstretched hands, but was so shocked at her appearance that he would not let her say a word before she was thoroughly rested and refreshed. Then, the waiter having withdrawn, he drew up his chair and begged her to tell him what he could do for her.

To this old friend, whose mottled hair she had known when it was sleekest, jettiest raven, she now opened her heart; beginning from the time when, almost against her will and certainly against her better judgement, she had yielded to the specious assurances of Bowes-Smith and his kind, and had consented to Richard becoming the inmate of a public lunatic asylum. – 'Never should I have let him get into their clutches!' – But so much had been made of the treatment, the individual nursing he would receive there, and the beneficial effect this would have on him, that she had sunk her scruples. Afterwards had come the stoppage of his letters, the dead silence of his imprisonment, and her growing doubts; followed by her journey to town, her tragic discovery of his true state, the insolence she had had to put up with from the young assistant – 'Hardly more than a medical student!' – the beggar's calvary she had since been through. Not a living soul, it seemed, was willing to break a lance for Richard: once certified, a man might just as well be under the soil. On all sides she had been bidden to go home and live in peace. Knowing what she knew? Would other women have done it? If so, they were made of different stuff from her. She would think herself a traitor, if she did not fight for Richard's release as long as she had a breath left in her body.

Ocock let her talk: heard her out in a lawyer's cogitative silence, the while thoughtfully pulling at and stroking his chin. Even after she had ceased speaking he sat meditative – and so used was Mary, by now, to being instantly downed and dismissed, that this very silence fed her hopes. Hence when at last he broke it, his words had the force of a blow. For all he did was to bring to her notice a point which he very much feared she had overlooked. And this was that she was no longer a private individual, but a public servant in Government employ. Difficulties would certainly be raised from this side, too, did she apply – as she was bound to do – for permission to receive a certified lunatic in her home. The Department would hold that the efficient discharge of her duties and the care, at the same time, of a sick man, would be irreconcilable ... impossible.

At this repetition of the word that had dogged her every step, something tipped over in Mary. Passionately flinging up her head, she looked full and squarely at Ocock: pinned with her own what Richard had been used to call 'those shifty little black boot-buttons of eyes!' And then, almost before she knew it, words began to pour from her lips, things she could not have believed herself capable of saying – to anyone, let alone Henry Ocock, now so far above her. (In after years of a sleepless night she would suddenly feel her face begin to burn in the darkness, at the mere remembrance of them. Spiritual blackmail would have been Richard's name for it.)

It was of herself and Richard that she had meant to speak; of the tie between them which no living creature had the right to break. But Ocock's presence seemed to bring the whole past alive before her, and the past brought Agnes, and memories of Agnes – 'The dearest, truest little soul that ever lived!' – and of the murk and misery in which the poor thing's days had ended. And under the influence of this emotion everything came out. Not only, lost to shame, did she throw in her listener's teeth all she had done for Agnes: the expense she had been put to when she could ill afford it; the pains she had been at to save Agnes from herself: she also stripped the veneer off his own conduct, laying bare his heartlessness, his egoism, his cruelty, yes, even brutality: how, in order to keep up his dignity, save his own face, he had wantonly sacrificed his wife, abandoning her when she most needed love, pity, companionship; shutting her up to drink herself to death – even barbarously shipping her off to die alone, among strangers, in a strange land. Not a shred of self-respect did she leave on him: he should see himself for once as others saw him: and she went on, pouring out scorn on his hypocrisy and pretence, till she had him standing there as morally naked as he had come physically naked into the world, and would one day go out of it. Before she finished the tears were streaming down her cheeks . . . for Agnes; her own troubles completely forgotten for the moment, over the other's tragedy.

Her voice failing her, she came to a stop: just sat and stared before her, feeling, now the fit was over, cold and queer and shaky. But nothing would have made her take back a word of what she had said; not even though – as was only too likely – she had ruined her chances for good and all.

As, however, the silence that followed seemed to be going to last for ever, she plucked up courage to glance at Mr Henry. And she had the surprise of her life. For he was sitting gazing at her with a look such as she had never seen on his face; a kindly, indulgent, almost *fond* look; and – oh, was it possible? – with his eyes full of tears. More, these eyes were now as steady as her own, had quite ceased furtively to dart and run. And the crowning touch was put to this strange reception of her tirade, by his nodding his head, slowly, several times in succession and saying: 'A staunch and loyal advocate indeed! – My friend, a great fighter has been lost in you.'

Then he got up and went to the window, where he stood looking down into the street. Mary sat motionless, but odd thoughts and scraps of thoughts were whizzing round her brain. This then was how . . . stand up to him, *bully* him . . . if Agnes had only . . . but would never have had the spirit. And then his eyes . . . the shiftiness more than half fear . . . fear of discovery . . . and, once found out – But, oh! not praise for her eloquence. If she hadn't touched him . . . or had touched him solely in this way. . . .

Coming back to her he took her hands. 'What you are asking of me, Mrs Mahony, means difficulties of which you, as a woman, do not realize the quarter . . . the half. I will make you no fixed promises; which I might be unable to keep. All I will say is, that for your sake – your sake alone! – I will see what can be done.'

And with this single straw to cling to, Mary travelled home.

CHAPTER EIGHT

He had enjoined her to patience and patient she was – though week ran into week and month to month, in all of which time she knew nothing of what was happening behind the scenes, or what strings Ocock was pulling to upset the cumbrous machinery of medical law. She just dragged on from day to day, in ignorance and suspense. But her nerves often got the better of her, and then the children felt her heavy, hasty hand. While, in her official capacity, so set did she become on her 'rights', so unblushing in making her voice heard, that her name grew to be a by-word in the service: 'That tartar at G.G.' (which was the morse call for Gymgurra) was how she was familiarly spoken of.

In this dreary time, when her narrow walls oppressed her to breathlessness, but from which there was no possible escape for her, one piece of good fortune came her way. The house at Shortlands found a tenant; and so the money which she had laboriously scraped together for the following quarter's rent would not be needed. Hence when at last the tide began to turn, with the substitution of 'highly dangerous', and 'a most risky experiment', for the maddening 'impossible', she actually had a small sum in hand with which to make her preparations. And she set about these forthwith; building on her recently acquired knowledge of men and their ways. She could look for no complete *volte face* on their part. Only in this grudging, half-hearted fashion would their consent be given.

Help in the house she must have, was she to be free to devote what time she could spare from her office-work to Richard. Her first thought was naturally of her poor old ageing sister, and she wrote to Zara, offering her house-room in exchange for her services. But though in her last situation little more than a nurse-maid, Zara declined the proposal as stiffly and uncompromisingly as if she were rolling in money: dubbing Mary mad as a

March hare to think of removing 'our poor dear Richard' from safe control; madder still to imagine that she, Zara, with her delicate nerves, would be able to live for a single day under the same roof as a lunatic. Emmy, unasked, wrote begging to be allowed to help care for 'poor darling Uncle'. But quite apart from the mixed motives that underlay the offer, this was out of the question. You could not so take the bloom off a young girl's life. There would be things to do for Richard – unfit things ... And it was here that Mary bethought herself of the woman she had befriended on her journey to town, whose son had died soon after. So, in the same terms as to Zara, she wrote to 'Mrs Bowman at Sayer's Thack' – though it did seem rather like posting a letter into the void. Almost by return, however, came an ill-spelt scrawl, joyfully accepting the job; and a little later Mrs Bowman herself got out of the coach, with all her worldly goods tied up in one small cardboard-box, but carrying with her, as a gift, a stringy old hen (fit only for the soup-pot) and half a pound of dairy butter. And in this poor, lone soul, Mary found yet another of those devoted, leech-like friends, who had starred her path through life.

The final surrender came in the form of a lengthy screed from Mr Henry, in which he informed her that, after surmounting difficulties and obstacles greater even than he had anticipated, he had at last succeeded in bringing the various authorities involved – medical, legal, postal – to agree to the plan of Dr Mahony's removal from control being given a provisional trial. That was to say, the patient would be accompanied to Gymgurra by two warders, who would remain while the experiment was made. In the event of it failing, they would immediately escort the patient back to the asylum. Followed, this, by four pages in which Mr Henry begged her once more seriously to consider what she was doing. It was still not too late to draw back. Should she, however, decide to go forward, he trusted she would further show her friendship for him by regarding him as her banker, if the expenses of the undertaking proved too heavy for her purse. He would be only too happy to assist her. – Well, thank goodness, owing to her little windfall, she need be beholden to nobody; although, at this pass, she would not have hesitated to borrow freely. But, Bowey's expenses settled, she had still enough in hand to cover the three fares up from town, and those of the warders back; as well as their board and lodging while in Gymgurra.

Only the day of arrival now remained to be fixed. But now, too, in the small hours when she lay waiting for the night mail, Mary was assailed by her first fears and apprehensions. It was not her ability to cope with, and control, and nurse Richard that she doubted. No, her fears concerned herself. Her own strength was already sorely taxed, she on the brink of those years when a woman most needed rest and care and a quiet life. Suppose *she* should fall ill? . . . need nursing herself? Or that she should die before him . . . be forced to leave him? . . . him and the children. This was the thought that haunted her nights; and though she drove it from her, fought it valiantly, it was often not to be got under till she had risen and paced the house.

When Cuffy heard that Papa was coming home, his black eyes opened till they seemed to fill his face.

'Do you mean he . . . he's coming back here? *Now?*'

'Yes. And you chicks must try your best to help me. I shall have more than ever to do.'

'But is he . . . isn't he still . . .' It was no use; his mouth was full of tongue; the 'mad' simply wouldn't come out. To which half-asked question Mamma said firmly: 'Run away and play.'

But they were moving his bed, and he saw them: saw, too, a new bed being carried into Mamma's room. 'What's that for? And where's my bed going?' And at the news that from now on he was to sleep in Bowey's room, the dismay he had so far bitten back broke through. 'Oh, no, I *can't*, Mamma! I won't! . . . sleep in the same room as her.'

'And why not, indeed?'

'She's . . . she's a *lady*.'

'Really, Cuffy! I do wonder where you get your ideas from. Pray, haven't you been sleeping all this time with Lucie and me? Are we not ladies, too?'

No, of course not – they were only just their two selves. But as usual he didn't try to explain. It was never a bit of good.

With Lucie, whose chubby face wore a harassed look, beside him, he sat on the back steps with his elbows on his knees, his chin hunched in his hands. The yard was mostly potatoes now – the floury sort that were so good to have for dinner, but left hardly any room to play. For you hadn't got to tread on them. Oh, *why* did Papa need to come back? They had been so happy without him . . . even though they had to keep a post office, and weren't *real* ladies and gentlemen any more. But nobody had once laughed at them – at him and Luce – since they came here, and they had had nothing to be ashamed of. Now it was all going to begin over again. Oh, if only there had been anywhere to run to, he would have run away. But there wasn't, only just long, straight roads.

Here Lucie put her mouth inside his ear and whispered guiltily: 'I don't b'lieve you're a bit glad!'

'Are *you*?'

Luce nodded hard. Mamma was glad, so she was too; or she'd thought she was till now. But Cuffy looked so funny that her little soul began to be torn afresh, between these two arbiters of her fate.

Cuffy wrinkled his lips up and his nose down. 'You're not *true*! I don't believe it.'

'I am!' But her face puckered.

'Well, I'm *not* . . . not a scrap! So there! And if you want to, you can go and tell.'

But she didn't; she only cried. Cuffy was always making her cry. He couldn't ever be nice and think the same as Mamma and her. He always had to be diffrunt.

It certainly *was* hard though, to keep on being sorry, when you saw how glad Mamma was. She smiled much more now, and sewed shirts, and got them ready for Papa; and she bought a new rocking-chair, specially for him to sit and rock in. And every day was most dreadfully anxious to know if there wasn't a letter in the mail-bag, to say when he was coming. And then she told them about how unhappy Papa had been since he went away, and how he had to eat his dinner off tin plates; and how they must try with all their mights to make up to him for it. And then she went back and told them all over again about when they were quite little, and how fond Papa had been of them, and how he thought there were no children in the world like his; and how, now he was old and ill, and not himself, they must love him much more than ever before. It made you feel *horrid*. But it didn't help; you *just couldn't* be glad. It was like a stone you'd swallowed, which stuck in you, and wouldn't go down.

And, at length, the suspense in which Mary lived was ended, by a letter definitely fixing a date for the arrival of Richard and his keepers. They would land at the neighbouring seaport, between eight and nine in the morning. It was on her advice, Richard being so excellent a sailor, that the sea route had been chosen for its greater privacy, few people, even at this time of year, choosing to undergo a buffeting round the wild coast. Now, all she had to do was to send word over the road to Mr Cadwallader Evans of the Bank. Long since, this kind friend had placed his buggy and pair at her disposal for the occasion.

She rose at six when the morning came, and was busy brushing and shaking out her clothes: she had not been over the threshold since her return from Melbourne. Not wishing to disgrace Richard by too shabby an appearance, she put on her one remaining silk dress with its many flounces, her jet-trimmed mantle, her best bonnet . . . in which still nodded the red rose he had been used to fancy her in. But her hands were cold and stupid as she hooked and buttoned and tied strings; and, having climbed into the buggy and taken her seat, she sat with a throat too dry for speech.

And after one or two well-meant efforts at encouragement, the chatty little man who was her companion respected her mood. He considered her 'a dam' fine woman for her age', and 'a dam' plucky one, too', but held the errand they were out on for 'a dam' unpleasant job', and one he had undertaken solely to please his wife, who thought the world of Mrs Mahony. He didn't dare even to hum or to whistle, and so, except for a passing flip or chirrup to the ponies, they drove mile after mile in silence, neither casting so much as a glance at the landscape, which both thought ugly and dull: once past the volcano – a knobbly bunch of island-hills set in the middle of a shallow, weed-grown lake – it consisted of unbroken grassy downs, which sloped to a sandy shore on which the surf broke and thundered.

The wide streets of the little port were deserted; but at the jetty quite a crowd had gathered. There stood passengers who had already been landed, several idle girls and women, a goodly sprinkling of larrikins. One and all had their eyes fixed on a small rowing-boat that was making for the shore from the steamer, which lay at anchor some way out.

Having dismounted and joined the throng, Mary asked of a young girl standing by: 'What is it? What's the matter?'

'Ooo . . . such fun!' said the girl, and tittered. 'See that boat? There's a madman in it. He's being put off here. They've had to tie his arms up.'

'Don't you think you should let me see to things? . . . and you wait in the buggy?' asked Mr Evans in concern. But Mary shook her head.

As the boat drew near, riding the surf, they saw that it contained, besides the oarsmen, two burly men who sat stooped over something lying prostrate on the floor of the boat. Mary hung back, keeping on the outskirts of the crowd, the members of which now pushed and pressed forward. But though the boat was alongside, its oars shipped, nothing happened – or nothing but a series of cries and shouts and angry exclamations, several men's voices going at once.

'They can't make him get up, that's what it is,' volunteered the girl, her pretty face distorted with excitement. 'I bet they'll have to tie his legs as well, and then just haul him out. What fun if he falls in the water!'

'I can't bear this,' said Mary in an undertone; she believed she could hear, as well, the sound of cuffs and blows. 'I must see what *I* can do.' And in spite of her companion's demur, she stepped forward. Bravely tossing her head, she said to those around her: 'Will you please let me pass? It's my husband.'

They almost jumped aside to make way for her; open-mouthed, embarrassed, or flushed a dark red, like the pretty girl. Mary felt rather than saw the nudging elbows, the pointing and whispering, as, herself now the gazing-stock, she walked through the opening they left. Outwardly erect and composed, inwardly all a-quake, she advanced to the edge of the jetty and went down three shallow steps to the landing-place.

The rough voices ceased at her approach, and the warders desisted from their efforts to shift a heavy body that struggled desperately to oppose them.

'Please, stand back, and let me try.' As she spoke she caught a glimpse, at the bottom of the boat, of disordered clothing, dishevelled strands of white hair, and a pair of roped hands working violently. Leaning as far over as she dared, she said in a low, but clear voice: 'Richard dear, it's me – Mary. Don't you know me?'

On the instant the contortions ceased, and a kind of listening silence ensued. Then came a palpable attempt on the part of the prostrate form to raise itself; while a thin, cracked voice, which she would never have recognized as Richard's, said in a tone of extreme bewilderment: 'Why, it's . . . it's Mrs Mahony!'

'Yes, it's me; I've come to take you home. Get up, Richard – but at once, dear! . . . and don't lie there like that. The buggy's waiting.' Again he made, she saw, a genuine effort to obey; but once more fell back.

'Take that rope off his hands.' And disregarding a warder's: 'Well, at your own risk, lady!' she added: 'And help him up.'

But this was easier said than done. No sooner did the men approach him than his struggles began anew. He would not be touched by them. It was left to Mr Evans and one of the sailors, who had not made off like the rest, to untie his wrists; after which, seizing him under the armpits, they hoisted him on to the quay. ('Mrs Mahony . . . why, it's Mrs Mahony!' piped the thin voice.)

'And now take my arm and come quietly . . . as quietly as you can. There are people watching. Show them how nicely you can walk.'

('Mrs Mahony . . . Mrs Mahony.')

With him a dead weight on her right arm, Mr Evans at his other side pushing and supporting, they got his poor old shambling legs up the steps and through the crowd. He was so cold and stiff from exposure that it was all he could do to set one foot before the other. He had no boots on, no hat, no greatcoat. Of the carpet-slippers in which they had let him travel, one had been lost or had fallen off in the boat; his sock was full of holes. In his struggles the right-hand sleeve of his coat had been almost wrenched from its armhole, his dirty shirt was collarless, his grey hair, long uncut, hung down his neck.

And the fear he was in was pitiful to see: he turned his head continually from side to side, trying to look back. 'Where are they? Oh, don't let them get the doctor! . . . *don't* let them get him!'

'No, no, my darling! . . . don't be afraid. You're quite safe now . . . with me.' And as soon as he had been half shoved, half dragged into the buggy, she sent her companion to warn the warders to keep out of sight. If follow they must, it would have to be in a separate vehicle.

On the drive home she took Richard's poor benumbed hands in hers and chafed them; she spread her skirts over his knees to keep the wind off, unhooked her mantle and bound it round his chest. His teeth chattered; his face was grey with cold. Then, opening the little bottle of wine and water and the packet of sandwiches which she had brought with her, she fed him, sip by sip and bit by bit, for he was ravenous with hunger and thirst. And though he quieted down somewhat, under the shelter of the hood, she did not cease to croon to him and comfort him. 'It's all right, my dear, quite all right now. Those horrid men are far away; you'll never, never see them again. You're with me, your own Mary, who will look after you and care for you.' Until, his hunger stilled, his worst fears allayed, exhausted, utterly weary, he put his head on her shoulder and, with her arm laid round him to lessen the jolts of the road, fell asleep, slumbering as peacefully as a child on its mother's breast.

And so Richard Mahony came home.

CHAPTER NINE

A week later Mary paid the warders off and dispatched them back to Melbourne. Not once had she needed them; there had been absolutely nothing for them to do – but hang about the hotel, eating and drinking at her expense. She went, besides, in mortal fear of Richard seeing them from the window, did they show themselves in the street, and of the shock this sight might be, undoing all the good she had done. So she handed out their return-fares and paid their bill, gladly . . . even though this came to a good deal more than she had expected, coarse brutes that they were! For their part, they could hardly believe their ears when they heard her report on Richard's behaviour since getting home; and they remained pessimistic to the end. 'Ah! you'll have trouble with him yet, lady . . . for sure you will,' were their final words.

But she laughed in their faces. Richard was a lamb in her hands, a little child, whom she could twist round her finger. Just now he spent his time weeping from sheer happiness, as he strayed from room to room of the little house . . . so wretchedly poor and mean compared with any he had known. But he was blind to its shortcomings. 'And all this belongs to the doctor? . . . it's *his* house? . . . he'll never have to go away from it again? And these cups and plates – do they belong to the doctor, too? . . . and may he drink out of them and eat off them? And is this the doctor's own chair?' Again and again she had to assure him and reassure him: he might sit where he pleased, do what he liked, use everything. With difficulty he took in his good fortune: at first, any unexpected knock at the door made him shake and try to hide.

Gradually, however – along with the marks and bruises that stained his poor old body – his alarms died out, and his eyes lost their hunted look. As long, that is to say, as Mary was with him, or he knew her close at hand: her presence alone spelt complete safety. It had been hard to make him understand that he was not to follow her into the office; he couldn't grasp this, and would often be found prowling round the office door, muttering confusedly. Even after he had learnt his lesson, she — hammering away at the key, or sitting stooped over her desk — would sometimes see the door open by a crack, and Richard's eyes and nose appear behind it . . . just to make sure. Then, if she nodded and smiled and said: 'It's all right, dear, I'm here!' he would go away content. His devotion to her, his submissive dependence on her, knew no bounds: a word of praise from her made him happy, a reproof bewildered him to tears. And was he really troublesome, she had only to warn him: 'Richard, if you're not good, I shan't be able to keep you,' for him instantly to weep and promise betterment. No one, not even the children, might in his presence handle any object that he looked on as her peculiar property: the teapot, her scissors, her brush and comb. 'Put that down . . . put it down at once! It belongs to Mrs Mahony.'

Fortunately he took quite a fancy to Mrs Bowman, and had no objection to being waited on by her — when the monthly 'statement' occupied Mary, or a visit from the Inspector impended. But then Bowey was capital with him, hit just the right tone, and never tried to order him about. She was a good cook, too, and, since he was prescribed small quantities of nourishing food, she was for ever popping in from the kitchen with a: 'Now, sir, I've got a nice little cup of soup here, made specially for you . . . something I *know* you'll enjoy!' And he would let her bind his table-napkin round his neck, and even, in default of Mary, feed him with a spoon, to avoid the pitiful dropping and spilling that otherwise went on. He invariably addressed her as 'the Cook', and spoke to her, and of her, as if she stood at the head of a large staff of servants. (Whose non-existence, oddly enough, he did not seem to remark.) For it was just as if a sponge had been passed over a large part of his brain, mercifully wiping out every memory of the terrible later years. He re-lived the period of his greatest prosperity; was once more, in imagination, either the well-to-do property-owner, or the distinguished physician. And since only those images persisted which had to do with one or other of these periods, his late-born children meant little to him: if he thought or spoke of them, it was as though they were still in their infancy. Sometimes, seeing them stand so tall and sturdy before him — a well-grown girl and boy of seven and eight – he grew quite confused. While, asked by Mary if he remembered his little lost daughter, he looked at her with stupid, darkened eyes, and could not think what she meant.

By seven of a morning, he was washed and dressed and fed. Eight o'clock, when the office opened, saw him comfortably settled in the rocking-chair. Here his day was spent. The chair stood by the window, which gave on the cross-roads and the main street; from it, he could see all that went on in the township. But his chief occupation was 'reading'. For his sake Mary subscribed to a Melbourne newspaper – though this was a day and a half old before it reached them. But, for anything it mattered to him, it might have borne the date of a month back. As often as not, he read it upside down; his spectacles perched at an impossible angle on the extreme tip of his long, thin nose. In this position he loved to proclaim the news, to whoever had time to listen: Mary, slipping in and out; Mrs Bowman, come to see that he wanted for nothing. And his information was invariably of some long past event: the death of Prince Albert, the siege of Sebastopol, the Indian Mutiny. And there good old Bowey would stand, her hands clasped under her apron, exclaiming: 'What doings, sir, what awful doings you do tell of!' – for, to throw his hearer into a state of surprise, even of consternation, was one of the things that pleased him best.

Tired of reading, he would talk to himself by the hour together; his clear voice, with its light Irish slur, ringing through the house. And hampered no longer by those shackles of pride and reserve which had made him the most modest of men, his theme was now always, and blatantly, himself. This self – to whom, as to everyone else, he referred only in the third person – was the pivot round which his thoughts revolved, he passionately asserting and reasserting its identity, in a singsong that was not unlike a chant. 'Richard Townshend-Mahony, F.R.C.S., M.D., Edinburgh, R. T. Mahony, M.D. and Accoucheur; Specialist for the Diseases of Women; Consulting Physician to the Ballarat Hospital!' and so on: only, the list having been sung through, untiringly to begin afresh.

In appearance, now that he was once more clean and well cared-for, he remained a striking-looking man, with his straight, delicate features, his cloven chin, the silver hair smoothed back from his high forehead; and often, on coming into the room and catching him seated and in profile – his gait, of course, was lamentable; he had never recovered the proper use of his legs –

Mary had a passing, ghostlike glimpse of the man who had been. It was his eyes that gave him away. There had been a time when these blue-grey eyes had looked out on life with the expression of a wantonly hurt animal. Still later, a day when they had seldom lifted, but had brooded before them, turned inward on torments visible to them alone. Now they met yours again, but as it were shrilly and blindly, all the soul gone out of them; nor ever a trace remaining of their former puzzlement over life the destroyer. He was now the least troubled of men. Content and happiness had come to him at last, in full measure. No more doubts, or questionings, or wrestlings with the dark powers in himself: no anxiety over ways and means (Mary was there, Mary would provide); never a twinge of the old passionate ache for change and renewal . . . for flight from all familiar things. He desired to be nowhere but here: had, at long last, found rest and peace, within the four walls of a room measuring but a few feet square; that peace for which he had sought, desperately and vainly, throughout the whole of his conscious life; to which he would otherwise have attained only through death's gates.

To see him thus was Mary's reward: Mary, grown so thin that she could count her ribs; with black rings round her eyes, 'salt-cellars' above and below her collar-bones; with enlarged, knobby knuckles, and feet that grew daily flatter. But she had no time to think of herself – to think at all, in fact – nor did she linger regretfully over what had been, or grieve in advance for what was bound to come. And Richard's condition ceased to sadden her: valiantly she accepted the inevitable.

It was another matter with the children, who had in them a goodly share of Mahony's own thin-skinnedness. Cuffy and Lucie never grew used or resigned to the state of things: their father's imbecile presence lay a dead weight on their young lives. And violently conflicting feelings swung them to and fro. If, at dinner, Papa was scolded for spilling his food, or for gobbling – and he was most *dreadf'ly* greedy – Luce's eyes would shut so tight that almost you couldn't see she had any: while he, Cuffy, red as a turkey-cock, would start to eat just like Papa, from being made so sorry and uncomfortable to hear a big man scolded like a baby. They kept out of his way as much as possible, being also subtly hurt by his lack of recognition of them, when he knew Mamma so well: they were just as much belonging to him as Mamma! And, home from their morning lessons at the parsonage, they withdrew to the bottom of the yard, where Mamma couldn't so easily find them. For she was always trying to make Papa notice them . . . when you knew quite well he didn't care. It would be: 'Show Papa your copybook . . . how nicely you can write now,' or 'Let him see your new boots.' At which something naughty would get up in Cuffy, and make him say nastily: 'What for? . . . what's the good? He doesn't *really* look!' But then Mamma would look so sorry that it hurt, and say: 'Oh, you must be kind to him, Cuffy! And try not to let him feel it.'

A doctor drove over once a week from Burrabool to write medicines for Papa, and he said Papa ought to take exercise, and it would be a good thing for him to go a short walk . . . every single day. And of course he and Luce had to do this, to help Mamma. For half an hour. The thought of it spoiled the whole morning – like a whipping.

'Does it matter which way we go?'

Cuffy never failed to ask this, as a sop to his conscience. But really they always went the same road, the one that led straight out of the township. For, if you got past the lock-up, where the constable's little girl might be swinging on the gate, you were quite certain not to meet anybody. To make sure she wasn't, you first sent Luce out to look, then fetched Papa and hurried him by. After that, though, you had to walk as slow as slow, because he couldn't hardly walk at all: his knees bent and stuck out at every step. You each held his hand, and went on, counting the minutes till it was time to turn back. And to find when this was, you had to get his watch out of his pocket yourself and look at it – which he didn't like, for he thought you were going to take it away from him. But it was no use asking him the time, because he said such funny things. Like: 'The time is out of joint,' or: 'A time to be born and a time to die!'

But when you said it was far enough and they could go home, and turned him round, he was glad, too; and the whole way back he talked about nothing but his tea, and what there was going to be for it. And when Mamma came to the door she didn't say what she would have said to *them*, that it was greedy and piggy to think about your meals so long beforehand. She just said: 'Tea's all ready, dear; and Bowey has made you some delicious scones.' He and Luce only had bread and butter, and didn't want it. They liked best to go and play like mad, because the walk was done, and they didn't have to do it again till next day.

But then came that awful afternoon when ... ugh! he didn't like even to *think* about it ... ever afterwards.

They had gone out as usual and walked along the road, and nobody saw them. And he was just going to fetch Papa's watch to look at the time ... or had he *tried* to and it wouldn't come, and he had pulled at it? He could never feel quite, quite sure: it remained a horrible doubt. And then, all of a sudden, quite suddenly Papa fell down. 'His legs just seemed to shut up, Mamma, really, truly they did!' (when she accused them of having hurried him). They couldn't stop him ... Luce nearly tumbled down, too ... and Papa fell flat on his face and lay there; and it had rained, and the road was dirty, and he lay in it, so that his clothes and his face were full of mud. And he called out and so did Luce: 'Get up, Papa, you'll be all wet and dirty!' and again: 'Mamma will be so cross if you don't!' and despairingly: 'Oh, dear Papa, *do* get up and don't just lie there!' And then he did try, but couldn't seem to make his legs work properly, and went on lying with his face and hair in the dirt – quite flat. And they tugged and tugged at him, at his arms and his coat, but couldn't move him, he was so big and heavy; and Luce began to cry; and he felt such a bone come in his own throat that he thought he'd have to cry, too. He began to be afraid the mud would choke Papa, and what would Mamma say then? And Papa kept on asking: 'What is it? What's the doctor doing?' And then he shouted out, like as if he was deaf: 'You've fallen down, Papa – oh, *do* get up! *What* shall we do if you don't!' And he said to Luce to run home and fetch Mamma, but she was frightened to; and she was frightened to stay there while he went; and so he felt his heart would burst, for they couldn't leave Papa alone. But just then a man came driving in a spring-cart, and when he saw them he stopped and said: 'Hullo, you kids, what's up?' And 'Whoa!' to his horse, and got out. And first he laughed a little, and winked at them, for he thought Papa was tipsy; but when they told him, and said it was their Papa who couldn't walk any more because his legs were wrong, he stopped laughing and was kind. He took hold of Papa till he made him stand up, and then he let down the flap of the cart and helped him in, and lifted them up, too, and they drove home that way, their legs hanging out at the back. And when they got to the post office Mamma came running to the door, and had a most awful fright when she saw Papa so wet and dirty, with mud on his face and hair, and scratched with stones where they had pulled him; and she sort of screamed out: 'Oh, *what's* the matter? What have you done to him?' (and they hadn't done anything at all). But she was so sorry for Papa, and so busy washing him clean and telling him not to cry, that she didn't have any time to think about them, or how upset they were. They went away and were together by themselves, at the bottom of the yard.

After this, though, they didn't have to take Papa walking any more. He never went out. — But the memory of the accident persisted, and was entangled in their dreams for many a night to come. Especially Cuffy's. Cuffy would start up, his nightclothes damp with sweat, from a dream that Papa had fallen dead in the road and that he had killed him. And, all his life long, the sight of a heavy body lying prostrate and unable to rise — a horse down in its traces, even a drunkard stretched oblivious by the roadside — had the power to throw him into the old childish panic, and make him want blindly to turn and run . . . and run . . . till he could run no more.

CHAPTER TEN

Thus the shadows deepened. For still some time Mahony contrived to cover, unaided, the few yards that separated bedroom from sitting-room. Then he took to shouldering his way along the walls, supporting himself by the furniture. And soon, even this mode of progression proving beyond him, he needed the firm prop of an arm on either side, was he to reach his seat by the window. Finally his chair was brought to the bedside, and, with him in it, was pushed and pulled by the two women to the adjoining room.

He never set foot to the ground again; was very prisoner to this chair. Nor could he stoop, or bend his body sideways; and did he now drop his spectacles, or let his paper flutter to the floor, the house resounded with cries of 'Mrs Mahony, Mrs Mahony!' or 'the Cook, the Cook!' Dead from the waist down, he sat wooden and rigid; and the light of the poor clouded brain that topped this moribund trunk grew daily feebler. His newspaper ceased to interest him; he no longer hymned his own praises: he just sat and stared before him, in mournful vacancy.

Oh, what a work it was to die! – to shake off a body that had no more worth left in it than a snake's cast skin, Mary could imagine him saying of himself. – Not so she. She clung jealously to each day on which she still had him with her; plodding to and fro on hot, swollen feet; gladly performing the last, sordid duties of the sickroom.

Then, gangrene setting in, he became bedridden; and she and Bowey united their strength to turn him from side to side, or to raise him the few necessary inches on his pillow. He was grown quite silent now, and indifferent to everyone; the sight of food alone called up a flicker of interest in his dull eyes. But the day came when even to swallow soft jellies and custards was beyond him, and a few teaspoonfuls of liquid formed his sole nourishment. And at length his throat refusing even this office, there was nothing to be done but to sit and watch him die.

For three days he lay in coma. On the third, the doctor gave it as his opinion that he would not outlive the night.

Beside the low, trestle-bed in which, for greater convenience, they had laid him, and on which his motionless body formed a long, straight hummock under the blankets, Mary sat and looked her last on the familiar face, now so soon to be hidden from her ... it might be for ever. For who knew, who could *really* know, if they would meet again? In health, in the bustle of living, it was easy to believe in heaven and a life to come. But when the blow fell, and those you loved passed into the great Silence, where you could not get at them, or they at you, then doubts, aching doubts took possession of one. She had sunk under them when her child died; she knew them now, still more fiercely. Death might quite well be the end of everything; just so many bones rotting in a grave. — And even if it was not, if there *was* more to come, how could it ever be quite the same again? — the same Richard to look at, and with all his weaknesses, who had belonged to her for nearly thirty years. She didn't believe it. If heaven existed, and was what people said it was, then it would certainly turn him into something different: a stranger ... an angel! — and what had she to do with angels? She wanted the man himself, the dear warm incompetent human creature at whose side she had been through so much. Who had so tried, so harassed her, made her suffer so. — Oh, as if that mattered now! What *was* life, but care and suffering? — for everyone alike. His had never been much else. Even though his troubles were mostly of his own making. For he had always asked more of life than it could give: and if, for once, he got what he wanted, he had not known how to sit fast and hold it: so the end was the poor old wreck on the bed before her. Now, death was best. Death alone could wipe out the shame and disgrace that had befallen him — the shame of failure, the degradation of his illness. Best for the children, too; his passing would lift a shadow from their lives ... they were so young still, they would soon forget. Yes, best for everyone ... only not for her. With Richard, the most vital part of herself — a part compounded of shared experience, and mutual endeavour, and the common memories of a lifetime — would go down into the grave. — Burying her face in her hands, Mary wept.

By day, for the children's, for her work's sake, she was

forced to bear up. Now there was nobody to see or hear her. The office was closed, the children slept: old Bowey dozed over the lamp in the kitchen. She could weep, without fear of surprise, alone with him who had passed beyond the sound of human grief; in this little back room where, by the light of a single candle, monstrous shadows splashed walls and ceiling: shadows that stirred, and seemed to have a life of their own; for it was winter now, and the wild Australian wind shrilled round the house, and found its way in through the loosely fitting sashes.

How long she sat thus she did not know: she had lost count of time. But, of a sudden, something . . . a something felt not heard, and felt only by a quickening of her pulses . . . made her catch her breath, pause in her crying, strain her ears, look up. And as she did so her heart gave a great bound, then seemed to leave off beating. *He had come back*. His lids were raised, his eyes half open. And in the breathless silence that followed, when each tick of the little clock on the chest of drawers was separately audible, she saw his lips, too, move. He was trying to speak. She bent over him, hardly daring to breathe, and caught, or thought she caught the words: 'Not grieve . . . for me. I'm going . . . into Eternity.'

Whether they were actually meant for her, or whether a mere instinctive response to the sound of her weeping, she could not tell. But dropping on her knees by the bedside, she took his half-cold hand in her warm, live one, and kissed and fondled it. And his lids, which had fallen to again, made one last supreme effort to rise, and this time there was no mistaking the whisper that came over his lips.

'Dear wife!'

He was gone again, even as he said it, but it was enough . . . more than enough! Laying her head down beside his, she pressed her face against the linen of the pillow, paying back to this inanimate object the burning thankfulness with which she no longer dared to trouble him. Eternity was something vast, cold, impersonal. But this little phrase, from the long past days of love and comradeship, these homely, familiar words, fell like balsam on her heart. All his love for her, his gratitude to her, was in them: they were her reward, and a full and ample one, for a lifetime of unwearied sacrifice.

Dear wife! . . . dear wife.

He died at dawn, his faint breaths fluttering to rest.

*

Close on two days had to elapse before relative or friend could get to her side: by the time Jerry and Tilly reached Gymgurra, she herself had made all arrangements for the last rites, and Richard was washed and dressed and in his coffin, which stood on a pair of trestles just outside the kitchen door, the doorways of the rooms having proved too narrow to admit it. There he lay, with a large bunch of white violets in his folded hands, looking very calm and peaceful, but also inexpressibly remote — from them all, from everything. Never again would the clatter of crockery or the odours of cooking flay his nerves.

The children, feeling oddly shy, sought their usual refuge; and when strange men came with the coffin, and there was a great walking about and tramping, they were told to keep out of the way. But afterwards Mamma called them in, and took their hands and took them to see Papa, who was all put in his coffin now, with a bunch of flowers in front of him and his head on a most *beautiful* satin pillow trimmed with lace. And Mamma kissed him and stroked his hair, and said how young and handsome he looked, with the wrinkles gone away from his face; but Cuffy only thought he looked most frightfully asleep.

Luce had to have her hand held every time she went by; but he didn't; he didn't care. And all the time Papa had lain in bed and was so ill, he hadn't either. Even when he heard he was dead, and saw him with a sheet pulled over his face, it didn't seem to make any difference. Or wouldn't have, if other people hadn't been so sorry for him. To see them sorry gradually made him sorry, too. For himself. And that night, when a great fat moon was on the sky, he went away and stood and looked up at it, and then something that was just like a line of poetry came into his head, and he said it over and over, and it went: 'Now the moon looked down on a fatherless child!'

Next day though, when Papa was put in and you couldn't help seeing him every time you went along the passage, it was different. And when Mamma got a large pocket-handkerchief and spread it over his face and hands (when you were dead you couldn't shooh the flies away, and they liked to walk on you), then he suddenly felt he wanted to see Papa again, most awfully much. So when nobody was about, he went and pulled the handkerchief off, and had a good long look at him: much longer than when he was alive; for then Papa wouldn't have liked it; besides him being too shy. Now he could stare and stare; and he did; till he saw a secret: Papa had a little black mole at the side

of his nose, which he had never seen before. This, and what
Bowey said: that they would soon come now and screw the lid
down (just as he was, with the little mole, and his eyelashes, and
everything), gave him a very queer feeling inside, and made his
knees seem as if they weren't going to hold him up much longer.
He had to look away . . . quickly . . . look at the violets, which
had been sent as a present: Papa was holding them just as if
he was still alive. And when he saw them, he suddenly felt he
would like to give him something, too. But only potatoes grew in
the yard. Potatoes had quite pretty little flowers when they did
have, white and purple, only they weren't come yet. But that
afternoon, when he was at the parsonage with a note and was
coming away again, he *stole* a flower (a *lovely* little 'polyanthers'),
his heart beating nearly to choke him from having to step on the
flower bed, which was all raked in lines, and in case he should
be seen from the window. It got rather crushed being in his
pocket, but it was *very* pretty, red and yellow, with bevelledy
edges, and soft like velvet. And when Mamma was in the office
and Bowey washing sheets, he went on tiptoe to Papa to put his
flower in. He meant to hide it under the violets, where nobody
but him would know; but doing this his hand touched Papa's –
and that was the end of everything. The mere feel of it, colder
– much, much colder – than a glass, or a plate, or a frog's back,
filled him with horror . . . he nearly screamed out loud . . . and
just dropped the flower anywhere and the handkerchief all
rumpled up, and ran for his life. And tore and tore, out of the
house and down the yard . . . to the only quite private place he
knew . . . where no one but him ever went: the space between
the closet and the fence, so narrow that you had to squeeze in
sideways. And he was only just in time. Before he quite got there
he'd begun to cry – as he'd never cried before. It came jumping
out of him, in great big sobs. – He was *glad* Papa was dead –
yes, ever so glad! – he told himself so, over and over. He'd never,
never, never need to take him for walks again. And nobody
would ever laugh, or point their fingers at them, or make fun
of them, any more. For if you were once dead you stopped dead
– he knew that now. Not like when Lallie died, and he had
gone on waiting for her to come back. Papa would never come
back . . . or walk about . . . or speak to them again. He was going
down into the ground, just like he was, with the shiny pillow,
and the violets, and . . . and everything. – Oh, no, *no!* he
couldn't bear it . . . he couldn't – even to think of it nearly killed

him. And he stamped his feet and stamped them, in a frenzy of rebellious rage. Oh, he *would* be good, and not care about anything, if only – if only . . . he'd take him for walks – anywhere! – yes, he would! – if only . . . Oh, Papa! . . . dear, darling Papa! . . . come back, come back!

Afterwards, he had to go out of the gate and hang about the road, till his eyes got un-red again: not for anything would he have let Mamma or Luce or Bowey know he had had to cry. – And it made him feel hot and prickly all over, when he went indoors, to see that somebody (Mamma most likely) had found the little tumbled polyanthers and picked it up and put it right in the middle of the bunch of violets. *That* hurt more than anything.

At the last moment, the doctor who was to have attended the funeral telegraphed that he was unavoidably detained. This left an empty place in the single mourning coach; and Tilly, scandalized as she was by the paucity of mourners, straightway fell to work to drape a streamer round Cuffy's sailor-hat and sew a band on his left sleeve – she had arrived laden with gifts of crêpe and other black stuffs. Open-mouthed, aghast, Cuffy heard his doom. But, though quaking inwardly, he clenched his teeth and said not a word: just stood and let her sew him. Because of Mamma.

It was Mary, suddenly grown aware of his silent agony, who came out of her own grief to say: 'No, Tilly, let the child be! . . . I won't have him forced. Richard would have been the last to wish it.'

But scarcely had Cuffy breathed again, when he was plunged into a fresh confusion. Men came to shut down the coffin; and then, while Mamma was saying good-bye to Papa, she suddenly burst out crying – oh, simply *dreadfully*! He felt himself blush over his whole body, to hear her – *his* Mamma! – going on like this in front of these strange people, so fierce and don't-carish, and with her face all red and wrinkled up like a baby's. But she didn't seem to mind, and didn't take a bit of notice when he poked her with his elbow and said: 'Oh, hush, Mamma! They'll hear you.' Or of Uncle Jerry either, who put his hand on her shoulder and said: 'It's all for the best, old girl – believe me, it is!' Aunt Tilly blew her nose so loud it hurt your ears, and winked and blinked with her eyes; but what *she* said was: 'Remember, love, you're not left quite alone; you've got your children. *They'll* be your comfort. From now on they'll put aside their naughty ways and be as good as gold – I know they will.' (Huh!)

The hearse stood at the door, its double row of fantastic, feathered plumes, more brown than sable from long usage and the strong sunlight, nodding in the breeze. Brownish, too, were the antique, funereal draperies that hung almost to the ground from the backs of two lean horses. The blinds in the neighbouring houses went down with a rush; and the narrow box, containing all that remained of the medley of hopes and fears, joys and sorrows and untold struggles, that had been Richard Mahony, was shouldered and carried out. The mourners – Jerry, the parson, the Bank manager – took their seats in the carriage, and the little procession got under way.

Rounding the corner and passing in turn the fire-bell, the Rechabites' Hall and the flour-mill, hearse and coach, resembling two black smudges on empty space, set to crawling up the slope that led out of the township. From the top of this rise the road could be seen for miles, running without curve or turn through the grassy plains. About midway, in a slight dip, was visible the little fenced-in square of the cemetery, its sprinkling of white headstones forming a landmark in the bare, undulating country.

Amid these wavy downs Mahony was laid to rest. – It would have been after his own heart that his last bed was within sound of what he had perhaps loved best on earth – the open sea. A quarter of a mile off, behind a sandy ridge, the surf, driving in from the Bight, breaks and booms eternally on the barren shore. Thence, too, come the fierce winds, which, in stormy weather, hurl themselves over the land, where not a tree, not a bush, nor even a fence stands to break their force. Or to limit the outlook. On all side the eyes can range, unhindered, to where the vast earth meets the infinitely vaster sky. And, under blazing summer suns, or when a full moon floods the night, no shadow falls on the sun-baked or moon-blanched plains, but those cast by the few little stones set up in human remembrance.

All that was mortal of Richard Mahony has long since crumbled to dust. For a time, fond hands tended his grave, on which in due course a small cross rose, bearing his name, and marking the days and years of his earthly pilgrimage. But, those who had known and loved him passing, scattering, forgetting, rude weeds choked the flowers, the cross toppled over, fell to pieces and was removed, the ivy that entwined it uprooted. And, thereafter, his resting-place was indistinguishable from the common ground. The rich and kindly earth of his adopted country absorbed his perishable body, as the country itself had never contrived to make its own, his wayward, vagrant spirit.

*Some more Australian Penguins
are described on the
following pages*

THE LETTERS OF RACHEL HENNING

EDITED BY DAVID ADAMS

WITH A FOREWORD AND DRAWINGS BY NORMAN LINDSAY

Rachel Henning's letters were written between 1853 and 1882. They give a vivid and fascinating account of life in colonial Australia as seen through the eyes of a previously sheltered young Englishwoman.

At first repelled by the rough texture of life in Australia she eventually resolves to 'make a do of it' and, as Norman Lindsay says, 'took to pioneering with amazing gusto. The long journeys on horseback, the campfires at night with damper and quart-pot tea, the sleeping under the stars with a saddle for a pillow, enchanted her.' The letters have been brilliantly edited by David Adams to make a story that reads like a novel.

Not least of this book's attractions are Norman Lindsay's superb pen drawings.

THE ART OF AUSTRALIA

ROBERT HUGHES

This is a comprehensive account of Australian art between the founding of the colony in 1788 and the latest developments of the 1960s.

The author, whose art column in *Nation* and whose contributions to the *Australian* proved sharp questioners of established values, traces the twin threads of the desire for independence in Australian vision and the obsessive influence of European and American models. In his view Australian painting is a phenomenon to be discussed, for good or ill, within the total context of contemporary art. He is thus led to reappraise many established reputations, and to suggest channels through which Australian painting may yet emerge as a world force.

Robert Hughes has been described by the art critic of the *Sydney Morning Herald* as 'the brilliant *enfant terrible* of Australian art and letters'.

'This book will inject into the often ungenerous and sluggish body of the Australian art world a dose of love for, and an excitement about, painting which is far more important than all the authoritative research on the size of Streeton's boots' – Eric Westbrook in *Walkabout*.

A Pelican Original